THE DREAD PRINCE

LAUREN CATE LEAKE

ALSO BY LAUREN CATE LEAKE

THE DREAD DESCENDANT SERIES
THE DREAD DESCENDANT
THE DREAD PRINCE
THE DREAD KING
DREADFULLY YOURS

MURDEROUS LOVE: AN ANTHOLOGY
FEATURING MARRY, KISS, KILL

COVER ART BY JESS KUESPERT

ISBN 9798992059236

This book is for everyone who lost a parent. I see you.

And for my dad. If one beautiful thing was born from mom's death, it was me finding my way back to you.

Content Warning

This book is much darker than the first. If you thought these characters were morally grey before, they are, as a result of book one, now pitch black. This book contains MANIPULATION, SUICIDAL THEMES, GRAPHIC LANGUAGE, VIOLENCE AND SEXUAL CONTENT.

Chapter 25 is marked with a serpent. This chapter contains sexually explicit content that can be skipped with no impact on the plot and story.

PLAYLIST

Pain by Three Days Grace
House of Memories by Panic! At the Disco
The Haunting by Set it Off
Killing In The Name by Rage Against the Machine
Blood//Water by grandson
If You Could Only See by Tonic
If I'm James Dean, You're Audrey Hepburn by Sleeping with Sirens
Sleepyhead by Jutes
All Around Me by Flyleaf
Red by Taylor Swift
Just Pretend by Bad Omens
Strangers by Ethel Cain
All I Wanted by Paramore
The Archer by Taylor Swift
Pretty Girl by Sugarcult
Better Off by Trousdale
Numb by LINKIN PARK
Nightmare by Set it Off
I Will Always Love You by Chase Holfelder
Darkest Part by Red

PRONUNCIATIONS

Maeve *like wave*
Malachite *like kite*
Abraxas *sis not sass (though...he has that)*
Reeve *like leave*
Vaukore *vow/core*
Vexkari *vex/car with letter "E" sound*
Ambrose *like gross (I can assure you he is far from it)*
Spinel *spin/elle*
Peur *pure*
Zimsy *zim/zee*
Orator *or/uh/tor*

Elven Lands
The Dread Lands
Sinclair Estates on Earth
MOUNT MORTE
THE DARK PEAKS
CASTLE MORANA
THE BERYL CITY
THE TOWERS
THE GREYWOOD

SANCTUM
THE CELESTIAN PALACE
Heims
CRYSTALMORE
The Dark Planet
Atema
LOWER ATERNIAN TOWNS
THE BLACK DEEP
Vaukore

15

PART ONE

Chapter 1

Malachite

"What did you see, Emerie?"

Roswyn's impatient and demanding tone rang across the room. But his wife did not hear him. Or, if she had, she chose not to acknowledge her husband.

Her forehead and back pooled with sweat, drenching her pajamas. The Witch gripped the satin sheet beneath her with clammy and shaking hands. When she did not answer her husband a second time, his hand slammed around her throat.

She barely flinched under his firm grip. Nor did she cry out as her head slammed into the headboard. But the death grip she held on the sheets beneath her remained.

Malachite clicked his tongue as his eyes slid to Roswyn. Roswyn released her.

"It's alright, Emerie," said Mal. "I'm not going to hurt you." He seated himself on the edge of the bed and smiled softly, in the menacingly beautiful way he had mastered. "But you will tell me what you saw."

Emerie was no fool. Mal knew she'd prayed for years to see the future, as her ancestors had before her. She'd gone her entire life without so much as a flicker of prophetic Magic. So long that her own family had abandoned the idea that she was a Seer. She was the bad end of an even worse joke to them.

Seers had once been the most valued Magicals there were, but as the prophecies ran dry, they became irrelevant in the Magical's world.

At least, until Emerie Videntis woke at the Witching Hour, her eyes glazed black, speaking about The Dread Descendant with prophetic certainty.

When Emerie still did not speak, Mal understood. He looked

over his shoulder to Roswyn. "Leave us," commanded Mal.

Roswyn's lips pulled into a thin line, but he didn't dare disobey his sworn Prince. He scowled at his wife before he turned and briskly left the room. She'd pay for that later.

The door clicked shut behind Roswyn, and Emerie spoke before Mal turned his attention back to her.

"You are not the only Dread Descendant the ancient prophecy spoke of, the one my ancestors professed. The youngest to point a single finger. . . has not arrived."

Mal's head snapped towards her.

She didn't stop.

"You will create Magic that is unstoppable, that will break the curse of this land and unite all realms." Emerie took a steadying breath. But she was not done. "He will be the catalyst that plunges the Magicals into further darkness. A storm unleashed and a beast unchained."

Mal stared at Emerie with a solemn expression. His hand twitched slightly at his side. "The youngest to point a single finger?" he asked with slow precision.

Emerie swallowed hard.

He watched her with piercing, dark eyes as she tried to relax.

His face remained cool as Emerie breathed heavily and nodded. He stood and paced across the room, his back to her.

His voice grew dark. "You will not speak of this to anyone."

Emerie began shaking once more. "I will not, my Prince. But. . .there is more, my Prince."

Malachite stepped back towards her and examined her intently for the first time, feeling for her Magic as his head cocked to one side. Emerie couldn't bring herself to meet his gaze, a fact he enjoyed.

His Dark Dread Magic pulsated towards her. A blatant threat. "Recite the entire prophecy," he commanded smoothly.

Chapter 2

Lennon Moon

"Any Portal issues?" asked Orator Moon.

"No, sir," replied Doggbind. "There have been no reported breaches. A minor disturbance every few weeks-a small bird from The Dread Lands."

"For her?"

Doggbind nodded.

"What kind of bird?" Moon asked, a slight nervousness leaking into his voice.

"A jay. I am certain. It slips back through before I can grab it, but I am able to divert the messages all the same."

"What do they say?"

"Nothing of importance. Her cousin, the Rosethorn boy, writes her. He never says anything other than that he misses her, and wonders if her nonexistent reply is lack of deliverance, or her state of mind."

"Good," said Moon. "Well done. Keep up the good work."

"If I may, sir?"

Moon nodded. Doggbind looked to Leslie Loxerman.

"Loxerman and I were discussing the possibility of writing back to him."

Moon didn't interject, so Doggbind continued.

"If we could make it appear it is from Sinclair, then perhaps we could receive some insight into their plans."

"Fake a letter?"

"Exactly," said Doggbind. "Her signature isn't a problem. We have a copy from her Bellator paperwork. But the letter itself is another story."

"The pair know one another well," said Moon. "Convincing the Rosethorn boy that it is indeed his cousin who writes to him will be far more complicated than matching handwriting."

"What if you allow one of his letters through to her?" asked Doggbind. "Let her write back, and then begin re-intercepting them?"

"Hmm," said Moon, "that is a thought."

"What if she doesn't write him back?" asked one of Moon's secretaries. "You said it yourself, Premier Doggbind, she is not her former self."

Moon contemplated for a moment.

"Arman," he said after a moment.

Ambrose Sinclair's former Captain looked up from his lap. "Sir?" He responded emotionlessly.

"She trusts you?"

Arman shook his head slowly. "Not anymore."

"Drat," said Moon, "I was hoping you'd be able to convince her to write back. You no longer train with her?"

"She has not maintained her position as Optimum. So, no," said Arman.

Arman had, however, maintained his position as Captain of the Magical Militia under the new Premier Doggbind, and swore a new oath to the Double O.

"Good," said Moon with a forced and uncomfortable chuckle.

Arman continued. "In fact, she barely trains with the Bellator at all. And when she does, she is at a fraction of the strength she once was."

"She remains loyal though? Despite all this?"

Doggbind barked a laugh. "I know a beaten soldier when I see it. She needs new guidance."

"I don't agree," said Moon. "I do not think it's wise to reignite her flame. The longer that boy is gone, the farther away from power she is." He looked to Leslie Loxerman. "She may even agree to marry at this point."

Loxerman nodded. "Reluctant though she may still be, I think you may be right. I just wish I could make the child understand. This is for her greater good and the good of us all."

Moon drummed his fingers together anxiously. "Perhaps it was a mistake for my predecessors to suppress the truth of the Shadow War. These children don't know what fear is."

Chapter 3

Maeve

Maeve Sinclair ran down the hallway towards her father's bedroom. She didn't remember the hallway on the second floor of Sinclair Estates being quite so long. But now, it never seemed to end as she barreled towards the door. The floor began to crumble beneath her, snapping in half, sending shards of glittering white marble in every direction. She inhaled sharply and flung herself over the collapsing floor.

She had to get to his room to be sure he was alive. She successfully reached the door of his chamber, as the house crumbled behind her. She hesitated. She knew what was on the other side. She dreamed that very dream nearly every night, and she dreaded opening that door.

She dreaded seeing the truth sprawled before her.

She reached for the crystal doorknob as a familiar voice spoke loudly.

Wake up, Maeve.

She whipped around. Mal's Dread Locket slipped from around her neck and slammed onto the floor, shattering into hundreds of tiny gold flecks as Sinclair Estates collapsed into ruin.

The dream state vanished in a flash of white light. She bolted up in bed, breathing heavily. Moonlight beamed through the sheer curtains in her London Townhouse.

Her hand flew to her chest.

Mal's Dread Locket was not there. Just as it had not been for months.

She steadied her breathing and pushed her hair out of her face, knowing it would be impossible to fall back asleep. She threw on her dressing gown and grabbed a book off her nightstand. Downstairs, a small fire dwindled in the large, white brick fireplace. She took up in a comfy chair next to it and tried to distract herself from her dream.

Wake up, Maeve.

The voice had been clear as a bell, and Maeve didn't need to speculate whose voice it was.

Malachite Peur visited her thoughts frequently over the previous months, both while she was sleeping and awake. At least, what little sleep she got.

She lifted her hand, and the fireplace in the townhouse Ambrose purchased for her shortly before his death roared into a full blaze.

Shortly after his death, Maeve discovered that he had also opened a separate bank account in her name, with the fortune she was always promised to receive upon marrying. Every single ruby and gold piece accounted for, despite her refusal to marry Alphard Mavros.

Zimsy shuffled sleekly into the room as Spinel jumped in Maeve's lap, purring loudly.

"Can I make you a tea?"

"No," said Maeve, staring into the fire. "You should go back to bed. I'm sorry I woke you."

Zimsy shook her head with a yawn and started towards the kitchen. She'd make them some anyway, Maeve was certain.

She had been surprised when she arrived at the London townhouse and Zimsy was frantically unpacking all of Maeve's things.

"What are you doing here?" Maeve had exclaimed. "I set you free!"

"Correct," she snapped. "Free to go wherever I want. Do whatever I want."

Zimsy had then started aggressively pulling things out of trunks and muttering to herself about how ungrateful Maeve was.

"Do you know how difficult that spell was?" Maeve had asked incredulously.

Zimsy had scoffed.

Maeve never protested her presence in the lavish townhouse. It was too big. Too empty. Zimsy filled it with warmth, like she filled all things.

When the sun rose, a hawk rested outside on the window's ledge, pecking at the glass. Maeve opened the window and took the letter. She recognized the bird as her Grandmother Agatha's, which she had trained to fly all across the country delivering mail.

Tea today?
-Agatha

Without a second thought, Maeve discarded the parchment on the overflowing stack of letters that piled up on the table by the window. Agatha incessantly asked her to visit, and Maeve had not responded to a single letter.

Maeve only went one place if she wasn't at home: The Bellator Sector.

Where she trained and fought. Where she listened to whispers about The Dread Prince and her father, the dead Premier. Where she ignored them all. Where she looked traitors in the face and smiled.

Where she pretended she wasn't Mal's second anymore. Where she lied and agreed that Mal, the now deemed villainous traitor, had killed her father.

She did as she had been instructed to do while she remained in isolation on Earth. The Double O closed all Portaling on Earth shortly after Ambrose's death, with no warning, separating Maeve and Mal.

That was six months ago.

Abraxas also remained in The Dread Lands, as well as a handful of others and a large portion of Bellator that were in training under Mal.

While Maeve was stuck on Earth with the rest of the Bellator and Roswyn.

Her thumb ran up and down her bare ring finger absentmindedly, desperate to feel the trickle of Magic that once lingered there, courtesy of Mal's Dread Ring.

She swallowed the anger that crept up in her throat and as the fire cracked and wafted, she wondered if she'd dreamed Mal completely. And that his Magic was something entirely out of reality.

She slipped her hand into her pajama pocket and pulled out the small sliver of parchment Mal had enchanted for them at Vaukore. It lay blank.

Just as it had been for six months.

Six months of torture. Of suffocating in her own thoughts. Without him.

When the piles of letters by the window cascaded to the floor, Maeve finally relented and visited Grandmother Agatha for tea.

"Your hair is too long," said Agatha upon seeing her.

"What a warm welcome," said Maeve cooly.

The two Sinclair women poured tea and sat across from one another in the sunroom. The heat through the glass felt nice against Maeve's skin.

"I figured you'd ambush me, and there would be more people here," said Maeve.

Agatha huffed. "Anyone in particular you're avoiding seeing?"

Maeve looked away, her voice cold. "Feels more like I'm being avoided, but I'd rather not discuss that."

Agatha sighed in a way that annoyed Maeve.

"Alright," said Agatha. "I'll only say one thing. I wish I'd gotten to see the look on Clarissa's face when you put that hag in her place."

Maeve spit her tea into the cup and genuinely laughed for the first time in months. Agatha laughed too. The rest of their time together was pleasant. Before Maeve realized it, the sun was setting, and the uneasy feeling that night brought to Maeve crept in on her.

"How about you come and see me once a week, and we can tend to that Greenhouse back there together," said Agatha.

"Alright," said Maeve softly.

Agatha launched into what a mess the Greenhouse was, and how Maeve would have her work cut out for her. Maeve looked up into the orange and violet sky beyond the glass panels of the sunroom, wondering what Mal was doing that very moment. He was preparing The Dread Lands, just as the plan had always been. She knew that.

But his absence ate at her mind, and in the void of his Magic, fear festered.

"When the time comes," continued Agatha, "I'll truly be devastated to lose such a fantastic gardener."

"What?" asked Maeve, her attention snapping back to Agatha.

"He's Human," she replied. "You know that."

"No," said Maeve. "I mean that you want to reside in The Dread Lands?"

"My birthright," huffed Agatha. "Once they are restored and liveable. Oh, yes."

"You'll leave all of this? Your gardens, your mansions, the home Grandfather lived and created and died in?"

"Yes," replied Agatha with another huff, then she laughed. "You think I won't have these things there? You think I won't take his painting and place it atop a new fireplace? Oh, yes." She leaned back in her seat. "I will return to the land my sweet Alyicious dreamt of. I will see it before I die."

Maeve looked out the pale green paned windows once more. "I can feel it," she muttered, "even now I can feel the darkness, the lifelessness of that place."

"And you no longer wish to rule it?"

Maeve didn't answer. Only after a quiet moment passed did she say, "There is something there. Something unnatural. And not the kind even I like."

Agatha raised her brow.

Maeve sighed. "You don't understand."

"How could I? Less than a year ago you were beginning plans to take back the Dread Lands and now-"

"Now my father is dead and. . ."

"And?" pressed Agatha.

Maeve's jaw tightened. "And it seems Mal has moved on without me perfectly fine."

Agatha rolled her eyes. "Even you don't believe that."

Maeve stared at her. "Why wouldn't he?"

Agatha shook her head. "Don't start disappointing me now, sweet child."

"He's deep in those mountains."

"The Dark Peaks," Agatha nodded.

Maeve kept her gaze out the windows. "That's where he said he had to go. And then we stopped being able to Portal off Earth and I haven't heard from him in months–"

"Heavens!" Agatha nearly shouted, sending herself into a coughing fit. She dabbed her mouth with a linen handkerchief. "You think he is not coming back?"

Maeve's shoulders dropped. "I think it doesn't matter anymore."

Agatha sat silently for a moment, and when she spoke again, her voice was soft. "You know, when Alyicious passed on, I thought I'd never feel anything but darkness again. I couldn't see how I could ever move past his absence. And then when I finally did, nearly a decade of grief behind me, I felt guilty for being alright again."

"I'm sorry–"

Agatha shook her head. "I am not seeking your pity, Maeve," she said gently. "I am telling you, the road ahead is long. If you do not seek the light, everything will remain in darkness. There is an end to the turmoil inside of you, but I will not lie. . .the path ahead of you will not be journeyed quickly, and should not be done alone."

Maeve didn't look at her grandmother. "You think he is coming back?" she asked quietly.

Agatha smiled. "Seek the light. The answer, you know very well, is buried within you." She refilled Maeve's tea, the milky brown color swirling as she added lavender. "Now, I ask you: is he coming back for you?"

Maeve watched the steam rise from her teacup as the swirling mist twisted into a serpent like shape.

"Filii Magicae Numquam Soli," said Agatha.

Children of Magic are never alone.

Chapter 4

Maeve

"The Dread Mark is hereby banned. Any Magicals bearing such a terrorist marking, contributing to the perpetuation of any such marking, will be found in treasonous contempt and held to the standards of the law."

Hellming Hall glowed in the morning light as Orator Moon stood at the podium in front of a massive tapestry that held the Double O's new emblem. It hung from the ceiling and covered the three stained glass windows of Magic at Vaukore.

Moon wore a tailor-made, pale blue suit, nicer than any she'd ever seen him wear. Each of the fine rings on his fingers were worth more than a year's worth of the Orator's salary. At his side was Doggbind, the new Premier and former head of Magical Law.

He wore a shiny Premier badge, vastly different from her father's. Though rumor had it, the new Premier was outraged when the pin her father had worn, which was centuries old, came up missing. The new design matched the Double O's new branding and insignia: two connecting O's that slid together like a narrowed set of eyes.

And eyes there were.

Doggbind had not been voted in the way her father had. In light of recent events, stemming all the way back to Kietel's grip on Magical society, The Orator's Office declared Militia Decree. The assassination of a Premier was more than enough reason for their panic. So they said.

Under such emergency actions, no election was needed. The Bellator were given law enforcement positions, and the Committee of the Sacred now occupied Orator Moon's cabinet of advisors and legislators.

Mal's coronation, and the subsequent death of her father, had been deemed an act of terrorism.

The Dread Prince was enemy number one.

His face was plastered on every newspaper, day in and day out, and in the windows of bookshops and tea parlors. The Magical Antiquities Museum published an editorial on the dangerous and deadly Dread Artifacts he "stole" from Magical society that were now at his disposal to destroy Magicals entirely. The only positive byproduct of their smear campaign was that Jema, Vetus Willus' Elven servant, was never charged with the murder Maeve and Mal pinned on her. Out of pity, guilt, or perhaps just for publicity's sake, the Double O ordered her Enslavement Curse be broken, and she was freed.

Maeve had never felt so relieved that her own plan for ensuring Jema was acquitted and freed was no longer necessary. Her Magic was weak as of late, and casting a spell to alter the minds of many in order to atone for her sins had seemed a daunting task.

Despite the fact that Doggbind spit each time Malachite's name was said or the fact that posters of him with "beware" written across his face were plastered across the door of her favorite tea shop, Esmarelle's, there were a constant rumble of sympathizers for the Dread Prince.

None of the new rules and regulations stopped Magicals from rebelling against the Double O. Mal's Dread Mark was found scarred in Magic on the doors to the Double O Headquarters. The Magic was so deep, they had to replace the entrance altogether.

And so, the Dread Mark was banned.

For the Orator's speech, Maeve was dressed in all black, tactical, Bellator attire. The Optimum pin still gleamed on her chest, though she had not deserved it in months, a fact which earned her many nasty glances.

Doggbind kept it on her all the same.

It was a bribe. A token of guilt. A consolation prize.

It was anything other than earned.

Maeve found it difficult to duel, to fight at all was a battle within herself. The power she awakened in her father's death, if it was ever real at all, now lay dormant once more, stifled by grief and loneliness.

She was weaker than before Mal trained her.

Moon's voice flooded back into her ears as his speech boomed out across Helming Hall.

Being there was torture. A sacred place of knowledge and exploration. Where she had become a Supreme. Now trampled with memories too precious to recall.

Moon gestured back at her, and she stepped towards him, reminding herself that her facade was part of a greater plan. That it was necessary to ensure the Magicals left on Earth were safe until Mal's return. Until they knew who poisoned The Dread Goblet.

Moon continued his speech to the students of Vaukore with her at his side.

"The falsely self acclaimed Dread Descendant is nothing more than a delusion of grandeur. This man named Malachite Peur committed treason by executing the murder of our beloved Premier, Ambrose Sinclair. His daughter, Maeve Sinclair, has turned away from her vows as the right hand of this imposter after he brutally murdered her father. He manipulated her mind with the power of the Dread Artifacts. She stands here today to denounce her ties with this sad attempt at rebel alliance and encourages all Magicals to trust their Orator. Trust their government to protect them from these radicals that seek to destroy everything we have worked for here on Earth."

Moon took her hand in his and held it high.

Dirty fucking politician.

Maeve smiled and repressed the thought of how easy it would be to reach over and slit his throat with just two fingers.

She wondered every night who it was that poisoned that goblet. The possibilities were endless. The Orator's mind was completely closed to her, not that she had the strength to dive into it, regardless.

The crowd at Vaukore cheered as his speech ended.

Moon released her hand and clapped her on the back. She stepped away from him, letting him and the Premier pass by her as they were ushered off the stage. Arman, once her father's captain and now Doggbind's, trailed behind the new Premier.

Maeve did not look at him.

Zimsy shook Maeve's shoulders, waking her from her nap.

"Roswyn is here," said Zimsy quietly.

Maeve looked over her shoulder. Roswyn stood in his Magical Militia uniform.

"What?" asked Maeve, dropping her head back to the soft pillow of the couch and closing her eyes.

"Get dressed."

Maeve did not move.

"It wasn't a question, Sinclair," said Roswyn.

"I don't answer to you," she replied lazily.

"You forget I am not the one commanding."

Maeve's eyes popped open and she stared straight ahead at the wall. Zimsy sat next to her and took her hands. Maeve didn't look over at the beautiful Elf.

"Go," she whispered. "You need to get out of the house."

Maeve rolled her head towards Zimsy. She smiled softly and squeezed Maeve's hand.

Freedom looked immaculate on Zimsy. Her skin glowed more than it ever had at Sinclair Estates. Her silky hair was shorter now, the way she always wanted it. But Clarissa had always insisted long hair suited Zimsy best.

Her pointed ears were jeweled with earrings she picked from Maeve's personal collection. Fine stones that she had never been allowed to wear.

"Is that my blouse?" asked Maeve sleepily.

Zimsy looked down at her and smiled. "Peach is not your color."

She squeezed her hand once more. "Go," she urged, "and when you return, we can go to that new tea shop."

Maeve pushed off the pillow and stretched. "You only want to go there to look at that Human who makes the special teas."

Zimsy looked away from her and smiled triumphantly. "He likes to look at me, too."

Maeve stood and grabbed her overcoat from a nearby chair. "Well, he makes horrible tea."

"You're awfully quiet," said Belvadora in her normal, monotonous tone.

Maeve looked up at her. With a sigh, she shifted her gaze to Roswyn. "This isn't my meeting."

Mumford scoffed. "Since when does that prohibit you from speaking your mind?"

Maeve didn't look at him. She stared at the paintings and tapestries that hung in Roswyn's manor. "What's the point of this? It's the same thing over and over again. Recruit. Move in secret. Repeat."

"In case you haven't noticed," Mumford fired back, "there are three new Bellator here tonight that have joined our cause."

"Whoo-hoo," said Maeve dryly.

Mumford's mouth fell open as he geared up to chastise her.

Roswyn spoke before he could. "Shut it. Both of you. Maeve's right. This isn't her meeting."

Maeve nearly laughed. Only Roswyn could side with her and take a dig at her in the same breath.

"If I may?" asked one of the new faces.

The girl looked at Roswyn to continue. He nodded. She turned her attention to Maeve. "Despite this not being your meeting, I believe I speak for all of us, especially those of us new here, when I say we want to hear your opinion."

Maeve stared at her for a moment before she spoke. "Why are you here?" she asked gently.

The girl didn't hesitate to reply. "Because I believe The Dread Prince is being wrongfully assassinated. His character, I mean. I believe the Double O is corrupt and full of liars."

"My father was part of The Double O," Maeve said tensely.

The girl nodded. "And that is why many of us do not trust that we are being told the truth. That is why I wish to hear from your mouth what we are doing. You stand beside him."

Maeve's brows pulled together. The girl continued.

"Moon and his cabinet all repeat the same rhetoric. That Mal killed your father because the Premier would have been in his way."

"Watch your mouth," warned Maeve.

"Hear her out," said Belvadora. "She is here, isn't she? Don't shoot the messenger."

Maeve's jaw tightened as she held her tongue, despite her desire to tell Belvadora to shove it. The new recruit looked at the boy next to her.

"We are here because we think that's a lie. That everything they are saying about you, and Malachite, is a lie. I didn't get into Vaukore. My scores weren't even close. I didn't know any of The Sacred before I made it into the lower sector Bellator. But I know what is said about you. And I know that you can't possibly truly stand at Moon's side and accept his propaganda. So that is why I am here."

She paused.

"Anything else?" asked Maeve.

The girl shook her head.

"First and foremost," began Maeve, "you do not call the Dread Prince by such a familiar name. He is your Prince, and Prince alone. Secondly, I'm not exactly sure what any of you want from me. You want to hear me say it? That I want to slit their fucking throats each time they speak my father's name? That every new decree they order makes my skin crawl?" She knew she should have stopped there, but as the words poured from her mouth, she didn't care. "That I am playing my part until Mal's return? Or are you all here wondering where he is? Wondering why Roswyn is leading this pointless meeting and not him? Because if that's the question you are seeking an answer for, you are absolutely out of luck."

Belvadora smiled across the table at her. "There she is."

Maeve shot her a mocking smile.

"Listen," said Roswyn tensely, addressing the room. "My orders are clear: I am to build an army here on Earth while Mal finishes readying The Dread Lands. His coronation didn't go as planned..." He paused and looked at Maeve. "So here we are. We must keep the Magicals loyal to his cause on Earth safe, until The Dread Lands are ready for them."

"But you don't know when that will be?" asked the new boy.

"No," said Roswyn. "And it isn't our place to question the Dread Prince's timing or orders. When the blight that drove our ancestors here three hundred years ago has been pushed back into the shadows, he will return, and we will be in the promised land at last."

Chapter 5

Maeve

Doggbind smacked on a piece of chewing gum as he stalked across the training arena in the Bellator Sector with Arman hot on his heels.

"Listen up," he bellowed, quieting the room. "New Militia Decrees have been passed." He hopped onto a training platform. "I said, 'listen up'!"

The room fell fully silent under his harsh stare. He reached in his mouth, pulled out the piece of gum and jerked his arm towards Arman. The blond Captain did not hesitate to take, with his bare hands, the saliva covered piece of candy from his Premier.

Maeve couldn't control the look of disgust plastered across her face.

"They already banned all travel on and off Earth," muttered Roswyn. "What now?"

Maeve didn't meet his gaze as she brushed past him and stepped further towards Doggbind and Arman.

The new Premier raised his voice, ensuring all could hear his news.

"Orator Moon will make a public announcement later, but I can tell you now that another Militia Degree has been ordered, signed, and executed."

Doggbind pulled a scroll from his inside jacket pocket and whipped it open.

"The first order: The word Dread is banned."

A hush of whispers shot across the hall of Bellator and Magical Militia.

"Silence," called Doggbind. "Under the Unity of Magic act, The Orator's Office decrees there shall no longer be talk of such Magic."

His eyes scanned down the parchment as he continued.

"Second order: any unapproved private session or conspiracy to undermine The Orator's Office will be met with the highest penalty of treason."

Maeve's shoulders lifted. She did not dare a glance back at Roswyn.

Doggbind rolled up the parchment and shoved it back in his coat pocket.

"No questions," he barked. "Bellator are dismissed and Supreme Militias are to go with Arman."

Doggbind dismounted the platform and stalked towards the exit, leaving Arman with his used piece of gum.

Maeve waited out of sight for Roswyn to round the corner. When he did, she silently snagged his arm. She Obscured them to her townhome in a twisting mist of Magic. Roswyn jerked from her at once, gathering Magic at his fingertips. He looked over her with heavy breathing.

"Relax," she said, annoyed. "I know you aren't dumb enough to go blabbing."

Roswyn shook out his hand and stepped away from her. "Well someone is," he grunted.

He crossed over to a long table, filled with glass topped stands, and reached for one filled with cookies.

Maeve's Magic popped across his knuckles, forcing him to withdraw his hand.

"Those aren't for you," she said.

Roswyn snorted. "Let me guess, they're for the multitude of guests you entertain regularly."

"Quit whining. Primus and the Seven Realms, you are obnoxious."

Roswyn turned towards her in defeat and without a cookie. Maeve continued.

"Either one of your little recruits is talking, or they are just paranoid."

Roswyn smiled. "Only one way to find out."

"It's going to look incredibly suspicious if we go knocking on doors this late at night, interrogating a very lengthy list of Mal's sympathizers."

Roswyn's smile widened. "Who said anything about knocking?"

For all the brute strength he harbored, Roswyn, for once, had been quite clever to ensure that each recruit and member of their little underground rebel society gave him Magical permission to enter their home by Obscuring.

On the fifth residence they Obscured into, Maeve had grown tired of the incessant startled scream that greeted them. By the twentieth, she had given up on even trying to assure them they needn't scream.

Not yet, anyway.

Though, by the end of their interrogations, Maeve's head spun from determining if nearly a hundred memories were true or false, and Roswyn was angry he didn't get to pound on anyone for being a snitch.

"There's always tomorrow," he said as he Obscured her back to the small garden behind her townhouse.

She slipped quickly into a small chair and held the sides of her face, rubbing the aches as Roswyn made a plan for keeping their meetings a better secret. But Maeve felt deep in her core that there was no snitch or traitor among them. The thought brought her no joy. It was far more worrisome that there was no snitch.

The Double O was merely making sure all Magicals felt the weight of their watchful eyes.

Too many eyes were on Maeve Sinclair. And the set of dark ones she desired on her were fading from memory.

"Stop being such a child," snapped Agatha, as she pulled poisonous moraspera needles out of Maeve's hand. The floral bush was over three hundred years old, and the only plant native to The Dread Lands that would successfully bloom on Earth.

"It hurts," protested Maeve.

"You've had worse," stated Agatha.

Maeve had a hard time arguing.

Agatha finished removing all the needles from Maeve's skin and set aside the sharp tweezers.

"There," said Agatha. "Pips swears he's stuck himself plenty of times and never felt the poison."

Pips was Agatha's gardener. He was a Human with such an incredible green thumb that Agatha deemed him worthy to know the secrets of the Magicals on Earth. In fifty years, Pips had never uttered a word of Agatha's heritage or abilities.

Maeve rubbed a healing potion over the affected skin as she said, "Imagine, the Optimum of the Bellator taken down by a plant that doesn't affect an old Human." Agatha laughed heartily.

"I haven't made Optimum in months," said Maeve. "Not honestly."

"Are you not training?"

"Sometimes," she replied quietly.

Agatha huffed. Maeve eyed her.

"Look at me like that all you want, child," Agatha began. "You already know I'm right."

"Optimum. Captain. Section commander," said Maeve. "None of those titles matter to me."

"Have you considered going back to Vaukore to finish your schooling? Academia and Practical Magic always suited you."

Maeve shook her head. That was out of the question. The

memories she harbored from Vaukore were nearly too much to bear. She couldn't imagine returning to school there.

"All's well," said Agatha. "The reforms The Orator's Office have implemented are hogwash, anyway."

"Reforms?"

"The Militia Decrees for the school," said Agatha.

Maeve shook her head.

Agatha frowned. "I paid for your newspaper subscription–"

"Zimsy uses them in the garden beneath the soil."

Agatha's mouth fell open. "Well, that's very rude."

Maeve smiled softly. "I never asked you to buy me a newspaper subscription."

Agatha's lips pulled into a thin line. "I thought it was a kindness to keep you up to date about the current affairs of the world."

"There is nothing that gossip column prints that would update me."

"I'm afraid you're incorrect there. Lies though they may be, I still want to know what webs they are weaving."

"Circle back around, Grandmother. What reforms at Vaukore?"

"The Headmaster position is gone, replaced by that fool Doggbind. A puppet to control, no doubt. Larliesl tells me most of the staff are under strict new Magical guidelines in the classroom."

Maeve didn't look at her grandmother. They sat in silence for a moment.

"Have you been to Sinclair Estates?" asked Maeve.

She had not been to her home since the night she left.

"No," said Agatha roughly. "Not since. . ." Agatha trailed off, clearing her throat before changing the subject from Ambrose's funeral. "The house itself kicked Clarissa out. Her Magic was completely useless in the estate. If she walked into a room, the firelights immediately died out. If she ordered Trudy to bake something, the house burned it."

Despite how pleasing this information was, Maeve looked across the table sadly.

"Grandmother," said Maeve, "why don't you talk to me about him? He was your son."

Agatha inhaled shakily. "He was not my first son lost."

Maeve looked down at her fingers, rubbing her wounded skin. She traced over her black veins.

"Some advice, Maeve darling," said Agatha, smiling. "Not everyone will grieve like you, even when your loss aligns. You can trust this old bag."

"Grandmother," said Maeve with a soft laugh.

Agatha winked at her. "How about we bake some lemon cookies today?"

Chapter 6

Maeve

Lists of Bellator lay sprawled across Maeve's dining table, the ends of the parchments curling up on themselves. Their names were divided into loyal, loudly disloyal, and those who remained malleable.

She and Roswyn studied their updated lists over dinner, discussing who he'd move in on next to begin feeling out their intentions. The Double O's ever changing laws and legislation made moving in secret harder all the time.

With Doggbind and Moon breathing down Maeve's neck, Roswyn had far more success at working behind the scenes.

"She's pregnant," he blurted out as Maeve thumbed through scrolls.

She paused and looked up at him. "Emerie?"

He didn't smile. He tore a piece of bread on his plate and popped it in his mouth.

"How can you tell?" asked Maeve. "You haven't seen her in over six months. She's in another realm."

"I'm a Pureblood aren't I?" he answered.

Maeve set aside the parchment and looked down at her food. "I suppose I thought they were lying about that."

"Well, they weren't. I can feel her Magic growing every day. Even across realms."

Maeve's brows flicked up. She couldn't feel Mal's Magic across realms.

"Apparently I can feel that it's a 'her,' too."

Maeve didn't smile. "I always pictured you having boys."

Roswyn cleared his throat and changed the subject.

"How many Bellator do you estimate will go to the Dread Lands?"

"At least a third," she answered. "Maybe half."

"Good," he said with a nod.

They fell silent as they finished their dinner.

"Have you talked to him?" asked Roswyn finally.

Maeve looked down at her nearly empty plate.

"No," was all she said.

"I figured based on that snappy response you gave the new girl."

Maeve looked at the table between them. Her stomach twisted. "Have you?"

He scoffed. "You think he'd speak to me over you if given the chance to communicate with us?"

Maeve sighed.

He set his fork down. "You do," he said, a smile pulling up at the corner of his lips.

"Don't sound so pleased." Maeve pulled her napkin from her lap and tossed it on the table, eager to retire.

His face pulled together, almost in a scowl. "You're practically dead inside aren't you?"

"Practically?" she asked. She shook her head.

A glass of Dragon Whiskey appeared on the table before Roswyn, courtesy of her enchanted townhome. He slammed it back at once.

"That's how I felt after Antony," he said, biting the sting of the liquor.

Another glass appeared in front of Roswyn.

And one in front of Maeve. She looked down at it.

"I don't remember how I felt after Antony anymore," she said. "It's all one blur of death."

Roswyn picked up his glass and raised it. "Drink that."

Maeve shook her head and didn't reach for the glass of liquor.

"Come on, Sinclair," he said sternly. "The house wants to help you."

Maeve stared at the glass of brown liquid the house gifted her. It had been months since she drank anything stronger than tea. Years before that.

Roswyn raised his glass slightly higher. "To Antony and

Ambrose."

Maeve grabbed the glass before she could talk herself out of it, and downed the contents in one swift gulp without toasting with him. The warm liquid burned her throat before she even swallowed. A harsh and fiery sensation slipped into her stomach.

Roswyn tossed his back.

The drink betrayed her, triggering her stomach to flip over and over. Maeve leaned over sideways and vomited beside the chair.

Laughter filled the room. She had never heard Roswyn laugh with enjoyment like that before. She wiped her face with her napkin and sat up. Nausea rolled through her.

She had never seen him so relaxed and joyful. He leaned back in his chair and looked up at the ceiling.

"I watched your brother do that the first time he ever drank Dragon Whiskey too. Except he vomited on my mother's antique rug. She still gripes about the stain." He paused and his voice lowered. "I was never so grateful for a stain." Roswyn's eyes landed back on her. "You don't look like him."

Maeve looked away from him.

"Except your eyes. You and Arianna both have them."

Maeve rested her elbows on the table. "I know."

She looked like her mother. She had seen her in her father's memories. They were old, whispers of thoughts, but Maeve had been able to make out some of her face just once.

Roswyn looked down at Maeve's hand, where her Sinclair family ring sat glistening.

"He had one similar," he said, lost in thought.

"I forget," began Maeve, "that you were friends. I dream about him. I think it's him, at least. Did you ever see his wolf form?"

Roswyn shook his head.

"Hmm," she said. "Well, I think it's him."

Roswyn pushed back in his chair, cleared his throat, and stood. "I'll see you tomorrow."

Two more glasses of Dragon Whiskey appeared between them.

Roswyn's brows raised. His smirk reappeared.

"I don't think that's a good idea," she said.

"Who said anything about good ideas?" He laughed. "If we're stuck here together, we might as well make the most of it."

Maeve didn't smile. "Don't start acting kind towards me out of pity."

Roswyn picked up one glass and handed it to her. "I've always pitied you." He picked up his own.

"Pity?" She almost laughed. "Is that what it is?"

"Just drink the damn whiskey, you insufferable woman," said Roswyn.

She looked down at her drink. "I think I'd prefer something—"

The house obliged her before she finished her request. The dark liquid in her cup swirled, turning a clear color.

Maeve sighed.

Three more shots later, Roswyn was still holding his own. Maeve was not.

He sat on the rug while she laid out on the sofa.

"Have you ever been drunk around Mal?" He asked.

"No," she said, swirling the green cocktail Roswyn made her in her hand. "I haven't been drunk in years."

"Do you remember that party at Vaukore when Alphard bet that Irish boy he could knock him out in one punch?"

Maeve laughed, causing the room to spin. "Alphard missed. Liam was sober and clocked him square in the face."

"That was the night Abraxas got those imported candies, remember?"

"Barely," said Maeve. "That was the last illicit substance I allowed Brax to coerce me into trying."

Roswyn grinned. "I remember now. You were puking until 3 a.m. in our bathroom. Alphard held your hair for hours."

Maeve looked over at him. "Was Mal there?"

Roswyn shook his head. "No. He and Abraxas always roomed together."

Maeve nodded, remembering their room was further down the hall. She roomed with Lavinia that year. She was always leaving Maeve little, uplifting notes.

Mal and Maeve barely interacted that year, aside from a few snide remarks.

"Where do you think he is?" she asked as she looked up at the ceiling.

"Somewhere deep in those lands, trying to restore our home."

Maeve sighed. "Home," she repeated quietly.

Roswyn moved like he was going to speak and then didn't. Maeve looked over at him. "What?"

He took a sip of his drink and didn't meet her gaze. "It's not worth it."

"What's not?"

"What I want to say to you."

Maeve sat up, ignoring the spinning room around her and spoke. "Now you have to."

Roswyn sniffed sharply and looked over at her. "I think you should just be his second. Nothing more."

"Why?" pressed Maeve coldly.

"Because it gets in the way."

"In your way?" she muttered darkly.

"No," he said, looking over at her with a scowl. "In yours and his."

Maeve took a steadying breath. Roswyn downed the rest of his drink and grabbed a bottle of Immortally Brewed Bourbon. He tossed the bottle back in his mouth, not bothering to use his glass any longer. He swallowed hard and pointed at her.

"This plan is bigger than you. It's about all of us. And you're wallowing because he hasn't been at your beck and call. Because he's out there fulfilling our destiny."

"I am not wallowing," she began.

"Then what are you doing?"

"What I am told," said Maeve bitterly.

"Since when do you need to be told exactly what to do?" he fired. "Get in there and tear that government apart. Pull Magicals to our side with that charm everyone seems to think you have. Or just trick their minds into it. Whatever works."

He downed the bottle, the house disposing of it at once.

Maeve stood in the entry hallway of the Hapswitch House. There were no firelights.

Her body felt heavy under the effects of the alcohol she already regretted drinking. She knew better than to cope that way.

Moonlight illuminated her back through Mal's old flat.

Most of Mal's personal belongings were gone, moved to Castle Morana before Portals to and from Earth were closed. The apartment was still fully furnished, housing many of her Uncle's things that didn't have a home.

The last night she'd spent there had been beautiful. Mal left early in the morning, long before sunrise. He trailed kisses down her neck as she sleepily stirred.

"Come to Castle Morana when you've had enough sleep," he had whispered gently. "Abraxas is already there."

Maeve looked down the hall into the bedroom.

That had been the last moment she spent with him before their communication was severed.

She turned their shared parchment in her pocket over. No Magic drifted from it. No green glow. No words.

Maeve had forgotten what a hangover felt like. Zimsy made her a special potion for her morning tea.

"I used to make these for Arianna," she said with a half smile.

The Sinclair sisters hadn't spoken since Maeve left Sinclair Estates and moved into the townhouse, but she knew Titus and Arianna moved to the Dread Lands before Portals and travel were closed.

Thanks to Zimsy's potion, her headache dulled by the time she reached the Bellator Sector. Her mood, however, was not so easily adjusted.

"Sinclair needs a partner," a voice rang out, bringing her to reality.

No one volunteered. No one ever volunteered to train with her.

A new recruit stepped forward with a smug expression on his face.

"I'll spar with her," he said happily, stepping towards her. "I don't know why you're all still so afraid of her," he said with a laugh. "Guess fucking the man who murdered your father will put a damper on one's Magic, huh?"

He and a few of his friends laughed.

Roswyn looked at Maeve, but her eyes were on the boy.

"What's your name?" she asked.

He opened his mouth, but Maeve interrupted him.

"Nevermind," she said with a sigh. "I don't care."

Her fist made contact with his face, shattering his nose instantly as dirty and Dark Magic slipped through her knuckles. Crimson red splattered into her vision. He fell to the floor at once. She crawled on top of him and reared her arm back and pounded once more, each time letting the sharpest Magic she had whip from her. Again. And again. The boy fell slack beneath her. She pulled her fist back once more as fingers snagged her forearm.

She Obscured in an instant, slipping from Arman's grip and placing herself behind him. She slammed two fingers into his back, bringing him to his knees. He growled in pain.

She stepped away from them. The training arena was silent. All eyes on her.

"Don't fucking touch me," she said lowly.

She didn't look at the boy, but she knew he was unconscious, and that blood poured from his cracked and mangled face.

A deep chuckle came from behind them. Arman turned as Doggbind walked towards them.

He kneeled beside the boy. He placed his hand on the boy's chest, and then looked up at Maeve. "Within an inch of his life."

His face was full of pride. As though she was his protégé. As though he took credit for her ferocity.

"Roswyn," he snapped, straightening to his full height, his eyes never leaving Maeve. "Get him to a healer."

Roswyn obeyed without hesitation, obeying Premier Doggbind without a glance at Maeve.

Doggbind seemed pleased with the look on her face. "Someone woke up, it seems." He crossed towards her. "If you want to make them bleed, Sinclair," he began as heat rose through Maeve's body at the use of her father's last name, "you do so under my instruction." Maeve looked up at him, unable to hide the scowl on her face. "Is that understood?"

Maeve's eyes slid to Arman. She suppressed the urge to hex both the traitors at once. "Yes," she said, looking back up at Doggbind.

"Yes, what?" he asked with a smile.

Ice moved through her veins, begging her to strike.

"Yes, Premier," she said at last.

Doggbind nodded in triumph and looked over at Arman. "Arman will be overseeing your training today. Perhaps he can be a positive influence on both your temper and your mind, Sinclair." Doggbind looked back at her. "Back to training, all of you!"

Maeve moved to step away from him, but he snagged her arm sharply, yanking her back in place. His lips moved to her ear.

"Do not forget your place," he muttered.

Maeve looked down at his hand on her sleeve for a moment and then looked back up at him. His eyes faltered only for a moment as she smiled softly, the way Pureblood women were taught to control a weak man.

"It's right here," she said gently. "Every day. Here on Earth. In this training arena. Right. By. You."

Doggbind's satisfied power-trip faded. He swallowed and dropped her arm roughly. He marched away, barking instructions at a few of his section commanders.

Maeve turned towards Arman.

"I have no intention of training with a traitor," she said.

The Bellator around them fell silent. Arman's eyes narrowed at her.

Something stirred inside her.

"Watch how you speak in the Bellator Sector, Maeve," he warned.

"There are always ears."

Maeve stepped towards him and readied two fingers at her side. "I fucking hope so."

Fuck the plan. Fuck the idea that she was supposed to smile and pretend she was okay. Fuck them all.

Chapter 7

Malachite

The Entrance Hall to Castle Morana flickered in hazy green candlelight. The marbled stone beneath Mal's feet reflected the Magical lights that lined the ornate walls.

He moved through the castle, the Dread Magic he'd become one with, cleansing the land beyond the castle walls, lingered around him, trailing him like a ghost. Twilight was endless in The Dread Lands. He had no idea the hour, if it was late or early. He passed the vaulted windows, looking out over the dueling area floors below. It remained empty, just like the halls around him.

He stepped inside Abraxas' office in Castle Morana, the only light illuminating the room was a set of twin tapers on either side of the desk.

Abraxas' quill dropped at once and he stood. "My Prince," he said, throwing his first over his heart. "Are you alright?"

Mal smiled softly and nodded. "How are things?" He paused. "Has Maeve arrived?"

He waltzed across the study and sat in one of the armchairs opposite Abraxas' desk. He released a hefty sigh, still riding the high of Magic he'd encountered on his journey.

Abraxas didn't return his smile. "Much has happened since your journey into the darkness of the Dread Lands."

Mal's smile faded, his stomach sinking. "How long have I been gone?"

Abraxas looked down at the desk, flipping over a calendar. "You don't know?" he asked, trying to sound casual.

Mal shook his head. "When I am infiltrating and altering the Magic here. . . I have no sense of time. It feels like I have only been gone for hours. A day at the most."

Abraxas whistled and placed his palms flat on the desk. He sighed and looked up at Mal. "Well, your hours were two months' time here at Castle Morana."

Mal's fingers gripped the armchair as his head reclined into the backrest. The euphoric feeling of triumph slipped away as his insides sank. His eyes closed as he spoke quietly. "How much time is that on Earth?"

"It varies," said Abraxas, opening a drawer of the desk and pulling out a glass vial filled with opal liquid. "But if my calculations are correct, about six months."

Mal's eyes popped open and he ran his hands over his face.

"Here," said Abraxas, rounding the desk and offering him the potion. "Astrea made it for you."

He leaned forward in the chair and buried his face in his hands. "Six months," he said slowly. "Have you spoken to her?"

Abraxas paused. "No. The Double O suspended all travel and communications to and from Earth. Magic cannot cross the lines of the realms. I've sent my mothers jay through small Portals I make, and I've written Maeve. Though, I'm not sure she's even getting them."

Mal looked up at him. "Six months," he repeated.

Abraxas leaned against his desk. "Can you not feel her Magic?"

Mal shook his head. "I've never been able to feel her if I was here and she was on Earth." He stood and ran his hands through his hair, pacing away from Abraxas. "I knew I should have kept her here. You and Roswyn insisted she needed to be on Earth to sway the Bellator to fight for me."

Abraxas looked down. He did not bring up the fact that Maeve had not come willingly to Castle Morana since the night of Mal's coronation. "I have no doubt my cousin is safe. Before the Double O shut everything down, she was playing her part perfectly."

Mal turned back towards him. "I am not concerned with that. She's the most powerful being occupying that realm." He turned away once more. "I left her for six months to bear the grief of her father's death. Alone."

"You couldn't have known that much time would go by."

"I couldn't bring her with me," he muttered.

"She knows that," said Abraxas. "She knows it was dangerous. She couldn't breathe when you took her beyond the gates."

They stood in silence for a moment as Mal collected himself. He turned towards the door and walked away from Abraxas.

"Where are you going?" he asked.

Mal didn't look back at him as he said, "To get my second and bring her home."

Chapter 8

Maeve

Magic exploded down Maeve's spine. She halted in the dark townhouse, where she paced restlessly in the night. She blinked, certain she was wrong about the feeling.

It grew and grew. Its taste and scent familiar and safe and–

She turned as small sparks of green light twisted in the hallway.

A mighty Portal swirled before her with blues and greens illuminating the floral wallpaper. She squinted in the light. The center of the vortex cleared.

Mal stepped from the blinding light.

His Magic moved through the Double O's restrictions with ease. He didn't even look affected by the Magic needed to Portal through realms.

"Hello, Maeve," he said softly.

Maeve's chest rose and fell slowly. She didn't move towards him.

He was in all black. A tailored set fit for a prince. Silver chains draped between his shoulders, encasing the Dread Locket that hung around his neck. A long black cloak draped to the floor.

The scar she had given him stood prominently across his brow and eye. Jagged, white skin that nearly blended into his pale complexion split his eyebrow.

Mal stepped towards her and held out his hand. The Dread Ring sat on his finger. She didn't take it.

"Your Magic is…different," she said stiffly.

Mal nodded. "It's stronger."

Maeve looked at him and swallowed the tears of rage begging for release.

Mal's shoulders fell. "Maeve–"

"Get it out then," she said. "Tell me why I've been sitting in the shadows for seven months."

"I came as soon as I could. Abraxas said. . ." He sighed. His voice was soft. "Seven months? Truly?"

Mal stepped towards her, stopping short as she stepped back from him.

"It's me, Maeve," he said.

She loosed a shaky breath but didn't retreat from him as he stepped towards her again.

"I know you are mad and scared. I can feel it all screaming at me," he said. "Just take my hand, and I promise I will never leave you in a different realm again."

Maeve looked down at his outstretched hand as he moved closer to her once more. The watch she'd gifted him gleamed softly in the dim light.

"Where are we going?" she asked as she looked up at his breathtaking face.

"Home," said Mal sincerely. "Our home."

The Entrance Hall at Castle Morana swirled into existence around her. She'd only been there once for Mal's coronation. The black stone floor reflected the firelight chandeliers above.

Zimsy stepped behind Maeve.

"There are hundreds of chambers and suites here, Zimsy," said Mal. "Any one of them is yours."

Zimsy looked up at Mal and thanked him. She turned to Maeve and took her hand. She squeezed it gently and ventured into the castle to explore.

Mal stepped forward, and Maeve hesitated. He turned back towards her. She looked past him down the long vaulted hall towards the Throne Room.

The last place her father drew breath. Where blood pooled from his eyes and mouth and nose. Where she felt his Magic fade from existence.

But there was new Magic at Castle Morana. Magic she had not been expecting to feel and sense.

"Maeve."

Mal's voice brought her out of her trance.

She looked up at him. His eyes were watchful and his face was calm.

She opened her mouth to tell him she wanted to leave. That she wanted to be anywhere but there. But a head of bright blond hair appeared through an archway at her side.

Abraxas walked into the Entrance Hall reading a large book. He looked up at Mal, and then he stopped promptly upon seeing her. His bright, silver-blond hair was longer, and the ends were slightly wavy. His serpent pin that signified his position as Hand gleamed on his chest.

Maeve's throat snagged as a jagged breath escaped her lips. Her eyes filled with tears.

The book in his hands hit the floor with a thud. Abraxas quickly closed the gap between them and slammed into her, silently embracing her. She shook and wrapped her arms tightly around him. Her jaw tightened, desperate not to cry. As she pulled away, her cousin's hands took her own.

"Oh, how I missed you," he said.

Maeve looked down at their hands. A shining silver band sat on his left ring finger. She couldn't look up at him.

"Engaged?" she asked with concern.

Abraxas forced his face into her line of vision. He smiled wickedly, wiping away a tear that had escaped down her cheek. "Don't feel sorry for me, feel sorry for her."

Maeve laughed. And Abraxas' chest swelled.

"Who?" she asked.

"Juliet."

It was likely Abraxas, being Mal's hand, had been able to pick Juliet. It was no secret the pair had indulged in many experiences together. Abraxas was wise to pick someone supportive of his lifestyle.

Maeve ignored the guilt in her stomach. She had refused her duty. And Abraxas was not given that privilege.

She smirked softly at him. "Wonderful. More blond Rosethorns."

He grabbed her in another embrace. "You've no idea how happy I am to see you."

Maeve sighed. "I missed you, Brax."

They pulled away and Maeve stepped back. Abraxas turned towards Mal.

"I believe everyone is here, My Prince. Except for Alphard, of course."

"Good," said Mal. "We'll be just a moment."

Abraxas scooped up his discarded book and continued across the Entrance Hall.

"Where's Alphard?" she asked.

Mal didn't look at her. "He's in Aterna."

"With the High Lord?"

"With Reeve, yes."

Maeve looked up at him. "You want his allegiance."

Mal didn't look over at her. "For starters," he said with calculated ease.

Tension sat thick between them.

"Come," said Mal, crossing the hall where Abraxas disappeared, "there is much I do not know."

Maeve followed him, somewhat reluctantly.

Roswyn and Mumford were already happily seated at the large circular table when Maeve and Mal arrived. Abraxas put out his cigar as they joined them. He looked to Mal, who gave him a short nod, and Abraxas began their meeting.

Roswyn relayed information about the Double O, Vaukore, and all the Magical restrictions on Earth. Once he was finished Abraxas spoke.

"It will only be a matter of moments before Moon, Doggbind, and the Double O realize Mal has returned," said Abraxas. "And more-so, how easily he got to Earth despite their Magical blockades."

"Thousands of Magical Militia are ready to come here," said

Roswyn.

"Wonderful," said Abraxas. "That will be our next order of business: ensuring all Magicals who wish to come to The Dread Lands are able."

"Is the city habitable yet?" asked Mumford.

Abraxas answered for Mal, who was preoccupied with watching every single breath that rose and fell through Maeve.

"Some of the manors and estates closest to the castle are, yes. The Beryl City I believe is next?"

Abraxas looked to Mal. He peeled his eyes away from Maeve for long enough to say, "Soon."

Abraxas nodded. "Any Magical citizens who need immediate placement in the Dread Lands can reside here at Castle Morana until then."

"And the Double O?" questioned Mumford. "We just allow them to carry on?"

"For now," replied Mal.

"Vaukore as well," said Abraxas. "If Doggbind holds the academy captive, we must be careful. Alphard is in our sister land, Aterna, making friends with Reeve and his court."

"Is that code for spying?" asked Maeve dryly.

Roswyn nearly laughed. "Since when is Al an ambassador?"

Abraxas smiled. "Since I appointed him one."

"Reeve's alliance was through my father," said Maeve. "What if he has no desire for such a companionship now?"

She could feel Mal's eyes on her.

"The hope is that the High Lord of Aterna will still desire to be our friend," said Abraxas, "and has valuable knowledge about the Dread Artifacts."

"Only two Dread Artifacts remain out of my possession," said Mal. "And we are going to find them."

"The stone and the spellbook remain," said Abraxas with a nod. "The stone's last known location was on the Dark Planet."

"How do you know that?" asked Maeve.

"Alphard may be struggling to get close to Reeve, but there are entire cities of thousands of Immortals. Many of whom were delighted to tell him what they know."

"And how long has it been since they were last known to be on The Dark Planet?" she asked.

"Over four hundred years," said Abraxas.

Maeve sunk into her chair at that daunting information.

"Do you remember our visit to Vetus Willus?" Mal asked.

She looked over at him. His angelic face studied hers. She nodded.

"I did not expect to walk out of that gaudy mansion with three Dread Artifacts in hand."

"No," said Maeve. "Like calls to like."

He nodded back at her. "Like calls to like."

They stared at one another until Abraxas broke the silence.

"The spellbook is another obstacle entirely," he said. "There are no leads for its whereabouts."

"What about Hiems? Kier loved Mal last I heard," said Mumford.

"King Kier from Hiems is still thrilled about our realms being open to one another."

"And Lithandrian and the Elven Lands?" asked Maeve.

Abraxas looked up at her, forgetting she wasn't aware of their current relations. "Oh," he said. "Right. Developments there have. . .slowed. Xander is dead."

Maeve's jaw loosened. She looked to Mal. His eyes didn't deny it.

Her heart swelled as a small bit of his Magic brushed up under her chin. It was apologetically possessive.

"And?" she pressed, fighting the natural urge to kick her head back and close her eyes.

Abraxas snapped his fingers, and a single scroll appeared in his hand. He slid it across the table towards her. She pulled it open, pinning the curling edges in each hand.

Abraxas Rosethorn,

I send our deepest gratitude for your letter. As Hand to the Prince, I imagine it bears heavily upon your heart to bear witness to a time when Hands, such as my Prince brother was to me, are so easily killed.

Maeve's stomach tightened at the threat.

I am no fool. I understand the reason my brother died. I warned him not to pursue Maeve Sinclair, the Dread Prince's Viper. My words fell on deaf, and eager, ears.

To answer your call, I am willing to maintain open communication in pursuit of your Dread Prince's vision for us all. However, be warned, Hand of the Prince, that I am wary of this new world dawning. There is a reason the Elven Lands have been sealed for centuries.

Please pass on my condolences at the great loss of the beloved Ambrose Sinclair. I can think of no one less deserving of that fate.

Lithandrian
Queen of the Elven Lands, Daughter of Luxeron

She looked up at Abraxas. The parchment disappeared with another snap of his fingers. "But the Dread Stone and Dread Spellbook are not all I have been searching for." He looked at Mal and Maeve. "Finding your little friend Ismail would prove very convenient."

Maeve had forgotten the exotic Witch.

Abraxas continued. "No one has seen or heard from her since she repaired the Finder's Stone for the pair of you."

Maeve looked to Mal, suddenly understanding. "You think she is hiding in Aterna?"

Mal's eyes never left hers and he smoothly said, "I think it's a possibility that Reeve was never an ally."

Maeve looked down at the table and ran her hands across her face. A moment of uncomfortable silence passed.

"Do you think there is any chance he did it?" asked Abraxas gently, his eyes sympathetic.

Maeve didn't look up at her cousin, hating the fact that her father's murder was even a topic of conversation, and replied. "I would be lying if I said I hadn't thought about it."

Chapter 9

Maeve

"These chambers were not meant for me," said Maeve. "They are meant for you."

She stood in the doorway of the Crown's Quarters in Castle Morana, the suite meant for he or she who wore the Dread Crown. Carved onto the threshold and the door handles were markings of Vexkari. Some old. Some new.

"It's the safest place in the castle," he said. "The ancient Magic in this room is holy. It is of my blood. I want you here."

Maeve stepped inside the bedchamber. It sat high in Castle Morana, overlooking the jagged cliffs of the Dark Peaks. The large windows should have shown her such a landscape, but it showed the cliff-side in Scotland. She halted.

The cliff-side around Sinclair Estates.

"It's. . ." she began, speechless at once.

"Enchanted. Just like the one in your old bedroom," said Mal cooly.

And like the one in her father's study.

Maeve crossed to the window. Her fingers pressed against the cool glass. "You did this?"

"Yes."

She didn't look at him. The gesture was wonderful, but nearly unbearable. A memory of her father surfaced. She did her best to repress it. Spinel scurried across the room, making himself comfortable in a chair by the green fire.

"It's very well done." She ran her finger up and down the windowpane in an attempt to distract herself. "Solid Magic."

"You should get some rest," said Mal.

"No, I'm alright."

"You haven't been sleeping."

"How do you know that?" she asked, looking over her shoulder.

Mal answered calmly. "I can feel it."

She looked back at the enchanted window. "I heard your voice so often," she began. "In nightmares when I felt as though I was drowning. When I dozed off in the bath and slipped into the water."

She turned from the window and surveyed her chambers. They were decorated with deep blue, nearly black, bedding and rugs. The armchairs were a pale green color. And the vanity along the far wall boasted a large gold framed mirror. She looked up at the painted ceiling and spoke.

"My mind. . . it's not connected to you like I became so accustomed to." She turned back to the window and tapped the glass twice with her knuckle. The cliff side shook silently and vanished, mist covering it fully. A new view appeared, the true view outside her chamber. Heavy rain blurred the Dark Peaks. "I am in your presence at last and I have never felt more alone."

Maeve brought her fingers to her chest, where his Dread Locket once hung.

Mal stood across the room. His gaze burned a hole in the side of her face.

"Look at me," he commanded slowly.

She obeyed. His face was soft as he stared down at her.

"I shouldn't have let you stay on Earth."

"Well, I didn't want to be here," she fired back.

Hel hid the wound her words created well. He spoke coolly, as he always did. "I believe you need genuine sleep."

"I can't–" she started, her voice breaking.

She looked back out the window, her pride and anger refusing to cry before him.

"Why can't you sleep?" he asked quietly. "I tried to see your dreams, but your mind is closed to me."

Maeve didn't answer right away.

"I have this recurring dream," she said quietly. "That I'm at my house, my old home, but it's different. It's broken and falling apart and dark. Nothing like it truly stands." She paused. "Or ever stood." Her voice grew quick. "And I know why I'm there. I'm supposed to save him. But when I make it to him, he's in this empty bathroom, stumbling around, confused and bleeding, and he doesn't even know who I am–" She shook her head, tightening the grip on her emotions. "And then I turn and Antony is there, watching, looking horror-struck. And when I turn back to my father, he's in this old bathtub, sitting hunched over himself, naked, shivering, and shaking in filthy water, and he still doesn't know who I am. And I watch him. And know that no matter what I do. . . he will die in my hands."

Mal was closer now. "It's only a dream, Maeve."

Maeve couldn't look at him. "Is it? If it is, it is so close to reality I can no longer remember which is which. My choices. My negligence. His death." She held herself tightly. Her body nearly shook. "I cannot block the memory of him myself. I want him gone from my mind." She turned towards his strained face. "Can you just–"

Mal spoke calmly, disregarding her words. "No," he interrupted. "I will not block those thoughts and memories. You must face them."

Maeve turned back towards the window once more. Pale green mist rolled over the mountains across the lands. She looked up. Three moons in perfect alignment sat across the sky. She wondered if her father had seen these moons the night he died. She wondered what he pictured for his own life in the Dread Lands.

He had been so proud that his daughter was the Dread Prince's second. His Dread Viper. Destined for power.

"Seven months. And not a word," she muttered, barely above a whisper. She didn't look at him. "Not even a glimmer or glimpse of your Magic."

The tether Mal kept on his temper slacked.

"If you had wanted to feel me, you would have. And if I recall, it was you who asked me for solitude, you asked me for time."

She looked over at him. "Not this long."

"Time is different deep in these lands, Maeve. I had no sense of how much time had gone by."

Her eyes raked over him. She shook her head. His Magic felt so unfamiliar. So foreign.

She swallowed and looked away from him. "Roswyn says that he thinks you and I shouldn't be more than The Dread Prince and his

Sword. That we all benefit from a purely platonic dynamic in power."

Mal's brows lifted. "You're listening to Roswyn now?"

She didn't answer right away.

"Maeve."

She didn't look at him. Wouldn't. Couldn't. "I pledged myself to you. To fight for your life and your crown. And I intend to until my final breath." She paused. "If you'll still have me as your second, I desire to be that and that alone."

He was silent. And then a cold wind fluttered from behind her. She turned, and he was gone. All the light around her faded, save for the pale green twilight of the Dread Lands.

Chapter 10

Maeve

The Bellator and Magical Militia, loyal to Mal, now resided at Castle Morana. Maeve stood in the castle, overlooking the desolate-looking stone court below, with Mal tensely at her side. The Supremes laughed and joked among themselves, practicing new Magic and debating techniques.

"They're yours," he said. "Yours to command. Yours to train. As you see fit."

Just as they had been her father's.

"I don't think–" she began.

"I didn't ask what you thought."

Maeve's jaw tightened. He spoke gently.

"They want you," he said.

Maeve looked out over the training arena below. "Roswyn is better suited."

Mal turned towards her and reached into his pocket. He pulled out an intricately carved silver box and extended it towards her. She lifted the lid without removing it from his hands.

On white, satin fabric lay her father's Premier badge.

Maeve's hand dropped at once. Her head shook slowly. "I cannot."

"Perhaps not today," replied Mal calmly. "But it belongs to you."

Maeve swallowed and looked back down at the Bellator. Belvadora and Mumford were sparring.

The box snapped closed.

"I'll have it sent to your chambers," said Mal.

She knew she wouldn't be able to look at it, let alone wear it, but she didn't argue with Mal.

"What do you want them to be?" she questioned, nodding down at the Bellator below. "A royal guard? An army?"

"I have those closest to me," he replied. "I need the rest to be unwavering in strength. It is unlikely the Elven Queen or Aterna's Senshi Warriors will be on our side in the wars to come. We must prepare as they have."

"Wars to come?" she repeated. "Plural?"

Mal nodded. "I can feel it. All on the horizon. Barreling towards me."

"Our numbers are few. I imagine far less than that of Aterna."

Mal nodded. "Mumford has been recruiting across Earth. Many of them don't have ties to this land. They are afraid to come here."

"All the Sacred families are here?"

Mal nodded. "The Towers are fully restored. Even the home your ancestors lived in, should you want to see it."

She'd often imagined what The Great Towers of The Dread Lands were like. The home of her ancestors, and all the Sacreds, stood scattered across the land, all of them tall towers of wealth and glory. The Tower of Avondell was the Sinclair's.

Maeve looked away from him. "And what of Human-borns? Will they come to be citizens here?"

"Their place here is yet to be determined."

"Why?"

Mal didn't respond right away. She looked up at him.

"Mal?"

He watched the Bellator below. "Do you think they have a place here?"

"Without question," she answered. "Many of those fighters down there are Human-born."

"I know," said Mal.

"Then what question is there?"

Mal sighed. "You were scheduled to be in the training court five minutes ago."

Maeve turned towards him. "Are you seriously suggesting perpetuating the bigoted views of The Committee of the Sacred?"

Mal's eyes narrowed. "Humans struggle to breathe here. Many Human born Magicals, in turn, give birth to Humans."

"You can make it so they can breathe here," she argued. "You doubt that?"

He looked down at her. "I doubt much about this place as of late."

She opened her mouth but Mal turned sharply on his heel.

"Dismissed."

Maeve's mouth fell open at the taste of her own choices.

"What happened to your nose?" she asked Roswyn when she arrived at training.

"It's fucking broken," he sneered.

"I can see that," she retorted. "Why haven't you seen Astrea to heal it?"

He stormed past her. A bright blue strand of light snapped from her fingers and slipped around his wrist, whipping him back towards her.

"Your commanding officer asked you a question, Roswyn," she said darkly.

He stepped towards her with a hateful scowl.

"He can't heal it." Abraxas' voice came from beside her, where he appeared.

She looked over at her cousin. He continued.

"He was given strict orders not to."

Roswyn stormed away. Maeve turned to Abraxas.

"By Mal?"

He nodded. "It appears our Prince meant his last threat to Roswyn where you are concerned."

"Ah," she said quietly, understanding it was her words that landed Roswyn his broken nose.

"What are you doing, Maeve?" Abraxas asked, disappointment rippling from his voice.

"Apparently leading the bloody Bellator," she muttered.

"Not in the training court," sighed Abraxas. "With Mal."

Maeve didn't look at him. "That's none of your business."

Abraxas scoffed. "I am Hand to the Prince. Everything is my business."

"I bet you genuinely believe that," she said softly.

"Maeve," he said, reaching for her arm.

She slipped away quickly and rounded on him. "Don't."

Abraxas shook his head. "You are making a mistake."

Maeve stepped back from him. "Then it is my mistake to make. And not yours."

Abraxas recoiled at her cold words. "Maeve," he started quietly, pity dripping from his voice.

"You are his Hand just as you said," she continued. "You are his, you've sworn it, I can feel it radiating off your chest, same as mine. You've always chosen him. Since he came into our lives, you pick him. What should make me believe this is any different? That your guidance comes from a genuine place of love for me?"

Abraxas' face hardened. "Business it is, then," he quipped.

"Is Larliesl planning to reside here?" she asked, happily changing the subject and ignoring their spat.

"It's delicate," said Abraxas. "He is loyal to Mal, though he desires to remain at Vaukore."

"He's sworn it though? An allegiance?"

Abraxas nodded. "He received Mal's Dread Mark."

A mark now banned by the Double O.

"Call him here," she said.

"He wants to be at Vaukore, and it's important he remains our eyes and ears there–"

"I am second in command," she said gently, looking over at him. "Call him here."

Abraxas smiled softly, both of them already forgetting their quarrel. "As you wish."

Larliesl arrived at Castle Morana with a twinkle in his eye and pride in his stride.

"Miss Sinclair," he said with a small nod as she greeted him at the gates. "Mr. Rosethorn."

Abraxas and Larliesl shook hands.

The Dueling Master looked up at Castle Morana behind her. "A magnificent sight."

"Tell me if you don't want to be here," she said, getting straight to the point. "If you want to return to Vaukore when term begins, I will understand. It's just that. . . I need you here. The Bellator who are just learning to fight need you here."

Larliesl smiled at her. He held his chin high and his shoulders dropped. "I am at your service, Dread Viper."

Maeve nodded, words of appreciation stuck in her throat. "Shall we begin?" she asked, gesturing down the path before them.

"Can I still be called Master of Duels?" he muttered to Abraxas, who chuckled and nodded.

Maeve left Larliesl to train the Bellator. She had no interest in participating. Though she was certain she'd hear from Mal about it. She wouldn't tell him it was because the various thoughts of the Bellator slipped into her head without her consent.

That had never happened before.

It was much quieter in the desolate hallway as she followed that new yet familiar Magic that greeted her upon arrival at Castle Morana.

She stood before a large chamber door in a far wing of the castle where many non-militant Magicals resided, patiently waiting for their future homes to be restored and livable. She realized, as her knuckles rapped the door, who stood on the other side. Like calls to like, after all.

Arianna opened the door hastily, as though she too knew her sister stood on the other side long before she knocked. She looked at Maeve with a vacant expression.

"I was wondering how long you could avoid me," said Arianna.

"It's a large castle. I could have managed."

"Well, soon you won't have to," she said with raised brows. "Our home in the city is almost habitable."

"Grandmother is going to live with you?"

Arianna nodded. "The Avondell has a lavish guest quarters, with enchanted gardens she can help restore. I didn't want her alone."

"She could have stayed here," said Maeve.

Arianna turned. "This place is far too large and far too militant for an old lady," she said over her shoulder.

Maeve stood awkwardly in the doorway.

"Come," said Arianna. "I have been keeping secrets."

Maeve's head cocked to the side as she stepped towards her sister.

She motioned Maeve across the room to where a beautiful, oversized bassinet stood.

Maeve stalled. Her heartbeat slowed.

That new and yet familiar Magic fluttered up around her.

"Twins," said Arianna, looking down at her babies.

Maeve took in her niece and nephew. Their tiny breaths and rosy cheeks were captivating. "I see that," she said softly. "How old…"

Arianna hesitated. Maeve looked up at her. Her sister's face washed over with sorrow.

Maeve spoke softly after a few silent calculations. "You were pregnant that night then. Why didn't you tell me?"

Arianna ran her finger gently across the girl's cheek and then the boy's. "And overshadow his crowning and your honor?" She looked up at Maeve. "I would have never heard the end of it," she finished with a brave smile.

Maeve looked up at her sister. "Agatha made me come," she lied playfully.

Arianna scoffed, but her eyes were soft. "No one makes you do anything."

Maeve looked back down at the twins. "What are their names?"

"Anselm and Aislin."

She sat in one of the leather chairs and invited Maeve to sit opposite her with a quick gesture. Maeve watched the twins sleeping peacefully for a moment longer, and then took up in the chair.

"I'm glad you came to see them," said Arianna. "I've been wanting to talk to you."

"Are you alright?" asked Maeve in an attempt to avoid whatever conversation her sister was planning to have with her.

Arianna paused. "Yes. Alphard and Astrea's mother Irma

delivered. Astrea actually assisted. Her soothing lotions were heaven-sent post birth."

"Hmm," said Maeve. "Good, I mean. I'm glad."

"I'm sorry for what I said that night. Our last night at home together," she blurted out.

"Please, Arianna, I don't want to–"

"Well, I need to say it, Maeve," she snapped. "It's not always about you."

Maeve rested her head against the back of the chair and took a long breath.

Arianna fiddled with the ring on her finger. A sapphire stone like Maeve's own ring, gifted from their father. Like Antony had as well.

"I'm sorry I let our mother dictate how I treated you."

"She wasn't my mother," said Maeve delicately.

"She didn't create or bear you, but she was, for all intents and purposes, your mother. And I know she didn't treat you kindly for it."

Maeve looked over at the twins, still sleeping soundly. "Where is she now?"

Arianna hesitated. "She is on Earth."

Maeve nodded, still watching as her niece and nephew's little breaths sucked in and out.

"She is not allowed in the Dread Lands," said Arianna.

Maeve looked at her sister. "How do you know that?"

"You think Abraxas could hold that little bit of gossip secret?"

Maeve scoffed with a smile. "Was that Mal's doing?"

"Of course," said Arianna. "I can't say I blame him. Though, I am able to travel to see her whenever I want. I wanted her to meet the babies soon. For that, I am grateful."

A moment passed as Maeve contemplated her words. Mal's protectiveness. His desire to fight for her. She couldn't wrap her mind around the time passed. She couldn't let go of the notion that he had truly abandoned her for seven months.

"Do you like it here?" Maeve asked.

Arianna nodded. "I feel a pull here. My Magic is more powerful. My children were the first born here in three hundred years. That is a legacy I can be proud of."

"Primrose chose to stay? Or was she denied her place here as well?"

"Chose," said Arianna with a nod. "Our Prince was good on his word, and Grandmother Primrose has never spoken ill of you again, I am sure."

Maeve looked over at her sister and chewed her lip. Arianna's brows raised.

"Thank you for the apology. I am not innocent."

Arianna laughed. "That's for damn sure."

Maeve smiled softly.

"You are running the new Militia?" Arianna asked.

A sigh rolled through Maeve. "I am supposed to be."

"What does that mean?" She asked.

"It means I'm delegating that responsibility elsewhere. This should have been Roswyn's job. He is better suited for his type of thing, anyway."

"Did you just bestow him a compliment?"

"Hardly," said Maeve.

"But you're still his superior officer, yes?"

"Yes."

"Abraxas' too?"

A smile pulled at the corner of Maeve's lips. "Brax too."

Chapter 11

Maeve

Larliesl worked the Bellator relentlessly. No one doubted why the Dueling Master was there. Those who attended Vaukore had only seen a fraction of his knowledge. Larliesl instructed them with fire in his heart and a true conviction that she'd never seen from him at school.

Weeks into his command of the Bellator, he introduced a technique of Magic that left everyone with wide eyes.

"At Vaukore I had a professor of Offensive Magic, died years ago, poor old chap, but he swore he'd known a Magical that could breathe Magic."

Fawley's eyes widened. "Like a dragon breathes fire?"

"Exactly like that," replied Larliesl with a grin. "Our fingers are beautiful, wonderful conductors of Magic, but it flows through the whole body. Who is to say you cannot use more than your fingers to expel Magic?" Larliesl placed his hands behind his back. "Anyone already experienced such a technique?"

There were a few murmurs through the crowd. The older, more trained Magical Militia spoke up, announcing their success with such advanced fighting. The green and inexperienced recruits listened eagerly.

"You may not have even realized it," continued Larliesl. "But your Magic is yours to bend. Yours to manipulate."

The way Maeve's Magic had burst through her knuckles as she pummeled that boy unconscious.

"Mr. Hendrix?" Larliesl asked, gesturing towards him.

Fawley stepped up at once.

Larliesl gave him a nod and slid one foot across the stone towards him. Magic swirled across the ground.

Fawley shifted back, sliding on his heels. He quickly caught his balance and looked up at the Dueling Master.

Larliesl flicked up two fingers, levitating a stone from the courtyard. He dropped the large, smooth rock in both his hands. Without hesitation, he slammed his forehead into the stone. With a pulse of Magic, it shattered into dozens of pieces, crumbling to his feet.

"These are highly advanced Magical Combat skills. But you will all be expected to perfect them," he said.

Larliesl placed the experienced Magicals with one another to spar and duel, and sent the recruits to meditate and begin to understand the pathways of Magic within their bodies. They left the training courtyard with gloomy expressions as they realized they wouldn't get to jump into the fight.

Larliesl observed, corrected and demonstrated for the entire morning and into midday.

When he dismissed them, he turned to Maeve.

"Mr. Peur–" began Larliesl. He laughed with pride and corrected himself. "The Prince has asked that I train you privately," he said, with a smile. "It seems you can't get out of training so easily."

"Did he?" asked Maeve softly.

Larliesl nodded. "I've noticed his efforts lie outside of these castle walls, as they should, truth be told. He fears he does not have time to train you."

Maeve swallowed the lie and didn't argue.

She hadn't seen Mal in weeks. She didn't know when he'd arrive back at Castle Morana. Or if she'd even know when he did. The castle was dark and quiet when she roamed its corridors late at night in solitude. The endless twilight of The Dread Lands made for no day or night. It was one long, green haze of time.

Mal was right. Time was different in those lands.

And it played tricks on her mind.

She pressed past her daze of thought and nodded at Larliesl.

Minutes later, his two fingers landed on her temple. "You aren't even trying."

Larliesl dropped his fingers at once.

"It is difficult to fight without causing serious injury."

Larliesl nodded and walked back towards his shoulder bag. "These were a gift when I graduated from Vaukore." He pulled out two silver bracelets and slid them along his wrists.

He clicked them together and a wave of Magic passed over his body, creating a shield.

"Those are quite a rarity," said Maeve. "Elven steel. Passed down in your family?"

Larliesl was, after all, part Elven.

Larliesl turned back towards her and shook his head. The Magic was familiar. And she realized.

"My father gave you those."

Larliesl halted. "Actually, your grandfather did," he said gently.

"Why?" she asked.

Larliesl smiled softly. His pale blond, graying hair dropped over his eyes as he looked down at his wrists. "I was the best. Guaranteed Optimum and top of the Bellator before I even left Vaukore. Much like yourself."

"No one gave me any trinkets," she muttered.

"You, much to my dismay, opted not to finish your studies," he replied lightheartedly. "Though I've never seen a Supreme with such academic inclinations take to combat so well."

Maeve accepted the compliment.

"Let's continue, shall we?" Proposed Larliesl. His face grew serious. "Aim to wound, Miss Sinclair. Do not hold back."

Maeve sat and listened to each Sacred Seventeen family voice their opinions and concerns over the revitalization of The Towers and The Beryl City.

None of them had hesitated to take their place in The Dreads Lands. They were all eager to slip out from beneath the Double O and the Committee of the Sacred's grip. But as some of their concerns revolved around who would rightfully receive what land and the opinion that Human born Magicals shouldn't reside in The Towers, she found it difficult to sympathize.

She and Abraxas sat on Mal's throne in his absence. Literally.

The oversized chair fit them both with room to spare.

"House Sinclair is no more," said Roswyn's father, Wyndyl.

Acid rose through Maeve's stomach. Her bones ached at the words.

Wyndyl continued. "Human born Magicals residing there is a disgrace to the legacy of the Sacred."

Maeve shifted her gaze to him. He avoided hers.

"The Tower on Avondell should go to a new family, one that can continue bloodlines," he continued.

"The Avondell, which belonged to the Sinclairs, should be ours," said Lillian Davenport. "It borders the land my ancestors claimed."

"Precisely," said Wyndyl. "A half-blooded Magical residing there? It would be a disgrace. Only those with Pureblood should occupy a place of such rich Magic."

"Then what of my blood?" asked Maeve, speaking at last.

The room fell quiet.

Wyndyl's eyes moved slowly to her. "An exception to be made."

"Why?" she fired back quickly.

Wyndyl looked down. "You are of greater Magical standards than the rest."

"How do you know that?"

"Because our Prince has deemed it so."

"Ah," said Maeve boredly. "So the others? The Magicals not of Pureblood? Where do you propose they live?"

"In The Beryl City."

Abraxas opened his mouth to speak, but Maeve was quick to overstep. "The Beryl City has not been restored."

Wyndyl forced a smile and looked at Abraxas.

"The Dread Prince's second speaks truly," said Abraxas, with some reservation in his voice.

Roswyn's father continued. "We have also discussed the Human-born Magicals residing on Earth, and only coming here when their duties as Bellator are needed."

Maeve laughed. Abraxas sighed.

"Are you unaware what the Bellator spend their afternoons doing?" asked Maeve, not expecting an answer. "Belvadora. To name one. A Bellator that fights for you. Who risks her life in the Dread Land's unpredictable darkness in order to restore those mansions you so deeply desire to claim. She is born of two Humans. A product of the desperation of our Magic. A product of perseverance. Her very existence defies the laws of Magic and yet you would have her remain on Earth. While you, with your prestigious blood, are too weak to even cross beyond the Barrier."

The Barrier was an impenetrable line of Mal's Magic that protected Castle Morana and the parts of their new world where the air remained toxic and remnants of Dark Magic brewed. Only he and the Bellator working to restore The Beryl City and the Greywood Forest passed beyond the Barrier, and only with Mal's Magic assisting them.

"The Dread Prince has left these matters to us," Wyndyl replied.

"He has left them to me, actually," interjected Abraxas, "if either of you would let me speak."

"Apologies to the Hand," said Wyndyl reverently.

Maeve looked over at Abraxas and whispered, "Sorry, Brax."

He spoke with authority. "The Tower of Avondell is Maeve's and Arianna's by birthright. Truly, it's Agatha Sinclair's most of all as matriarchy of the family. See how nicely she sits and doesn't yap? If they see fit to use it for housing Bellator, then so be it. The Magic there is no one's to tamper with but their own. That said, there isn't enough space for the entire rank in The Avondell. So they remain at Castle Morana until The Beryl City has been restored."

"Human-borns residing in this holy Castle?" asked Wyndyl incredulously.

"I don't recall stuttering," said Abraxas plainly.

He stared at Roswyn's father and then popped a smile.

"If I may?"

All heads turned towards Mr. Mavros.

Abraxas looked over at Alphard and Astrea's father and nodded.

"Not everyone here shares the same sentiment as the Roswyn family. I have no qualms living amongst those who willingly fight for future generations of Magic to flourish."

Wyndyl scoffed subtly as many families agreed with Mr. Mavros.

"The Prince himself admitted he is concerned about Human-borns living here!" Wyndyl exclaimed to Mr. Mavros.

"I have heard your concerns," said Abraxas. "Many times. However, the Prince is not concerned with Human borns living in The Dread Lands. He is concerned for their safety here."

"And where is he?" fired Wyndyl hotly, realizing as the words slipped from him that his aggression was out of turn and quite out of line. His cheeks flushed red.

"That doesn't concern you," said Abraxas plainly.

"Of course," said Wyndyl, bowing slightly at the waist.

"Is that all you have for the Crown today?" Abraxas asked.

No one spoke. Roswyn's father turned and left the hall before any of the rest, a trail of bickering hot on his heels. Once the hall cleared, Abraxas propped his elbow on the arm of the chair and rubbed his eyes.

"You listen to this garbage every day?" asked Maeve.

"Yes," groaned Abraxas. "And you were no help either."

Maeve huffed. "Well, you're the one who invited me here."

"Because I thought if you were here that they'd shut up about it," said Abraxas dryly. "This Artemis Tower, The Crescent Tower, on and on, as if I don't have relations with four other realms to concern my time with."

Maeve sighed. After a moment, she spoke. "Where is Mal?"

Abraxas shot up with a single brow raised. "Why? Do you miss him?"

Maeve ran the tips of her fingers down the arm of Mal's throne. The lack of his Magic told her he rarely sat there, if at all.

Maeve looked over at her cousin sadly and changed the subject. "Your wedding is soon."

Abraxas stood and didn't press her on the topic of Mal and further. "That reminds me, I need your help with a few invitations."

Chapter 12

Maeve

His steps reverberated through the floor, snaking towards her. Each smooth stride drenched her in more Magic than the last. Applause and exclamations of joy carried out from the hall.

She rounded the corner, and Mal stood at the center of the hall.

With his eyes already on her.

Her knees bobbled as she took in the Dread Crown atop his head.

He was heavenly.

His high set cheekbones sucked in shadows, making him appear all the more deadly. His suit rivaled any attire of the evening. He dripped with an elegant darkness that fit his lean body.

King Kier from Hiems stood close by him, chattering endlessly, desperate for even a glance from the beautiful prince.

The Magic coursing through her veins begged her to run to him. To feel herself melt into his hold and be held captive by his dark eyes, silently admiring her. To remember what it felt like for his Magic to be one with hers.

Pride seemed too trivial a reason why she did not move towards him, despite her sleepless nights of wishing he'd return to Castle Morana. Perhaps it was her climbing heart rate, spiraling out of control with the feeling of so many eyes on her and their unwanted and unspoken condolences.

All the same, she did not go to him.

His eyes slid away from hers as he disappeared down a corridor with Kier in his ear.

She gathered her gown in her fists and made for the other side of the Entrance Hall, nearly barreling through arriving guests in an attempt to escape the pounding of thoughts slipping through her mind against her will. Her breathing quickened as they grew loud.

Cool evening air washed over her face as she stepped across the marble entrance and made for the castle steps.

"Maeve!"

She turned as Arianna hurried out of the castle. "Where are you going? I need your help with the flowers still." She gestured back inside the castle.

"Can't Grandmother help you?" she asked, panting slightly. "Or Juliet's mother?"

Arianna looked her over. "What's wrong?"

"I just need some air," she replied. "Just. . . I'll be there in a moment."

Arianna nodded. "It's alright. Agatha can help me. Can I help you?"

Maeve shook her head quickly, stepping back from her sister.

Arianna hesitated and then retreated back into the castle.

"Hello, kitten," purred a voice behind her.

Her mind fell silent.

Maeve turned, and there, standing in full Senshi armor with the moonlight at his back, was Reeve. She didn't even have time to stop herself before her mouth fell open. He looked divine, like something truly of the Gods who granted him power.

His hair was different. It was longer, half of it tied in a knot at the top of his head with silver embellishments wrapped around it.

Maeve faced him fully and cocked her head to one side. "You're overdressed."

Reeve's eyes moved down her body, then flicked up to her own. "As are you."

Her brows pulled together as she smiled placatingly. She stepped closer to him until she could see her own reflection in his black and amethyst plated armor. His giant sword hung nicely at his side.

She forgot how tall he was. She whispered up at the High Lord, "Why are you wearing that?"

Reeve looked around the party behind her, and much to Maeve's surprise, dropped his facade as he bent down and looked her dead in the eyes.

"Because sometimes I have to remind all these fuckers, including little Dread Vipers like you, who I am."

"Why not show them that beast form to remind them?" She retorted.

She'd only seen a glimpse of his dragon form the day Kietel kidnapped her from Vaukore. To most Magicals, that divine form of destruction was merely speculation. After all, they'd never seen him snarling with his long, gangly, barbed neck whipping out fire.

Reeve alone was graced with such a power. No Immortal with powers of Aterna had ever been able to fully transform into something of such unholy Magic.

His voice brought her out of her daze. "Picturing it?"

She looked up at him and ignored his satisfied smirk. "So? Why not show them?"

"Because that beast takes rage," he replied. "Do I look enraged tonight, kitten?"

"Stop calling me that," said Maeve sweetly.

Reeve merely shook his head.

Before she could respond again, two men rounded him on either side. They were fully suited up as well.

Eryx, Reeve's General, donned two broadswords.

His glistening, part Elven eyes were on the party behind her. The misty twilight illuminated his glowing pale skin and long, silky-white hair. He wore the finest gold and silver jewelry she'd ever seen. All of it Elven.

His glare was as sharp as the daggers tucked into his boots.

She recognized the other. She'd seen him before at the Hexadic meeting and at Mal's coronation. A white bow and sling of arrows rested on his back.

The archer was a small framed boy, who didn't look a day over fifteen. He had long, bony arms and pointed features. Drystan was his name.

"Weapons? At a wedding?" Maeve clicked her tongue.

Drystan smirked.

"We haven't met," said Maeve. She stepped towards Drystan. "Not officially, anyway."

Drystan bowed his head slightly. He looked over at Reeve and then back at Maeve.

Alphard Mavros emerged from behind the three men of Aterna. He stepped around Reeve and smiled at Maeve.

"Welcome back," said Alphard.

"You too," she said.

But Alphard's eyes were already on the party behind her, and Maeve was certain he was scouring the crowd for one red-head in particular. Victoria was finally his fiance.

Alphard's head turned towards Reeve as a smile blossomed across his face.

"Enjoy yourselves, boys," he said.

Reeve's mischievous grin did not return as he walked past her into the party. Eryx and Drystan followed him.

"Thank you for the invite," he called back to her.

"He came," said Abraxas, watching Reeve across the hall as he prepared to take his place for the ceremony. "I'll be damned."

"It's your wedding," said Maeve. "He's always liked you."

Abraxas shook his head. "No. That's not it."

Maeve looked at her cousin with raised brows.

"Just as I suspected. He is rather. . .taken with you."

Maeve shot her cousin an incredulous look and fired back quickly. "He is taken with his ego, with making sure I stay beneath him."

Abraxas swirled his drink with the slow rotation of his fingers and didn't reply.

"What?" she pressed.

He didn't look at her. He smiled and politely toasted a guest across the hall. "Be careful with that one, Maeve."

She shook her head. "He's not stupid. You're misreading him."

"No," said Abraxas hollowly. "One doesn't inherit the power of thousands of Immortals and retain control for hundreds of years by being stupid. No." He downed his drink and set it on a floating tray, quickly swapping it for another. "A ruler with no heirs. A ruler with no idea who will inherit his God given power, or, for that matter, when. A powerful being with the inability to stay away from you, it seems."

"He's here for Mal," she fired back.

"He has denied our invitation for months, declining to come here every single time. Except now you are here. Now you are the one extending the invitation and he is here."

"He's not—"

"He came for you. At Vaukore."

"None of that—"

"I am merely suggesting you be careful."

"Stop interrupting me," she huffed.

Abraxas raised his brows and waited for her to continue.

When Maeve had nothing to say Abraxas laughed. "Watch yourself. Around them all. That includes King Kier and Lithandrian if she ever deems us worthy of her presence. I fear they all want a taste of you."

Chapter 13

Malachite

The newly wed Mr. And Mrs. Rosethorn had the distinct honor of being the first wed in Castle Morana in over three centuries. Mal officiated their vows with a smile he grew tired of long before the night was over. He'd only just returned, and sleep desired to claim him. But as hundreds watched him with adoring, curious, and wary eyes, he did not falter.

He toasted the newlyweds. Juliet was a beautiful blonde bride. Abraxas was the most dashing groom anyone had surely ever seen. They both wore all white, as was the tradition for Magical weddings. Abraxas had opened his mouth shortly before the ceremony to suggest, perhaps, a pale blue, but one look from Maeve's Grandmother Agatha had him quickly closing it.

As always, Abraxas ensured the drinks flowed, and the music played. Though, when Mr. Iantrose tried to take the stage to make a toast with a glass of Dragon Whiskey in each hand, Abraxas took his arm gently and muttered, "Absolutely not."

Maeve wore green. The color she was crafted to adorn. Her marks of Vexkari peeked through the sheer fabric along her neck and arms. His marks.

They betrayed her anxious heartbeat.

His fingers ached with the desire to sedate the chaos running blindly through her.

Respecting her wishes was far more tortuous than listening to the endless flattery from Magicals and Kier and his council. If she had deluded herself into wanting separation, he'd play along. At least until she broke or he did.

Damn Roswyn and his constant opinions. A Supreme in the making with the thickest head and jealousy to match. Breaking his nose wasn't punishment enough, but hearing the bone snap did give

Mal some satisfaction. If nothing else, it reminded Roswyn that Mal was true to his word.

The apology flowed before Mal ever even twisted a finger.

It seemed the entire rank of Bellator knew of their distance.

But Mal knew it was only a matter of time before she broke. And when she did, he would be there to put her back together and show her just how infinite his loyalty was.

"Mal," said Abraxas, touching his arm gently and pulling him from his thoughts. He balanced a glass of dark liquor and a cigar in one hand.

Mal attempted to listen as Abraxas introduced him to someone he was certain his Hand deemed rather important. But the only guest of importance to Mal had just slipped out onto the balcony.

Chapter 14

Maeve

Dinner was a lively affair. Kier presented Abraxas and Juliet with a set of ice crystal goblets, carved from the ancient ice of Stalakta Fortress, and Reeve brought a hundred bottles of Aternian Absinthe, enough to intoxicate the entire party.

"You're supposed to sip it," Drystan muttered to Abraxas, who was on his fifth glass.

Abraxas' flushed cheeks paled. "What?'

Drystan laughed. "Don't worry. It's cool."

Abraxas shook his head, fanning his flushed cheeks. "It's quite warm, actually."

Eryx chimed in then with a booming laugh. "He means it's alright."

Maeve looked sideways at the young-looking Archer. "That's not Aterna vernacular, is it?"

He shook his head and Eryx answered for him.

"Drystan spent a lot of time on Earth. Specifically, North America."

"Have to be more specific than that, Eryx."

"Where were you then?" Asked Maeve.

"A city called New Orleans," he replied with a smile. "It was unlike anything I've ever experienced."

"He still whines about being back in Aterna," said Eryx.

"Why did you return then?" asked Maeve.

Drystan shrugged. "They called a Hexadic. And Reeve asked me to come home."

"So you were there until recently then," Abraxas remarked.

"For about twenty years."

Abraxas gasped and smiled with intrigue. "Gods, how? You're but a babe."

"The many moons I have seen would surprise you," answered Drystan.

Maeve smiled. "Incredible. I must admit I'm jealous. You can travel the entire universe in that Immoral life of yours."

Drystan's face paled slightly. Maeve looked to Eryx, but his eyes were on Drystan.

The smile faded from Drystan's boyish face. "I actually lost my Immortality in battle. When I was fifteen."

"Apologies," said Maeve softly.

"No reason to," said Drystan. "The best thing that ever happened to me was that."

"But you. . .are Immortal," questioned Abraxas.

"I am now," said Drystan, "yes. But it is not my Immortality keeping me alive."

Maeve's eyes traveled to the harsh and ancient markings that shot across his partially shaved skull, perfectly symmetrical and wrapping the base of his head. Though they looked like tattoos, Maeve knew them to be more than that.

They were Vexkari.

"Those marks are traces of powerful Magic," she said. "Did you take someone's Immortality?"

Drystan smiled patiently at her words. "No. It was given to me."

"Apologies again," said Maeve. "I meant no offense. I'm just. . .so curious."

A few exclamations from Bellator nearby drew their attention down the table. They stood around Reeve as the High Lord boasted his sword. Their faces were lit with awe as he laid it across the dining table.

"The power resonating off this thing," said one.

Along the center of the blade were markings.

"What does it say?" asked another.

"Death before dishonor," said Reeve. "Loosely translated."

They oohed over the sword as an even larger crowd swarmed the High Lord of Aterna.

"What do you call it?" asked one of the Bellator.

"Shadowslayer," he said proudly.

The Bellator grinned.

"Shadowslayer," repeated Maeve.

Reeve's eyes popped to hers.

"That's quite a name," she continued.

Reeve welcomed the challenge in her voice. He patted the thick hilt of the sword. "It got the job done."

"Victory over the darkness that nearly killed off an entire race of Magic must come so easily to one blessed by the Gods," said Maeve. "If only our ancestors had such a savior."

Reeve held her gaze. "There is blood in the water, Miss Sinclair," said Reeve gently. "It needs to be purified."

Maeve didn't reply. It was Mal who spoke with regal boredom from the head of the table.

"I would see it turn the darkest shade of crimson before any blood was cleansed from those who dirtied it in the first place."

His eyes bore into Reeve's like a dare.

Reeve nearly smiled. "Is that why our friends in the Elven Lands have remained distant?"

Abraxas laughed, a lighthearted attempt to break the tension. "The Elven Queen and you seemed far from close at the Hexadic my late Uncle called."

Maeve's insides twisted.

Reeve's eyes moved to her briefly, then to Abraxas. "She and I have had our disagreements, but I believe she was genuine in her desire to join your plight for a Magical utopia until her brother died mysteriously on the floor at Sinclair Estates."

Maeve looked up at the ceiling, biting her tongue.

"Something to say?" asked Reeve.

Mal's Magic swelled to attention. Maeve anticipated its move towards her, but it remained with him.

Abraxas' mouth opened, but Mal, his eyes never having left Reeve, spoke. "Lithandrian's brother died because he tried to take something that wasn't his."

Silence fell. Too many eyes were on Maeve. Mal continued casually. "I rid Lithandrian of a fool for a Hand."

The blatant confession spilled from Mal's tongue with sensual ease.

"I see. Only a fool would touch what is yours," said Reeve quietly, no trace of fear in his voice.

Mal smiled charmingly. "At last, we agree." He grabbed his crystal goblet and toasted the Immortals. "An honor to have you at Castle Morana."

The ballroom was loud. And growing louder as everyone drank themselves into the night. Fragments of thoughts and memories slipped into her mind. All of them unfamiliar and unwanted. She moved against the wall, bracing herself as she tried to silence her mind. She closed her eyes and rested her head back. Her mental shields were up. They were tighter than she'd ever kept them.

And yet, the mindless and drunken streams of consciousness from those around her flooded her mind.

She dropped her shields.

Nothing changed.

Except-

Magic swirled into her mind, gentle and cool.

She looked across the ballroom.

Mal's eyes were already on her. Kier's mouth was moving rapidly, but Mal was fixated on her.

The voices lingered in a garbled mess of thoughts. But one rang clear across her mind. The voice, mesmerizing and calm.

She is my never ending thought.

Maeve's breath caught as she stepped forward. Mal's expression lifted in shock as he realized her mental shields were down. He nodded once to Abraxas, who ushered Kier away, and then his eyes were back on her. He extended his hand out and spoke into her mind.

Would you do me the honor?

At his call, she forgot the party surrounding them and stepped steadily across the ballroom. As if in a trance, she forgot the Immortals that lurked in the shadows. And she forgot the tension and distance between her and Mal.

She forgot the floors were stained with her father's blood.

She forgot the past months of solitude and the pride that kept her there.

All strain between them faded in her mind as her fingertips brushed Mal's.

She forgot the Double O. Forgot the Sacred Seventeen and the Bellator she was meant to lead.

There were only his eyes on her, and his bare fingers against her own.

Maeve stiffened once more as the entire room's attention turned towards them, their thoughts growing louder. Their thoughts about her.

Pity. Jealousy. Distrust.

Her grip on his fingers pulled back. He held her in place with gentle control.

The ballroom darkened, a small beam of light cascaded softly down around them, shadowing Mal's sharp features. A soft laugh of gratitude escaped her lips as she took in his Magic that altered her view of the party.

"It's just me, Maeve," he said softly.

She stepped in towards him, inhaling his leather and spice scent as he placed his hand around her waist. Her chest rose heavily under the weight of his presence. With a gentle push on the small of her back, he began to dance them around the hall.

He looked down at her. "It never bothered you before to dance with me."

Maeve looked up at him. His dark eyes did not look away. "It's not you," she whispered. "It's their gaze, their thoughts screaming at me. I can hear them clearly. Their Magic betrays them."

Mal's eyes sharpened. "That's new."

Maeve nodded. "It only started happening shortly after I arrived. It's like their thoughts slip into my mind. I can't even pick or control what I hear or don't hear. I can go days without anything, then suddenly it's everything."

He continued to dance her slowly around the ballroom, their bodies stiff and formal with room to spare between them.

"And right now?" he asked.

"It's everything."

Mal removed his hand from her back and held it out between them. "May I try something?"

She nodded.

His hand closed to a fist, then burst open. Magic shot around them and the room full of thoughts fell silent. All that remained was the quartet of music.

She looked around them with relief.

"Better?" he asked.

Maeve nodded. He dropped his free hand to his side, keeping their palms pressed together in the other.

She stepped towards him with a steadying breath and placed her hand back on his shoulder, pressing her chest against his. His left hand slipped around her back, settling lower than before. Mal's palm twisted smoothly across hers, pushing her fingers apart with his until they were completely intertwined. They resumed their dance in silence until Mal spoke.

"How are the Bellator going?" he asked quietly, his eyes anything but casual.

"I wouldn't know," she answered honestly. "Larliesl trains them."

"So I've heard," he replied.

"Then why did you ask?"

Mal's hand slipped lower on her back, pressing her against his front.

"To hear your voice, Little Viper."

Maeve relaxed into him. His movements slowed, bringing them to a halt by the green glass-paned doors that led outside. Maeve looked up at Mal. With a wave of her hand, the doors clicked open for them. He turned and pulled her outside. She followed his lead without hesitation, the music following them out onto the balcony.

He did not remove his hand from hers as they stood looking out over the courtyards of Castle Morana.

"These were once great gardens," said Mal. "At least that's what the books tell me."

"The books?".

Mal nodded. "There are only a few written texts left here. The Magicals took all they could when they fled to Earth."

"Yes," said Maeve. "I noticed."

His finger tips brushed across her knuckles.

"But there are a few stories, mostly from healer records left in the Healing Hall, about this place before the blight. Before the waters were poisoned and the air turned toxic."

Maeve looked down below at the barren terrain. Vines of thorns wrapped the trellis and flowerbeds. What remained of any previous plant life was but a mangled mass of dead branches.

"The gardens could be restored. Just as you breathed life back into the air, so can you the ground."

Mal didn't look at her. "Would that bring you joy?"

She swallowed and looked over at him. "I can't even recall such sentiment."

He looked down at her, and his eyes scanned her face. "Oh, that I could make you remember."

She faced him and yielded a step. He mirrored her movement. His free hand moved from his side. With calculated control, his fingers slithered slowly up her arm.

Her eyes fluttered to a close beneath his delicate touch.

His fingers moved across her exposed shoulder, and up her neck, sending chills prickling across her skin. She looked up at him as he cupped her cheek. His thumb moved across her jawline with sleek precision.

"The gardens would be a start," she whispered.

Mal looked back and forth between her eyes. "Then gardens you shall have."

They stared at one another until Abraxas stepped out onto the balcony.

"Apologies for interrupting," said Abraxas genuinely. "Mal, Kier is leaving. He's lingering. I assume he wants your ear before he goes."

Mal dropped his hand and nodded. He didn't look away from Maeve.

"I'd like to retire," said Maeve. "If that is alright."

"Of course," said Mal softly.

"Will the spell follow me upstairs?" she asked.

Mal nodded. "If you need more assistance," he said, placing a single finger on her chest where her Dread Mark lay beneath her gown, "you need only call."

His Magic seeped into her, curling her toes.

She nodded softly. "Thank you," she whispered.

"Goodnight, Maeve."

He stepped away from her towards Abraxas. He stopped rigid as Maeve spoke.

"Goodnight, my Prince."

Mal's chest swelled. He stepped back into the castle without another word.

Maeve looked at Abraxas. "I don't believe I've said congratulations. You threw quite a party."

"My speciality," he replied with a smile.

Maeve didn't return it. Her eyes followed Mal across the hall inside.

"Going to bed?" Abraxas asked.

She nodded.

"I suppose it is rather late. And I do have some de-flowering to accomplish."

Maeve looked at him and even he couldn't keep a straight face at his dramatic words.

"She did not wait for you," said Maeve dryly.

"A technicality. Waited for me? Yes. For marriage? No. After all, there were only so many names on the list. It wasn't like anything was going to change."

Maeve didn't need reminding. It had taken months for her to manage to break her engagement to Alphard Mavros.

"You love her?" asked Maeve.

Abraxas smiled. "In my own way. It's a duty I am happy to fulfill." He sucked in a breath. "My preferred option doesn't bear me children."

"That's quite a selfless act."

He shrugged it off and smirked. "Is it? I can still enjoy her. She's quite witty and beautiful. I have a brain and a cock."

Maeve's mouth fell open as her brows pulled together. She waved her hands in front of her. "Brax," she whined with a genuine burst of laughter.

Abraxas smiled triumphantly. "At last," he said.

He held out his arm for her. She shook her head and laced her arm through his own.

"Let's send you to bed," he said.

The scent of gardenia hit her as she crossed her chamber towards the bathroom. The oversized tub filled with bubbling, blue water as she undressed and hung her gown over the back of the dressing chair.

The water was her preferred temperature as it hit her skin. She melted into the bubbles, resting her head against the edge.

The blue waters remained warm long into the night. Though, telling time was difficult in the Dread Lands. The perpetual green twilight that gleamed through the bathroom windows made the hours pass endlessly while her thoughts lingered on Mal. His hands against her skin once more. The desperation in his eyes to fix it all.

She'd never seen defeat on his face before.

It would be easy to call his name.

Her Dread Mark tingled. A silent beg.

She forced her eyes closed and tried to forget their dance, praying the warmth of the water and exhaustion would at least allow her some sleep.

And sleep she got.

As her mind drifted into dreams, she was once more forced to view the image she hated most. Her father sat naked in a bathtub, confused and terrified, as Antony, in his wolf form, whined with bright blue eyes set between black fur.

But that time, in the reoccurrence of her dream, they were not the only ones watching Ambrose.

Another stood lurking in the shadows of the dirty and tattered room. A woman with pale skin and icy hair. Maeve couldn't look at the new and unknown addition to her dream, but she knew she lingered there all the same. Her eyes remained trapped on her father. As they always were.

Wet panic washed over her as she plunged into the bath water. Feeling somewhat grateful to have been ripped from the reoccurring nightmare, she rubbed the water from her eyes with labored breathing as she pushed out of the water.

The warm waters had grown cold, sending bumps across her skin. She hastily dried off, throwing on her robe and quickly scurrying to the fireplace in her bed chamber. She curled up into the chair, re-kindling the flames with the twist of her fingers.

Spinel emerged from the shadowed corners, dipping into a deep stretch with sleepy eyes. He gracefully jumped to the arm of the chair, chattering with expectant demands. Maeve obliged and rubbed his cheeks and scratched behind his ears until his eyes closed.

Spinel sat in her chair, still enjoying the fire long after Maeve had resigned herself to the fact that sleep was impossible for her. She contemplated another bath, perhaps reading. But all of her options seemed too daunting of a task.

The hour was late. Too late to be pacing and unable to sleep. The Crown's Quarters were silent and loud all at once. Nothing but the calm darkness surrounded her, and yet it ate at her mind all the same.

Spinel rolled further onto his back, tucking his paws across his face. Maeve sighed, feeling ridiculous for being jealous of her cat's ability to sleep so soundly.

She wondered if she'd ever sleep again like she slept at Sinclair

Estates. Rainy afternoon naps in her hidden reading tower. Sun-drenched evenings dozing off early on the balcony.

She was homesick for something that would never be again. Her life was now nostalgia, nothing but a memory of something so beautiful that it was heart-shattering to grieve it.

Mal, she called silently and without care as small tears slipped down her cheeks.

A cool breeze shifted into the room, raising the sheer curtains that lined her chamber and swirling them into a mass of black Magic.

He stepped from the cosmic mist.

His eyes raked over her slowly, as though he sensed the very direction her blood flowed in her darkened veins.

She wiped her cheeks with her palms.

His velvety smooth voice was a welcome sound in the bleak and sleepless bedroom. "Are you alright?"

Words halted in her throat. She hugged herself tightly in the cold night air.

"Talk to me," he said quietly.

She pressed her fingers into her biceps.

"I can't sleep," she relented.

He stepped towards her. "Are you still hearing thoughts?" He stopped an arm's length from her.

She shook her head up at him. "I just. . .want to sleep. I feel like I haven't slept in months. I don't know if it's this room or. . .my mind."

She didn't reach for him. She crossed the room towards the bed and looked back at him. He watched her closely.

"Can you make me sleep without dreaming?"

Mal nodded, his expression calm.

Maeve turned from him and slipped under the covers. He didn't step towards her.

Soothing Magic slithered over the sheets and wrapped around her. Her eyes found darkness before she could ask him to join her.

Chapter 15

Maeve

Alphard and Abraxas were already seated in her cousin's study when she arrived early in the morning. Abraxas poured a potion into his tea as he held the side of his face.

"Thank the Gods and Primus for your sister," said Abraxas to Alphard. "Otherwise I'd never survive a hangover from that Aternian Absinthe. Curse Reeve, that bastard."

Alphard whistled. "That Absinthe doesn't mess around. My first night in Aterna, Reeve poured me so many goblets I couldn't stand. It hardly affected him, though."

Abraxas signaled for Maeve to join them. "Good morning, cousin."

He poured his drink and suppressed the urge to gag.

Alphard looked over at her and didn't stand.

"Hi," he said with a soft smile.

A smile she hated. A smile that plastered everyone's lips lately. A smile of sympathy.

Maeve couldn't muster one back. Alphard's smile faded.

"I'm sor–"

Maeve pulled her lips into a thin, tight line and shook her head.

Alphard paused, and nodded.

"I hear you've been in Aterna," she said, taking a seat. "What's it like?"

"The cities are a marvel, but nothing beats Reeve's castle in Crystalmore. It's in the name. Built into the side of these massive crystal formations, mountain like."

"It's made of crystal?"

"Basically," said Alphard. "Nothing fragile about it though. An absolute fortress."

Mal rounded the corner to the study briskly. Alphard and Abraxas shot to their feet. Maeve was slow to rise.

Alphard stood with his fist over his chest in salute.

Mal's eyes raked over her. "Are you rested?"

Maeve nodded. "Yes," she replied. "Thank you."

Mal nodded and looked away from her. "Swiftly, Abraxas," he said. "I am heading back into the Peaks today."

He was leaving, perhaps for weeks, again.

Maeve settled back into her chair. Abraxas looked at her.

"You're the way in with Reeve. He wouldn't let Alphard close. But he will let you in."

Maeve's lips parted. "You want me to spy?" She looked to Mal.

He met her gaze only for a moment before he looked back at the windows. "Spy is the wrong word. You need to get him to slip, let his guard down."

Her mind drifted to the first and only meeting she'd been privy to with her father and Reeve.

"Reeve does not trust me or my judgement," she said.

"He doesn't need to trust you in order for you to manipulate him," said Abraxas plainly.

She looked over at Mal. He didn't look at her.

"You want me to go to Aterna?"

"No," said Abraxas quickly. "Alphard will remain our ambassador. He is guarded around Alphard because he knows why Al is there. Hopefully, that will help drop his suspicions around you."

"And what information in particular do we need? Are you just wanting to know if he poisoned that goblet?"

"That and much more," said Abraxas. "We need to know about his Inheritor. His power. The number of Senshi Warriors they have. A secret kept incredibly well, I might add. We lost history and knowledge when our ancestors fled to Earth. Aterna retained it all. We have two Dread Artifacts we must find."

Mal still would not look at her.

"You are quite clever and charming when you want to be," continued Abraxas.

Maeve frowned.

"Can I speak to you in private?" she asked Mal.

Mal nodded towards Abraxas. He and Alphard took their leave without complaint.

"Are you serious?" she asked as the doors closed behind them.

"What's not believable about it?" Mal asked tensely. "I'm told you had his gaze most of the evening."

"Is that what your little speech was about?"

"Don't patronize me," he said lowly.

Maeve leaned back in the leather chair and looked up at the green-glass ceiling vaulting above them.

"I thought the goal was cooperation," she said softly.

"Cooperation would have been a dream," said Mal pointedly.

Maeve looked at him.

"I've realized something, Maeve. I've realized how weak I must have looked that day. Willing to take the scraps of a throne. It was easy for them to kill Ambrose because I made it easy."

Maeve's eyes lifted back to the ceiling as her throat dried.

"I didn't boast that I had killed every last man of Kietel's. I didn't tell them I'd murdered my own father and grandparents out of pure spite. I didn't show them what lengths I am willing to go to. And in return, they saw me as nothing more than the descendant of some barren land, with no true reign. I didn't ask for anything but this throne, and they were thrilled that's all I wanted. It was nothing to give it to me. But now I see. I see so clearly what needs to happen."

"And what is that?" Maeve asked softly.

"All of it."

Maeve's heart kicked as she finally met his gaze. "All?"

Mal nodded. His relaxed, dark eyes were set on her. "All."

Maeve sat forward in the chair. "You want Reeve to bend the knee."

Mal shook his head. "I want them *all* to bend the knee."

Her brows pulled together, and she spoke gently. "That is not what we presented before your coronation. That is not the world we said we wanted."

"The world we wanted is gone, Maeve. It was destroyed the night of my coronation. Destroyed by fear and greed and hunger for power that was not earned."

He crossed towards her and continued.

"I've spent many nights wondering what Dark Magic lingered in that goblet. Was it meant for me? Was it purely by chance it was laced with poison? But I already know the answer, and so do you."

Maeve swallowed. Mal's words were ice in her blood.

"This is something I'm sure Reeve and Lithandrian can understand. The divine right to rule is something I was born with. And it does not stop with this crown."

Maeve looked up at him.

"Your father supported my desires," continued Mal.

"Please don't talk about him," she whispered desperately.

Mal paused and then said, "You must find out who his Inheritor is."

She met his gaze. The tension between them sat sharp again. It dug into her stomach with constant precision.

"I cannot protect us if I do not know who all my enemies are."

Maeve nodded. "I understand."

Mal nodded in response. "If there is nothing else. . ."

Maeve stared up at him with words desperate to flee her mouth. Desperate to fly into his arms. But she bit all those urges back.

"You did not punish Alphard the way you punished Xander," she said.

His expression didn't change as he said, "You think so lowly of me now that you believe I would kill a man you love?"

Maeve's mouth opened, but Mal was faster.

"Xander is dead because he was no one to you. Alphard is alive because he does matter to you. I know you are the reason he finally has Victoria. I know because he sat on his knees before me, broken and begging for me to intervene and break his engagement with you. Make no mistake, I reminded him of his transgressions where you are concerned. Anything else?"

Maeve shook her head and suppressed the desire to ask how long he'd be gone that time.

Chapter 16

Maeve

DECEMBER *1945*

"How long has he been in power?" Maeve asked her father as she stared at the chessboard between them.

"Since the Senshi Rebellion, after Reeve's father handled the Shadow War, and the deterioration of their society post-war, in popular opinion, poorly."

"Does he have any children of his own yet?"

Ambrose shook his head.

"But when he does, will they rule when he dies?"

"No," said Ambrose. "His Inheritor will rule after him. The next to gain the power of Aterna is a matter of fate. And always one of cruel fate."

"But you used the word 'rebellion'?" She asked, moving a piece in their game.

Ambrose studied the board for a moment and then spoke.

"Reeve's father did not give his power to his son willingly, despite Reeve being his ordained Inheritor. Reeve was forced to take it from the maddened King."

"King?"

"Reeve is the first High Lord of Aterna. I am told he refused the title of King after his father wore the crown."

"And you were also told he was forced to take it? How do you know he didn't steal it for selfish purposes?"

Ambrose sighed. "If you are set on hating him, I cannot make you see him how I do."

"And why should I see him like you do?" she asked casually, trying to hold a poker face at the terrible move she just made.

"Because I have known this man my entire life, Maeve. I trust him explicitly."

"I would argue that's foolish."

Ambrose smiled. "There are those you trust explicitly, are there not?"

Maeve sighed. "Yes."

Ambrose's eyebrows flicked up in victory

"So his Inheritor gets all the Magic of Aterna, that dragon form, power and all?"

"Not exactly," said Ambrose. "Power of Aterna, yes. Reeve holds the Magic of hundreds of thousands of Immortals. But the curse on him that creates that beast of a dragon was not inherited."

Maeve stilled and looked up at her father.

"Curse?"

Ambrose smiled. "I don't think that's my story to tell."

"Oh," whined Maeve. "Just when things were getting good."

Ambrose laughed softly. "Ask him about it if you want."

Maeve shook her head slowly. "I don't think he cares for me much."

Ambrose moved his piece. "Sometimes the best political partnerships are built upon differences."

Maeve scrunched her face like she didn't believe that. "Why didn't you sit down and talk to Kietel then?"

"I did. Twice."

Maeve's hand froze on her chess piece, and she looked up at him.

Ambrose leaned back in his chair. "Of course I did. I tried for peace. I tried to see his side, and tried to get him to see mine. I hoped we could come to a common ground."

"Obviously that didn't work."

"No," said Ambrose. "In that instance, Kietel would not budge. He was a strange man. So much power. A clear plan for the Magical's dominant future on Earth. And yet, he did not see Mal coming. He did not foresee the consequences of taking you."

Maeve looked down at the board.

"He allowed me to write you that letter, you know?"

"What?"

"The letter I managed to get to Rowan before the bombs were

dropped and Vaukore nearly fell. He told me a great secret I don't believe he meant to. He was very knowledgeable on ancient Magic and the seven realms. How all seven realms were connected, and even you, all the way on Vaukore, would be able to feel what he was about to do with those bombs. It was the second dropping that enabled him to do so much damage to Vaukore." Ambrose checked her King, and said. "And so, you never know what value can come from a simple conversation with your enemy."

Chapter 17

Maeve

Reeve attended many parties at Castle Morana. It was a season of weddings and celebrations of birth and new lives in The Dread Lands. Abraxas ensured that life in their new realm was just as lavish and extraordinary as it was on Earth.

Mal remained across the party, smiling diplomatically at King Kier. The ruler of Hiems brought his oldest daughter with him. Her skin was stunning against the bold ivory gown she wore.

"Go," hissed Abraxas as Reeve moved to the bar. "Do your job."

He disappeared before Maeve could argue further.

She moved across the hall, straightening her back and tossing her hair behind her shoulders.

"No gorgeous blonde Immortal this evening?" she asked as she arrived at Reeve's side.

Reeve's shoulders pulled up and he took a swig of his drink.

Maeve smiled and chuckled. "Couldn't find anyone in Aterna that suited your fancy? Or have you just been through them all?"

Reeve's eyes sparkled behind his glass.

Maeve's smile dropped. "What?"

"Nothing."

Maeve looked down at her dress, searching for an imperfection.

"Look at you all frazzled beneath my gaze," he murmured.

She stopped and narrowed her eyes. "It is far from frazzled that your gaze incites."

"You haven't danced at all," noted Reeve.

"Not really in the mood," she replied as she took a glass of sparkling water to her lips.

"I sense distance between you and the Dread Prince."

"Really?" she replied dryly. "Was it the obvious entertainment of

Kier's daughter? Or the even more obvious ignoring of my presence that gave it away?"

"The course of love never did run smooth,"

Maeve scoffed. "True love," she corrected. "The quote is 'the course of true love never did run smooth.'"

"You know Shakespeare?"

Maeve laughed as a smile began blossoming on her face. "*You* know Shakespeare?"

"Of course," said Reeve with a grin. "One of the greats."

Maeve's face scrunched in disbelief.

"Is that so hard to fathom?" asked Reeve.

Maeve stammered.

Reeve continued. "Is it that I enjoy reading or the arts?"

Maeve sighed. "I only meant he's a playwright from Earth. You're from a different world."

Reeve nodded. "A realm with art and poetry and stories from every realm and planet that dates back farther than Earth's own existence."

Maeve's mouth fell open slightly. "Is that true?"

"Aterna has the largest library in the universe, as far as I know. Keepers of time, as they are called, protect its knowledge with their lives."

"It's in the city?"

Reeve's smile faltered, his pupils shrank, and the spark in his firelight eyes flickered out. He chose his response carefully, and Maeve knew why.

It burned deep in her stomach, the disappointment that crept into his expression, the realization that they played nice, but she was potentially his enemy. And the possibility that he was hers. The High Lord was not going to give her and her Dread Prince any more power than they already possessed.

Maeve's jaw clenched and she straightened. She pushed him, knowing she had already failed at manipulating the information from him. "Your majesty?"

Reeve loosed a breath. "But break, my heart, for I must hold my tongue," he said, quoting what she knew must be more Shakespeare.

Ice shot down Maeve's spine, and she knew Mal watched them across the hall.

"What's that from?" she asked.

"Hamlet."

"I haven't read that one," she said with strain.

Their eyes locked together.

"It's. . .one of them."

"A good one?"

Mal's gaze was not letting up.

"Again," said Reeve. "It's one of them."

She could feel his jealousy crawling across the floor towards them. She looked up at him, but his eyes were on Kier and his daughter.

She refused to acknowledge the implications of Kier introducing them and bringing the beauty all the way from Hiems.

"Who was she?" Maeve asked softly. "Your mate?"

Reeve's Magic tensed, and she looked up at him. His eyes were pained.

"My wife died in the Shadow War."

"She was a Warrior?"

Reeve shook his head. "She was a healer."

Maeve looked away from him. "How long were you together before…"

"Twenty years."

"I've read mates can speak mind to mind," said Maeve. "Of course, they haven't existed for Magicals in centuries. Earth stifled all that Magic."

"Am I wrong that you and the Dread Prince are able to communicate silently?'

Maeve shook her head gently. "The walls are down because we make it so. I allow him in my head. There is no force great enough to penetrate the walls of my mind without my permission."

"I have heard that of Pureblood Witches, and I mean no offense Maeve, but your mother was not of the Sacred."

The thought had plagued her for months, wondering how the barriers in her mind were so strong despite not being of Pureblood.

"Do you have any thoughts on the matter?" she asked. "With all that Immortal wisdom?" She smirked.

Reeve loosed a laugh.

"Did you know her?" asked Maeve.

Reeve's mask truly fell for the first time. Maeve didn't smile in triumph. She wasn't pleased with herself.

The corners of her mouth pulled up as sadness swarmed her blue eyes. "You did, didn't you?"

Reeve's jaw tightened. His mouth opened and closed in a frustrated groan.

Tears brimmed her eyes with the realization that the lie was deeper than she had yet to realize. She pushed away from the bar before they could fall down her cheeks.

Another nail in the wall of secrets, this one signed with her father's name too.

Reeve was casually on her tail, matching her quick stride effortlessly thanks to his long legs.

"I can't explain," he said.

Her eyes narrowed. "What?" she asked, not looking over at him.

"Maeve," he said in a frustrated growl.

She whipped towards him, putting space between them. "What?" she snapped unapologetically.

Reeve's chest rose and fell. His jaw clenched tightly as a glimmer of pain shot across his face. "Listen to my words."

She frowned up at him, her brows softening as she considered his tense muscles.

"I *cannot* explain," he said once more with a slight grimace.

His body relaxed. His eyes scanned the room behind her.

"There is Magic holding your tongue," she said softly, realizing the meaning of his calculated words.

Reeve looked back down at her. She shook her head.

"More secrets. More masks. More questions with no answers."

"If it would unburden you, I would speak them all," he said slowly.

Maeve took another step back from him. "I have a feeling your truths would be, by far, the most burdenous part of you."

"Imagine how I feel," said Reeve.

"I do try to see your perspective, it is just difficult to see anything with one's head that far up one's ass."

Reeve nodded in approval, his smirk growing. "That was good. You've been taking lessons on wit from your cousin."

Maeve couldn't endure his company any longer. His endless arrogance and his ability to laugh everything off. . .There was little worth laughing about with Reeve as far as she was concerned.

He created more questions than answers.

As she turned from him, she didn't know what bothered her more: the idea that Reeve knew her mother, or that her father chose to tell him. And not her.

Maeve found it difficult to keep pressing Reeve as he accepted her every invite to Castle Morana. Even for the simplest of gatherings for cigars with Abraxas, he held his secrets close. If he couldn't talk about her mother, she doubted he'd ever spill the secrets of his Inheritor.

Maeve was not suited for diplomacy or the mind games Mal and Abraxas insisted were necessary to establish their place in the world.

Alphard returned to Castle Morana from his latest visit to Aterna, with less information than Maeve even.

"What about the university there?" asked Abraxas. "They have quite a large college of literature and law."

"It's nothing like Vaukore," said Alphard. "There was little information there outside of the arts."

"What about Aterna's library?" offered Maeve.

Alphard looked over at her. "What do you mean? They have

nothing to search."

Maeve shook her head. "That's not true. Reeve told me Aterna boasts the largest known library."

Alphard looked to Mal.

"When did he tell you this?" Abraxas asked with a slight look of confusion.

Maeve shrugged. "I don't remember. Not that long ago."

"When?" questioned Mal.

Maeve looked at him and opened her mouth. Then closed it. She looked down at the table, realizing her mistake. "At the banquet for Emerie and Roswyn's daughter. It slipped my mind."

Mal shifted in his seat, swapping his crossed legs and didn't look at her. "Strange. I thought memories were your speciality."

Maeve looked at him sharply, despite his resolve not to meet her gaze.

Abraxas spoke. "You're certain you didn't misunderstand him?"

Maeve opened her mouth to reply once more, but Mal spoke over her. "I'm certain Maeve listens to Reeve with such intensity it would rival your own, Abraxas."

Abraxas' eyes slipped to Mal, his lips curling together.

Maeve didn't look at either of them.

Mal stood, sliding his chair back. Everyone stood at once. Maeve was slow to her feet.

"Return, Alphard," he said as he walked behind her and towards the door. "Find the secret library my Second suddenly decided to remember."

Maeve looked across the table at Abraxas. His brows lifted quickly, and he looked rather satisfied. "Close your mouth, cousin. You look like a trout."

Maeve entered Mal's study without an invitation, flinging the doors open with a flick of her hand.

"Have I offended you?"

The doors slammed close behind her, but it was not her Magic that moved them.

Mal didn't look up from his work.

She waited a moment and then spoke. "Mal," she said softly.

His eyes lifted to hers. "My court addresses me as their Prince."

Maeve shook her head in disbelief, tearing her eyes away from his.

The walls of his study were lined with many of her father's things. Books, essays, ancient and rare Magical artifacts.

Magical wills were a marvel. The things Ambrose wanted to leave to Mal were now Magically there. Just as much of Maeve's London Townhouse had been filled with the things he left her. And how her chambers in Castle Morana now were.

She crossed the study, her low heels clicking across the floor as a framed picture caught her eye. Next to a stack of leather-bound books, was a picture of her.

A picture that once occupied her father's mantel piece.

"He gave me that before he died," said Mal calmly. Maeve looked back at him. "I was too distracted by it to pay attention, he said."

Maeve looked back at the framed photo taken on the balcony at Sinclair Estates.

"That was his birthday party," she said quietly, remembering the evening perfectly, knowing she'd never celebrate a birthday, let alone anything, with him again.

Pressure built in her throat and head. She turned from the shelves and made for the doorway.

"Maeve."

She swallowed hard and forced the tears threatening to slip from her eyes away. She turned towards him and held her chin up proudly.

Mal stood and crossed beside his desk. "Why did you come here?"

She sighed shakily. "Because you instructed me to do a job. I did that job and you are angry at me for it."

Mal's head cocked to one side. "I am not angry with you for finding out about the Library in Aterna."

"Then why are you?"

Mal replied without hesitation. "Because he made you smile."

Maeve's mouth opened to retort before his words took hold. She snapped it shut.

"What-" she stammered, feeling her cheeks flood with warmth.

"He made you smile," Mal repeated plainly.

Maeve looked down at the floor between them. Mal's voice was regally calm.

"I haven't seen you smile once since you got here."

Maeve looked back up at him, anger festering in her core. "You asked me to get close to him."

"And it was my first mistake as your Prince," he said smoothly.

Maeve nodded, ready to argue further. "You leave for days at a time. No communication. No idea if you are alive or struggling. You come back and speak in riddles to me, in cryptic messages about this darkness out there. I haven't got the faintest idea what it is you are subjecting yourself to."

"As my second, you should worry about your training and protecting this realm. Abraxas can handle the politics of it all."

"Politics?" She laughed. "I'm not concerned with that nonsense. I want to know what it is you're doing out there." She pointed out the window at the lands beyond. "What have you seen? What do you know? What has you so distant and so certain–"

"What has me distant?" Mal's nostrils flared.

Maeve fell silent.

"You chose this distance, and you chose to be separated from me," he said with a lethal calm. "Don't you dare ask me such a foolish question."

Maeve turned on her heel and made for the door. Magic covered the locks as they clicked into place before she reached it.

"I haven't dismissed you," said Mal lowly.

Maeve turned back towards him. "I cannot fathom how it is so easy for you to continue as though nothing has happened–as though he's not dead and everything is as it was supposed to be."

"I am pushing forward because that's where Ambrose wanted us to be."

"Do not presume to know what my father wanted."

"I do not presume," fired Mal. "I had many conversations about the future of Magicals with him. I spent many nights in his study, in his basement, rolling through all the possibilities for our future, Maeve. Mine and yours."

Her chest tightened.

"I am not your enemy," he continued. "If you desire separation, so be it. But do not chastise me for holding all of this together when it could so easily crumble. Do you truly believe he would have wanted his death to be the catalyst for collapse?"

"No," she said through her teeth.

"No," Mal repeated. "But that is what our true enemies want."

"And who are they?"

"As far as I'm concerned, anyone that isn't you and I."

"Even your court? Those boys devour even a glance from you."

"They are driven by my power, hungry for a taste of it, desperate for a place on top in the future I am creating."

"I, too, was once driven by what your power offered me."

Mal's eyes softened. "But it was replaced by deeper Magic."

They took long, steadying breaths together.

"Show me, Mal," she said calmly. "Show me these lands I am meant to protect. I am going mad in this castle with all these thoughts and dreams that do not belong to me."

Chapter 18

Maeve

What remained of two giant serpents marked either side of the entrance to the long lost Beryl City. Their great bodies twisted into the sky, together forming an arch.

Great towers and walls shot into the sky, their stones dark and decaying, crumbling to the pavers along the wide streets. Cobwebs clung to the stone and ash covered the streets. The air was barely breathable, but it didn't burn her skin. A mask of fabric laced with Mal's Magic draped across her mouth and nose, allowing her to breathe normally.

Maeve turned on her shoulder. "It feels like something is here."

"Something is here," said Mal. "All our kind lost is here. All the abandoned Magic."

Mal wasn't wrong, but Maeve felt something else. Something that skirted down the streets alongside them, something awake and aware of their every move.

"No," she said. "Something. . .dark."

Castle Morana was covered by dark green mist and shadow on the horizon beyond as they climbed the winding passages and roads in Beryl City, passing by the remains of shops and homes, their windows and doors intricately carved and created. Crystal doorknobs and gilded windows sat dull and dusty.

"Can you imagine what this place once was?" she asked, stopping at a square. A dried up fountain sat at its center.

"I can," answered Mal. "And I can see it all, born again."

She watched him step towards what appeared to have once been a hat shop. He looked back at her.

"What sacrifice is made to achieve this goal?" she questioned.

Mal's eyes drifted away from hers. "Sacrificing for our future is a great honor." His eyes slid back to hers as he turned around. "Do you want to see The Avondell Tower?"

His question wasn't asked flippantly. It carried weight. The Sinclair home of The Towers was her birthright. Or, it once had been. The house of her ancestors was holy to her.

She nodded, feeling an excited shift in her Magic for the first time since arriving in The Dread Lands.

When they are at The Avondell, Maeve moved to pull the fabric down from her nose and mouth. Mal's hand shot to her face at once.

"I haven't fully restored the air here," he said.

Maeve nodded. "I know," she replied. "But I can feel it's weak enough for me to breathe here."

He dropped his hand and allowed her to remove her mask. The Magic supplying her oxygen pulled from her lungs. Mal watched her cautiously as she took a breath on her own.

He smiled softly. "Perhaps it is just you who is stronger here."

Maeve moved towards the once ivory gate, the path beyond wild and overgrown. She pulled the thorny vines away with her gloved hand, revealing a metal placard with ornate letters.

THE TOWER OF AVONDELL: SINCLAIR

"No," said Maeve, her fingers lingering over the cold metal. "It is the remains of them that were stronger."

She dropped her hand and looked down the straight path. She'd wondered since childhood what this home would be like, what Magic it would hold. She dreamed of returning there, filling one of the rooms with her things. How grand it was in her mind.

Now it sat, seven stories tall with shattered glass windows and a broken down door, looking desolate. Thorny vines twisted up the structure, climbing the chipped windowsills and wrapping the oversized gargoyles.

"Can I go inside?" she asked quietly.

"Of course," he replied behind her.

Maeve twisted two fingers, bringing the iron stakes from the ground that allowed the gate to swing wide.

She stepped onto the paved path with a large inhale as Magic exploded around them in a screech.

There was nothing warm and welcoming about it. The burst of energy blasted straight into her stomach, knocking her into the air. Mal's dark shield consumed them as he Obscured and placed himself behind her, catching her swiftly in his arms before she hit the ground.

Her eyes squeezed shut as she balled in on herself against him. The Magic swirled at her stomach, dispelling after a few tight breaths.

She groaned into his chest, forcing her eyes to open. She looked back at The Avondell. Everything was just as it had been. The gates slowly closed themselves.

Mal's eyes were wide as they silently watched.

Maeve's head turned heavy as she fell back against his chest. Mal looked down at her as her eyes fluttered closed. "Your stamina is low," he noted. "You haven't been training like you should."

"My Magic is not as strong without your presence," she admitted weakly.

Maeve looked up at him, his chiseled face blurred in and out of shape. Sharp breaths caught in her lungs.

"No," said Mal, "you have never needed me."

His lips pressed down on her forehead, cold and healing Magic slipping down her neck and arms. It settled peacefully in her stomach, numbing the pain.

Her eyes fluttered to a close. Astrea's voice faded in and out in the darkness.

"She's alright." Astrea's voice sounded in the void. "No traces of Magic remaining."

Maeve felt her move away.

Mal's voice was quiet. "Thank you, Astrea. I'd like you to check her every day."

"Do you think I'm wrong?" asked Astrea. There was no arrogance in her voice. No wounded pride.

"I think the Dark Magic my Dread Viper consumed is cunning. And it wouldn't be the first time she hid it from me."

"Forgive me," said Astrea quietly, "I just don't understand. I thought the blight was purged from The Tower of Avondell, like the rest."

"As did I," said Mal. "The darkness that lingers across this land was, and still is, eradicated from The Avondell. This is some other Magic."

Astrea's footsteps clicked across the tile. A door clicked shut.

Mal's cool knuckles brushed down her cheek, sending her back into a deep slumber.

Astrea's healing hands hovered over Maeve for, what Maeve hoped, was the final time.

"What's that face for?" Maeve asked Astrea as she helped her up on the healing bed.

Astrea smiled curiously. "Strange Magic," she remarked. "I have felt it in Mal."

Astrea's eyes traced over Maeve's darkened veins.

"Yes," said Maeve, tugging her sleeves down her hands in an attempt to conceal the marks.

Astrea pulled her eyes away and began placing glass toppers back on the vials of potions she'd used on Maeve.

"The Magic that runs through you," she started, "it is twin to Mal's."

"Like calls to like," said Maeve.

"It is more than that," said Astrea. "It has another twin. One I can't see, but there is a place for it beside yours and Mal's."

Maeve stilled. "Have you told him that?"

Maeve's eyes shifted to Astrea's chest, where she knew the Dread Mark lay beneath her clothes. Astrea held a high honor at Castle Morana as Mal's healer.

"Of course, I have," she replied.

Maeve contemplated Astrea's words for a moment. "A third," she whispered. "What did Mal say?"

Astrea hesitated. "He seemed. . .unconcerned."

Maeve nodded. "And he knows you are pregnant?" She asked calmly. "Congratulations, by the way."

Astrea's hand stilled on a bottle of dark liquid. "How can you tell?"

"The Magic radiating from you is almost nauseating," said Maeve with a small smile. "Why hasn't it been announced?" she asked casually.

Astrea continued working diligently to organize her potions and ignored her.

Maeve's mouth opened as she realized. "I'm sorry."

Astrea's fingers halted and she looked up. "I don't think I've ever heard you use those words."

Neither of them smiled as they held one another's gaze.

"Whose baby are you carrying, Astrea?" Maeve asked quietly.

She handed Maeve a small bottle of pale grey goo. "I think that's all you need for those wounds. They shouldn't scar if you keep applying that potion."

Maeve hopped off the healing table and grabbed Astrea's wrist as she turned.

Astrea snatched it away. She didn't look at Maeve as she began putting various small boxes and jars of ingredients into a chest. "I have not forgotten it was I who married my father's brother's son, my cousin, and it was you who married no one."

The metal clasp on the chest snapped shut. Astrea turned to Maeve, her face resumed its normal mask of harshness. "I can't expect you to understand my position."

Maeve pulled her shirt on with a sigh. "I wasn't judging you," she said. "Believe it or not, I am on your side."

"My side–" she began incredulously.

Astrea snapped her mouth tightly shut and closed her eyes. "Apologies. I am still growing accustomed to you as my superior."

Maeve smiled softly and muttered, "I was always your superior."

Astrea fought back a glare.

Maeve laughed. "Now, go ahead," she said. "Go ahead and tell me what our new stations prevent you from freely speaking."

Astrea did not hesitate. "I am lucky enough my cousin has no desire to touch me. Can you imagine if that was you and Abraxas?"

Maeve grimaced. "It's no secret the bonds of marriage made for us are not willingly vowed."

"Does that make it any less horrible that I had to vow them?"

Maeve paused. "No."

Astrea pushed her hair out of her face with a sigh. "I am grateful you ensured my brother got to be with the one he loves. If only we all had that power. All eyes are on you, Dread Viper," she said. "If you are immune to the enslavement of Pureblooded Witches, you could at least try to free the rest of us."

Maeve smiled, but it did not meet her eyes. "I am not of Pureblood."

"What am I missing?" Maeve asked Abraxas as he poured her a cup of tea.

"They're been told to procreate as quickly as possible, if that's what you are referring to."

"So nothing has changed?"

"Everything has changed," Abraxas argued back. "We are here, in these lands, reclaiming them."

"You know this wouldn't be a problem if everyone would stop arguing over the Human-borns' place here. Then there would be plenty of children being born to repopulate this realm."

"Do we even know that their children will be born Magical?"

"So what if they aren't? Is a world with diversity so terrible? Is Zimsy only here because she is my friend?"

"Many of the Sacred do not want such a world," he said with a sadness in his voice. "You've heard them."

"Well, maybe the rules and culture set forth by the very people who got us into the mess of corrupt government we seek to escape may not be the best foundation on which to lay our new society."

Abraxas sighed. "I can't argue with that."

"You are so bright and brilliant. Do not let them push you into what is best for them. Mal chose you to decide what is best for his Dread Kingdom. Make it so."

Maeve arrived at her training with Larliesl with little spirit in her fight. The nightmares Castle Morana offered were worse than her own. Larliesl had scarcely begun when Mal appeared in the training court.

"I can take it from here," said Mal smoothly as he walked towards them.

Larliesl placed his fist over his heart and bowed. He excused himself silently.

"I thought you didn't have time to train me," said Maeve.

Mal smiled. She fought the one on her own lips.

"You were weaker out there than I ever saw you at Vaukore. I thought it necessary."

"I'm sorry," she said with a dry laugh. "I wasn't expecting to be attacked by a house you told me was safe."

"Perhaps if your senses were sharpened you could have been ready on the offensive."

Maeve didn't have a reply and so she looked away from him.

She didn't want to face the gates of Avondell again. She buried the desire to return deep in her mind and pretended like it wasn't devastatingly embarrassing that her ancestors' home had rejected her, when Mal was able to enter freely.

"I am not of Pureblood," she blurted out quietly.

Mal sighed and lowered his chin. "That's not why that happened, Maeve."

Her gaze lifted.

"Many Bellator, some Human born, have crossed those lines of Magic without issue."

"I don't want to talk about it anymore," she said, tossing her hair behind her shoulders. "You came here to train me."

Mal didn't press her on the issue. "Did you not continue training on Earth?"

"Only what was required of me in the Bellator, and sometimes not even that."

"Duels?"

Maeve shrugged.

"Larliesl says you barely try. Perhaps the Dueling Master is going too easy on his former student."

Maeve smiled placatingly.

"Have you jumped?" he asked matter-of-factly.

"No."

Mal sucked in a long breath, steadying and readying his Magic. "Let's begin there. Enter my mind and jump."

"Where to?" she asked, stalling.

"I don't care," he replied. "But maybe try just getting inside first, and staying inside."

Maeve breathed deeply and accepted her forthcoming failure.

Mal nodded once at her, and her pulse quickened.

She pressed into his mind, darkness flooding her senses. She pressed further and met solid steel walls of power. Her Magic flowed useless against his strength.

She was not the only one more powerful in The Dread Lands.

But that power was not enough. She was too weak to slip into his mind.

Larliesl was right.

Mal's voice echoed across the darkness.

You're not even trying.

Maeve sighed and whipped her Magic out. It crackled against his shields.

Better.

She prepared once more to fire on him, but a freezing cold whip slashed across her mind.

Maeve recoiled at once, pulling from his mind. Her fingers shot to her temples. Mal's expression shifted into confusion.

"What was that?" Maeve asked breathlessly.

"What was what?"

Maeve shook her head, trying to rid herself of the daunting feeling. She closed her eyes, making certain of what she felt.

She looked up at Mal's face of concern. "You. . .attacked me."

Mal shook his head. "I did not move to hurt you."

"Well, something did," she fired back.

The sharp pain still lingered in her mind, like the tip of a blade pressed against either temple.

"I'm sure it was just your strength failing. I've told you-your Magic is weak–"

"Seven months without any real challenge will do that," she muttered.

Mal looked away from her and clicked his tongue. "Try again," he commanded, a bit of annoyance seeping into his tone.

Maeve wanted to argue further, but the defeated look on Mal's face silenced her tongue. She stepped towards him and readied herself for more, praying she wouldn't feel such haunting darkness from him again.

Chapter 19

Maeve

Maeve sucked in a frustrated breath as her heels echoed down the corridor towards the ballroom. Guests were already in attendance by the hundreds. She could feel all their racing thoughts, slamming through her without permission.

She paused in the long stretch of castle, and a nervous sigh slipped from her lips as she begged herself to swallow her pride. Reeve's allegiance and trust were crucial. She'd try a new tactic. One that never failed to gain a man's attention.

She ignored him completely. All evening.

She moved onto the balcony where it was far less likely her mind would be flooded with the random musings of guests, in search of a moment's peace before returning to the never ending charade.

It didn't take Reeve long to join her. Just as she hoped.

"If you look hard enough, you can see the crystal peaks of Aterna."

Maeve looked across The Dread Lands. Castle Morana sat high in the Dark Peaks, overlooking the world around them. Aterna sat across the Black Deep. Too far for her to recognize.

"You can see Aterna from here?" she asked.

"Can you not?" he replied.

Maeve laughed. "It's all the way across The Black Deep. Even if the haze was lifted and the Magical barrier dividing your land from ours was gone, it would be a stretch for me to see your crystal palace from here."

"How do you Magicals   manage without such heightened senses?"

Maeve smiled at him. "Perhaps the same way you manage to keep your head upright despite having an inflated ego."

Reeve smirked. "Clever, clever."

"I did want to know something though, since you are here."

Reeve's brows raised, and he took a seat opposite her on the balcony.

"There is little left on record here about such things, and at Vaukore we weren't taught anything about the Dragons. My father told me there was a war centuries ago when Dragons fought Magicals. I didn't want to believe him when he said my uncle killed the last of them. The skull was in our home."

"I remember," said Reeve.

"I insisted that because of you, they must still be real," she continued. "But then I remembered a conversation with my father. He said your dragon form was not natural Magic. It's a curse."

Reeve listened intently as she continued.

"How could my uncle do that?" she asked softly.

"Hunting Dragons was a sport for many Magicals."

"Doesn't that bother you?"

"Of course it does," said Reeve. "They were driven to extinction. Just as they drove Magicals of Shadow Magic to extinction."

"What a depressing, endless cycle. I fear we are next," she muttered.

"Why do you care what curses I carry?"

She shrugged. "Because after you. . .they are no more."

He was quiet for a moment. Maeve gestured to his neck.

"Tell me why they call you Shadow Slayer. Where did you get that scar?"

He answered without hesitation, like a rehearsed speech.

"The Shadow War. A gift from its namesake herself."

Maeve's head cocked to one side. "Namesake?"

"She was a creature of Darkness, Queen of this land. I called her Shadow. She was the last known Magical with the abilities of the long lost Dark Planet, thought to be long gone from the Dragon's war."

"She possessed Shadow Magic?"

Reeve nodded. "The last known wielder."

"Looks like she didn't manage to take your head off though."

He shook his head. "No, despite her greatest effort she did not see one very powerful and pointed arrow coming towards her."

"Your little archer?"

Reeve laughed. "He's hundreds of years your senior."

"Well, he looks fourteen," she said with a smile.

Reeve's eyes pulled from her as his smile faded. His lips hesitated on the brim of his goblet. "He was that day." He was silent for a moment. "Actually, freshly fifteen, I believe."

They sat in silence for a moment until Maeve spoke. "I'm sorry if I opened an unpleasant door."

Reeve shook off his daze, and looked back at her. "The door is always open in my mind. I will never forget the power that oozed from her. It was more alive than any Magic I have ever felt."

"At Brax's wedding," began Maeve, "Drystan said that his Immortality had been lost in battle. Shadow destroyed it?"

Reeve nodded. "She didn't just take it. She absorbed it."

Maeve's brows raised. "She was that powerful?"

"A product of Shadow Magic."

She sat for a moment. "Like Vexkari?"

Reeve contemplated her question. "Not unlike Vexkari I suppose."

"Drystan also said Immortality was gifted back to him," continued Maeve. "I am assuming that was a gift from you for stopping her final blow." She motioned one finger across her throat.

"It was," he replied.

"So that's why he stopped growing and aging then?"

"So inquisitive this evening," he said with a mischievous smile.

Maeve shrugged. "You're on your third goblet full I figured I might pry."

Reeve laughed. "You think three goblets of this weak Witch's Wine will loosen my tongue?"

"A girl can dream," said Maeve with a playful smile.

Reeve's eyes locked with hers. "What an honor to occupy The Dread Viper's dreams."

Maeve looked back down at his throat. "She made that slice with a single finger I assume."

"A sword," corrected Reeve.

"She used a sword? But if she held Shadow Magic, why did she see fit to use such a weapon on you?"

"The sword belonged to my grandfather. It was re-forged for Orion the Dread on the day of his coronation."

Maeve hesitated. "Mal's ancestor?"

Reeve nodded. "So it would seem."

"There was Magic in the Sword?"

Reeve shook his head. "I felt nothing when she moved to remove my head from my body. It was merely the blade. I believe she felt it… poetic."

Maeve looked away from him and pondered in silence, looking at the party guests dancing and drinking.

"What do you know about Shadow Magic?" Reeve asked.

She shrugged and shook her head. "Nothing, really. Just that it died out three hundred years ago." When Reeve didn't reply, she looked over at him. "What do you know about Shadow Magic?"

He was already watching her closely. He didn't answer right away, and when he did, his voice was smooth. "I know to fear it."

"Why?" she pressed.

His expression saddened. "Because it is deceit so natural that when faced with it, I cannot tell if reality is my own."

Maeve looked away from him once more. "They didn't teach us anything about Shadow Magic or the war in school."

"The Double O was formed as a way for Magicals on Earth to start over. They were terrified of repeating the past. Ignorance is bliss."

"There is one thing I don't understand. You are the most powerful of us all. Why was she nearly able to kill you?"

"I did not hold the power of Aterna during The Shadow War. My father did. On the battlefield, I was merely a Senshi Warrior with a blade pumped full of as much of my father's Magic I could handle."

"And Drystan's arrow?"

"The same."

Maeve shook her head. "Where was he?"

Reeve's brows raised.

"Your father," she elaborated.

Reeve's eyes moved away from her. "He was fleeing."

"I thought those that inherited the power of Aterna were meant to be worthy of it."

"I have never asked the Gods why either of us were deemed fit."

"And your Inheritor?"

Reeve didn't look over at her, after a long pause he spoke, a sad resignation in his voice. "How could I forget how seamlessly you carry conversation to gain the upper hand of knowledge?"

"Born and bred," said Maeve with a sigh, not attempting to deny her manipulation.

Reeve looked over at her. "Enjoy the rest of your evening."

He stood from the settee and made for the doors to the castle. Maeve didn't call after him.

Abraxas appeared before her a few moments later. "You alright?"

She nodded. Abraxas handed her a water.

"Deception takes a toll," she muttered. "He sees through me in the end."

"Ah," said Abraxas, taking a seat next to her. "It bothers you being a spy."

"Wasn't entirely unproductive," she said. "He may not have been forthcoming about his knowledge of his Inheritor, but he was about the darkness that drove Magicals to Earth. Darkness I'm certain Mal will want to know about."

"You'll have plenty of time to discuss it with him when the pair of you get back from Hiems."

Abraxas pulled a small folded piece of paper from his pocket and handed it to her. It was icy blue with her name written across it in white stamped letters.

"You read my mail?" she asked with narrowed eyes.

"The Hand reads all correspondence," he said casually.

Maeve Sinclair,

The Dread Prince has graciously accepted my invitation to dinner. I would be truly honored for the Dread Viper to see our beautiful realm and dine at Stalakta Fortress with my family.

Looking forward to your reply,
King Kier

Maeve dropped the letter into her lap and looked up at Abraxas excitedly. "The ice planet?"

Abraxas nodded with a smile. "I thought that might make you happy."

Chapter 20

Maeve

Maeve's first visit to Hiems was as expected: freezing. The ice planet was covered, as it had been for as long as the history books remembered, in endless winter. Green and blue waves of light draped across the horizon in an icy glow.

They Portaled directly to the ice covered steps that led to the shining, white castle of King Kier. Stalakta Fortress it was called. Mal wore an all black ensemble, complete with a high neck to keep out the cold. Alphard stepped out of the Portal behind her.

Upon the castle landing sat a bright white wolf with red eyes. Behind him, a dozen more wolves waited. Their thick fur boasted all shades of black and grey.

The white wolf sniffed. His head shifted to one side.

Then his oversized paw stepped forwards, and he bent onto his back legs, his white nose pointed at the snowy steps.

"Your grace," he said.

Maeve's entire chest rose as her eyes grew large.

The wolf's red eyes lifted to hers. "My name is Mordred of the Kings Guard. It is an honor to greet you on behalf of King Kier." His voice was like gravel crushing together.

She couldn't believe her eyes. Before her was a talking wolf.

The pack behind him all bowed in the same fashion Mordred had. Maeve looked up at the winding, icy stairs. At least two dozen wolves sat along the pathway to the castle, perhaps more than her eyes could see.

"I was hoping to make your acquaintance, Dread Viper," said Mordred.

Maeve looked back down at him. "The honor is mine," she said stiffly.

She resisted the urge to speak into Mal's mind, and question why she was face to face with a talking wolf without warning. So her guards remained up all the same. Alphard, who had visited Hiems before, avoided looking at Mordred.

Mordred led them towards the castle. The fortress stood slender, with ice covered towers that shot high into the white backdrop of ice walls surrounding it. They crossed a bridge of pale blue ice that arched high over a frozen river.

As they crossed the threshold of the castle, Maeve prepared herself to feel an encapsulating warmth of Magic, but it never came.

She'd nearly forgotten Hiems boasted no Magic. She pulled her coat closer. Kier stepped towards them with open and welcome arms.

"Malachite!" he exclaimed.

"Kier," said Mal with a charming smile as they clasped hands.

Kier turned towards Maeve.

"Maeve Sinclair," he said. "The Dread Prince couldn't have picked a better second if Primus or Merlin himself came back from the dead!"

Maeve forced a smile, anticipating his next words and praying they wouldn't be spoken.

"A tragedy, your father's death. You have my condolences."

Maeve nodded, unable to form a reply.

"Your chef still the same as my last visit, Kier?" interjected Alphard, interrupting them before Kier spoke further. "I could kill for one of those cakes."

Kier laughed. "Come. To the lounge. We shall stuff our faces. I have a gift for you, Dread Prince."

Kier instructed one of the servants to have his gift brought to the great hall as Maeve looked at Alphard and mouthed a silent *thank you*.

He gave her a brief nod before following after Kier and striking up another conversation.

Maeve shivered.

Mal looked down at her as they followed closely behind Kier and Alphard. Mordred trailed them with silent steps. She looked over her shoulder at the wolf, and wondered if Antony had been able to talk in his werewolf form.

She pulled her arms around her center as the castle grew colder with each step.

They followed Kier into an intimate dining area with large fires at each corner of the room. Mal slid his coat off his shoulders in a fluid motion. A man with a stern face took it from him at once.

Maeve welcomed the warmth the fires provided, though she still had no desire to remove her coat.

Mal's eyes scanned over her quickly. "Kier?" he called in a friendly tone.

The ruler of Hiems turned towards him with raised brows.

"Might the fires be larger?"

"Of course!" Kier clapped his hands and two men moved from either side of the door, adding firewood until each fire was blazing hot and stretched high into the stone holes they sat in.

Maeve looked up at Mal. A smile pulled at her lips. His Magic drifted towards her in intoxicating confidence. She stepped towards him and opened her mouth just as Kier called her name.

"My daughter," said Kier, gesturing to the girl now at his side. "Wren. I believe the pair of you failed to meet at her last visit to Castle Morana."

Wren did not acknowledge Maeve. She bowed her head at Mal and spoke directly to him. "Your grace. It is wonderful to see you again."

Mal smiled at her in a way Maeve hated.

"And my sons, Gerald and Kax."

The two little ones bowed respectfully and looked to their father for approval. Kier nodded, and they relaxed.

"Wonderful to meet you all," said Maeve, plastering on a smile.

"Please, sit," said Kier, gesturing towards the table.

Maeve took her place at Mal's right as Kier sat at his left.

An older woman shuffled into the hall, carrying a large box covered in dark fabric.

"Wonderful, wonderful," said Kier as she made her way across the hall to him.

She stood silently between her king and Mal.

"Go on," said Kier, motioning for Mal to remove the draped

fabric.

With a fluid twist of his hand, the fabric disappeared, revealing a large birdcage with an inky colored bird on a small branch.

Wren gasped and awed at Mal's use of simple Magic. Maeve's stomach knotted at her gleaming expression. Another twist of his fingers and the cage door slipped open. Mal extended his slender hand towards the opening. The sleek bird fluttered slightly and stepped onto his outstretched finger.

"A raven," said Kier. "One of the oldest on Hiems."

Mal studied the sleek bird with his head cocked to the side. It rested on his long finger with perfect ease. Mal's eyes moved to Kier. His brow raised and the corner of his mouth tugged up.

"I travel all this way and you gift me an old bird?"

Kier smiled.

"The Magic within her is deep," said Mal.

"Yes," said Kier. "She can camouflage herself entirely and repeat Human speech. She can Obscure as well."

"She can jump the way we Magicals can?" asked Maeve.

Kier nodded. "She is touched by Fauna."

Mal looked to him. "Touched by Fauna?"

"Fauna were Gods that visited Hiems many evolutions ago. They blessed our planet's creatures with their Magic. Mordred, and most of the creatures that roam freely on Hiems, hold Fauna's power. Evaneskca, as she is called, now will bless you with her unique Magic."

"All of the animals on Hiems are blessed with Magic?" Maeve asked.

Kier smiled at her and nodded. "In one way or another. It's not simple Magic."

Maeve wracked her brain for any semblance of a lesson at Vaukore about Fauna or her gift of Magic. But none came.

"But there are no. . ." she began, struggling to find the words.

Kier laughed. "No Humans here possess Magic abilities no. Though we've managed for quite some time." He smiled.

"Were the Dragons from Hiems?" Maeve asked.

Kier's smile faded, but he commended her all the same. "Smart girl. The Dragon's tyranny lasted many years on Hiems in the ancient Magical world. Back when Vaukore was still the home of King Primus, the first Magical. They were driven off this rock and exiled to The Dark Planet." Kier's eyes widened. "Your uncle killed the last of the wretched beasts, I am told?" he added with praise in his voice.

"So I am told as well," she replied.

"Yes," continued Kier. "I remember now. Your father showed me the skull and skin."

Maeve's insides twisted. The bowl of stew that was now placed before her seemed inedible.

It didn't take long for Kier to steal Mal away. That was, it seemed, the King's favorite pastime. Maeve walked the icy halls of Stalakta, studying their portraits and paintings with Mordred at her side.

The wolf's back met her hip. His paws were far larger than her own hands.

"How does a wolf and his pack come to serve as a King's Guard?" she asked casually.

"By being the best," he replied. "Much like how you came to stand at the Dread Prince's side."

Maeve hummed in agreement. "May I ask you something that I am uncertain if you will take offense to?"

Mordred grunted in approval.

"Were you born this way? Or were you once Human?"

"I am, what the books would call, a werewolf," he said. " But here on Hiems with Fauna's Magic I am able to move freely between man and wolf as I please. No moon cycle dictates my transformation. Admittedly, this form feels more natural to me. I have not been in my Human form in forty something odd years."

"In Vaukore's realm, there are mermaids in the glacier lakes. Would they be touched with that same Magic if they came here?"

"Hard to say," said Mordred. "I've never been to the small realm in question."

"Fauna did not bless the Humans with Magic, and yet Kier rules above you all."

Mordred chuckled. It was deep raspy. "There are many species on this planet. None of them trust another to rule."

Maeve smiled softly. "I see."

"The boy who has come before. Mavros. He told me tale of a friend of his who was part-wolf, part-man."

Maeve nodded. "He was my brother."

"Earthlings are not kind to my kind, I have heard."

"No," she said weakly. "They are not."

Mordred's eyes softened. "I am sorry for your brother's death."

"Why do The Double O hate your kind? Why the push to eradicate that particular deviation of Magic?"

"The ancient ways are not forgotten by those who sought to maintain order of the Magicals on Earth. The Shadow War was only three hundred years ago, and your ancestors remembered the mangy beasts and four legged hounds from hell that crept out from the blight. It is my understanding they were likely afraid of the Magical gene your brother possessed."

"Hounds like you?"

"More like my fallen comrades brought back. Never dead. Never to live again. Only to destroy Magic."

"The Immortals, the High Lord of Aterna, they vanquished those armies and ended The Shadow War."

Mordred moved in a shrug-like manner. "There is always darkness waiting to rise."

"My home, back on Earth, my family had unicorns there. My father said they'd once been here on Hiems. But they could not speak. Were they not touched by Fauna?"

"Speaking is not the only gift of Fauna," he answered. "A being touched by Fauna inherits special abilities, otherwise impossible. I boast no abilities to move through space like your Prince's new raven. Nor can I conjure ice like some spiders, but they cannot speak or move between forms. That said, the unicorns of your family possessed everlasting blood, did they not?"

"So I was told."

She reflected on the water demon, the creature that nearly claimed her life.

"Are there other creatures from Hiems on Earth?"

"Of course," said Mordred, boredly. "How do you think your brother came to be a wolf? There is Magic from every realm on Earth by now."

A brown and white wolf appeared around the corner. Maeve nearly startled at his silent appearance. The wolf sniffed and huffed.

Mordred gave him a clipped nod.

"Excuse me," said Mordred.

He didn't look up at Maeve as he followed the wolf around the corner. Maeve stepped forward and watched them until they disappeared around another corner.

"I couldn't stop staring at them, either."

Maeve looked up as Alphard stepped beside her. She looked away hastily. He continued.

"My first time on Hiems, I couldn't sleep for days from the sight of them. Thinking about Antony. . .what he would have looked like in his wolf form."

"I'm fairly certain you aren't supposed to be alone with me," she said, her eyes back on the wolves.

"An error I apologized for," he replied, and then muttered. "And paid for with honor."

Maeve scoffed. "You apologized to Mal," she said. "Not to me."

Alphard paused. She turned towards him boldly.

"I'm sorry," he said sincerely.

She nodded and extended him her hand. "Then we speak of it no more."

He suppressed a grin, but he took her hand and shook it in agreement.

"One last gift before you go," said Kier as they stood outside the castle where Mal Portaled them in.

Mal smiled fully. It was so impactful Maeve was certain if he commanded it, Kier himself would fall to his knees.

"You've done enough, my friend," said Mal graciously.

Kier shrugged.

A solid black mare huffed in the freezing night's air as it emerged between two forms of ice.

"I imagine she'll do well in the Dread Lands," said Kier. "Your ambassador here tells me it remains cool most moon cycles."

The horse stepped straight to Mal. She was massive. Larger than any Clydesdale or Shire Maeve had ever seen on Earth.

"I feel the deep Magic within her," said Mal, his hand brushing along her mane. "She is of Dread Magic. This is too gracious a gift."

"Nonsense," said Kier. "You are a Prince. I look forward to your reforming the Dread Lands. It has long been overdue."

"Your kindness will not be forgotten," said Mal.

"No," said Kier. "And nor will my proposal, I hope."

Mal's charm did not falter as he said. "Of course."

Chapter 21

Malachite

"A marriage proposal," said Abraxas. "Bold. But as I suspected. Did Maeve hear?"

Mal shook his head. "Mordred was giving her a tour. And I think we'd know if she had."

"Normally, I would agree. But lately my cousin hasn't been exactly forthcoming with her thoughts."

Mal did not need reminding of her distance. Every breath she took felt farther and farther from him. Each day that she avoided his gaze, every dinner and every training, her walls were completely up.

"Is she pretty?"

"Who?" asked Mal as Abraxas' words pulled his thoughts from Maeve.

"The ice Princess," Abraxas replied with a laugh.

"Irrelevant," said Mal. "It's out of the question."

Abraxas pulled a box of cigars from his desk. "You don't have to tell me. She'd kill us both." He lit the tip of it with his fingers and relaxed.

Mal stared off into the study, not concerned with Kier's daughter or his proposal of marriage to her.

Maeve consumed his thoughts. As she always did. "I should have told her about the wolves."

Abraxas exhaled a ring of smoke. "She would have taken it hard seeing them with or without prior knowledge."

"I know she was looking at them and thinking about her brother. What could have been and the life she should have had as a family. With both of them taken from her. . ."

"She's been visiting Arianna and the twins more."

Mal looked over at him. "Has she?"

Abraxas nodded as he continued to smoke. "Strange to see the pair of them taking walks through the castle together. Zimsy says they frequent Agatha often as well. I can't remember the last time they were happy to be in one another's presence. Of course, it is Zimsy's presence she chooses to be in the most."

"Who else's presence does she enjoy that I am unaware of?" asked Mal, a slight bit of contempt slipping into his tone.

Abraxas smiled softly and turned his head to the side. "No one's in the way you are insinuating, Mal."

Mal looked away from his Hand. "Tell me truly Abraxas," he began, "if she was never to come around, would it be wise to accept Keir's offer?"

Abraxas' face saddened. "No."

"And why is that?"

Abraxas set aside his cigar and sighed. "If I was to set aside my cousin's happiness, and your own, I would not advocate for your marriage to the bloodline of Hiems. I would pursue the Elven Queen's daughter. They have the largest cities, army, and the greatest wealth. That said, she will come around, Mal. You just need to find her again."

"You've put a great deal of thought into that idea, it seems."

Abraxas shrugged. "That's my job."

Mal looked away from him. "'By the time I was your age, I already had two sons.' That is what Kier told me."

"You have plenty of time for that, down the road," said Abraxas. "When the pair of you have lived your youth and restored balance."

"She doesn't want that," said Mal softly.

"She doesn't want to be forced," Abraxas argued. "There is a difference." He leaned forward in his seat. "Mal," he said sincerely, drawing the Prince's attention towards him. "Just because the King of some frozen realm pressures you to move quickly on something, doesn't mean you must. Kier's motives are his own. He's not concerned with ensuring you have an heir in order to protect your bloodline. He is concerned with his bloodline being incorporated with yours."

Mal sat silently for a moment. "Your uncle warned me they would do this."

"Do what?"

Mal stared at the photograph of Maeve that had once occupied Ambrose's study.

He could feel her all the way on the other side of Castle Morana. She wasn't asleep. She rarely slept without his assistance. Assistance she didn't even know he provided.

"Use me."

Chapter 22

Maeve

The Barrier loomed ominously before them, separating the habitable part of the Dread Lands from the part still plagued with a dark blight. Much of The Beryl City was still wrecked with dark Magic, and it was crucial they restored the lands and made room for the Magicals seeking a place in The Dread Lands.

The Double O was growing desperate on Earth, but refugees from their tyrannical grasps at power fled to Castle Morana through Mal's secret and powerful Portals every day.

Obscuring around the Barrier was still dangerous for many of the Bellator, and so they traveled on horseback as they used Mal's Magic, which was supplied to them through their Dread Marks, to restore life to the ancient lands. Mal rode on the massive horse Kier gifted him, who he appropriately named Obsidian.

"What does it say?" asked Roswyn through his mask, squinting at the painted writing on a stone wall.

"Should have paid attention in Latin," muttered Belvadora.

Roswyn glared at her. Maeve smiled under her mask.

"Professor Schuyler would be so disappointed," said Fawley.

"Shut up," snapped Roswyn.

"Do not wake the sleeping shadows," said Mal. "That's what it says."

Maeve looked at him. "Umbra. Singular shadow."

No one commented on Maeve's correction.

"I guess they didn't call it The Shadow War for no reason," said Mumford, uncomfortably averting his eyes from the sloppy letters.

Mal reached for Maeve's mask once they crossed the serpent archways and pulled it from her face, his fingers brushing her skin. She resisted the urge to look over at him as she inhaled with ease.

"We can breathe here," she announced.

Belvadora pulled her mask from her face and opened her mouth to speak. The words caught in her throat as she inhaled.

Her brows pulled together as she placed the mask back over her face.

"Speak for yourself," she said, after Magic filled her lungs once more.

Exhaustion claimed them, and they traveled most of the journey back to Castle Morana in silence. Maeve spoke as the mist parted, and the moons of The Dread Lands presented themselves high above the path they traveled.

"Is it just those three?" she asked Mal.

"Yes," he answered.

"Can you ever see the stars?"

"High on Mount Morte, you can actually."

Maeve looked over at him. "A different galaxy than Earth?"

He nodded with a soft smile. "Entirely."

She looked back up at the sky, wishing she could see the new constellations above her.

"I'll take you there one day," said Mal, bringing her attention back to him. "Once it is safe."

Butterflies shot through her stomach at the way his dark eyes searched hers.

"Can you see Aterna from there too?"

Mal's face hardened. He looked away from her.

"You're interested in visiting there?" he asked, failing to hide the jealousy in his tone.

"I-" began Maeve, before stopping herself.

She looked away from him with a clenched jaw.

"Reeve proposed such a thing, I assume?" he questioned icily, not looking at her.

Maeve's insides twisted as she shook her head. She stopped herself from laughing at how ridiculous he sounded.

"And what of Kier's proposal for you to marry his daughter?" she fired at him.

Mal didn't look at her. "I didn't think you knew about that," he said coolly.

"I didn't," she replied, her eyes forward, "until now. I couldn't conjure another reason for his overbearing display of affection and loyalty."

"At least I know you are still sharp as a thorn," he muttered.

"Did you decline?"

Mal looked over at her. "Excuse me?"

"Did you decline?" she repeated plainly.

Mal reached down, grabbed the reins on Spitfire, her father's black and white speckled mare, and brought them to a stop. The others continued on ahead of them, not noticing their halt.

"Look at me," he said.

Maeve did not obey.

"That was an order from your sworn Prince," said Mal.

Maeve looked over at him, defiance burning in her stomach.

"Ask me that again," he dared, a dark glimmer in his eyes.

Maeve opened her mouth to speak, not concerned with the Magic swirling up around them. His Magic.

"Did you decline?" she asked through gritted teeth.

He frowned at her. "I have been so patient," he said. "So incredibly patient. And you repay me with such faithless insinuations."

He let go of the reins on Spitfire and continued down the path.

A tight and slow breath rose through Maeve, but it was not enough to calm her. "Seven months," she seethed, her voice growing louder. "Seven months of solitude, practically exile."

The others turned back towards them, realizing their argument at last, then hastily continued. Mal turned back towards her, Obsidian's large black frame blocking her path.

"Maeve–" he started.

She pressed forward on Spitfire. "I've heard all the excuses and the reasons."

"I'm going to ignore this outburst," said Mal, "and acknowledge that you are drained and tired." He turned on Obsidian and pushed forward.

Maeve scoffed. "Ignoring the problem seems right up your

alley."

Darkness swirled around her, prickling up her arms in ice and blackening her vision. Her back touched down on cold ground. Mal hovered above her, pinning her arms against the chilly earth as his chest pressed into hers. Maeve didn't fight him.

Her breath rose and fell hastily at his close touch.

"I did not decline," he said lowly, "because I cannot decline. You know very well I cannot. I need allies in this world. I cannot isolate Kier. Not now."

Maeve looked up at him, cursing the tears that fell from the corners of her eyes. Her voice broke as she spoke. "I'd wager my cousin believes it's a good match."

Mal's grip on her arms softened. His eyes scanned her face, watching as she swallowed her tears. His shoulder relaxed and his face dropped.

"Maeve—" he began softly.

She inhaled sharply and Obscured out from under him, not looking back as she stepped hastily towards Spitfire where he waited. Wiping her face with the back of her hand as she hoisted one leg over the saddle. She took the reins and squeezed her legs tightly. Spitfire took off towards Castle Morana at full speed.

The water in her bath had long gone cold. She didn't have the energy or care to reheat it. Her eyes burned, though her tears from her conversation with Mal were dry. Zimsy stayed with her until all the bubbles were gone. Her beautiful friend insisted she wasn't nodding off on the edge of the tub, and it took much convincing from Maeve for Zimsy to go to bed.

"Okay," she finally relented. "But I'm not far if you can't sleep and want me to bake you some lemon cookies."

"I just made lemon cookies for you," Maeve had argued.

Zimsy's full lips pulled together. "You add far too much flour," her musical voice said with a gentle smile.

Maeve forced herself from the freezing bath water shortly after Zimsy went to bed.

Her pajamas and silky robe were warm compared to the water as she slipped into the soft fabric.

She pushed the bathroom door wide and stopped. A soft green glow illuminated across her chamber, coming from a drawer in her vanity. Spinel rubbed against the legs of her vanity.

Her bare feet prickled with cold across the dark floors. She pulled the parchment from its place in the drawer, and fell into the desk chair, pressure building in her face.

I did not decline, Little Viper, the words scrolled elegantly across the parchment. *Nor did I accept.*

Maeve held the sliver of enchanted paper in her shaking fingers.

It would be so easy to run to him. She merely needed to call his name, and he'd appear. But as hot sorrow soaked her cheeks, she could not bear to have him see her so beaten.

He'd seen her cry in the week after her father's death. She had cried endlessly. She wiped her cheeks as his words vanished. She grabbed a quill and dipped it gently in the inkwell.

Your lack of an answer is an answer to me in and of itself, she wrote back.

The words disappeared at once. She felt the pull of his Magic on the other end.

She couldn't go to him. She couldn't stomach the floodgates of despair that would burst open at his sympathetic touch.

She stared at the blank slip of parchment. And stared. And stared, waiting for his reply. Finally she wrote:

Are there any others?

A moment passed. Her writing faded and was replaced with a reply from Mal.

Others?

Maeve sighed and scribbled quickly.

Proposals.

No.

You don't have to keep things from me. That isn't going to make this part go any faster.

Is there such a trick to hasten time?

The quill fell from her hands and clattered on the desk. She placed her face in her hands and sucked in a tight breath. Her tears fell in a steady rhythm.

Mal's Magic swelled through the parchment, a silent plea for her reply. She grabbed the quill once more and wrote:

First, you would need to reverse it.

His reply came without hesitation: *If only I could.*

Maeve leaned back in the chair as more of Mal's words appeared.

Come to me.

She sat forward and prepared to write a message of protests and excuses.

Don't argue, appeared on the parchment.

She didn't let herself think.

She placed two fingers on her chest, where his Dread mark lay beneath her clothes. She Obscured in an instant, snapping away from her chamber, and a new room came into focus.

Mal stood before her.

She looked up at him, begging her emotions to swallow themselves.

He stepped forward and wiped each tear away with cool fingers. His touch calmed her erratic breathing and consoled her scattered mind.

His fingers brushed across her cheek in a flowing motion. "I don't want her, Maeve. I want you."

Maeve sniffled. "My father always said wants in marriage were not something Pureblood Magicals could afford."

"Then it is a good thing we are not of Pureblood." He smiled gently as his thumb rolled over her bottom lip. "I want to show you something."

He dropped his hand and extended it to her. She took it, holding onto it firmly, hoping more of his Magic could calm her nerves.

The walk across Castle Morana was silent, but every few turns and stairs, Mal ran his thumb over her knuckles. He could have Obscured her to their destination, she knew that. But they took their time, and he never released her fingers from his.

When they reached the glass doors to the courtyards, Mal flicked his wrist in a slow, fluid motion. The doors pressed open with a long and steady rolling sound.

Maeve's breath caught.

The gardens of Castle Morana had changed. Shiny green life bloomed in abundance. A vast majority of the paths were now lined with green and blue hydrangeas.

She stilled at the threshold, hesitant to move forward lest the vision fade. He had done it. He said he would restore them for her. She had, truthfully, not thought of them since. . . but there, before her eyes, were flowers.

And they were the most beautiful sight she had seen in months.

"Your grandmother Agatha and her green thumbed, Human gardener were crucial in the restoration." He walked in front of her, running his hands along the vibrant green leaves. "Still not flourishing without my help, but as long as I will it, they will bloom."

She stepped across the intricate stone pathway and hesitantly brought her fingers up to one of the pale green ball of blooms.

"They're real," she whispered as her skin met the soft velvet petal of the flower.

Mal's eyes were on her. She looked over at him, forgetting her jealousy and pride. Her hand fell to her side, and she walked steadily towards him. He turned towards her as she reached him and placed her hands on his chest. He scooped them up in his own and lowered his forehead to hers.

"Please understand," he began. "It was not seven months for me. I left you on Earth, took a breath, and returned. And you. . . Everything changed in that breath."

Maeve swallowed. He continued.

"And now I am trying to find my way back to you." His hands cupped her face. "And you are so far away. Tell me what to do to find you again, Maeve."

Her head shook in defeat. "I do not know," she answered sadly. "I am but a shadow of myself."

His thumbs caressed her cheeks, sending electric energy buzzing through her body.

"The gardens are beautiful, Mal," she said, the words choking out of her. "I am honored by such kindness."

His finger tilted her chin upward. "I'd move mountains if they blocked your view, Little Viper." His fingers moved, cupping her neck between his hands. Maeve rose to the tips of her toes, brushing their noses together. "I'll bend the world for you."

Calming Magic seeped into her skin as his lips brushed hers. Her bones vibrated with a soft electric glow. He kissed her so tenderly, and with such supple control, that her body melted into his. Her eyes fluttered to a close as she pressed back into his smooth lips with equal delicacy.

His lips pulled away gently and the backs of his fingers slid down her cheek. He watched her bask in his touch for a moment, thoroughly pleased to finally hold her in his arms once more.

She looked up at him.

"It's late," he hummed. "I need to move out."

"Take a walk with me," she said softly, twisting her fingers through his. "Once through the gardens. The darkness of the night can wait."

Mal obliged. They walked, hand in hand, through the new bushes and blooms until a yawn escaped Maeve's lips. He led them around the castle and to the stables.

Spitfire greeted her with a small huff. She slid her fingers down his face as Mal saddled Obsidian and Maeve crossed towards him.

"Abraxas will travel to Hiems tomorrow to decline Kier's proposal," he said.

Maeve's eyes shot up at him. She struggled to find her words as he straddled the silky mare. Maeve played with her long, wild, black mane. Mal took the reins and positioned Obsidian towards the gates.

"You are a Prince now," she said at last. "There will be others."

Mal looked down at her from where he sat high on Obsidian, a steady breath rising through him. He spoke coolly, the corners of his lips pulling up ever so slightly as he replied.

"And they will all find me unequivocally uninterested."

His Magic pressed against her lips in a kiss-less goodbye.

The gates to Castle Morana flew open wide, gusting icy wind around her. Obsidian kicked back, and flew towards the arching metal at incredible speed, leaving Maeve in the wake of Mal's exit.

Chapter 23

Maeve

One.

Two.

Seven.

Sixteen.

Twenty-nine.

Maeve stopped counting the days Mal was gone at thirty. She was unable to bring herself to acknowledge that he'd been gone for a month. She'd fallen asleep with warm cheeks after their moonlight garden stroll.

Now she fell asleep knowing the nightmares that awaited her.

The gaunt woman with long white hair and sunken eyes visited her dreams the most. Sometimes she stood at the foot of Maeve's bed, watching her. In truth, she preferred the ghostly woman to the vivid, and gut wrenching dreams of her father and Antony.

Maeve was certain she'd awake soon and the nightmare would be real.

Sometimes she wished it was.

She shot up with a sharp inhale, palms flat against her clammy cheeks. Her vision focused on the figure at the foot of her bed. Wet, warm tears slipped from the corners of her eyes, one after the other, in a silent cry.

Mal shifted into view before her.

His face was pained. And she was certain he had seen the dream.

It was the same as always. The bathtub and the disoriented look on her father's face.

She stiffened and clenched her jaw tight, pressing down on the cry barreling up her throat. It was suffocatingly tight in her room. She threw off the covers and nearly bolted from the bed, as if it was to blame. She rushed across the room and forced open the glass doors of her balcony with a sharp wave of her hand.

She didn't stop until her hands gripped the cold stone ledge and she sucked in the freezing night air. Three more steadying breaths and her grip loosened. The endless haze parted just enough for her to see three moons that sat in perfect alignment, though each in different phases. Something entirely impossible on Earth.

The sky was a dense shade of green, as it had been since she arrived.

She felt Mal at the threshold behind her, his eyes on her.

"Will there ever be pure sunlight here?" she asked quietly.

"Possibly," he answered gently. "There is in Aterna I am told."

Maeve didn't look back at him. "It's hard to tell time here."

"Even harder out there," said Mal.

Maeve bit her tongue, knowing she was being selfish.

"Speak your mind," he urged.

Maeve shook her head. He didn't fight her.

Mal appeared at her side, surveying the mountains and the vast lands before them. His hands tucked at his back. "Astrea can make you a potion for the dreams."

"Is that how you sleep through the night?" she asked, a little too bitterly.

"Not when your thoughts are screaming at me, I don't," he replied smoothly.

She looked up at him and spoke genuinely. "I'm sorry I woke you."

Mal turned fully towards her and inhaled deeply. "I wasn't asleep, Maeve."

She resisted the urge to run her fingertips over the faint white scar across his eye and brow. The scar she had given him. "Abraxas says you rarely sleep now."

A small smile pulled at the corner of his mouth. "And here I thought you no longer cared about me."

"You don't think that," she fired back softly.

Mal scanned her face. "No," he said finally, "your cowardice has not yet completely blinded you."

Maeve paled and dropped her hands from the bannister. She

turned towards him fully. She'd be damned if that scar didn't make him more exquisite.

"I am not a coward," she said with a strained calm.

Mal stepped closer. "No?" he questioned. "You refuse to train with me since our first attempt. You do not train with Larliesl despite being the one to bring him here. You don't read. You don't care what the Double O is doing. You don't care to find the one responsible for your father's death. So tell me, what are you being?"

"Realistic," she snapped, with little fire in her tired voice.

"You are running," he corrected. "And I've told you before, that is beneath you."

"Maybe sometimes running is the only way to stay alive," said Maeve.

Mal's eyes widened. "Alive? Is that what you wish to feel?"

He was closer now, his scent and his Magic swirling up around her. She didn't answer.

Mal's two fingers tucked slowly under her chin, angling her head upwards. His eyes moved back and forth between hers. He nodded subtly.

"I'll see you in the morning for training. Not a request," he said and dropped his hand, leaving her on the cold balcony.

The Throne Room of Castle Morana was filled when Maeve arrived early in the morning for her training with Mal. She halted in the archway, her eyes scanning along the large room. The entire ranks of Bellator were present. They lined the walls along tables and stadium-like seating. They filled the rafters and balcony boxes above.

Mal stood at the foot of his throne with his hands tucked behind his back.

"Have I misunderstood something?" she asked.

Mal's reply came calmly. "Your training this morning will be spectated."

Maeve's head slid to the side as she eyed him. Mal did not smile. Her back straightened.

"You're serious?" she asked quietly.

"Perhaps an audience is required to make you feel a spark of something lost."

Excitement shot up her spine, but it was quickly drowned out by her quickening pulse.

Coward. Mal had called her.

The words burned deep in her stomach. It was the antithesis of her father. Of what he raised her to be. It was the greatest insult that could be thrown at her.

She stepped towards him across the shiny emerald tiles. Magic seeped from her feet as fury built deep in her core. Mal may have thought she wasn't paying attention to Larliesl's trainings, but Magic slipped from her every step, crackling across the castle floor. His eyes traveled down her body, but his calm scowl remained.

She faced him boldly, pushing down every resentful thought that scattered across her mind.

That it was his fault.

Mal's head cocked to one side as his chest rose. Maybe he had heard her.

She was glad of it.

Mal nodded as a wicked look spread across his haunting features. Dark Magic swirled behind him. They stepped towards one another in synchronicity, both drawing their Magic to their sides. Bitterness surged through her two deadly fingers.

It was not a shield that either of them produced. They fired Magic with intent to hurt upon one another. The thick sparks of light crashed together, shooting into walls of ethereal Magic between them.

Mal's Magic broke through hers quickly, knocking her back. She Obscured before her back slammed into the ground, righting herself on one knee.

A heavy breath slipped from her lips. One spell and he'd nearly exhausted her. She stood and straightened her spine. Her eyes found his like a magnet.

He fired again, and this time she threw up a shield and swiftly dodged the blinding burst of Magic. He fired again and again. Each time pushing her further back in the hall. Each shield was weaker than her last, and each time she dodged and struck back at him, she was a second too late.

Sweat dripped down her back. He was ahead of her every step of the way. Their minds were far from fused. Far from the dance they once shared.

Her arms fell to her sides in exhaustion as his pursuit did not halt. Icy and breathtaking Magic struck her. Her vision blurred as she stumbled to the floor.

She wondered if she was just weaker. Was it the Dread Artifacts he wore? Or was she never a match for him at all?

"Why did you run?" he asked, circling her as she stared up at the ceiling, gripping her wounds and aware that too many eyes were on her. She squeezed her eyes shut and laughed, the sound hollow as it echoed across the hall.

She pushed off the floor and glared up at him.

"I didn't have a choice."

Mal shook his head. His expression was nothing short of terrifying.

"You stopped choosing me," he pressed towards her. "But you never stopped being mine. You will always be mine. Buried six feet deep or soaring through the sky you belong to me, Maeve Sinclair. And I have allowed you to think otherwise for far too long. Now, get up and gather your strength or I will pierce your skin further until you understand that you will never, ever, run from me again."

Maeve pushed to her feet and ignored the tension in the room.

"Do not yield to your emotions," said Mal, another curse cracked through her weak shield. "Do not bend to me."

Dark swirls of Magic, twisting like vines, spiraled towards her. She pressed her feet into the ground and braced herself, shielding her face with her arms.

His command rang out over the shattering of her shield. "Do not bend to any of them."

His Magic was indeed paramount. It was stronger than the Dark Peaks and deeper than the Black Deep. He was nothing like her school companion.

Shaking heavily, dark tendrils sliced through her before she could even try to retaliate. She doubled over with a scream. Her head shot up as he fired towards her again. She Obscured, placing herself at his backside.

Mal swirled towards her, and gathered more Magic at his fingertips. "Anger is more useful than despair." He fired on her, filling the room with bright green light.

All that barreled across her mind was anger. At him. At Reeve. At Abraxas. At herself. So foolish. She'd been so naive and foolish.

She blocked successfully, but her counterspell fell weak against his shield. He fired on her again, Magic slamming through her in a wave of slicing ice.

Each fire of his Magic came quicker than the next. He wasn't giving her a moment to even breathe. She wished he'd suffocate her fully. Drown her in his possession.

But he was gone so often. And that place was dark and shadowed.

Frustration swelled inside her as she narrowly escaped another powerful blow.

"Wrath is far more powerful," he said louder, taunting her, growing her resentment and pushing her hatred.

The Magic she fired back at him was weak. Pathetic.

That of a coward.

His Magic pushed her backwards, then forwards, leaving her no room to find an offensive position. Her breathing was fast. Her heartbeat shook through her.

"And rage," said Mal. "… rage is more devastating."

The room darkened as fury swelled inside her.

What did he know of rage?

They took her father from her. They took her life, her future, and the one person she knew who'd love her without stipulation or gain. She'd be damned if they made her a coward. She'd be fucking dammed if that anger denied her Mal and her rightful place, slaughtering at his side in the name of her father.

He was hers. The Prince was hers.

His voice bellowed across the Throne Room, "Don't you want to devastate them?!"

A scream exploded from her throat before she realized she'd even inhaled. Electricity spiraled down her arm, sparking at her fingertips. Hot. It was so hot. But she was alive at last.

Mal was on her in a blink. His hand gripped her wrist tightly, redirecting the bright green lightning blast towards the ceiling. Maeve's legs gave way, and she fell to her knees, bringing Mal with her. With a sharp inhale, her Magic too collapsed, and Mal released her wrist. Her palms slammed into the cold emerald marble floor as she heaved a sob.

Her scream echoed across the hall as she cried with a broken voice, "Why did it have to be him?"

Mal remained kneeling before her. He studied her for a moment. His face was distraught. "I am sorry, Little Viper," his voice hummed. "I am more sorry than you'll ever know."

She fell forward into his chest and buried herself in the crook of his neck. His arms snaked around her back as she released nearly a year's worth of repressed remorse. Her tears flowed, hot and free and loudly against him. She didn't care that they weren't alone. She didn't care that the hall was filled with piercing eyes. Her Bellator. His court and their new world.

He brushed the back of her head and rocked her slightly, hushing her cries.

"I promise you are safe," he whispered. "I promise I am here. I am yours. Please, let me be."

His hands moved to her face, and he gently forced her gaze up at him. She shuddered and tried to sedate her sobs.

Mal placed his forehead on hers. "Let me help you, please." His eyes begged. "Say you'll let me help you avenge the death of the closest thing I had to a parent. Say you want me to slaughter them all. Say the word and my Magic is yours to command. Just tell me who to kill first and they won't live to see the sun rise."

Maeve wiped her nose with the back of her hand and spoke with conviction. "Orator Moon."

Chapter 24

Maeve

Jumping through minds was like shifting her fingers through water. Everything bent to her will. Pureblood minds. Mal's own mental shields. None of them stood a chance. Mal insisted it was her own reserve, but Maeve knew better.

Magic was merely the will of the mind to do the impossible.

He glowed with Magic the longer they resided in The Dread Lands. A halo of energy surrounded him. And he wasn't the only one.

Abraxas was sharper than ever. His ability to retain and extrapolate information was unbelievable. Alphard and Roswyn were unmatched in training. They packed on muscle at an alarming rate. Astrea's fingers healed with ease.

And Maeve. Maeve slipped through their minds as though she were their own shadow. She summoned lightning from her fingertips at will.

The unexplained and rare Magic she possessed perplexed them all. Bellator that had not been present for Mal's coronation didn't believe she could produce lightning. That is, until it screamed from her fingers and shattered a chunk of the Throne Room ceiling.

Finding Orator Moon would be different, though. He was in a different realm. And failure to find him was not an option for Maeve.

Failure was no longer an option. She'd forgotten how addicting Mal's praises of satisfaction were. The way his eyes swam with wicked thoughts when their Magic collided. She endured his brutal training and tests without a single yield.

It was worth it for every smile of approval he looked down at her with.

Abraxas' spies on Earth reported Moon made little public appearances since Maeve's disappearance. They lied about the number of Magicals fleeing to Castle Morana in secret, and certainly didn't admit to the public that a large portion of their Bellator and Magical Militia had deserted the Double O and taken new oaths with Dread Marks branded in Magic across their chests.

The Magical Times printed her vanishing as a kidnapping. That the evil and desperate Malachite Peur had stolen her away in the night.

Pale green light cascaded through the tall windows of Castle Morana. It was the most light she'd seen in months. Abraxas paced up and down the Throne Room. Maeve opened her eyes with a sigh.

"That's not helping, Brax."

He huffed and turned towards Mal. "This is a bad idea."

Mal's entire force of Magicals stood at the ready in and outside of the castle. They were prepared for anything that could possibly come their way as Maeve attempted to locate Orator Moon.

"They cannot Portal here at will, Abraxas," said Mal calmly.

"The room full of Bellator suggests otherwise," he pressed.

"They are here to observe," lied Mal smoothly.

Abraxas looked between them in exasperation. "I'm being left out of some bit of information and that absolutely infuriates me."

Maeve smiled softly and looked at Mal.

He was right, of course.

Abraxas huffed again, but placed himself on Mal's throne dramatically and didn't argue further.

Mal crossed to where Maeve sat cross-legged on the Throne Room floor. He crouched before her in a predatorial way. Her stomach lurched as she fell trapped in his captive gaze.

His fingers gripped her chin gently, ensuring her attention was on him. "You stop before your body gives out," he commanded.

She nodded. Mal's fingers pinched together as his brows raised. She fought a grin.

"Yes, my Prince."

Mal's solemn expressions slipped into a smirk. He released her chin and crossed the Throne Room back towards Abraxas.

Her cousin's worried eyes remained on her.

"Barlow," called Mal.

The woman stepped forward at once, slamming her fist into her chest. She was in her fifties, and a decorated soldier for the Double O. Her salute fell and her eyes landed on Maeve. With a single nod, Maeve prepared to enter her mind.

Finding Moon's location could take four jumps. Or forty jumps.

He wasn't in hiding just for fear of Mal's retribution for the Double O's slanderous lies. No. Maeve was certain Moon was hiding from *her.*

And there was only one reason she could think that her father's friend would fear his daughter.

Finding him was a matter of patience and endurance. Getting him to Castle Morana would be a test of just how far her Magic could go.

She slipped into Barlow's mind as darkness consumed her. Memories flowed by at will. She jumped to another mind, of a Magical Militia, one who remained on Earth. Doggbind stepped into view in the training exercise memory. He drilled them relentlessly, with the force of a dictator with something to prove. No man with an earned title barked like him.

One traitor at a time, she reminded herself.

She ignored Doggbind, and slipped into another's mind. Many of them had never had a personal conversation with Moon, and finding a strong enough connection to slip into Moon's own mind was the challenge.

She'd never jumped this many times. She'd never soared through so many muddled minds. Dead end after dead end had her stomach turning to acid. She looked upon their faces.

All of them were liars and cowards who remained content licking the boots of a corrupt and overstepping regime. Rage swelled inside her at their thoughts. Power hungry and misogynistic and ruthless in all the wrong ways.

So she shattered them all without a care before jumping to the next. There were no innocent among them.

Her pulse slowed after the first few.

Mal's voice rang clear across the hall. "Maeve."

She didn't stop at his warning. She pressed farther and farther, slicing and destroying everyone in her path.

Blood poured from her nose, slipping across her lips.

Abraxas pushed to the edge of the throne with a tight jaw. "Maeve, stop. That's enough," he said, panic slipping into his voice.

But Maeve didn't stop. Training with Mal paid off. She was moving through mind after mind, her Magic jumping without hesitation.

"Maeve," said Abraxas once more, pushing from the throne and jetting across the hall to his cousin. He gripped her shoulders and shook her gently.

She persisted despite his and her body's cries for rest.

Her bones ached. Her Magic begged for release as it shriveled into nothing.

But she was so close.

She could feel him in her blood.

Traitor, it hissed as Moon's Magic barreled towards her.

At last, she saw him in real time.

But her ace was still up her sleeve, and locating him was not her only objective.

Her arm shot forward and a small spiraling Portal, just big enough for her hand, sparked into existence. Moon jumped as his eyes shook with fear. Her fingers latched around his throat on the other side of the Portal as she sent paralyzing and electric Magic through the tips of her fingers.

He couldn't even scream against her onslaught.

The Portal grew larger and larger, her grip never faltering as the swirling mass of Magic revealed Orator Moon on his knees before her in the Throne Room. The Portal dissipated and Maeve's grip loosened as her Magic flickered out.

Mal strode down the throne stairs towards them.

The Orator squeezed his eyes tightly shut and the muscles throughout his face twitched and squirmed. His body thrashed beneath her power.

Maeve's hand fell limply into her lap. Her white eyes faded and closed as she collapsed backwards into Abraxas' arms.

Chapter 25

Malachite

Mal stilled.

Her heartbeat flickered. And then stopped. Maeve wasn't moving. Abraxas held her closely, frantically, as her head rolled limply back. Astrea moved quickly across the hall towards Maeve.

His heart pounded slowly as Abraxas spoke.

"She's not breathing."

Mal's hands tensed as blood drained from his face. He couldn't feel her Magic at all.

Mumford had Moon shackled with steel restraints laid with moonstone to numb his Magic as he cried, begging for his life.

Astrea worked over Maeve, chanting spells Mal didn't recognize. Healing was never his speciality.

He could feel Roswyn's Magic, willing Maeve not to wake. His hatred for her was unbridled. And then a shift, as Roswyn realized that Maeve's demise meant Mal himself would come completely unhinged. He'd tear the world apart until there was nothing left if she was gone.

She was his. She would always be his.

Astrea worked in vain. Maeve remained without breath.

Little Viper, Mal called silently.

The Magic of his that ran through her darkened veins did not answer.

Astrea panicked, pure fear radiating from her. Fear of losing the girl her brother loved at her own hands, and fear of Mal. She knew his wrath would be unending if she failed to save her.

Little Viper, he called silently again as he stepped towards her.

Abraxas was praying, to whom Mal did not know, but he prayed over his cousin in an ancient and purely Magical tongue, reciting it as though he had known the words since he was a child.

Each one of them held their breath as Mal passed.

Astrea screamed in frustration as Mal reached them.

"Give her to me, Abraxas."

Abraxas looked up at Mal defiantly, tears swelling up in the corners of his eyes. He gripped Maeve tightly and stifled a cry. This was his first time seeing his beloved cousin at the threshold of death.

But it was not Mal's.

Mal took her body in his arms and gently pulled her away from Abraxas. Her Magic was cold, barely there, like a stifled fire begging to be rekindled.

He was gone before any of them could blink.

He cradled her body against his.

Maeve's eyes were wide as she looked up at him. One large breath swelled in her chest and Mal's insides shook with relief.

Maeve opened her mouth to speak, but Mal sunk his lips into hers fiercely. She sucked in sharply through her nose as he forced her mouth open wide. He pulled away from her and brushed the back of his finger down her cheek, trailing down her neck and across her black filled veins.

"Was I dead?"

He pressed his forehead against hers. "Close to it."

Her Magic cascaded around him, thanking him. He sucked it in like a starving man.

He *was* starved of her.

"Where are we?" she asked.

Mal didn't move to show her, wanting nothing in that moment but to keep holding her, feeling her Magic as it was meant to be: unyielding.

"I am not sure what this place is," he answered. "But the Magic here is alive."

Maeve turned her head from him. Down pale white stairs were three trees that twisted together as one. They held small, shimmering leaves. The ceiling was carved with ancient markings.

"You aren't angry with me?" she asked, turning back towards him.

Mal looked over her angelic face, her pale skin flushed pink.

"I couldn't feel your Magic at all," he said. "I've only felt such a level of dread twice in my life, when Vaukore fell and I thought I might lose you. . .when Kietel took you. And when you nearly drowned in those mountains."

She looked up at him, her blue eyes swimming with regret.

"I can't lose you, Little Viper," he said. "It terrifies me what I would do if you were taken from me. I don't think I could control my rage."Mal shook his head and looked up, a breathy sigh escaping him. "I told you to stop before you broke, even if it meant we didn't grab him this time."

"But they would have known and he–"

"It was a command. What good is his death if it costs you your life?"

She paused and frowned. "I'm sorry."

He sat her up so that they kneeled before one another.

"You swore an oath as my second, to honor and obey," he said, no trace of anger in his voice. "You're so rebellious, so brazen, and so cunning, and those traits draw me to you as they always have. But you will get yourself killed if you do not listen to your Magic. You knew you were close to breaking, and you failed to control your bloodlust. It is valuable, yes, like rage and fury. But you mustn't let those things control *you*." He pulled on the fabric around her neck, bringing her closer, and gripped the back of her head. "I will tear apart the fucking world without you."

Magic slammed between them, and Maeve's eyes fluttered to a close. She moaned in pleasure as his promise swept over her.

Mal smiled triumphantly at his effect on her. His hands moved to her forearms, where he gripped tightly. He sent burning ice into her skin. She smiled and laughed audibly, tossing her head back and sighing sensually.

"How can I get through to you when pain delights you?" he asked with a smirk, pulling her closer.

Maeve looked up at him, and his breathing snagged at her enchanting expression. She was triumphantly gorgeous. Dark, beautiful, deep, and dirty Magic swam in her eyes. Those were his eyes. Those eyes that could halt him with one look. He was a man possessed. And if she ever pushed him away again, he'd show her just how much control he used each day not to succumb to the tortuous desires he had for her.

"Tell me more of how you will destroy the world over me," she said with an angelic grin.

His chest tightened. He buried his lips in hers, dropping her arms and wrapping his own around her fully. She pressed into him, her lips smooth and ready against his.

Her fingers twisted through his raven hair. Mal breathed her in fully as they trailed over the back of his neck, bringing every hair to attention. The ground was warm against his back as she pressed down on him.

His hands moved to her hips, pushing her down into him. Maeve's soft moan was so satisfying to his ears, he did it again. And again. And again, until her lips pulled from him as he forced their bodies to grind together.

"Mal," she whispered between sharp breaths.

His hold tightened and he sent Magic, soft as a feather, through his fingers. He wouldn't be able to restrain for much longer. The throbbing need to reclaim her grew as she tossed her head back, exposing all her darkened veins that marked her as his. He'd never intended to scar her in such a permanent way, but now, as her delicate fingers trailed sensually across her chest, he desired to mark her further.

Her eyes landed back on his.

"I should be punishing you for trying to run away from me," he said, still sliding her hips in a torturous motion across his growing desire.

Maeve smiled.

And he lost control.

In a swirl of black Magic, their clothes were gone and his hands moved up her torso, gripping her throat. She tensed beneath his hold as he pulled her face to his. She was so warm, and already dripping against his hardened cock.

"Apologize," he said darkly.

Her brows pulled together as her lips parted, desperately attempting to breathe. A high whine was the only sound that slipped from her as he constricted her airway.

I'm sorry, she slid across his mind.

"Sorry for what, Maeve?"

He moved his hips, thrusting forward, sliding his cock between her spread legs.

For trying to run.

Mal nodded, one hand loosening from her throat and moving to her face. He continued his slow thrusts beneath her. Each time the head of his cock flicked against her clit she dropped lower on him, writhing as much as his hold allowed.

"You cannot run from me," he said, his fingers rolling over her pouting lips. "And if you do so again, I will make you crawl to me across the Throne Room for all to see."

His hands moved swiftly to her waist, lifting her off him. His stomach tightened at the sight of her smooth skin gleaming, already wet from her own arousal as she suspended above him. Her long inhale was cut short by a cry, as Mal positioned himself at her entrance and pushed the tip of his cock inside her from below.

His neck rolled, forcing his head back and a sigh to escape his lips. Maeve's hands grabbed his biceps, clinging to them desperately as he stretched her.

The desire to slam into her raced across his mind. To bury himself so deeply within her, she'd never have the chance to run again. He'd failed her. And he would not do so again.

She moved her hands lower, dragging them across his chest. His muscles tensed beneath her fluid touch and he relented, pushing further into her. Her eyes closed and her lips pulled together.

"Eyes on me," said Mal, slowly thrusting further into her.

Maeve obeyed with scattered breaths. He released her waist, and she fell into him fully. Her cry brought a rush of wicked thoughts through his veins. She pulled her hips forward and back, forward and back, without hesitation. He fisted a handful of her hair and yanked her lips to his.

That's a good girl, he praised her silently as she rode him.

His free hand moved to her lower back, pushing her further in rhythm. Her pace quickened and his fist tightened. He'd nearly forgotten how absolutely addicting she was.

She winced as he bit into her lip and then licked over the tender skin. She slowed her hips, bringing them to a steady roll on top of him. Mal inhaled slowly, sucking in every ounce of her Magic oozing from her.

But he wanted more. More of her intoxication. More of her pain. More of her pleasure. Magic thrummed at his core, pleading for just fucking more.

He pulled his lips from hers. "Do you want to really feel it?"

Maeve nodded.

She leaned backwards, groaning as he filled her still. He took her wrist in one hand, flipping her palm towards him. With a single finger, he sliced across her palm. She twitched, sucking in sharply as the cut spread open. Bright red blood slipped from the wound.

Maeve didn't hesitate, She took his hand and placed two fingers on his palm, creating a matching cut to her own. He bucked into her as she sliced the skin. Maeve released him, and raised her bloody palm.

"Pour toujours," he said.

Forever.

"À tout jamais," she replied.

And always.

She bent towards him, slamming their lips together as their bloody palms met. Electric sparks shot through him as their blood fused. His heart sped forward, chasing every ounce of euphoria that raced through him until she shook on top of him, coming hard and chasing her own rush of satisfaction.

He gripped her bloodied hand tightly in his as he spilled inside her, singing her name.

Chapter 26

Malachite

Maeve was in a deep sleep. Mal could feel it all the way in the dungeon beneath Castle Morana. She hadn't slept so contentedly without his Magic sedating her since she'd arrived there. Each night she spent tossing and turning, her dreams becoming more vivid as she cried out restlessly.

Now she lay in his bed, high in the north tower, surrounded by soft silks with a resting heart-rate. The dreamless and deep sleep she deserved at last.

He'd left her two gifts for when she woke. The first was his Dread Ring, which he slipped on her finger before he left her. Back where it belonged. And the second was the Dread Locket, which lay beside his bed in a crystal, velvet-lined box. She'd worn it briefly before his coronation, but he longed to see it drape across her chest once more.

As Orator Moon shook before him deep under Castle Morana, Mal envisioned her wearing them both and taking the Orator's life.

Moon's wrists were chained above his head. Mal had removed each of his fingers with the Dread Dagger. Blood drained down the Orator's arms from the bloody stumps at his knuckles.

Roswyn delivered a punch to the Orator's face after tightening his chains. Mal's eyes moved to the inscription on the dagger. He read the ancient language with ease, the foreign tongue rolling off his. He looked up at Moon and asked, "Do you know what that means?"

Moon's head hung, his distant gaze on the stone floor.

"Forever wounded," said Mal. "No Magic can heal you, even if someone was coming to your aid."

Blood dripped from the dagger in Mal's hand, where he leaned against the dungeon wall.

"Which, it doesn't appear that they are," finished Mal.

"Why did you wait so long, Malachite?" asked Moon, his voice weak.

Mal answered without hesitation. "Because I wanted to share the taste of revenge with my Dread Viper. It has taken me months to resurrect the fearless and feared Witch you squashed with your recklessness."

"There is no one to blame but yourself for the death of her father," said Moon, blood spilling from his broken nose and busted lip. "Or do I not recall that you handed him that goblet."

Mal's lip curled, but he refused to take the bait. "I don't have many questions, but you will answer them."

"I won't," Moon spat. "You can bring her in here to look into my mind, but I won't voluntarily speak."

Mal smiled. "I never said it would be voluntary." He pushed off the wall and stepped towards Moon, bending over until their eyes were level.

Moon's body relaxed. His face flushed as Mal's Pathokenesis abilities took hold.

"Did you think she was my only means of discerning the truth?"

"Truly," said Moon earnestly, no longer in control of his own desire or emotions.

"Did you know it was poisoned?"

"We didn't know for certain," replied Moon.

"We?"

"The Committee of the Sacred. The Double O."

"They ensured the Dread Goblet made it into my hands?"

Moon nodded desperately. "It was my plan. They ensured the St. Beveraux girl made it to your side."

"Did Ophelia know?"

Moon sighed and smiled up at Mal, as though he was so pleased to be hanging himself. "I haven't the faintest idea. It didn't matter to me."

"Dirty fucking politician," sneered Roswyn from the corner.

Moon beamed at Roswyn. "She was just a means to an end."

Mal placed the tip of the Dread Dagger under his chin and forced the traitorous man to look up at him. Moon shook as the steel blade made contact with his skin.

"Why Vetus? Why do all that when you could have gifted it to me yourself?"

Moon swallowed. "You did not trust the Orator's Office. Neither did Ambrose. Not anymore."

"How could you have known I'd give it to Ambrose?" asked Mal.

"I didn't," said Moon. "You alone were meant to die. No others needed be harmed."

Mal clicked his tongue. "Do you take me for an idiot? No one at my coronation mattered to you. Do not feign as though that was a concern. You allowed a deadly weapon that anyone could have drunk from to be presented to me."

The constrictions around Moon's neck tightened as Mal recalled the many occasions he and Maeve shared a glass of sparkling water. "Maeve could have drank from it."

Moon's eyes grew large, his neck turning a brighter shade of crimson as his jaw fell slack under asphyxiation.

Mal continued. "Can you imagine the pain I would inflict upon you had you caused such a thing? If you had taken the one I love?"

The word slipped from him before he'd even registered it as such.

Moon thrashed against the chain as his eyes slid closed.

"You have destroyed her entire world," said Mal. "And now I am going to destroy yours."

Moon's heaving and gasping breath filled the dungeon as Mal stepped away. He coughed and choked until he could finally speak freely.

Mal's Pathokenesis abilities lifted.

"My children," he pleaded, "I will do anything to ensure they are not harmed."

"Such a vague word, 'harmed'," said Mal. He turned back towards Moon. "Open to such interpretation. Besides, your 'children,' as you call them, are soldiers in the Bellator Sector. Perfectly capable of discerning who they are willing to die for at such an age."

With the wave of his hand, darkness encased Moon's suspended body, slashing his skin slowly with Dread Magic. Mal turned on his heel, Roswyn close behind him. The orb of Magic remained around Moon.

Mal did not look back at the disgraced Orator as he delivered his final words. "We may have been born into your world, but you will die in ours."

Maeve stirred as his fingers brushed her cheek. Her brows pulled together and a small groan resonated from her throat.

Mal pressed taunting Magic into his fingertips, trailing them down her neck and across her chest. Her pale skin prickled to life beneath his touch.

Her eyes fluttered open.

"Hi," she said groggily, her eyes finding the windows along his chamber wall. "What time is it?"

The round tower sat high in the castle. Dark walls circled the small space.

Mal leaned over and hovered above her. "Late. Early. It doesn't matter." He pressed his lips to the soft spot of skin between her neck and shoulder. "I want you all the same."

Maeve craned her neck to give him better access, a smile blossoming over her lips. He pulled back, taking in her content expression.

"You said I needed rest," she muttered.

He lowered himself onto her and slipped his hands down her stomach, gripping her hips. "I'm the Prince. I changed my mind."

Maeve chuckled. "I suppose I can't deny the Prince his pleasures."

"You most certainly cannot," he agreed.

His lips pressed against her soft and sweet mouth, rolling over until she was on top of him.

Chapter 27

Maeve

Maeve touched the Dread Ring on her finger. Mal's Magic was deliciously stronger than ever. The locket around her neck kept her attention on him and his sultry gaze as Abraxas laid out the Double O and The Committee's reaction to the abduction of Orator Moon.

"Vaukore has been turned into a refugee center," said Abraxas, gathering the papers before him and straightening them with a clack on the table. "Doggbind is there, with hundreds of Magical families, and a vast majority of his remaining Bellator."

"I'm sorry," said Maeve. "Did you say refugee center?"

Abraxas slid a tan flyer towards her. She pulled it close.

BY ORDER OF THE PREMIER

ALL MAGICALS ARE TO EVACUATE TO REFUGEE CENTER:

THE UNHINGED AND   FALSE PRINCE, MALACHITE PEUR, HAS ATTACKED EARTH. ORATOR MOON WAS TAKEN PRISONER AND IS PRESUMED DEAD. THE ORATOR'S OFFICE FEARS PEUR WILL RETURN AND WILL NOT BE SATISFIED UNTIL EACH MAGICAL ON EARTH IS TAKEN TO THE DREAD LANDS TO BE SACRIFICED TO THE DARKNESS. VAUKORE ACADEMY OF MAGIC HAS BEEN DESIGNATED AS THE PLACE OF PROTECTION BY YOUR PREMIER AND THE MAGICAL MILITIA.

NO MAGICAL SHALL REMAIN ON EARTH BY ORDER OF PREMIER DOGGBIND.

YOU ARE HEREBY ORDERED TO EVACUATE BY MIDNIGHT.

Maeve looked at Mal. Abraxas continued.

"The Committee and the rest of the Orator's Office are there," he said. "They are hiding behind thousands of citizens and children in hopes we will not attack them there."

"Shame," sniggered Roswyn.

"Make no mistake," said Mal, his eyes peeling away from Maeve, "not a single innocent dies. I will not make orphans out of these Magicals that have been lied to and used as a shield."

Roswyn's smile faded.

"Does Moon know about the Dread Stone or Spellbook?" asked Abraxas.

"No," said Mal. "Not the faintest idea."

"That doesn't mean someone on The Committee doesn't," said Abraxas. "You'll want their secrets as well."

"How do we get there without them knowing?" asked Alphard, who had just returned from another trip to Aterna.

He was no closer to discovering Reeve's secrets than Maeve was.

Mal smiled knowingly. He looked to Maeve. "It just so happens I know a way in."

"You've got to be joking me," asked Maeve as Rowan waited for them on the other side of the secret and unknown Portal between the realms of Vaukore and The Dread Lands.

Rowan's unreadable expression didn't falter. "Disappointed I'm still everyone's favorite spy, Miss Sinclair?"

Abraxas stepped forward and shook Rowan's hand.

Maeve had never forgiven him for his negligence in leading her straight to Kietel and causing her near death.

"Sorry cousin," said Abraxas. "The Double O still believed him in their pocket." Abraxas smiled and reached for the former headmaster's cheeks. He pinched them together as Maeve's mouth fell open. "But really, he's in my back pocket."

Rowan's eyes slid dramatically to Abraxas with a glare. Abraxas returned his stare with a dazzling smile.

Abraxas dropped his hold and turned back towards them.

"Evening Rowan," said Larliesl, clearing his throat.

Moon stepped through the Portal behind them, Alphard and Roswyn flanking him on either side. His wrists were no longer bound with moonstone and Elven steel. Mal's Magic wrapped his bloodied hand stumps and gagged his mouth. Dried and fresh blood slid from his scalp, his stomach, and his arms.

Rowan looked satisfied. "Hello, Lenny."

Moon stared down at the cave floor.

"How many are there?" asked Mal,

Rowan looked to Maeve. "Far more than your father ever had stationed here to protect you."

Maeve didn't smile. "I suppose that makes us a greater threat than Kietel and his Human war ever were."

Rowan nearly rolled his eyes, but he looked back at Mal with respect. "Doggbind knows you are coming. He just doesn't know when. The castle is filled with Magicals. No corridor or classroom is spared."

"They are hoping civilians get hurt," said Abraxas plainly.

Rowan nodded.

"Arman is here with Doggbind?" asked Mal.

"Never leaves his side," said Rowan.

Mal smiled and extended his hand to Maeve. She placed her fingers in his palm. His lips touched down on her palm. "We do not need to be present in order to kill."

"I will not be satisfied watching him die from behind shadows," said Maeve.

Mal chuckled and kissed her fingers once more.

Footsteps rang from the spiraling stone stairwell that led from the small cavern in the mountains into the castle above.

Hummingdoor bounced towards them, clapping his hands rapidly. He zoomed towards Mal, forgetting himself, and quickly stepped back.

"Apologies," said Hummingdoor, bowing his head as his cheeks flushed red.

Mal smiled at the Alchemy Master. "No need, sir."

He may have already been crowned, but Mal's charm was so innate that it never left him.

"Larliesl," said Hummingdoor. "My dear friend, what a welcome it is to see such a long familiar face."

"How are the students?" asked Larliesl.

"Fine, fine," said Hummingdoor. "I am assuming you mean to get them off realm the same way you came?"

Mal nodded. "Those willing. The Portal to the Dread Lands is secure."

"They may not all go willingly, my Prince," said Hummingdoor. "The smear campaign against you is strong."

"There are whispers," said Rowan. "More Magicals speak up for you. They did not all come here willingly."

"No," said Hummingdoor, "and they are punished for it each day. The cells beneath the castle from King Primus' day are full. Students even."

"How will you sort those who have secretly remained on Earth for you from those who swap sides when they realize they are on the losing one?" asked Rowan.

"I'm not concerned with that right now," answered Mal. "They can all be sorted later." He looked back at Maeve and smirked. "We have such an easy time detecting lies."

Chapter 28

Malachite

It was easy for his Dread Viper to locate Doggbind. Two jumps from Rowan and she found him standing in the courtyard outside the castle. The fighting commenced as soon as Mal's Bellator emerged into the foyer. Mal and Maeve breezed past them all with sights set on the courtyard.

A rage of emotions radiated from the civilians that lined the halls as they observed him. Some held their fists up proudly. Some clutched their children while muttering prayers to all the Gods and King Primus himself. Conflict and fear wracked most of their faces though. Some ran, making for the upper floors of the castle. Mal cast a shield over them all as they passed.

It was their choice if they bowed to him. They certainly didn't deserve to suffer for his agenda.

Suffering was reserved for certain names on a list. Names Maeve had given him. He was happy to deliver her their heads. He had plans for all of them too, past granting his vengeful Second's wishes.

Roswyn and Alphard led the charge through the castle, leagues ahead of them when they came across the pair in the entrance hall.

"Found this on her," said Roswyn as his Magic held Leslie Loxerman down.

He extended Belvadora a small vial with his free hand.

Maeve laughed as Belvadora examined the bottle of poison.

"Couldn't bring yourself to do it?" Maeve asked Loxerman. "You must truly be delusional to think what awaits you is anything less than hell."

She looked back to Roswyn. "Remember: they all remain alive."

Roswyn looked back at her, annoyed.

Mal wanted to whip him for daring to glance at her that way. But his hatred for her rolled off Maeve, as it always did. So carefree of others' opinions.

"As were your orders," Maeve reminded him.

Mal suppressed a smirk.

Loxerman looked up at her in surprise.

Maeve squatted before Loxerman and answered her unasked question. "I have many questions for you before you die."

"And yet you killed the Orator," she replied.

"Oh no. I wouldn't dream of depriving you of your place spectating." Said Maeve dryly. "He has already been drained of his knowledge. Just as I will drain you."

Maeve stood and addressed Belvadora. "Keep an eye on that one, Bella," she said. "Can't have her offing herself before I've had the chance to replace all her happy memories with ones made of nightmares."

Mal wanted to slam her against the wall and bury his mouth in hers right there, forcing that hag Loxerman to watch him fuck her blind.

Electricity zapped between them, and Maeve looked up at him with daring eyes.

He pressed against her mental shields, realizing she had them completely down for him. She smirked in satisfaction and spoke into his mind.

There's time for that later.

When they reached the dim courtyard, Doggbind stood looking up at the statue of King Primus. Arman was mere steps away.

"Did you think hiding behind a school would stop us from coming for you?" asked Mal casually.

"You are outnumbered and out-manned," said Doggbind.

"How terrible," said Mal boredly.

Doggbind glared over at him and stepped away from the statue. His expression was wild. That of a desperate animal. Mal pitied him, only for a moment. For he, too, knew what it felt like to be so close to something great. . .and have it sliced from your hands.

"I alone could wipe you and all your traitorous Bellator from existence with the sheer will to do so," said Mal.

"Then why not be done with it?" Doggbind asked, standing tall.

"It is, of course, much more satisfying this way," replied Mal.

Doggbind took in Moon as he stumbled to his knees behind them. He snarled.

"Arman!" barked Doggbind.

The Magical Militia Captain stepped in front of the Premier. Doggbind smirked nastily.

"Are you willing to die for your Premier?" asked Doggbind.

"I always was," answered Arman, his eyes on Maeve.

"Poetic," said Doggbind. "Two right hands in a duel for–"

His words stopped short, a gargling noise choked from him as he gasped for air. Maeve pushed him to the edge. In a blink he was within an inch of his life.

Doggbind stumbled forward as she released him. He sucked in desperate air and staggered backwards, his body shaking and limp all at once. Arman caught him as his legs gave way.

Arman's eyes were on Mal, his hands tightly around the usurper Premier.

Mal didn't smile as they looked at Ambrose's former Captain. "Maeve."

Arman's eyes snapped to Maeve's.

"I promised you the victor," Maeve said. "Take your spoils."

Arman withdrew his hands from Doggbind. Blood splattered his face as Doggbind gagged and staggered. He crumbled at Arman's feet. Crimson soaked the stone around him like wine as blood from Arman's single fingered deadly slice poured from him.

Arman did not watch him fall. He did not observe the blood that poured from his mouth and neck as he took his final breaths.

Arman's fist formed over his heart, his eyes never leaving Mal as he said, "My Prince."

Mal's cold expression remained, but his head dipped towards Arman.

Arman's gaze slid to Moon. The Orator's eyes were round at the dead body between them. Moon froze, his frantically fearful face paled.

Arman stood tall. "Did you truly think I would stand by you when you tarnished the name of my Premier, my Commander, and used his

Bellator to take control for yourself?"

Moon's shoulders shook.

"Fear looks good on him, doesn't it?" said Mal casually.

"It is all he reeks of," answered Arman.

"How many of the disloyal remain?" asked Mal.

Arman placed his black boot on top of Doggbind and nudged him over with his foot. Doggbind rolled limply beneath him. "I have been busy on Earth, my Prince. All that remain here are loyal to you, except for those who have been gathered in Hellming Hall awaiting your judgment."

Arman twisted two fingers. Doggbind's Premier badge ripped from his uniform and floated into the air. Arman's fist clenched as it shattered.

Chapter 20

Maeve

Arman's words were true. Hellming Hall held a small portion of the Double O's remaining militant forces. They lined the four walls on their knees.

Mal's Bellator, new and old, made themselves comfortable on the dining tables. They stood and cheered as Mal entered the room, beating their fists over their Dread Marks. Mal smiled humbly and held up his hand.

They quieted at once. The waves of adrenaline that pumped through the room nearly lifted Maeve off the floor. Moon was already at the center of Hellming Hall. It was clear more of the Bellator had taken some jabs at him in their absence as the castle was searched and secured.

Abraxas and Arman organized gathering all the citizens and getting them home. Wherever that was. Vaukore was huge, and there were thousands of Magicals there.

There had been no close battle. The loyalty for Mal was overwhelming, and the hatred for the Double O, unbridled. Moon, Doggbind, and the Committee had grossly miscalculated their upper hand. It crumbled beneath Mal's claim to the throne.

Still, the ease of battle made her nervous. Something lurked in the back of her mind, the whispering thought that this was just the beginning of bloodshed.

She forgot her worries soon after Mal took her hand and escorted her upstairs.

"Mine or yours?" he asked as they reached the landing.

"What?" she replied, her brows pulling together.

His head tilted to the side. "Pick one."

Maeve's mouth fell open as he continued, closing the small gap between them and taking her chin in his hand. "My room? Or yours?"

he asked coolly.

She picked his.

Mal's voice brought her thoughts back to Hellming Hall and out of the delicious way he had devoured her in his old dorm room.

His hand was extended towards her where he stood by the disgraced Orator.

Come and claim him, Little Viper, he said into her mind.

Her chest tightened.

Come and show them all what happens when we are crossed.

Every powerful step across the floor rang through her body. The sound echoed against the three stained-glass depictions of Magic, creating tones of musical Magic.

Moon jostled weakly at her advance, as though he sensed death walking towards him.

"Mercy, mercy," he pleaded through broken breaths.

His panic grew as Mal stepped aside, giving him a full view of his executioner.

"I beg of you, Maeve, he was never meant to die," cried Moon.

"Is that supposed to make me feel better?" .

He averted his eyes and hung his head low.

Mal's Magic slithered under Moon's chin and forced his face up as he placed himself at Maeve's side.

"You will look at her while you die," he said, his voice calm.

Moon's lip trembled as he begged one final time. "Mercy."

The word moved through her like a dagger's tip. *Mercy.*

"In what world," began Mal, "do you think that you are permitted mercy?"

His fingers brushed down Maeve's cheek as her eyes, full of resentment, remained on Orator Moon.

Mal stepped behind Maeve. A single finger trailed down her spine, sending his own Dread Magic into her veins.

It surged through her, a glimmer of his power, begging to destroy and rip. She pointed two fingers at Moon, red electric light bouncing between the tips of her fingers.

Mal's Magic was alive and racing through her, tripling her heartbeat.

Rage, pure and unbridled, swarmed through her as she took on Mal's own fury coupled with her own.

They took her father. They took her life.

They took the promises of new dreams and destroyed them with one careless and evil action.

Mal's Magic turned unbearably cold as it begged her for release. Her skin crawled with destruction as it barreled into her fingertips.

Mal was right.

Anger felt better than tears.

Wrath felt better than grief.

And rage felt better than guilt.

Mal's fingers brushed across the serpent pin on her chest.

Do it, Mal's voice said into her mind. *For Ambrose.*

There was no scream of triumph that erupted from her throat. She held bated breath as she pointed every ounce of blame and fury at the man her father once called a friend. The man who was elected as their voice of freedom.

Moon's eyes slammed closed. Bright red light flashed through the hall as vibrant lightning shot from her fingertips and shattered through Orator Moon.

He crumpled to the floor and did not move again.

Her own Magic spiked in all directions, targeting each soldier whose loyalty lay with The Double O. They dropped to the floor as she shattered their minds all at once. Her balance faltered as every bit of her strength drained from her veins.

Mal's arm slid around her waist, supporting her. He smiled down at her with pride.

"There she is," he said, his eyes glistening darkly.

He took her hand, still pulsing with Magic, and ran his tongue from her elbow to her wrist. He looked over the hall of bodies as her vision faltered. Her head rolled back against his chest, exhaustion settling into her bones.

The hall erupted in one synchronized agreement:

"For Ambrose."

It was late when they arrived back at Castle Morana, despite the endless, hazy twilight. But Abraxas insisted on a small celebration. He ensured the drinks flowed and indulged in his other favorite pastimes. There was nothing "small" about it.

Maeve lingered for longer than she would have liked, watching as everyone drank themselves unconscious in the late hour. Her mind slipped to what her father had said one evening. She couldn't remember the party, but he said he'd be worried if his Magical Militia *didn't* engage in celebratory revelry now and again.

Those were now her fighters.

The ones who came by the thousands to his funeral. Who called his name out as she killed one of the many responsible for his deaths. Who now toasted goblets full of his favorite brandy late into the morning.

Save for Mal.

He sat on a large throne-like chair in the lounge, which suited him, as he was the victor. Maeve watched him smirking at something Roswyn said, and she wished they were alone.

His eyes met hers as ice swept down her spine. She'd wanted him to hear the thought. She stood and broke their gaze.

"I'm going to bed, Brax," said Maeve to Abraxas, who sat next to her playing a game of cards which he had placed a rather high bet on. The smoke from their cigars made her brain fuzzy.

"Goodnight, cousin," he replied.

Without looking away from the game, he blew her a quick kiss.

Maeve walked into the foyer and paused, knowing Mal would be on her heels. She reached the foot of the spiraling, oversized stairs as she heard his voice behind her.

"Turning in so early?"

"I believe it is so late that it has become early," said Maeve, turning towards him. The large clock in the atrium read close to six in the morning. "I'm tired. And," she reached for the locket around her neck, "still adjusting to this new power."

Mal nodded. They stood in the silence together with nothing to say, but neither wanting to part ways. Mal stood only a few feet from her as what little moonlight could cascade through the windows shadowed his face.

Maeve stepped in closer until she could see him properly.

"Thank you," said Maeve softly.

"I hope you truly understand now that, next to me, you can have anything you want, Maeve." He reached out and touched the side of her face. "You should fear nothing."

His eyes held her captive as she leaned into his touch. Swirling dark orbs of power she couldn't bring herself to look away from stared down at her.

"Did you look inside?" he asked quietly, with a nod towards the locket around her neck.

She hadn't even thought to.

Feeling foolish, Maeve reached down and pulled open the clasp. The slim locket slid open. Inside was a small portrait of Ambrose, leaned against the balcony railing, smoking a cigar. On the other side was the picture of Mary Gagner that had been in Mal's uncle's house. Mal's mother was merely a child in the photo.

Maeve's breathing hitched and her eyes quickly became watery.

Relief and grief were too similar of words. Moon and Doggbind may have been dead, and The Committee not far behind them, but he was still dead. He was still gone.

As satisfying as it was to topple the entire Double O and stage an entire mutiny, she was still lost inside her mind. Desperate to find a way back to him. Back to someone that did not exist.

Mal wiped a small tear that escaped from the corner of her eye.

"We will make them proud, Maeve."

She swallowed the groaning cry that pressed against the walls of her throat. His hand lingered on her face, despite the fact that Mumford rounded the corner and came to a quick halt upon seeing them.

Mal's eyes remained on Maeve as he spoke calmly. "Did you need something, Mumford?"

"Yes, My Prince," stammered Mumford. "A private word, please."

Mal's eyes traveled down to Maeve's lips, his thumb following. She breathed deeply, inhaling the Magic pushing towards her, not caring that they weren't alone.

Sleep in my chambers, he spoke into her mind.

A smile tugged at the corner of her lips.

Don't make me wait long, she replied.

His hand fell and he walked towards Mumford, motioning him to follow. Maeve placed the back of her cool hands against her hot cheeks and turned towards the staircase and headed for the North Tower.

184

185

PART TWO

Chapter 30

Maeve

"Good morning, cousin," said Abraxas brightly.

"You're awfully cheery at this hour," she said, taking a croissant off a tray and pouring herself a cup of warm tea.

"The Prince was up early and eager to begin his day out in the Dread Lands," said Abraxas, nose deep in a newspaper from Earth. "Tell me, how's the view of the Dark Peaks from the North Tower?"

Maeve nearly choked on her tea. She grabbed a napkin and dabbed her mouth as she looked across the table.

Abraxas wore an innocent expression. "Is it a nice view?"

Maeve lowered her chin at her cousin. A smirk developed across his face.

"Well," started Maeve, "since you're such a damn know-it-all, I can't believe you don't already know."

Abraxas laughed. "Too early for a good comeback? Maybe I should let you eat first and then you'll be able to generate a clever response."

Maeve held up her middle finger to him and resumed eating her breakfast.

He ran his hand through his silver blond hair. His voice was genuine when he spoke. "You look well."

Maeve didn't look up at him. "I was mad at you, too."

"I wrote to you," he said softly. "I tried."

Maeve nodded. "I know that now."

"And Mal," he continued. "He had no idea–"

"Brax," said Maeve gently. "It's past. I want to lay it to bed."

Her cousin's smug expression returned, and his brows raised. "Clearly."

Maeve bit her lip and fought a smile.

Abraxas continued. "Poor Roswyn and Mumford–having guard

duty outside the doors all week. A torturous existence."

Maeve looked up at him.

"Do with that what you will," he continued. "Though I think it would be sinfully egregious if they weren't forced to hear you screaming our Prince's name."

Maeve's mouth fell open. "I have never screamed his name," she argued with a scoff.

"Belvadora was on guard duty last night and *begs* to differ. Though I hear you did that too."

Abraxas' bright white smile mocked her.

"You're evil," said Maeve, shaking her head and holding her hands up in defeat. "You win."

His smile softened. "I jest, cousin. I hope you know that no one will ever be in your corner quite as happily as me."

"And you? How is marriage treating you?"

Abraxas frowned slightly. "Talk of marriage? How boring. Might as well ask me about the weather." He cleared his throat. "Well, Maeve, it's green and hazy outside, but there's a chance tomorrow will be slightly less green and hazy. More misty, if you will."

Maeve didn't press him farther after his deflection.

Abraxas snapped the newspaper closed. "Now that the fun is out of the way. Business."

With the flick of his fingers, a small scroll of parchment slid across the table towards her. The pale violet seal was already broken.

Maeve took it and examined it closer. "A dragon?"

"An invitation to Aterna."

"From the High Lord?"

Abraxas nodded. Maeve opened the letter. It was addressed to Mal. Abraxas spoke as she read over Reeve's words. His handwriting held a sharp elegance.

"You've been extended a great honor," he said. "The Gyeoltua was a duel of excellence in the ancient kingdoms of Aterna.

"Yes, I remember from Professor Vinn's class," she muttered softly, reading over Reeve's words.

They were without fluff or exaggeration, written almost as though he'd put little effort into drafting it.

"What do you think?" she asked Abraxas.

"You'll be the first in over three hundred years to fight Aterna's best."

"You don't think it's just a formality of sorts? We invited him here. He's inviting us there."

"No," said Abraxas swiftly. "I believe, given the events of late, the High Lord would like to see what reborn strength the Dread Viper has."

"You think they just want to see my power?"

"Without a doubt," said Abraxas. "They can wrap the invitation up in fancy parchment and call it whatever festival they want. But this is about assessing you and Mal against their own forces."

"Reeve has seen me lose control of my power," she argued, her chest tightening.

"But he's never seen you control it," he replied with a proud grin.

"You're far too excited about this. We just took out The Double O. He's probably set some trap for us to ensure we don't have the ability to turn on them too."

Her cousin's grin widened. "He'd never do that to you."

Maeve frowned at him, and looked back down at the parchment as she muttered under her breath in a mocking tone, "I'm Abraxas. I think I know everything."

Mal returned to Castle Morana within two day's time. His appearance in the training courtyard snagged her attention and landed her a stinging jab from Belvadora.

"Ow," said Maeve with annoyance, her eyes snapping back to Belvadora.

The blonde shrugged and didn't smile. Maeve's eyes were already back on Mal where he leaned in the archway watching her.

"Dismissed," said Maeve.

Belvadora didn't hesitate to move on to sparring with another.

Mal disappeared from the archway as Maeve crossed the courtyard. The corridor was dark and shadowed as she followed his unknown path. Two corner turns and she stopped, Magic dancing down her arms.

Slender and firm fingers grabbed her waist from behind, pulling her backwards into the darkness. The marbled wall was chilly against her back, but Mal's lips were ice against hers. She sucked in sharply at the extreme temperature.

"My," she said with a shaky breath as he pulled away. "Your Magic is. . .."

The faintest image of a smirk appeared on his face in the darkened corridor. "Yes?"

Maeve swallowed. "It's captivating."

His fingers brushed her face tenderly.

"You are handling the darkness well, it seems," she said.

"More so now than ever," he replied. "Your presence here has changed everything."

Maeve smiled. "Talk to me about this party at Crystalmore."

Mal brushed her hair behind her ear. "I told Abraxas you'd be wary of it. He insists we attend."

"You are the Prince. It is your call."

Mal's fingers moved down her cheek, bringing her eyes to a close. "He is my Hand. I trust his judgment."

Maeve sighed heavily under the Magic resonating from his fingertips.

"You do not wish to fight?" he asked.

"I will fight," she answered calmly. "I fear they have ulterior motives."

Mal's fingers tucked under her chin. Her eyes opened.

"Then let them," he said. "There is no trap you and I will not claw our way out of."

"I want to be as strong as possible."

"We have a few weeks," said Mal. "I will make sure of it."

She angled her face up and he responded graciously.

"Still no sign or indication of the Dread Stone or Spellbook?" She asked as she gathered her clothes from the floor in the Crown's Quarters.

Mal placed one hand behind his head where he lay reclined on the bed. "No." He paused and watched her. "I'm sorry I've been gone so long. Thank you for not holding it against me."

Maeve's head cocked to the side. "What do you mean? It's only been…two days."

A look of confusion shifted across his face for a brief moment before it slid into frustration.

"How long does it feel like you've been gone?"

Mal shook his head with a lengthy sigh. "At least a month."

Maeve's mouth fell open. No wonder he'd been so eager to undress her. She crossed towards him, sliding a thick sweater on. She crawled on the bed and sat next to him.

"Hey," she said as she took his face in her hands. "You're doing wonderfully, Mal. We're still learning."

"I promised you," he said.

She brushed her thumbs across his cheeks. "What?" she asked softly.

"I promised I'd never leave you alone for so long again."

Maeve slid closer to him.

"How can I keep that promise when I am upside down out there? With no correlation or connection to the passage of time beyond the Barrier and here."

They sat in silence. Maeve looked over at her vanity.

"Take the parchment with you," she said, taking his hand and displaying the wristwatch she'd given him nearly three birthdays ago. "And we will write to one another each night at midnight. Tallying the days."

Mal slid from her grip and twisted his fingers around her own. He brought them tenderly to his lips. "What a clever little Second you are."

"We can keep track," she continued, "and if I need you to come home, I will tell you."

Mal's chest fell quickly as a small breath slipped through his lips. "What did you say?"

She leaned forward and pressed a kiss to his forehead. "Home, my Prince. You are my home now."

She pulled back as his hands trapped her face. Mal's dark eyes held her hostage.

His Magic slithered up her body, bringing her eyes to a close. He didn't need to speak a word. She felt them all. But he spoke them anyway.

"There is no love I can fathom that is greater than what I feel for you."

Maeve's eyes shot open. Her mouth opened to return the sentiment, but Mal's Magic sealed her voice. He smiled.

"I already know, Little Viper. I see it in your dreams. It screams at me from your blood. I alone hold your heart. And I do not intend to ever let it go."

Chapter 31

Maeve

Maeve sat in the chair Arman provided her, opposite of where Leslie Loxerman curled in the corner of her cell.

Maeve crossed her legs. "Do I need to force you?"

Loxerman watched her with tired, red eyes. Maeve may have insisted Loxerman and the rest remain alive for interrogation, but that hadn't stopped Mal from enjoying their pain.

Loxerman shook her head.

Maeve wasted no time.

"Who was my mother?" she asked.

"She was no one of importance," replied Loxerman.

"Did you ever meet her?"

Loxerman shook her head. "Your father kept her far from us."

"But you knew who she was?"

"I knew she existed."

"Did you kill her?"

Loxerman looked down at the cell floor. "No," she said at last.

"That doesn't sound very convincing."

Loxerman looked up at her, a strange glaze cast over her eyes. "I. . . agree."

Maeve watched her for a moment. "I don't believe you."

"Then dig through," said Loxerman. "You will find no recollection of her beyond Ambrose's admittance of his mistake."

"Bet you forced Clarissa, just like you have forced women to marry and breed and lie for decades."

"The Committee of the Scared backed his plan for Clarissa to pretend you were hers, and you should be grateful such an opportunity was given to a half-blood Witch. You alone bear those three stars on your wrist despite your dirty blood."

Arman had not spoken to Loxerman once since their interrogation began, but his voice hummed in the small cell, "Watch your mouth, Leslie."

Loxerman swallowed as a bit of power slipped from Arman. Perhaps Mal wasn't the only one who had visited her previously.

"Moon said the Dread Goblet was your idea as well," said Maeve.

Leslie breathed a laugh. "He came to me scrambling for a way out. You know, I advised him to accept the reality of Malachite's throne. That he, Lenny, could perhaps still hold rank and power within a new world. Maybe even maintain his position as Orator on Earth. But he was insistent that Malachite die."

"A costly error," said Maeve.

"Indeed," agreed Loxerman.

"You didn't answer my question."

Loxerman did not meet her stare. "The goblet was technically my idea, yes."

"Did Vetus Willus and the St. Beveraux's know about its poisonous nature as you did?"

Loxerman looked up at her. "You sent Moon and Doggbind into a tailspin when you killed Vetus and so perfectly got away with it, too."

"You know what pleases me?" asked Maeve. "In all your evil plotting and planning, you were too stupid to realize Vetus held three Dread Artifacts. And all three fell into Mal's hands with desperation to be in the control of royalty once more."

Loxerman opened her mouth, but Maeve cut her off quickly with succinct words.

"Did the St. Beveraux's know?"

"Marguerite did, yes."

Maeve sat for a moment. Rage swam through her, quietly begging permission to shatter Loxerman's mind. Even that seemed a mercy.

"And Ophelia?" She asked at last.

Loxerman's brows pulled together. "I have no idea."

Mal leaned against the doorway. "You're up late."

Maeve looked out the window. It was still impossible to differentiate day and night in The Dread Lands.

"Go to bed, Maeve," came Mal's voice.

She returned her gaze to the work before her. "I'm not tired."

Mal's Magic moved behind her, running down her shoulders and arms in a soothing way.

She'd spent the entire day running through Loxerman's mind, desperately searching for any semblance or sign of her mother, and verifying the things Loxerman had admitted.

"It just doesn't make sense," said Maeve. "Why is there no record of her? Why do they remember her existence, but not one detail of her. My father had her buried so deep in his mind, even he barely remembered her."

"But Clarissa, she knew of her existence. She knew you weren't hers."

"I know," said Maeve. "It's as though they knew of her, and nothing more."

"What about your grandmother?"

"Grandmother Agatha swears she never even knew I was born of another woman."

More of his Magic pressed into her back, relieving her tense muscles and nerves.

The thought of this phantom of a mother plagued her. Was she even alive? If she was, how could she have abandoned her so easily to be raised by another?

Maeve looked over at him. He was dripping in Dark Magic. A breath escaped her lips and she stood at once, crossing her chamber towards him. "You need rest, Mal."

He looked down at her with hooded eyes, his fingers looped around the Dread Locket that hung elegantly from her neck.

"When can we kill her?" he asked.

"Soon," said Maeve. "I just want more time in her mind. Maybe she has convinced herself of such a lie, that it appears real and I must break it."

Mal nodded. "I can't promise I won't keep her on the edge of death."

Maeve smiled and took his hand in her own. Her Sinclair family ring brushed against his Dread Ring as electric and icy Magic traveled up her arm. She led him to the oversized chair by the dwindling fire. He pulled her to his lap at once.

Maeve traced her fingers along his sharp cheekbones. "I have more information that may help satiate your bloodlust."

His brows raised. "Whose is the next name on your list? Allow me to deliver them to you."

"Marguerite St. Beveraux."

Mal's hands stilled. He looked away from Maeve as his head rested against the back of the armchair. He didn't speak for several moments.

"It's not your fault," Maeve said softly.

Mal nodded and licked across his teeth. His eyes were locked on the fire as he said. "I was a fool."

Maeve began to argue but Mal's eyes silenced her.

"I need to feel this, Maeve. It's the only way I'll learn the lesson."

She nodded and sighed. "I have one more name."

Mal waited for her to name them. Guilt slipped into her stomach.

Mal smiled, sensing the deep-rooted jealousy within her. "You want Ophelia."

"Now tell me again you aren't going to deny me that."

His smile faded. "I wouldn't dream of it."

Maeve dropped her hand. "Even if she is innocent?"

Mal chuckled. "'Innocent' is a broad term. You have already decided she is not."

"And if I am wrong?"

Mal pushed her hair behind her shoulder. "She delivered the Goblet to me, regardless of her intentions. Her naivety and negligence cost us greatly. There is no world in which you are unjustified in your hatred."

"Is that a yes?"

"In the coming weeks, families from across Earth will come here to begin a new life in The Beryl City. Many of them eager to please their Prince. The St. Beveraux's are no different. I'll have Abraxas move their court appearance up."

"They will think they are coming here as honored guests?"

"Yes," said Mal.

His face moved towards hers, their noses brushing.

"I know you desire her," said Mal softly. "If it is blood that you crave, you need only name the bleeder."

Chapter 32

Maeve

The Dread Mark was woven intricately into the banners along the Throne Room. Deep emerald fabric reflected the firelights, matching the cape now pinned at her shoulders that too bore Mal's mark.

She was not merely a daughter seeking vengeance.

She was the Dread Viper.

The Throne Room filled with Bellator, Magical Citizens, Sacred Seventeens, and those on the Committee who were, for the time being, still alive. Mal sat on the throne he rarely occupied, with sensual ease.

Abraxas stood to his left, and Maeve to his right.

The doors to the long hall opened with a stout elegance. Led by a handful of Bellator with capes just like Maeve's, Marguerite and Ophelia nearly skipped towards the throne. They were both dressed in what Maeve could only assume was their absolute most expensive attire. Marguerite had more gaudy rings shoved on her fingers than her Aunt Vetus had when she died.

Ophelia's excited eyes were locked on Mal.

Abraxas welcomed them with a sly smile.

They bowed dramatically at once. Mal did not speak.

Lifting up, Ophelia stiffened upon seeing Maeve. Her eyes grew large behind her stylish glasses. Along her cheek was a small scar, one Maeve had given her.

Maeve's blood boiled. Her two fingers drifted together.

Don't look so pleased, Maeve said into her mind. *The fun part hasn't even started.*

Ophelia's mouth dropped wide open.

"You remember, Maeve, of course," said Abraxas cordially.

Ophelia looked to Mal, her excitement quickly dwindling.

He offered her no sign of intervention from his throne. He sat, with the Dread Crown glowing atop his head, and one leg crossed over the other.

"You have been called to Castle Morana today in exchange for permanent residence in the Dread Lands," said Abraxas.

"And we are beyond humbled at your generosity," said Marguerite, Ophelia's mother, turning towards Mal.

She bowed dramatically again.

Ophelia's eyes were back on Maeve's fingers as her Magic pulsed with animosity.

"According to Leslie Loxerman, you knew the goblet was poisoned," said Maeve.

Marguerite paled. A fearful laugh slipped between her teeth. "I don't understand," she said in her fake French accent.

Marguerite looked to Maeve. Maeve looked to where Leslie Loxerman sat crumpled at Arman's feet. "Isn't that right?"

Marguerite followed Maeve's gaze as her expression shifted to one of horror.

"She made me," said Marguerite shakily, her accent slipping.

"No," said Maeve plainly. "She did not."

Marguerite looked back at Maeve as her throat bobbled. "She was blackmailing me."

"And you chose to do her bidding instead of facing the consequences of your actions for the affair you were having with Doggbind."

"He threatened my daughter," she snapped.

Maeve shook her head. "I will do more than merely threaten."

Ophelia grew redder by the second.

Marguerite looked to Mal. "He was a bad man. He took me against my will–"

"Is that why when he was head of Magical Law you were directly involved with passing new Enslavement Curse legislation? Because the curse you held on four Elves, two Humans and one Magical weren't enough? You wanted guarantees that all their offspring were Magically enslaved to you as well? And those laws you were campaigning for just happened to be signed by Doggbind?"

Marguerite's knees wobbled.

"Oh, see," continued Maeve, smiling in an unsettling way, "you screwed up. Because you held these conversations in front of Jema. And it gnawed on me for months that I had to frame her for Vetus' murder in the moment. So when she was freed I brought her here, she was more than happy to expose you and her previous master's secrets. You'd been sleeping with Doggbind for years." Maeve laughed. "So I'm sorry that I'm a little enraged by the idea that you were willing to kill my Prince so that your affair wasn't publicized."

Marguerite's skin turned a pale shade of green as she became too stunned to speak.

"I've replayed the memory over and over. Vetus made a point to instruct Mal to drink from it the night of his coronation, you nagged her endlessly to use those words."

Ophelia stepped towards Mal, her arms stretched wide in a pleading motion. "Please, Mal," she began.

Abraxas interrupted her. "You will address your Prince as such."

Ophelia nodded quickly and closed her eyes. She opened them and thick tears dripped down her cheeks. "My Prince, I beg of you. I did not want this."

Abraxas looked to Mal. He still did not speak.

"And my mother, please, she waz only trying to protect me from the Committee."

"They poisoned the Dread Goblet?" asked Abraxas.

Ophelia frantically shook her head, still looking at Mal through wet lashes. "They knew zat it was laced with ancient and deadly Magic."

Her words confirmed Moon's confession.

Ophelia squealed. "I tried everzing I could to keep you away from Aunt Vetus. I never wanted to hurt you, or the Premier," she cried. "I-I love you."

Mal didn't react to her words. He spoke at last, his voice low. "And Maeve?"

Ophelia sniffled, and her shoulders shook.

"What if my Second had drunk from it?" he asked. "Or was that not of your concern? See, I remember vividly an evening where you commented that she and I frequently shared a glass." Mal's voice dropped. "Her lipstick would leave a mark on the rim, and you took every opportunity to insult the shade. Why was that?"

Ophelia trembled. "I-I just wanted. . ."

"I know what you wanted," said Mal. "I have seen your mind. You hate her for everything she is, that you are not. And you will not convince me that you hadn't hoped she would drink from it and not I."

Thick droplet tears streaked Ophelia's face. She gripped her skirt tightly at her sides.

"I could find out so easily," he continued. "But I fear the answer will make me snap your neck right then. And I promised my Dread Viper she could claim you."

Ophelia's cry cracked across the throne room. "Mercy, please," she begged Mal.

"It is not I you need seek mercy from."

Ophelia looked at Maeve, attempting to hide her fear.

"Bow before her," said Mal. "Get on your knees and beg her for forgiveness."

Ophelia stared at Maeve defiantly. She didn't move. Maeve held her stare as Magic cracked at her fingertips.

"Ophelia!" Marguerite hissed, her voice losing nearly all of its affected, fake French accent. "Bow."

Ophelia reluctantly and hesitantly dropped to the floor, wincing as the stone tile pierced her bony knees.

"You are only angry wiz me because of our Dread Prince," said Ophelia quietly. "Because he will not let you hurt me the way you want to. I know it."

Maeve spoke at last. "Hurt you?" Maeve cocked her head to the side. "Ophelia, you have signed your death sentence tonight. Je suis ton bourreau."

I am your executioner.

"No, no," she stammered. "You promised," she looked back over at Mal. "You promised if we came to live here she wouldn't be able to hurt me."

Mal's expression didn't change as he spoke with a cool drawl.

"I made another promise, Ophelia. One that supersedes any hope

I had in you and your mother's innocence. I promised my Dread Viper she could have revenge, to name the name and I would see it done. Your mother's name is already on the list." The Dread Prince stared at Ophelia with unwavering resolve. "Would you like to add another name to the list?" Mal asked Maeve.

"If my Prince allows," she replied, looking over at him.

"Name them," said Mal.

Maeve looked back down at the beauty before her.

"Ophelia St. Beveraux."

She is yours, he said into her mind, *do not hold back.*

Maeve Obscured behind her and grabbed the back of her head, balling Ophelia's hair inside her fist.

"But first," said Maeve. "I'd like to show you something."

Maeve slammed through her without hesitation. Ophelia's cry was drowned out as Maeve pressed into her mind. A white void surrounded them. Ophelia remained on her knees.

Maeve conjured up a very special memory of her own for Ophelia to view.

The white void around them twisted and swirled until it formed Mal's chambers. The powerless girl's eyes darted around the room and then slammed closed when the image of Mal and Maeve appeared in the four poster bed.

Maeve's grip on her hair tightened.

"Open your eyes," said Maeve. "You'll miss the best part."

Ophelia's cheeks turned bright red as Maeve forced her gaze to the bed.

Ophelia watched, stunned, as Mal mounted Maeve, his head tilting back in pleasure as he pinned her to the bed.

Ophelia tried to push Maeve out of her mind, but she was no match for Maeve's strength. Not even close. She was an insect fighting a bird.

"Watch," whispered Maeve sweetly in Ophelia's ear. "My favorite part is coming."

Ophelia's face scrunched up as she shook her head with a frown.

Mal pulled Maeve up and turned her around. His hands joined together around her throat and his movements became violent.

"Stop it," whispered Ophelia, her voice cracking.

"I'm sorry," said Maeve. "Would you like to see something more tender?"

The room shifted into an array of colored mist that formed a montage of Maeve's memories: Mal running his hand along her jaw, his lips pressing against her temple, stroking her cheek, his hand placed on her thigh at the dinner table, his caring face as he healed her wounds in front of the firelight, and a memory of the way he smiled at her when she had a brilliant thought.

"You've made your point," said Ophelia with a clenched jaw.

"I don't know that I have," said Maeve coolly. "But I know I should have made it a long time ago. Perhaps if you had feared me as much as you feared the Double O and the Committee, my father would be alive."

Maeve held Ophelia's head still as the memories continued to flash. Ophelia fell silent and Maeve wandered further into her mind. Her own memories vanished and were quickly replaced by one of Ophelia's.

The room twisted into something new. Maeve's stomach dropped as she witnessed Ophelia push up on her toes and bring her lips to Mal's.

His hand swiftly moved to her jaw, gently pushing her away and holding her in his grip. Ophelia looked up at him with flushed cheeks, attempting to suppress her smile.

"You are beautiful," said Mal.

Maeve's heartbeat kicked at hearing him speak those words as Ophelia's smile blossomed.

"But you are not what I want," said Mal quietly.

Maeve sighed with staggered breathing. Ophelia's face fell flat as Mal released her chin and walked away. The memory vanished.

Maeve looked down at Ophelia next to her. The poor girl stared down in defeat. Her cheeks were just as red as they had been in her memory. A solid tear streaked down her face and her glasses fogged over.

Maeve withdrew from Ophelia's mind as burning hatred swelled in her chest. Ophelia remained on her knees with her head bowed.

The Throne Room remained completely silent.

"When was that?" asked Maeve, barely above a whisper.

Ophelia's voice was muffled by sobs as she spoke, but Maeve heard her clearly. "After the coronation, before the portals to Earth were closed."

Electric ice trickled down Maeve's arm, fury that Ophelia had dared to make such an advance on Mal in her absence, right after her father's death.

And perhaps even fury that Mal had not told her.

"You are not worthy of him," said Maeve.

Ophelia's eye slid to Maeve. "Why is that?" Her eyes narrowed. "Your blood is as pure as mine."

Maeve sucked in sharply through her nose and pointed two fingers at Ophelia. Bright red light burst across the hall, pulsing and whipping out with each lash Maeve administered.

Ophelia's shrill scream filled the room. She doubled over.

Marguerite attempted to shoot to her daughter's side. Maeve stopped her with her other hand, palm flat.

"Stop this, I beg of you!" Marguerite shouted. "She's just a girl!"

"Then what am I?" snarled Maeve. "Why is it that I must always be held to a higher standard?" Ophelia squirmed and twisted in pain under Maeve's Magic. "Why is it that I am the one to lose my family? And the pair of you expect to be pardoned for the role you played in my father's death? In the attempted assassination of my Prince?"

"Ophelia never wanted to hurt Malachite! She was desperate to keep him away from Vetus and her trinkets."

"And you? Can you say the same?" Maeve asked. "Or if I dive into your mind, will I find a shred of reserve as you pushed your daughter on Mal?"

Maeve scowled.

"My late husband wanted that engagement, he proposed her hand to The Dread Prince and knew nothing of my agreements with the Double O and Committee of the Sacred."

"If you are going to kill me," cried Ophelia, "please do it."

Maeve shook her head, and pointed two fingers directly at Ophelia's face. "Death, too, must be earned."

Magic surged through her, unbridled and free. It slammed through Ophelia, ripping apart every memory and shattering every bit of her mind. Ophelia's body contorted and she convulsed beneath Maeve's power.

She withdrew, and wobbled slightly.

Mal was in her head a moment later.

Do not falter, his voice commanded.

She sucked in a tight breath as her Magic back flowed, replenishing itself from her violent attack.

She met Mal's eyes where he sat on the throne.

His head lowered ever so slightly in silent praise.

Marguerite fell to her knees. "What have you done?"

"She shattered her mind," said Mal, his eyes never leaving Maeve.

Marguerite's sobs echoed across the hall.

"S'il te plaît, sois rapide avec moi," she said, begging for a swift death.

"No," said Maeve. "Your punishment is a lifetime of watching your daughter be but a shadow of herself. Unable to speak, unable to stand or clean herself. Unable to recall anything beyond each moment of misery. On Earth."

Mal looked to Roswyn and inclined his head.

That was the only command needed for Roswyn to march towards the St. Beverauxs and drag them from the hall. Maeve never saw either of them again.

"Well done," said Mal as he pressed a kiss into her back, slipping her clothes down her tired arms. His hands gripped her hips tightly, pulling her backside into him.

She groaned against him, collapsing into the bed and burying her face back into the sheets. She'd slept for a full day, regaining her strength.

His fingers pressed deeper, sending sharp Magic through her body. She winced and whined against him. She didn't need to look over her shoulder to know he was smirking, completely aroused by her pain.

Maeve flipped over onto her back and met his satisfied smirk.

"She kissed you," Maeve blurted out.

Mal stilled. His smile faded.

"Why did you keep that from me?" she whispered.

"You were already carrying such sorrow," he said. "I rejected her, and she never returned." Mal leaned forward and placed a kiss in the hollow of her neck. "Don't tell me you didn't think of hiding Alphard's advance on you from me."

"I considered it," she said.

Mal hummed into her throat.

"Don't act so pleased," muttered Maeve.

Mal hovered above her. "Nothing pleases me more than seeing you come unglued."

Her stomach pinched.

Mal's dark eyes held her captive as he said, "I want to create enemies just to watch you slaughter them."

Maeve couldn't help but grin up at him. "Then I better get to training. Our visit to Aterna is only days away."

"You are healing," said Mal smoothly. "Shattering Ophelia's mind took quite the toll on you. I am not worried about your appearance in Aterna." His bottom lips brushed hers. "You'll have me there."

Maeve hummed. "I don't want special treatment," she said with a smile.

"That's just too terribly bad," he replied.

Chapter 33

Abraxas

Abraxas called the Sacred Seventeen families to Castle Morana. They quieted upon his arrival. His hangover raged through his skull, despite the potion Astrea made for him. Arman walked swiftly at his side. Since his arrival at Castle Morana he'd taken to watching over Maeve without instruction to do so, and Abraxas spent the previous evening walking Mal off a proverbial ledge over it. Abraxas pitied the man who dared offer her a simple "good morning."

"Primus and the Gods, I am dreading this," he muttered to Arman as they entered the room full of Sacred families.

He slammed a stack of paper smoothly on the table and took up in a chair, rubbing his temples. He skipped formalities and got straight to business.

"Now that the Committee of the Sacred has been dealt with, there are changes you need to be aware of. The Elven people under Enslavement Curses will be freed, their curses broken, and, for those of you still clinging to such ways, reparations paid from your pockets. They will be given the freedom to choose life on Earth or a new life here in the Dread Lands, both of which come with a hefty sum of gold."

A shift ruffled through the room.

"Was that a groan?" snapped Abraxas dryly. "You are all incredibly appreciated and I am hopeful for our future here, but if you desire your old life, go back to Earth. I am not the Double O. I am not the Committee. My court will not be run by your gold."

He tried to avoid his mother's gaze, but caught her proud smile nonetheless.

"There is much I'd like to address today," he continued, Astrea's potion kicking in at last. He smiled. "Beginning with the newspaper production. A great idea by yours truly, if I must say so. Hillman, bring in the rest please, now that the nastiness is out of the way."

Hillman, a Bellator who stood at the door of the Hand's Hall, left and returned with a handful of Magicals from all sorts of backgrounds. Some Human-born, some part-Elven part-Magical. All of them looking to create a new life in the Dread Lands.

Zimsy was among them. She held a stack of papers in her long, elegant arms. She smiled brightly at Abraxas, who relaxed at her excitement, despite being in a room with some who saw her as less than. She held her ideas for the bakery she wanted to open in The Beryl City closely and took a seat at the table.

Abraxas smiled, recalling how Maeve desired to march in behind Zimsy to ensure no one tried to cross her friend, but Zimsy had insisted on coming alone.

The new world they were creating looked brighter all the time.

Soon he'd be setting foot in Aterna, something he'd dreamed of since childhood. Regardless of how ignorant they were to the knowledge of who was friend or foe, one thing he knew for certain was that Mal was not going to risk another Ambrose.

He was playing chess with long pauses between moves. There would be no haste in his choices, no glory to be found until he was certain they were safe.

The future barreled at him, at them all, but Abraxas didn't mind. Rumor told, Aterna had a plethora of enjoyable, exclusive substances he could try.

Chapter 34

Reeve

The Dread Prince stood in the grand Celestian Palace of Crystalmore. Reeve was certain no Dread bloodline would ever set foot in his home city again, not after the disaster of the Shadow War. But there he stood, nonetheless, with clothing fit for a handsome young Prince with little understanding of the world or the weight of his existence.

No crown sat atop his gentle, dark curls. Despite his lack of years, he played the game well. The Rosethorn boy, Abraxas, was at his side.

"Welcome to Crystalmore, Dread Prince," said Reeve.

Mal smiled with an easy charm as he shook Reeve's hand, and then Eryx's.

His entire staff nearly bounced on the balls of their feet to meet him.

Reeve gestured to the dark-haired woman at his side. "This is Melione."

Abraxas held out his hand. Mely, as she was affectionately called, took it with a sly grin.

"Abraxas Rosethorn. Hand to the Prince," she said.

Abraxas added his other hand atop hers. "Melione. We meet at last."

"Mely is my strategist," said Reeve. "She can smell conflict from a mile away."

"Beautiful," said Abraxas. "We'll be two peas in a pod, I am sure."

Mal stepped along the line of Immortals eager to meet him and shake his hand. Abraxas stepped away and trailed him.

"Maybe she didn't come," said Eryx under his breath.

"No," said Reeve. He inhaled deeply, feeling her Magic as it called to him. "She is here."

Eryx and Mely looked over the hall.

She appeared atop the stairs, Roswyn and Arman at her sides, just a step behind her. Shortly followed by Mumford and Alphard, and the young blonde girl who was always eager for Maeve's attention. Maeve paused and surveyed Mal and Abraxas below.

Magic cracked across the crystal floor beneath her feet as she descended the stairs. Reeve's eyes alone were fixated on the Magic flowing from her.

"Is that her?" Mely practically squeaked.

Reeve nodded.

Even with daggers in her eyes, she was radiant.

"She's beautiful," whispered Mely, her eyes lit with awe.

A smile tugged at the corner of Reeve's mouth. "That she is."

"Oh," said Mely under her breath. "I don't know why I was expecting to see her in a gown."

Maeve stepped down the stairs, her black laced boots stark against the pale crystal of the stairs. Reeve was certain the gold that plated them was real. Her pants were a thick brocade, her bodice fitted, and laced tightly, covering her arms and fingers. The high neck didn't shield all the dark scars that traced her veins, though it obscured most of them. He struggled to look at them. A deep emerald cloak pinned at her shoulders, with Mal's Dread Mark embroidered on the back that flowed to the backs of her knees.

She may not have been in a gown, but she was still dripping in her father's wealth.

The serpent pin that designated her position as his Dread Viper gleamed proudly on her chest.

"Will she duel?" asked Mely. "Given her attire?"

"Yes," he said. "I think it is safe to assume this is the form she will appear in from here on out. She is not his escort, Melione. She is his personal assassin."

"Beautiful palace," said Abraxas, joining Reeve at his side. "Dream-like." He laughed. "Castle Morana is so deliciously moody. All this bright crystal and sparkling stone hurts my eyes."

Reeve ignored his teasing and accepted the drink he offered. Together, they looked out over the party below.

"The Orator knew," said Abraxas. "The goblet was intended to kill Mal."

Reeve sighed and leaned his arms on the railing before them. "I assume you will take command of Vaukore, now that the Double O has fallen."

Abraxas interjected. "The destruction of The Double O as a whole was never the objective. It was always to root out corruption. That said, those who chose to remain on Earth will be free to travel between realms, if they so wish."

"And who determines Magical law on Earth? You cannot abandon thousands with such power to live harmoniously with Humans. There will be those who try to grab for it."

"I know," said Abraxas gently. "Mal is. . .hesitant to force his reign on those who do not wish it. His mind is elsewhere."

"Then you leave Earth a lawless land."

"Perhaps you'd like to rule it," said Abraxas with a side-eyed grin.

Reeve laughed. "Not a chance. Malachite and I have something in common. I did not want this crown."

"Jokes aside, I am aware we have caused a wrinkle in things."

"A wrinkle?" asked Reeve incredulously. He chuckled. "Abraxas, my friend, a wrinkle is not what you have caused."

"Don't look at me," he said. "I have no blood on my hands."

"Hand to the Prince, you have all the blood on your hands," corrected Reeve.

Abraxas frowned, but found it difficult to argue. After a moment, he finally spoke.

"He'll kill anyone she deems worth killing if it means she is herself again."

Reeve shook his head slowly. "She will never be herself again." He clapped a hand on Abraxas' shoulder. "Let go of the old version of your cousin. She was buried with her father."

Chapter 35

Maeve

The dueling arena in Crystalmore rivaled anything Maeve had ever seen. The crystal coliseum sat in a valley carved between two peaks. Seating surrounded the pit high into the sky, and giant pillars of iridescent, dark, smooth crystal jetted up past them, all bearing the Aterna Plate of Arms.

The pale floor of the arena bore numerous seven pointed stars, burned into the crystal with ancient Magic. White clouds billowed across the sky in the open arena.

Maeve looked up at Mal, where he stood at the edge of the arena on a tall platform. She placed her fist over her heart, where, beneath her clothes, lay her Dread Mark.

The ground began to shake, but Maeve maintained her footing.

Reeve stood from his seat.Excitement, nervous and ready, buzzed from the crowd. The deep amethyst stone around his neck began to glow. It grew and grew in intensity until it shot from him, splitting in all directions. The orb of light slammed into a large stone, working as a siphon for Reeve's Magic. From each pillar burst a web of light, of Aterna Magic. The webs were shiny and pale in color as they shot out, sending one beam towards each of the seven pointed stars. They sparked into the crystal floor as the shadow of a Senshi Warrior, its face masked, generated and stood from the sparks.

Maeve pressed her Magic towards him, feeling for Reeve's presence in it. The phantom was just that, nothing more. But it was Reeve who powered it.

The phantom bowed at her, waiting for her to follow suit. When she raised her head, the phantom shot forward, a bright swirl of flames spiraling towards her. She Obscured and placed herself behind him. With one blow, it shattered into a thousand tiny crystals.

Two more pale phantoms materialized on separate stars. She had no party tricks up her sleeve with these warriors, they had no minds to jump through or shatter. They did not bow as the first had, as one disappeared and one charged at her. Magic slunk behind her, quick and silent. Maeve flared her palm backwards, eliminating the threat.

She pressed her Magic towards the phantom charging her with violet fire at his hands and slammed up a shield. It quickly fired again, sending cracks across her shield of pale light.

More phantoms appeared in the arena, faster than she could eliminate them. With each one, more of Reeve's Magic hurled at her. She narrowly dodged an advance and soon sweat pooled at her brow and soaked the back of her bodice.

The phantoms grew stronger, managing to clip her shoulder and leg with blows of Magic. They surrounded her, one grabbing her arms tightly, dulling the Magic in her hands. She circled her foot along the crystal beneath them, pulsing Magic snapping across it. The phantoms surrounding her recoiled and slammed to the ground. She kicked her head back into the phantom behind her. Magic pierced its chest as it shattered with a satisfying clang.

She Obscured from the oncoming swarm around her and locked eyes with Mal.

With a winded breath, she raised her fist in the air and opened her palm. The audience's exclamations grew silent.

His voice rang across her mind, dripping with satisfaction. *You need assistance?*

Mal mirrored her movement, raising a single finger. With the curl of his wrist, sharp ice sliced across her palm, splitting her skin open.

She didn't wince from the cut as Dark Magic surrounded her, flooding her veins from the sacrifice of blood dripping down her wrist. She didn't feel the heat of its sting at all.

She turned on the phantoms. . .and unleashed.

Dark Magic poured from her, slicing them all, two and three at a time, as she pushed herself to the edge.

Careful, Little Viper, came Mal's voice. *Or you risk not walking out of this arena in triumph.*

She tightened her control deep in her core, the pulse of Magic begging her with each hit to let it conquer. She Obscured between them all, slicing through each one with two deadly fingers. Reeve's Magic surged around her, as the phantoms glowed with bright violet fire.

Finish it, said Mal.

And she did.

Lightning popped at her fingers, slithering up her arm like an electric serpent. With two pointed fingers, and one blast to the floor, the dozens of phantoms, and the webs of light between the pillars, shattered into millions of crystals.

The roar from the crowd of Immortals wasn't enough to drown out her own disappointment. The power Reeve pushed through his phantoms was nothing to him. It was a fraction of what she felt radiating off his dragon form that day at Vaukore.

Yet there she stood, panting and barely able to move, while he smiled and leaned back in his seat.

Reeve's swirling Portal wafted ethereally outside of the palace. The waters of the Black Deep pushed and pulled against the sparkling stone steps that descended into the black water. Ships with pale violet sails floated across the water in the distance. The Dread Lands were not fully visible, but if she squinted, she could see the top of Mount Morte in the dark peaks.

Reeve appeared at her side.

"For a moment, I thought we weren't going to get a light show," he said cordially, referring to her performance. "The crowd would have been devastated."

"Why did you invite me here?" she asked sadly.

Reeve paused. Maeve continued.

"Just to see what I'm made of? No, I think it was to show off your thriving society and beautiful palace."

"I'm sorry," he said dryly. "I thought you enjoyed fighting. Or is that only when revenge is pumping through your veins?"

Maeve looked away from him. Roswyn and Arman were already stepping through Reeve's Portal back to Castle Morana. Mal and Abraxas were saying their last goodbyes.

"I thought their deaths would mean more," she said.

Reeve did not look over at her. "Moon's and Doggbind's?"

"And Ophelia," she whispered.

"Avenging him doesn't bring him back."

Maeve's chest tightened as overwhelming nausea swept over her. She pushed down on the weakness surging through her.

"I wake up from these dreams that feel like anything but dreams, and I think only for a moment, but long enough for it to sting, that he is alive. And I am not hollowed out."

Mal smiled as Abraxas nailed the punchline to a joke. Eryx and his handful of warriors laughed.

"He smiles, and I am glad of it," she continued as they watched them. "But he did not die in that Throne Room that day. It was I who was stabbed through the heart. And I desperately want to feel myself again, to feel the steady beat of his affection. But it comes quickly, and I think 'at last,' only to have it strangled by the thought of my father's final strained breaths. I don't care who sits on what throne. I don't care what happens anymore. The only time I feel anything good at all is when I am fighting."

"I am to assume these are not words you utter to your Prince."

"What does my uttering matter?" she said. "He is inside my very skin."

She hid them well, beneath high collars and fingerless gloves, but the traces of Mal's Dark Magic still ran across her body.

"With time," said Reeve. "You will learn his absence. And it will be a joyful memory of life. His death will feel like the dream."

"I don't want to learn his absence," she said, her voice cracking.

They did not look at one another as Reeve said gently, "But you will."

Her tears betrayed her, as one slipped past her guard and rolled down her jaw. She wiped it swiftly and without acknowledgment. "Apologies," she said, in control of her voice once more. "I don't know what caused me to speak so candidly."

She still did not look at him as she thanked him for the invitation and his hospitality. She moved towards Mal and Abraxas.

"Maeve," he called after her.

She turned back towards him.

"It may not have filled the void you wanted it to, but do not let grief blind you from the fact that they deserved to die all the same. And I am glad it was you who killed them."

Maeve stared at him for a moment. "I hope you think that of me to come. But I do not foresee it."

He smiled. "Now you are a prophet?"

"You have eternity to mock me," she said with a small laugh. "Take the day off."

"Am I mistaken, and you are now Immortal?"

"Hardly," she said, "but I'm sure you'll speak of me long after my death."

Reeve's eyes raked over her like she was a meal. "There's that Magical arrogance you have perfected."

"You're disgusting," she said with a laugh.

"You've got quite a mouth," he said. "Someone should show you how to use it."

"Bite your tongue," she said, suddenly serious as her brows pulled together. "Mal will hear you."

Reeve stepped closer to her, his head cocked to one side, and his playful demeanor gone. "You so rarely disappoint me, Sinclair. But when you do, it's when you are afraid of him... and when you think *that I am*."

He passed by her, their arms an inch from touching. Maeve watched him walk towards Abraxas and Mal. She cursed him under her breath.

Chapter 36

Maeve

Loxerman jabbered on endlessly, her mind having grown weak in her solitude and Maeve's constant memory work. The old Witch had plenty of secrets, some Maeve herself didn't understand. Only one secret mattered to her though: the truth of her mother. The truth of the woman who bore her. The dark haired woman she'd seen in only glimpses of her father's mind.

She never told him what she suspected, what she came to know.

Loxerman's mind was more muddled each visit, making it difficult to work through. But finally, Maeve caught a glimpse of something interesting.

Loxerman herself was much younger in the snippet of a memory. Her hair was longer and full of life.

Loxerman whispered to a man in a mask. "The boy's name is Antony Sinclair."

"Gold upfront."

"The Zaichosky's have already paid you half, have they not?"

Maeve watched the decaying memory ten times before she pulled it from Loxerman's mind and said. "Care to explain?"

Loxerman mumbled. The chains binding her to the floor clattered beneath her as she scooted to the opposite wall, seemingly having a conversation that didn't include Maeve.

Maeve sighed, crossing her legs the opposite direction and letting a small burst of Magic slip from her. Loxerman startled as it hit her skin. She looked up at Maeve like she'd only just realized she was there.

"You paid to have my brother killed?"

Loxerman looked behind her warily. She turned back to Maeve and blinked rapidly.

Loxerman smiled. "I remember now. It was his birthday."

Maeve's stomach rolled over.

"Happy birthday. . ." Loxerman sang and then bit her lip. "Can't remember the name though."

It was so tempting to just dispose of the mental woman before her and be done with it all. But hope remained for some semblance of her mother's face. Some clue that could lead Maeve to understanding the circumstances of her existence.

Maeve dove back into Loxerman's mind, pressing the memory further, bending Loxerman's mind to bring forth more of it. The same small segment played again and again, each time becoming more fragmented and broken until it collapsed into nothing completely.

With a vocal cry of frustration, Maeve whipped from Loxerman's mind, propelling herself back into the dark cell. Loxerman's head hung limp. Her spine hunched over as her mouth foamed. Her dead eyes stared at the opposite wall.

Maeve's shoulders fell in defeat.

The gardens at Castle Morana were a hazy glow of dew and mist as Maeve walked the hydrangea lined paths. New blooms sprouted around them, flowers she couldn't identify and had certainly never seen on Earth.

The Crown's Quarters kept her awake. It may have been the most Magically protected room in the castle, but the ghosts of such an ancient place were loud. The albino woman with long white hair stood at the foot of her bed most nights until she forced herself from the chamber and wandered the castle in the quiet night.

Black vines snaked their way over one bush, suffocating and piercing its stems. Maeve pulled on the thorny weed forcing it to release the beautiful green bloom.

Magic trickled down her ring finger and down her front where the

Dread Ring and Locket sat. She looked over her shoulder as Mal appeared. He stood in a lingering, swirling shadow with watchful eyes.

The vine fell at her feet and turned to ash. She looked back at the blooms.

"Are you coming or going?" she asked softly.

"Going," he answered, stepping towards her. "Do you have your parchment?'

Maeve hummed a reply. "And I have another name."

Mal's brows raised.

"The Zaichoskys," she answered.

"All of them?" he asked without an ounce of judgment in his voice.

"They paid half of the hit on Antony," she answered.

Mal nodded. "I figured as much if you were naming them. But that isn't what I asked."

Maeve looked up at him. "I have no way of knowing who among them was innocent."

"Are you asking me to do it, so it doesn't weigh on your conscience that you killed innocents?"

Maeve nodded and he spoke with ease.

"They are in The Palen Tower, outside The Beryl City. They'll be dead before dawn."

He smiled down at her. She did not return it.

They stood in silence until Mal spoke once more.

"It is not enough," he said.

She looked up at him. His hair was growing long, she'd noticed he stopped cutting it. It framed his face nicely.

"What is not?" she asked quietly.

"Any of what I have to offer you."

Maeve's stomach sank. She stepped towards him, the moonlight shining on them both, and shook her head.

"Mal," she said, feeling that never ending heaviness in her chest lurking, "you have given me more than I ever dreamed for myself."

His eyes were somber. "But I cannot bring him back."

Maeve's jaw tightened. Mal continued.

"I feel your mind. I see the reality you try to slip away to in your head. You cannot sleep for wanting it. You cannot focus in training for desiring to be there."

Maeve didn't mention the ghosts of her dreams to him. He'd only consume himself with ridding the castle of something so unexplainable.

"Is that so terrible a dream?"

He stepped towards her and took her face in his hands and said gently, "It is not real, Little Viper."

She pressed towards him. "But what if I could make it real?"

"Even you are not capable of withstanding such a falsehood in your mind. Eventually it would snap." His fingers brushed through her hair. "It's a beautiful thought, darling girl. And if I could run away to a world where he lived, and you and I were together in easeful bliss, I would. There would be no more prophecy, no more darkness. . .I would lie with you each night and devour you each morning."

Warmth soaked her cheeks as her vision went blurry. Mal pulled her close, wrapping his arms around her.

"It destroys me that I cannot give you that," he continued, "and that our fates lie here, carving a place for ourselves in the world that has cast us aside."

Mal pressed his lips to her temple, inhaling softly.

"You are too hard on yourself," she said. "It's not your burden to bear. You are performing miracles here. I am selfish, and sorry for it."

"I handed him that goblet," he replied. "I think about the consequences of such a seemingly inconsequential choice endlessly."

Maeve couldn't look up at him.

"You don't have to hide from me," said Mal. "I spent too many days longing to merely share the same air as you."

"There is no one I want to view me as weak less than you," she admitted tearfully.

Mal pulled from her, keeping her in his grip. His eyes glistened darkly as his lips parted. "Your father told me once, 'fear is the absence of Magic'."

Chapter 37

Maeve

"He's never brought a date here before. Not once," remarked Abraxas as Reeve entered the Ballroom accompanied by a beautiful, blonde Immortal.

"Is that his mate?" asked Arianna.

"No," said Abraxas. "I heard his mate died long ago, years ago, an Immortal girl. Alphard said there's a statue of her at the entrance to Crystalmore."

"What a romantic notion," squealed Arianna.

Maeve looked at her with speculation. "It's ridiculous," she stated plainly.

Arianna frowned at her. "No, it isn't. It's no more ridiculous than the prophecy we are all here because of."

Maeve laughed and relaxed. "Fair enough."

She watched the High Lord cross the ballroom with the blonde beauty on his arm. She was strikingly unique, with the famous immortal glow, just as all the dates he'd brought to Sinclair Estates had been.

"Now that I think about it," said Arianna. "Back home, I've never seen him with any girls but blondes."

"Oh look," drawled Mal, "you stand a chance, Abraxas."

Mal smirked. Maeve looked up at him, biting her bottom lip.

Abraxas swirled his drink and couldn't even argue. In fact, he looked pleased by the revelation.

Maeve moved to go around Mal, heading for the balcony, fresh air, and any room that Reeve did not occupy. Mal's slender hand slipped around her waist and pulled her gently to him. His lips met her ear, and he spoke with a soft dominance.

"I expect a dance before the night is over."

Maeve looked up at him. "I wouldn't dream of depriving you."

He released her, satisfied, and she slipped by him. Arianna followed Maeve onto the balcony and staggered slightly.

"Are you drunk?" asked Maeve with a smirk.

"Maybe," said Arianna.

"You are," said Maeve with a laugh.

"Perfect time for you to tell me why the Zaichosky family are all dead."

Maeve's smile faded.

"Didn't think I'd know that was you?" asked Arianna.

"It wasn't me," replied Maeve softly.

"Mal did it then," she corrected dramatically. "You can't get by on a technicality, Maeve. If he did it in your name, the blood is on your hands."

"Fine," snapped Maeve.

Arianna frowned. "You're not going to tell me why?"

Maeve paused. "You know why."

Arianna looked away from her, quickly grabbing another drink from a floating tray. She took long sips, neither of them speaking until Arianna asked quietly, "But how do you know?"

"Because I saw it within Loxerman's mind. They paid someone to do it."

Arianna's drink paused at her lips.

"Down the whole thing at this point," said Maeve with a small laugh.

The corners of Arianna's mouth turned up. She looked over at Maeve with a slow and steady breath as she tilted the glass back.

"The blood on my hands is from bleeders of betrayal. I do not feel remorse for avenging our father and Antony."

Arianna pulled the empty glass from her lips, and nodded.

Maeve had, as promised, not forgotten her dance with Mal. In fact, on their fifth song when Maeve tried to step away from him, Mal's hand slid lower, bringing a quick gasp from Maeve's lips. She reprimanded him with her eyes.

"Something wrong?" he asked innocently.

"There are people watching us," she said with a smile.

Mal chuckled. "And which one is going to tell their Prince to take his hands off what is his?"

Maeve's smile blossomed as he bent towards her. Their noses brushed, and then he flicked his bottom lip across hers.

A moan pulled from her throat as her stomach tightened and heat rushed between her legs. Mal's satisfaction grew as he looked down at her darkly. The scar across his eye only fueling her fire.

His hand on her lower back tugged her closer as he pressed sinful Magic through his fingertips.

"That's not fair," she whispered against his parted lips.

"No," said Mal. "What's not fair is the way those baby blue eyes cut me from across the room. What's not fair is the arousing scent of gardenias that lingers in every room of this castle you occupy. What's not fair is the insatiable thought of licking across every darkened vein on your body and making you admit they all belong to me."

Maeve reeled and moved to press her lips against his. She hadn't realized he'd moved them from the ballroom and into the Entrance Hall until he pressed her against the marble wall, pulling his taunting lips from her before she had a taste.

His hand slipped beneath her hair, gripping tightly and forcing her mouth to angle up at him. She pressed her lips towards him again in a silent request.

He smirked down at her, completely satisfied with her desperation.

"Have you been deprived, Little Viper?"

His grip on her hair tightened, pulling her to the balls of her feet. She nodded earnestly.

Mal's free hand moved across her face with a calm expression. His thumb snagged her bottom lip, rolling it over.

He hummed in contemplation, his Magic forcing her legs to squeeze together.

"I can't decide what's more enticing," he started, staring down at her in a predatorial way. "Watching you squirm for me, or the way your mouth tastes." His hand trailed down her chest, sending her skin scattering with tingling Magic. "Because you taste like victory, Maeve. But watching you yearn for my touch. . .makes me want to start a war."

He pulled her from the wall, his grip never faltering as he backed her down the corridor.

"Where are we going," she whined.

"Someplace I can claim victory," he said with a taunting smile.

With a flick of his chin, a door slammed open behind her. Maeve gasped and Mal's grip on her loosened as the room they stumbled into was already occupied.

Arman pulled his lips from Arianna's swiftly. Maeve's sister paled and Arman straightened. Maeve's mouth fell open as a smile began to blossom across her lips. Mal stood tall, frozen next to her in the uncomfortable silence.

"Apologies," said Arman.

A soft exhale slipped from Mal. Maeve could hear the playful tone slip through his voice as he said, "Are you apologizing to your Prince for walking in on one of his Bellator enjoying himself? Or because it's my Second's sister your lips were locked on?"

"Or because you two were only coming to do the same?" asked Arianna with a loud, giggle.

"Arianna," hissed Maeve with a smile.

Her sister was indeed drunk.

Arman looked back over at her and cocked a brow. She shrugged innocently. Maeve's smile faltered as she pictured the twins and their blonde set of hair.

Her eyes darted to Arman. She understood at once. This was no mere moment in the dark.

He looked at her calmly, his eyes anything from denying it.

"I believe Arianna has acquired her limit, Arman," said Mal smoothly. "Please see that she reaches her old chambers here for the night. I expect you to keep watch all evening."

Arman's eyes flickered in shock for a moment. He fought to not return the smile dancing across Mal's lips.

Arianna was on Mal in a flash as she threw her arms dramatically around his neck. He looked over at Maeve with a shake of his head.

Arman's hand slipped around her waist, pulling her gently from Mal.

"Come, darling," he whispered as he brought his lips to her ear.

Arman pulled her from the room and Maeve stared up at Mal in complete shock.

"Did you know?" he asked her with a laugh.

"No," she said, covering her mouth.

Mal nodded. "This may be the one and only time that we know something Abraxas does not."

Maeve laughed as he placed his hands back on her hips, pushing her further into the room.

"Now," he said lowly. "Where were we?"

Chapter 38

Maeve

Maeve tossed up a shield, sending Arman sliding back across the stone courtyard, as they warmed up with one another. Larliesl observed them both from afar, watching others begin their day of training as well.

Their pace escalated as they fired sharper Magic at one another, moving across the stone.

"Did my father know?" Maeve quipped, already knowing the answer.

Shame flickered across Arman's face.

"There's no need to feel ashamed of hiding it," said Maeve, dodging his advance. "It was wise."

"You misunderstand, Sinclair," he fired back. "I am not ashamed for fear that my Premier would have been angry or disappointed in his Captain." He shot towards her, Magic shifting between his steps, nearly knocking her over, as she focused on his words. "I feel ashamed I never told him because I was more concerned with my appearance than honesty."

Maeve halted her advance and held her hand up. Arman stood straight. "You blame yourself for hiding it, but you never could have had her then. Not in the light."

"And now?" he questioned. "Are we in the light?"

She stared at her father's former captain, one of the only Supremes that matched her strength. That understood the crushing weight of power. The man her sister loved, it seemed.

"Maeve."

Abraxas stepped out into the training court, his voice short and winded as he called for her. He motioned for her to quickly follow with an impatient expression.

"Apologies," she said. "It wasn't my place to pry."

Arman shrugged. "No need."

"Maeve," hissed Abraxas, rocking on his feet.

Arman gave her a quick nod, and she turned from him. Abraxas vanished back into the castle, forcing Maeve to quicken her pace to keep up with his long strides.

"What's going on?" she asked. "Is Mal alright?"

Abraxas nodded. "Mal is fine. Gone still. We have visitors. And I think, if they are here, it means they come bearing quite the gift."

Maeve tossed her hair behind her shoulder and fanned her face, sticky with sweat.

They rounded the last corner into the large entrance hall of Castle Morana.

Alphard crossed the hall with Mordred at his side. The snowy white wolf padded silently across the marble floor. Maeve's brows lifted at his appearance. More wolves filed into Castle Morana. Between them was a Witch.

Maeve's mouth fell open.

Ismail walked towards her with hesitancy. Her smile was far from genuine.

"Maeve Sinclair," she said as they joined at the center of the hall.

"The Dread Prince is away?" asked Mordred, gravel in his voice.

Abraxas nodded. "Hello, Ismail. My name is Abraxas Rosethorn. I am honored to have you at Castle Morana."

Her lip bled, and there were four distinct rips across her clothing.

Abraxas smiled in an attempt to calm her fearful eyes. "Alphard, go and fetch Astrea, will you?"

Alphard didn't hesitate to go get his sister. Mordred sniffed loudly.

Maeve didn't speak. She was too stunned by the pack of werewolves before her that were, apparently, holding Ismail, who had either not come willingly or was hurt regardless, hostage.

"The Crown thanks you," said Abraxas, addressing Mordred. "I'm sure Mal regrets not being here to thank you in person."

Mordred grunted. Ismail stiffened.

"And the gold?" he asked roughly.

"I can take you there now," said Abraxas smoothly.

Alphard returned with Astrea, who was finally showing her pregnancy.

"Ah," continued Abraxas. "Perfect timing. Astrea, please take Ismail. If you'd like to follow me, Mordred–"

"No."

Mordred stepped between Abraxas and Ismail.

"She doesn't leave my sight until I am paid and the Dread Prince returns."

"Of course," said Abraxas casually. "Alphard, show our guests to their sleeping quarters." He looked to Astrea, "Let's get you healed, Ismail." And then he finally looked back at Mordred. "You are aware the Prince is gone for days, weeks, and even months at a time, yes?"

Mordred's snout tensed.

"King Kier is fine without his King's Guard indefinitely?"

Mordred didn't reply.

"A predicament," said Abraxas with a laugh. "Rest, Mordred. We will speak again at dinner."

Abraxas slipped his fingers around Maeve's wrist and pulled her with him as he turned sharply on his heel.

"What the hell is going on?" muttered Maeve icily.

Abraxas did not answer until he shut the doors of his study and leaned against them.

"Brax?"

His eyes found hers. "I put out a bounty on Ismail."

Maeve's mouth fell open. "What? She's bleeding, Brax!"

"I know that!" he hissed. "They weren't supposed to hurt her."

"She looks absolutely terrified." Maeve shook her head, coming to her senses at last. "I am going to her."

She moved towards Abraxas, and he grabbed her arms swiftly. "You can't."

Maeve huffed. "What are you not telling me?"

"I didn't tell Mal," he admitted in a garbled confession.

Maeve's shoulders dropped. "Alright."

"He's going to be mad."

"No," said Maeve, "he's not. She is here. We have been searching for her for months."

Abraxas looked past her and nodded, though his eyes were far from in agreement.

Maeve waited a moment before she said, "I don't trust them."

Her cousin's gaze landed on her at last. His chest rose and fell dramatically. "Kier's King's Guard?"

Maeve nodded. "There is something shifty about them. I can feel it. The Magic radiating off that wolf is. . .disloyal."

Abraxas dropped his arms and marched towards the desk, pulling out stacks of gold.

"How much did you offer?" she asked incredulously.

"I made each of the Sacred families pay for it, split seventeen, well sixteen now, ways."

The unintentional dig cut through her like a slice from The Dread Dagger, but Abraxas was too busy counting money to notice.

"Are you and he able to communicate when he's out there?"

"Yes," she replied.

"Wonderful," said Abraxas as he slid the gold pieces into a dark purple bag with gold strings. "Get him here, please."

Maeve reached into her pocket and pulled out the worn sliver of parchment. It lay blank.

"I'll leave out the part where you lied to him," she said sweetly.

"So generous," he muttered.

She grabbed a blue-jay quill from Abraxas' desk and scribbled a brief message.

We found Ismail.

The words lingered across the parchment only for a moment and then disappeared.

The Dread Goblet sat at the center of the table. Maeve stared at the ancient gold artifact. It shone regally.

Abraxas and Mal's mild tempered argument ensued in the background. Her thoughts were on Ismail and if she'd be able to tell who poisoned the Dread Goblet. The Double O knew it to be poisoned. Loxerman said there was tale that an ancient poison laced the smooth basin.

"How did Mordred find her?" she asked, speaking over their bickering.

Abraxas and Mal ceased their discussion.

"Speaking is not all they are blessed with," answered Abraxas. "Incredibly heightened senses as well."

"They tracked her across Earth," explained Mal.

"I don't like that they hurt her," said Maeve. "She's done nothing wrong."

Mal's hands landed on her shoulders. He planted a supple kiss on her temple. "I know," he murmured. "I told them."

He slid into the chair next to her as the doors opened and Ismail was ushered inside by two Bellator. She swallowed hard. Her wounds had been healed, but the uneasiness in her eyes remained.

Ismail's eyes locked on the Dread Goblet. Her shoulders fell slack.

"Please, sit," offered Abraxas as he took a seat next to Mal.

She accepted stiffly.

"Apologies for all the nastiness," said Abraxas. "Thank you for sitting down with us."

As though she had a choice.

"You are familiar with The Dread Artifacts, also called The Armor of Dread?" Mal asked.

Ismail nodded.

"Are you aware that I lack only two of them?"

Ismail looked up at him. "Two?"

Mal nodded once. "The Spellbook and the Stone."

Ismail's calculating eyes drifted away from Mal. "You'd like for me to locate them?"

"I would, yes."

"That is not my speciality," she said gently.

"When I met you, you said you were drawn to the broken Magic in my pocket. You can sense Magical artifacts, can you not?"

"Sometimes yes," she answered.

"They call to you."

She looked back up at Mal. "They do."

"Can you find the items I am seeking?"

"I can try," she replied.

Mal held her gaze for a moment before continuing.

"Unfortunately, Ismail," he said, his voice dropping, "trying will not be enough."

Ismail swallowed. Mal continued.

"There is plenty of time for us to discuss the plans I have for finding them both. But first, I have a question for you. And please understand, both my Dread Viper and I are capable of discerning the truth with or without your consent. It is in your best interest to be truthful."

Ismail chewed the inside of her lip.

"Is that understood?"

She nodded. Her eyes slipped to Abraxas as his brows raised.

"My Prince," she added. "Yes, my Prince."

Abraxas' brows fell in a look of approval.

"Why did you return the gold and vanish after you repaired the Finder's Stone?" Mal asked.

Ismail tensed, but she answered. "Shortly after you departed, I received a visit from The Orator's Office. They were far crueler than your four-legged friends."

"I am sorry, Ismail," said Mal. "I never intended for you to get hurt."

"I know that," she said, but her eyes were wary of the new world surrounding her. She hardly looked at Maeve.

"The Double O came to you?" prompted Abraxas.

Ismail nodded, her eyes still on The Dread Goblet. They turned glassy. Tears rimmed her charcoal smudged painted eyelids.

Maeve gasped, and Ismail's guilty eyes landed on her at last.

The room became swelteringly hot. Maeve's vision blurred. Her hands turned numb and her neck pooled with sweat.

"I didn't know until after I had confirmed the goblet was laced with poison," cried Ismail, thick tears streaking her cheeks. Her eyes snapped to Mal. "I didn't know it was meant for you."

"Breath, Maeve," said Mal calmly, his lethal eyes on Ismail.

But she could not. Her chest stung with a deep ache. Would there be no end to the betrayal?

"That is why you returned the payment and vanished? And why you have eluded me for so long?"

Ismail nodded, sucking in sharp breaths of regret.

Dark Magic fell from Mal like a discarded robe. It surged across the floor, wrapping Ismail in piercing, dark, energy, ready to strike.

"Who poisoned it?" asked Maeve, her pulse accelerating rapidly. "I know you know."

Ismail's teeth clattered together as she spoke. "I need not touch The Dread Artifacts in this room to know what Magic is stored within them. They scream at me. It was not meant to kill the Dread. It was poisoned to kill someone…something else. There are many guilty parties," she said, sucking in tightly. "Only one life force still remains."

"Who?" asked Mal sharply.

Ismail's eyes traveled from the goblet to Maeve's narrowed eyes. Maeve heard the accusation before it even rolled off Ismail's tongue. In fact, she didn't hear her at all. Sound faded from her senses as Ismail spoke the words that somewhere, deep in Maeve's stomach, she knew were coming. She only watched the Witch mouth his name, and all understanding became lost to her.

"Reeve of the Aterna."

There would indeed be no end to the betrayal.

How many silent moments passed, Maeve did not know. Nausea swept through her, tingling her spine and hands. The feeling of the chair beneath her seemed to vanish. Ismail continued quietly, though no one instructed her to speak.

"He poisoned it himself. More than three hundred years ago."

The words repeated over and over in her mind.

Mal was right. They had been foolish. They had been so foolish to think there were not enemies all around them while they danced and dueled.

She didn't know what happened in the room with Ismail after she accused Reeve of poisoning the Dread Goblet. Something snapped in Maeve's mind. She stood and left them as her vision blackened.

Ismail's scream followed her into the hall. She braced herself on the wall, stumbling into the cold stone. She pushed off the wall, shattering the frames of Dread royalty that hung in large frames. Their portraits shredded and hit the floor beneath her Magic.

Mal was behind her in a flash, catching her waist and forcing her face up at him with his free hand.

"Shhh," he soothed her.

I've got you, he said into her mind. *Breathe.*

Maeve clawed at his chest, gripping the fabric of his shirt until it balled beneath her fists.

She couldn't speak. Her throat was painfully dry.

Make it stop please, she begged silently. *It's too loud in my mind.*

His hand slipped from her face and slid around the back of her knees as his darkness consumed her.

The North Tower was quiet when she rolled over in Mal's sheets.

He was awake in a large chair, thumbing through an old hand written text. One of the few left behind in Castle Morana.

His eyes lifted to hers. Her thoughts were already consumed by Ismail's confessions.

"It was not meant to kill Dread," she said, reciting Ismail's words.

Mal closed the leather book and set it aside. He crossed the circular tower towards the bed. He sat beside her and brushed his fingers across her forehead.

Her mind ran through all of the possibilities, kicking her heart into overdrive. Reeve watched the Dread Goblet get presented to Mal. He was already disgruntled that Mal was traveling to the Dread Lands before his coronation.

He saw Mal hand her father the Dread Goblet. He had to have seen that. He had to have.

"Hey," Mal said softly. "Stop."

Maeve looked away from him and up at his dark ceiling.

"Do you trust Reeve?" she asked, desperate for an explanation.

"I already told you, Maeve. The enemies are anyone that isn't you and I."

She paused. "How could he. . .if he knew."

"'Only one guilty party remains', is what Ismail claims. He alone didn't poison that goblet."

Maeve ran her hands over her face, brushing Mal's away, and sat up, sliding her legs over the side of the bed. He watched her carefully as she slipped on her boots.

"Where are you going?"

"To Aterna."

"Maeve," he began.

"I want to know."

"And what will happen when he reveals he is indeed your enemy?"

"Maybe he'll kill me too," she muttered, gripping the laces with white knuckles.

Mal snatched her hands up and forced her attention to him, her body tense beneath his strong hold.

"Speak those words again and you will regret them," he said, his voice laced with a calm venom. Mal frowned at her, searching her face. He swallowed.

"He doesn't know we know. We must play this carefully. He knows where the Dread Stone is. I know it in my blood. If I can get him around Ismail I believe she will be able to follow that Magic."

Maeve ripped out of his grip. "I don't give a damn about that stone!"

Electric Magic crackled at her fingertips. Mal did not acknowledge them. His dark and solemn eyes remained on her.

"Don't," he said.

She scowled at him so furiously that for a fraction of a second, the endlessly calm demeanor he kept up, vanished. Pain slipped across his raven eyes. There was no fear. She was no match for him. They both knew that.

His mask returned.

"Finding the Dread Stone is one of the last pieces of the puzzle, Maeve," he said quietly. "It will ensure I keep you safe, and that we have a life that flourishes here."

"What good is a life here if I cannot sleep without your assistance? If I cannot see the sun?"

Her words stung him once more. And the broken part of her was glad of it.

He stood and crossed the chamber. Without looking at her, he said, "You are forbidden from traveling to Aterna. That's an order."

His back was to her as he Obscured in a black mist.

Chapter 30

Maeve

She paced the long hallways and corridors of Castle Morana. Sleep was a foreign idea. Far from reality. She called softly for Spinel, carrying his favorite treat in her hand. He'd been missing for a few days, which wasn't uncommon for the curious cat. But Maeve felt less alone in the Crown's Quarters when he was curled up beside her.

Ismail's confession replayed across her mind.

She'd known the moment The Double O began scrambling after her father's death that they were complicit somehow. She'd already come to resent the Committee of the Sacred long before then. Ophelia's brazen flirtation and desire for Mal was enough to hate her.

But Reeve.

How could he have known? How could he look her in the eye if he knew?

Faint Magic slipped from the nape of her neck to the small of her back.

It was Mal, and he was weakened. She could feel his fading Magic as easily as her own.

Her steps quickened across the castle, until she spotted him on his knees just past the Entrance Hall doors to Castle Morana. A dark cloud of Magic surrounded him. So dark it had Maeve stopping before she reached him.

It swelled at her presence.

Watching her.

The Magic was familiar but so unknown.

She held the darkness' gaze as it swirled above Mal and disappeared, but it lingered all the same as she crossed to Mal.

She kneeled before him. Her fingertips brushed against his exposed chest. He was cold as ice on Hiems.

"Mal," she called.

He stirred slightly.

"Mal," she said sharply.

He startled at once, trying to slide away from her. She gripped his shoulders and hushed him as his breathing quickened.

"Hey, hey," she hummed as her fingers moved to his face. "I'm here."

His eyes bounced across the room, finally landing on her own. They held a glimmer of green. She brushed it off and attempted to soothe him.

She held his face gently. "I'm here."

He didn't break their gaze. His cold hands moved across her own. Maeve nodded.

"Let's get you in bed," she said softly.

She moved to stand. Mal's hands moved to her own. The moonlight dipping into the foyer faded slowly and black swirls of misty Magic circled them. It spiraled above them and vanished with a calming, cool, swish, leaving them on Mal's bed in his chambers.

The thick curtains around his bed were drawn, putting them in their own world.

Mal's hand moved up towards her face. His slender fingers brushed against her skin. Her eyes fluttered closed, and she relaxed into his touch.

His hand stilled, and she looked up at his tired eyes.

"Do you want to tell me?" she asked softly.

His fingers moved down her neck. "There is not much to tell," he said. "I am succeeding in restoring these lands."

Maeve looked into his eyes. They had returned to their normal state, with no trace of green visible. "You're alright?"

Mal nodded and took her arms, gently pulling them both onto the fluffy bedding.

"I am," he answered.

She tucked herself close to him. His leg draped over hers.

"I'm sorry," she said softly. "For the way I acted last we spoke."

Mal did not reply. He ran his fingers lazily up and down her back, exhaustion pouring from him.

"Please," she said into his chest. "Please do not ever give more than you receive out there."

Mal's fingers pushed under her chin, drawing her gaze up at him. "Your father taught me better than that. I could never commit such a disservice to his memory."

"Dark Magic is not like the rest," said Maeve.

"We don't know what it is," he replied.

"Dark Magic comes at a cost," she said. "We know that much."

Mal moved his fingers down her neck, tracing over her darkened veins. "And yet," he whispered, "here you are."

"What did I trade for these marks?"

Mal's eyes moved back up to her own. "Your innocence."

"And what did I gain in return?"

A smile tugged at Mal's lips. "I've been wondering that myself." He looked back down at them. "I keep waiting for you to feel some power, a new surge from them. . .but your Magic has not changed."

"See," she said with raised brows. "I broke the rule."

Mal scoffed and brought his lips to her forehead. "We shall see."

Chapter 40

Maeve

The Grand Balcony at Castle Morana slid into view. The ever-present twilight surrounded the land beyond. Music drifted towards her from the Ballroom. The tune was familiar.

Something felt strange about Maeve's new dream. Dreams in Castle Morana never left her chamber. The gaunt albino woman was nowhere to be found as her mind wandered through sleep.

His back was turned, but he looked over his shoulder as she approached.

Maeve smiled at Reeve.

He heaved a heavy sigh upon seeing her, and subtly leaned against the bannister to catch his breath.

Maeve's smile fell flat. "Is something–"

"No," he interrupted her, attempting to smile playfully, but breathing seemed difficult for Reeve as she walked towards him. He looked at her in awe.

"Your Magic," he started as she stood before him. "It's. . .growing."

A small smile pulled at the corner of her lips. "I'm pregnant."

A heavy bit of Magic pressed into her as shock slipped from him. It was warm against her cheek. She looked up at him, never having seen Reeve so uncontrolled.

"Congratulations," he said, his voice strained.

She paused. "You don't mean that," she said, barely above a whisper.

It was true. He hadn't meant it. And the Magic pressing into her body from him felt like nothing but regret. Maeve's face softened.

"Of course I do," he replied.

Maeve's hand moved to her belly.

A long silence passed between them.

"I never got to tell you how sorry I was," said Reeve. "How sorry I am for your Father."

Maeve averted her gaze and Reeve sighed.

"That was selfish of me to say."

Maeve looked back at him. "It was honest. No one is honest with me anymore. It's all games."

Reeve gave her a soft smile that didn't meet his eyes. "Did you expect otherwise?"

"Nothing has gone how I expected at all."

"No," said Reeve, his half-hearted smile fading. "On that, we agree."

She looked up at him, his eyes dull. He didn't look himself.

"You seem. . ."started Maeve.

Reeve merely shook his head, as if to say he was fine.

"More games," said Maeve.

"You are quite good at playing them."

"Bred that way, remember?"

Reeve scowled. "Don't listen to a word those jealous Immortals and Magicals say. There was a time when Pureblood was so coveted that—"

"Well it's not that time anymore," interrupted Maeve as her voice broke. "And I am not of Pureblood."

Reeve eyed her carefully. Her emotions were skyrocketing at the mention of her bloodline.

A small tear slipped from the corner of her eye and rolled slowly down her cheek.

Reeve reached a hand towards her face but quickly halted when she spoke.

"Don't," she snapped.

His hand returned slowly to his side. A genuine smile slid across his face.

"You had me worried for a moment," he said. "But there you are. Still as stubborn and prideful as ever."

Maeve wiped the single tear as her emotions returned to normal. "I should return."

Reeve nodded. "I am at your disposal, Lady."

"I am his second, not Lady of the Dread House," said Maeve. "And I don't need your protection just because I'm with child."

"No," agreed Reeve. "If anything, you are more ferocious than I can ever recall having seen you." He smiled softly.

Maeve hesitated to leave him, a genuine smile blossoming on her lips.

Her stomach fell through the floor as Magic, white and hot, raced down her arms.

Bright light slammed into her vision, the beat in her head deafening.

Maeve pushed up out of bed in her darkened chamber. Something warm and thick slipped over her lip and onto her tongue. The metallic taste of blood pulled her from bed with haste. Magic ran towards her, slamming closer and closer.

The chiming clock above the mantel rang out. Then again. Then again.

She stared into the face of the clock, feeling foolish as her clammy hand found her flat stomach. A sigh of relief escaped her lips.

The balcony doors in her chambers flew open, slamming against the wall as a gust of icy night air chilled the floor beneath her bare feet, swirling the curtains in a twisting motion.

Something came swiftly. Magic she'd never felt and yet longed for all the same.

It was there.

She rushed onto the balcony and gripped the stone bannister.

The gates of Castle Morana were far across the grounds from the Crown's Suite, but she made out Mal's backside as he stood alone. She pushed off the railing and flew back across her chambers, out into the corridor and across the castle.

Mal alone could Obscure in and out of the castle with his Dread blood, and her sprint across the castle had never felt so long. The dark hallways tunneled on endlessly in her hasty pursuit.

When she reached the Entrance Hall doors, they already sat open. The chilling air of the Dread Lands prickled her face as she made her way towards Mal. He stood along the stone carved entryway below with his back still turned, blocking her view from whoever, or whatever, stood beyond the gate. His cloak flowed gracefully behind him in the piercing wind.

He'd felt it too.

She flew up beside him

On the other side of the Magical threshold stood a young boy. No more than two, maybe three.

Spinel meowed at the little boy's feet, rubbing against his legs with his tail curled high, acting as though he hadn't been missing for weeks.

The boy's eyes moved to Maeve. And he smiled.

Her knees weakened as she leaned towards Mal.

He was so familiar. His round cheeks brought her comfort. His eyes were a sharp shade of glimmering green.

Her Magic felt for his, unafraid and without caution. His defenses were as strong as Elven Steel, but warm with a glow of ancient Magic. His dark hair lay flat against his head, bangs trimmed perfectly across his forehead. His clothes were expensive fabric she'd never seen.

"Hello," she said with a nervous smile.

The gate between them slid open with the wave of Mal's hand.

"Are you from The Beryl City?" she asked. "How did you get all the way here?"

She looked behind him for any sign of his parents or a guardian. The night was still beyond the gates.

He hasn't spoken, Mal said into her mind.

The gates stood open wide. The child shivered, and Maeve stepped towards him.

"Gracious," she said, quickly slipping her robe off and sliding it around his shoulders and wrapping him in the much too large fabric. "You're freezing."

The boy glanced around her shoulder curiously.

Zimsy made her way towards them at a leisurely pace.

Maeve moved slowly, but he did not flinch from her as she placed her hands on either side of his small face. She pressed their foreheads together, and recoiled at once as his Magic pierced through her.

The boy didn't appear scared or surprised at her reaction.

"Maeve?" asked Mal tensely.

"I'm fine," she replied hastily.

Her hands fell to her sides. The boy's green eyes were mesmerizing in the hazy moonlight. Spinel chirped at her loudly.

Maeve reprimanded him with her eyes. He rubbed his lanky body against the boy again, purring up at Maeve.

Zimsy reached them a moment later. "You found Spinel," she said with a little laugh. Zimsy kneeled beside him. A smile blossomed on his face as he took her in. "And who might you be?"

The boy made a motion with his hand.

She looked over at Maeve. Maeve gave her a small, concerned shrug.

"I'll call a search of the Greywood," said Mal. "The Bellator need to make sure there aren't more children roaming in the night."

"Send some to the city as well," said Maeve. "Perhaps he wandered off."

They both knew how unlikely it was that a small boy, barely more than a baby, had made it from The Beryl City without freezing or getting hurt.

"I'm sorry, I must have woken you," Maeve commented to Zimsy.

"Slamming your chamber door open and barreling down the hall will do that," said Zimsy with a smile. She looked back at the boy. "Would you like some sweets? Three in the morning seems like a perfectly good time for little boys to have some cookies. I just made some with fresh lemons from the gardens."

Zimsy extended him her hand and he took it at once. She led him back towards the castle, Spinel hot on their heels with his tail perked in a high curl.

"What was that?" asked Mal when they were out of earshot.

Maeve shook her head. "I couldn't see anything. There is a shield sharper than my own around that boy's mind."

Mal pulled a handkerchief from his pocket. The linen was embroidered with his Dread Mark in the corner. He took her chin in one hand and gently dabbed at the dried blood between her nose and her lip.

"You weren't asleep?" asked Maeve.

Mal meticulously removed the blood as he answered. "I just got in."

He dropped her chin and waited before he spoke, ensuring Zimsy and the boy were out of earshot.

"Do you remember the last time you woke in the night with blood dripping from your nose?"

Maeve nodded. Mal looked towards Morana, where Zimsy walked with the child.

"He's just a boy," said Maeve.

Together, they silently watched the small boy until he and Zimsy disappeared into the castle.

"Like calls to like," said Maeve quietly.

Mal nodded slowly in agreement. "I felt it too." He looked back at her. "However, he got here, you were the coordinate. The same way Kietel found you."

"But Kietel found me because his Magic lingered in me. I have never encountered this boy."

A quick breeze bit at her exposed skin. She pulled her arms tight. Mal opened his cloak to her. She pressed herself against him as he wrapped the fabric around her.

"You just let him in?"

Abraxas puffed on a small cigarette and rubbed his eyes.

"Yes," said Mal.

"No idea who he is?"

"No," he answered again.

Mal had his back to them, looking out the green glass windows along his study. His gaze intensely on the Dark Peaks.

Abraxas' face scrunched and he looked at Maeve. "Didn't you chastise me for accepting the invitation to Aterna? Something about a trap?"

"That's different," she replied.

"How?" Abraxas pressed.

"Because I know he isn't a threat."

Abraxas scoffed. "Because he is barely not a babe? May I remind the pair of you that you were jumping minds and using Supreme level Magic at that age."

"This is different," she said again. She looked at Mal, whose back was still turned. "That boy is something different."

Abraxas looked back at her. "The threat doesn't have to bare its teeth to be considered a danger."

"Abraxas," said Mal calmly, finally turning towards them. "He stays."

Abraxas didn't argue a word further. "Where is he now?"

"Eating sweets with Zimsy," answered Maeve.

Abraxas looked over at her. "Did she make lemon cookies again?" His eyes sparkled and he forgot their disagreement at once.

Astrea arrived at Castle Morana and performed an exam on the child. She found no abnormalities or injuries.

"He is of Magical heritage," she informed them. "It flows freely, and in abundance within him. And there is something foreign. It's not prominent enough to truly feel, but I thought worth mentioning all the same. I can't place it."

"Any traces of a spell or curse?" Mal asked.

"None," she replied. "He is pure. But there is one more thing," she said. "He is not merely holding his tongue. He's mute."

"But you think he understands us?"

"Certainly," she said. "I asked him many yes or no questions. He shook and nodded his head appropriately. But I can feel he lacks the ability to speak."

Mal thanked her, and she took her leave back to her home in The Towers.

The Bellator searched the Greywood, The Towers, and The Beryl City for days. There was no sign or clue of where the boy came from.

Maeve sat and watched him draw on a pale yellow scroll of parchment.

Maeve leaned over the drawing. It was a cat.

"Is that Spinel?"

He nodded and looked down at his feet, where Spinel lay curled in a tight ball.

"He seems to like you," said Maeve.

The boy smiled up at her. He made a small movement with his hand then reached down and ran a hand along Spinel's soft fur. He looked back at Maeve and made the hand motion again. He pet Spinel once more, and stood. He made the motion a third time.

Maeve understood. She mimicked the small movement. "Cat?" she asked.

He nodded. Spinel purred loudly at his feet.

"What other words do you know?"

His smile faded and he looked back down at Spinel, then back up at Maeve.

He made the motion for cat again.

Maeve kneeled before him. "Is there a motion for your name?"

He pulled both hands together and made a motion.

"Slow," said Maeve gently.

He repeated the motion. He nodded as Maeve copied it.

He nodded and took the quill back in his tiny hand. He dipped it back in the black paint-like ink with deep concentration and wrote in perfect cursive: *Maxius*.

"Maxius," said Maeve as she read the word. She looked back up at him. "Hello, Maxius. Can you write any other words?"

He placed the quill back on the parchment. Maeve watched him curiously.

Cat, he wrote in slightly sloppier handwriting than his name.

Maeve laughed and reached for Spinel. She pet his head as he pulled his paws in tightly.

"I've been learning his language," she told Mal upon his return. "I believe it's what they use on Earth."

"Earth?" Mal asked.

Maeve nodded. "I asked him to write me his last name, his parents' names. He cannot."

"He doesn't know them or he won"t say?"

"No idea," she replied. "I can't get in his head."

"My Pathokenesis abilities are just as void on him," admitted Mal.

Maeve watched as Zimsy walked with him through the gardens with Spinel trailing them, as he always did.

"Who is this boy?" she asked quietly.

Mal fell silent a moment before he spoke. "Ismail has returned empty handed once more."

Maeve swallowed. Whether or not the unique Witch was searching for the remaining Dread Artifacts out of guilt or by force, Maeve didn't know. Nor did she care. Maybe it was Mordred and his pack of wolves nipping at her heels that propelled her.

"Reeve's been awfully silent," she noted. "No fancy party invitations."

"Abraxas is working on that."

"He will come here? And you will introduce him to Ismail?"

"Yes."

Maeve looked away from him.

"Does his innocence matter to you?" asked Mal after a moment.

"Yes," she admitted. "A great deal."

If jealousy spiked through Mal he controlled it well. Maeve continued.

"The hope that he did not falsely call my father friend, as so many have, is the single thing that keeps me from burning Crystalmore to the ground." She looked over at him. "His innocence matters, because, if he is not, then I am easily played a fool."

Chapter 41

Maeve

Emerie and Roswyn's daughter's birth celebration came months after her birth. She'd been in Irma and Astrea's diligent care since she was born early and with less strength than needed for an infant in the Dread Lands. Anndee was her name.

But the small baby with pale blonde strands of hair and pink cheeks seemed perfect in Emerie's arms as they gathered in the Tower of Sordell.

Maeve was certain she'd never seen Roswyn smile so consistently. He slipped his hand on the small of Emerie's back as she passed the newborn to Juliet, who puckered her lips at the small babe.

Mr. Iantrose teetered over to the happy new parents. He looked down at Anndee and smiled. "My great grand niece."

Emerie looked up at him and shook her head. "No, Mr. Iantrose, we aren't related."

"Oh," replied Mr. Iantrose, entirely unaffected by her words.

Abraxas stood over the bar, pouring a hefty concoction with a grin. "Come, Emerie," he called.

She stepped towards the bar, her eyes still on Juliet and the baby as Abraxas extended her the drink.

"Congratulations," he said.

She took the swirling silver liquid and thanked him.

"A toast, a toast," shouted Abraxas. "What better reason to drink than a baby," he said, raising his glass high.

Laughter flitted through the room.

"I jest," continued Abraxas. "I speak for The Dread Prince when I say we are honored you have chosen a life here and perpetuated such strong Magic here. May Anndee's Magic be true, and her days here long."

Mal raised his glass of sparkling water where he stood next to Maeve. "To Anndee."

"To Anndee," chimed the crowd.

Emerie beamed and placed the glass on her lips. Maeve looked up at Mal as they sipped their water.

Glass shattered across the floor. Every head turned toward the sound.

"What the hell?" said Roswyn, pushing through a few guests to get back to his wife and child

Shards of her wine glass sat at Emerie's feet. Her eyes were glazed black and her arms lay limp at her side. Roswyn grabbed her waist, holding her securely.

She spoke with a dozen voices, muffled and raspy, as she said, "The one to inherit the Power of Aterna has been chosen."

Emerie's eyes flooded with color as she sucked in sharply and fell forward into Roswyn. Her body gave way as he supported her, lifting her up into his arms. Astrea arrived at his side, placing her hands on Emerie's face.

Roswyn looked past Maeve. She followed his gaze to Mal.

The Dread Prince's expression was solemn.

"Is she alright?" Roswyn asked Astrea as she entered Abraxas' study.

She nodded. "She's fine. That exhausted her, though."

"The baby?" He asked with a strain.

"Perfectly healthy."

Roswyn swallowed.

It was not uncommon for the bloodline of Seers to have reactions to their family's prophecies.

"She remains completely unaffected," elaborated Astrea.

Roswyn didn't reply to Astrea. Maeve had never seen a flicker of fear across his brute features. She'd never questioned his love for Emerie. Whether he loved her or not was of no consequence to Maeve. But one thing was certain: he cared a great deal for that new baby girl.

He looked up at Mal.

"Go," said Mal, before Roswyn even had the chance to ask.

He placed his fist over his chest and left the study without another word.

"Thank you, Astrea," said Abraxas.

She took her leave in silence as well.

Abraxas pulled open the drawer of his desk and took out a long scroll of parchment. He picked a small, feathered writing quill and hastily wrote the date, and the exact words of Emerie's prophecy.

"Turns out, she is a Seer," said Maeve, sliding back into one of the comfy chairs.

"Yes," said Abraxas as he sliced the parchment by sliding his fingers across the tan paper. "No more jokes for me," he muttered.

Maeve's eyes moved to Mal. He sat before Abraxas' desk, reclined in an armchair. His eyes lifted to Maeve's.

Abraxas sealed the small bit of parchment with wax and filed it away.

"Now," he said. "Maeve could jump, see what they know."

"She's not jumping," said Mal cooly, as though he knew those exact words were about to come from Abraxas.

"But I could," said Maeve.

Mal's eyes slid to her. "No," he said calmly.

"They are on-planet, in-realm," she began to argue. "It wouldn't be like the last time–"

Mal's shoulders dropped, the vein in his neck twitched. Maeve looked away from his stern glare.

His Magic slithered down the desk between them and tucked under her chin, forcing her gaze back to him. He pressed into her mind.

I don't doubt your ability or your dedication to the cause.

I know that, she pressed back, *but at some point I need to try. I need to restrengthen myself.*

Abraxas continued talking as they communicated in silence.

Mal's eyes fell to the table. *You nearly died the last time.*

Because I pushed too hard.

His eyes lifted back to her. *You always push too hard.*

A smile kicked at the corner of her mouth. *It was you who trained me.*

Mal's eyes softened. She felt his pride through their bond. *You were a born fighter. I merely showed you the way.*

You brought me back to life once, I'm certain you can do it again.

Mal's chin sat atop his fingers.

Pour toujours, she slid into his mind.

Forever.

À tout jamais, he said in reply.

And always.

"Are either of you listening to me?" groaned Abraxas.

Chapter 42

Maeve

Most of Maeve's favorite shops still remained on Earth since they were Human owned. She had shown no interest in shopping or buying new clothes, so when she announced to Mal she wanted to travel to London and Paris, he fought back his fear of her traveling to their old planet and supported the small part of her that seemed like her old self.

Spinel was quite perturbed when Maeve wouldn't allow him through the Portal Mal created to Earth. He chirped at her feet and slunk into the darkness of the foyer.

Zimsy and Arianna accompanied her. The twins stayed with Grandmother Agatha, but Maxius had insisted on staying in Zimsy's arms. And so she carried him until she spotted a dress she wanted to try on. Maeve took Maxius in her arms. He was soft and warm.

Zimsy claimed she only somewhat liked the dress, but Maeve bought it for her, anyway. They enjoyed warm tea in a small shop as ice flurries blew by the window. The haze of winter clouded the sun from view, but Maeve relished in its presence, regardless. The Humans around her didn't know who she was. She was no one to them in the busy buzz of Paris just before Christmas.

She was grateful to be no one for a fleeting moment.

Maxius slept soundly against her, taking large breaths.

"No one has found his parents?" asked Arianna.

"No," said Maeve, ripping off a piece of her pastry. "He doesn't tell me anything about them. Or maybe I just can't understand him yet."

Maeve paused for a moment and then looked at her sisters casually. "How are. . .things?' she asked.

Arianna's eyes narrowed. But Maeve smiled.

"Guess you already told her," said Arianna, nodding over at

Zimsy.

Zimsy's poker face was non-existent. Maeve had indeed told Zimsy she walked in on Arman and Arianna.

"Zim," hissed Maeve.

"I'm sorry!"

Arianna's head lifted back as she laughed. "It's alright, Maeve. I'm the one who told Zimsy about that summer when you were eleven–"

"Shut up," said Maeve sharply, her cheeks growing hot.

Zimsy bit her lip. "Actually, Abraxas told me about that first."

Maeve groaned and swirled her tea. "You didn't even answer my question, Arianna."

Her sister smiled. "It's really nice."

"It's more than just a drunken fling in the dark, yes?"

Arianna hesitated and then nodded, shame filling her expression.

"Don't be ashamed," said Maeve. "I want to help you."

Arianna looked away. Maxius inhaled deeply and shifted against Maeve.

"This is not our old world, Arianna. If you want him, say the word, and I will see it done."

The Sinclair sisters' eyes met. It was silent, but there was an unspoken understanding between them. The past was over. The constant childish competition was over. Maeve was genuine in her desire for her sister to find happiness in Arman. They both lost their father, but if Maeve's gut instinct was correct, her sister and her father's Captain had been secretly acquainted long before his death.

"It's wrong to leave Titus," she said, still clinging to the life forced upon her.

"But not wrong to have an affair and carry another man's children?"

Arianna's eyes flashed with hurt.

"I just mean–" began Maeve.

"I'm aware of what you meant," said Arianna. "I don't want to argue. Just leave it be."

Maeve opened her mouth to speak.

"This is your problem always," said Arianna. "You can't just let it go.”

“Because you are in denial about what you could have,” said Maeve urgently. “What I can give you.”

“Not everyone wants to be a rebel, Maeve,” she scoffed in reply.

Maeve shook her head. “Fine,” she said, standing and pulling some Human money from her pockets, being sure to keep Maxius tucked snugly against her. “Have it your way.”

“Maeve, wait–” began Zimsy.

“I have some other things I’d like to do alone,” she said without looking at them. “Meet back at the Portal spot for Mal to bring us home.”

She left the little shop and threw up an invisible warm shield of air around herself and Maxius. Maxius didn’t wake at all until they turned the corner and Maeve leaned against the towering building behind her.

He looked up at her with sleepy eyes.

“Would you like to see my old home?” she asked softly.

Maxius yawned and nodded.

She held him tight as she Obscured them both to the edge of the Sinclair Estates property line.

“This is where my family is buried,” she said, as she walked with his tiny hand in hers, matching his short steps. The cliff-side drop to the stones and water below was sharp. The sun began to dip behind the horizon.

“It’s late,” she remarked. “And colder than I thought it would be.”

The property was no longer enchanted with a cozy warmth. Small patches of ice and snow stuck to the ground, crunching beneath their feet. The graveyard came into view, nestled back into the trees she and Mal spent a beautiful summer racing through.

“My old home is on the other side of these woods,” she said.

We go? he signed.

Maeve looked down at him, sadness barreling up inside her. “No,” she said at last, losing her nerve to see Sinclair Estates.

Maxius didn’t question further. They walked the rest of the way without more conversation. The iron gate of the cemetery opened for them silently, swinging forward majestically.

Past her ancestors, past Antony's grave, sat her father's mausoleum.

A breeze shifted around them, pushing barren leaves across their path through the graveyard.

The smell hit her before the realization of what she was seeing.

Maeve stepped in front of Maxius. He grabbed the back of her legs and peeked around her. She scooped him up into her arms and forced his head against her shoulder.

Before Ambrose's mausoleum lay a bright white unicorn.

Its neck was slit, and the ground beneath it spread with rot already.

She stepped forward hesitantly, red writing coating the creature's side.

Mortem ad Sinclair

Maeve gripped Maxius tightly as the words "death to Sinclair" registered across her mind.

Every instinct to flee overcame her as unknown Magic sparked around her seven times.

Seven hooded figures Obscured around the graveyard. Collectively, their Magic shattered the protective barrier around the graveyard meant to keep Humans and unwelcome guests from entering.

Maeve dropped Maxius to his feet and fell to her knees before him. With two fingers she pointed behind him. A Portal, the height of Maxius, swirled into existence, the greens and blues illuminating the cliff-side graveyard. The courtyard at Castle Morana blurred into view behind Maxius inside the Portal. She shoved him through as her other hand shot behind her, throwing up a shield in an attempt to deflect a curse that spiraled towards them.

The Magic required to make such a Portal surged through her, depleting the Magic needed to stop the curse from slicing through her back. She was without her full strength on Earth, that was evident quickly. Mal had both the Dread Ring and Locket. She was on her own.

Warmth drenched her clothes as the curse shook through her. She gasped a cry as her small Portal began to collapse on itself. She surged her Magic through the doorway between worlds, but it only shrunk quicker.

Maxius gripped her hand tightly, tugging on her with a fearful expression. She pushed him fully through the swirling Portal and ripped free from his grip.

She slammed the Magical doorway closed as he looked up at her in terror.

Her palms fell forward into the grass as her body shook and her vision blurred. The tips of her fingers were numb with ache. Creating a Portal on-planet was one thing. Sending Maxius across realms required much more of her strength. Nearly all of it. And the fiery Magic running down her back was another issue entirely.

She turned towards her attackers and stood tall, despite the blow to her Magical reserve, and the pain building through her. Her breaths were heavy and deep.

Their faces were all masked.

"And here I thought that Portal was for you to run with your tail tucked," said one.

"You talk of cowardice as though your identity is not hidden from me," she replied.

With the wave of their hand, their mask lifted and turned to mist.

"Remember me?" he asked.

The man was older than she was. In his thirties. She knew his face well, though now his expression was ridden with lack of sleep. He'd been to Sinclair Estates many times.

The son of Orator Moon. Leonardo. Moon had called him Leo.

Maeve's footing shifted under exhaustion.

"That Portal drained the little snake," one said.

"Who was the boy?" Leo asked.

"A child and not your concern."

"Is that where you draw the line? Children."

"A hard one," said Maeve, her vision white and hazy now. Blood soaked her back. She exhaled sharply. "I am worried I will pass out soon. So let me say this: your father deserved to die and I wish every day that I could kill him again and again."

Magic pierced her face, sending her sideways onto her elbows on the ground. Leo advanced towards her.

"How dare you make a widow of my mother."

Maeve scoffed, spitting blood onto the autumn leaves. "Your father made an orphan of me."

"Everyone knows that poisonous goblet was meant for that usurper you share a bed with."

"Too scared to say his name?" she taunted, praying she could bide her time with her tongue. "Afraid you'll summon him?"

His boot made contact with the side of her cheek, sending her face first into the cold earth.

"Leonardo," snapped one of the others. "You're going to kill her."

Maeve laughed as blood filled her mouth.

Two shaking fingers pressed into her chest as she searched for him across realms.

Mal.

She felt nothing in return. Maxius was her only hope of rescue.

"I dont give a fuck," said Leo. "If she dies, so be it."

"We have orders to capture, not kill," he argued back.

Leo turned his attention on the other, bowing up at him.

"Oh-ho!" she exclaimed with a bloody cough. "Is there a bounty on my head?"

"Three rubies to be exact," answered Leo.

"That all?" she asked.

She backed against the oversized headstone above her grandfather's grave, gripping her stomach and pressing what little healing skills she had into her wounds.

"It's against Magical law to kill a unicorn," said Maeve.

If she could keep distracting them, she'd be deadly again soon.

"There are no Magical laws left on Earth," said Leo. "There is no government, not an ounce of order remains."

"I don't mean the fucking Double O's laws, you idiot," she said with a groan. "A bad omen, truly."

Leo turned back towards her. "Yeah, that's what I wanted it to be. I can't believe we have you down," he said genuinely. "I was expecting to have to fight you out of our minds." He looked her over with pity. "But something in me says you've lost the ability for that little party trick."

Maeve's eyes narrowed.

"Or maybe you never had it," he said.

She replied, "How do you think I found and killed your father?"

Magic slammed into her chest, knocking her head back against the marbled gravestone.

Her teeth slammed together. Her eyes shifted to a close.

"Come on, Leo!" screamed one of the others. "We already agreed to split the bounty! Stop messing around and grab her before he comes for her."

"No," said Leo. "I want her to rot here with the rest of her useless lot."

He pointed two fingers at her, before toppling to the side.

Another hooded figure stood before her. "I'm collecting that bounty, you ass," said a woman's voice.

Darkness hissed through her darkened veins, and Maeve gasped.

Mal.

I am here.

Magic, dark and holy, barreled towards her, deep in her chest. It exploded with cosmic night.

Birds screamed and rushed from the treetops above. The orange sunset disappeared, hidden by inky black mist.

Mal appeared at her side as black Magic erupted from him. It swarmed around Maeve. The Magical before her vanished, misting into dark nothing as Mal ripped her apart. Leo scrambled backwards on the ground. The graveyard gates slammed closed as a new Magical barrier encased them, imprisoning her attackers.

Mal bent down before her. His mouth twitched as he took in her bleeding and marked face.

"Can you stand?" he asked her calmly. "Let's get you on your feet."

He lifted her off the ground by her waist and set her gently before him. His chest pressed against her back, one finger extended towards the rest and his free hand wrapped tightly around her center.

"Hello, Leonardo," said Mal darkly. "I thought I made it clear that if a hand was laid on her, every head would roll."

Leo opened his mouth to speak, but the words caught tight in his throat as Mal's chin jerked upwards.

"I didn't give you permission to speak." Mal shook his head. "I have tried to be understanding and patient. I have no qualms about what you do on Earth, only that you allowed my people and yours to travel freely between realms with immunity. And this is how you repay me? By attacking my girl when she is here paying tribute to her father? Pathetic. Seven on one? You couldn't even face her yourself."

Leo grabbed at his throat in frustration.

"Answer," commanded Mal, releasing his grip on the man's voice.

Leo gasped, choking on air until his breathing regulated. "You destroyed lives here on Earth. You killed many families in your attacks," he gestured to the man next to him. "You killed Kellon's sister. You killed my father. It is chaos on Earth, and you expected us to lay down and be happy for your so-called graciousness."

"I did not extend the sins of those around you onto you," said Mal. "For that I did expect gratitude. My mistake."

Dread Magic pulsed at his fingers.

"You were offered a place in my lands," continued Mal. "Despite your heritage. Despite that your father attempted to assassinate me, I offered you a new life."

Three of the still masked Magicals yanked on the gate of the graveyard to no avail, desperate to escape.

"Fuck you," said Leo. "Just kill me. Why do you hesitate?"

There is empathy resonating from you, Mal said into her mind.

I know what he feels. Every ounce of it.

What would you have me do, Little Viper? He would have killed you too.

One of the masked Magicals fell to his knees, begging for his life. "I only agreed to come for the bounty, your Grace," he whimpered. "My family needs the money. My parents were both killed in the battle at Vaukore by Doggbind and his men. My sister and I have nothing."

With a wave of his hand, Mal removed the mask. A young boy, no older than fourteen with tear stained cheeks, looked up at them.

"Is this who you enlist to do your dirty work, Leonardo?" Mal asked. "Children?"

Leo looked over at the boy. "He owes my family a debt," he spat.

The boy did not look at him.

"Dead men collect no debts," said Mal.

Leo glared up at him. Mal looked back at the boy.

"What's your name?"

"Jack, my Prince."

"If you would call me by such a name, why are you not in the Dread Lands? You were offered a place."

The boy did not look at Leo.

"I was afraid," he mumbled.

"Of me?" Mal asked.

Jack shook his head. "Of him." His eyes shifted over to Leo. "Of his father. If my family's debts were not paid, my sister would be fed to Moon's dogs."

Mal looked back at Leo. "Lovely."

Leo scowled at the boy.

"I'll make you an offer, Jack," said Mal.

The boy's red nose looked up at him.

"You and your sister will have a place in my world, if you want it. But your loyalties must be proven."

Jack swallowed. "She's only six. I can prove my loyalty and hers."

"Good. A real man already," said Mal. "Stand."

Jack stood at once and straightened his back. He looked at Mal with reserve.

Mal stared back at him. His heartbeat stayed in perfect rhythm as he said, "Kill Leonardo Moon."

Leo looked over at Jack and laughed. "He doesn't have the–"

Maeve jumped slightly as a bright flash of red shot from Jack's palm towards Leo.

The fallen leaves beneath him shuffled as he fell limply onto the cold ground, his eyes stuck wide.

Mal pointed four fingers out, and the remaining four Magicals sucked in their last breaths.

Jack looked up at Maeve and Mal.

"Go home and gather your things," said Mal. "My Hand will send someone to collect you and your sister shortly. There is an orphanage in The Beryl City, where you will be permitted to live freely."

Jack dropped to his knees. He placed a fist over his heart and bowed his head.

Darkness enveloped Maeve's vision. Maeve tucked her head into his chest as he pulled them through space and time to Castle Morana. Her feet touched down on the entryway.

"An orphanage?" she asked up at him.

Mal nodded. "It was created long before the restoration of those mansions."

Maeve used what little strength she had left to grab his face. "My Prince," she said with awe.

He pressed a kiss into her forehead and inhaled slowly.

Zimsy reached the foot of the stairway with Maxius in her arms. He pushed from her long, slender Elven limbs, desperate to reach the ground. Zimsy placed him on the tile and he ran towards Maeve.

Maxius tugged her down to her knees and threw his arms around her. She winced as she hugged him back.

Mal moved to press his fingers to his chest, "I need to call Astrea."

"I already did," said Zimsy, watching Maeve closely.

Mal nodded in silent thanks.

"How did you get here?" Maeve asked her. "And where is Arianna?"

"Mal sent Arman and the Bellator for us as soon as he came for you," she answered. "Arianna is fine."

Maxius pulled away from her. He made a swift motion with his hands and gestured to the blood staining her side.

"Blood?" asked Maeve.

Maxius shook his head.

"Hurt?"

He nodded and made the motion again.

Maeve smiled softly. "Yes, it hurts. But my friend will be here soon to heal me. And then I won't hurt anymore."

Maxius looked up at her, worry still running through his eyes.

"You are safe," said Maeve.

Maxius made a motion with his fingers. Safe.

"Safe," repeated Maeve, stifling her wince as she moved to stand.

Mal's hands slipped around her hips, stopping her from falling.

The castle doors swung open and Astrea appeared, her pregnancy almost at full term. Alphard trailed behind her. The two Mavros siblings looked more alike than ever as they entered their mid twenties.

Astrea moved towards Maeve at once.

Alphard's mouth fell open slightly at the beginning of a bruise on her face, his eyes trailing to her blood-stained clothes.

"Who the fuck managed to do that?" he asked, slight fear in his voice.

Mal shifted her body towards him and pressed his lips into her cheek. Icy Magic danced across the skin, penetrating the wound. The pain lifted at once.

"I was drained," Maeve answered. "There were seven of them, I think, and I used all my Magic making a Portal."

Alphard's brows raised. "A portal from Earth? To here? By yourself?"

She nodded.

"Damn," he said. "Astrea can't even make a Portal to the next room."

His sister looked back at him with a glare. He merely smiled back at her.

Astrea looked at Mal. "I need her lying down. Her back needs attention."

Chapter 43

Maeve

"You can't go to Earth anymore."

Maeve looked up from her breakfast.

Dark circles encased Mal's eyes. His lids hung low.

"You haven't slept," she replied.

"How can I, knowing that it's so easy for them to find you?"

"Earth is not the problem, they are."

They were quiet a moment. Mal's voice came low and drenched in sorrow.

"Portals are closed. The use of them is forbidden."

"No, Mal," she started, panic rushing through her voice. "You can't do that."

"It's already done," he said.

She shook her head. "No," she said once more. "No, I-you can't-you can't keep me from his grave-from visiting my home."

Mal looked her over sadly. "This is your home now."

Her throat tightened. "Please," she whispered.

He crossed towards her and leaned against the table.

"I can't feel you on Earth. I know you must have called for me. If Maxius hadn't made it back, I wouldn't have known you needed me. I can't bear the thought of you calling my name without reply, even thinking for a moment I am not coming."

"Mal," she said, reaching up and pulling his face towards her.

His hands covered her own and he spoke calmly. "It's done, Maeve. You cannot travel there again. It's time we left behind the ghosts of our past. It's time we embraced the world ahead of us. You are at my side, and I will do whatever it takes to ensure you remain there."

"I don't like this," she whispered.

"I don't care," he replied carefully. "I need to be able to feel you, and the only way that is possible is if you are on this planet, in this realm."

Maeve's hands fell to her lap.

"I want something in return," she said.

His head cocked to the side. "In return?"

"In return for not fighting you on this."

"It's a command, Maeve," he said.

"And I'm choosing to obey it."

Mal looked down at her in displeasure. Maeve continued, despite his sleep deprived demeanor.

"Make it so that all Committee of the Sacred arranged marriages are void unless both parties want to remain together."

Mal's brows lifted. "This is about Arianna."

"Yes," she said.

Mal looked down at her. "Jumping through minds, creating powerful Portals, and master negotiating." His hands cupped her face. "My Dread Viper."

He pressed a soft kiss to her lips before pushing off the table.

"Where are you going?"

His fingers brushed her hair behind her ear. "I won't be gone long."

"That didn't answer my question, Mal."

A soft smile played at the corner of his mouth. "I need to go alone. You need to stay here and heal."

"I am healed," she argued. "Let me accompany you."

His lips pressed down to her forehead as his hands found hers. Cold steel brushed her finger tips. He pulled away and she looked down, the Dread Dagger now in her hand. She looked up as Mal turned the corner and disappeared from sight.

Abraxas sent out the new decree with Mal's sharp signature before noon. Titus left Arianna before dinner and she moved back into Castle Morana with the twins. Arianna never brought it up to Maeve, but the smile on her sister's face as Arman met her at the foot of the stairs was satisfaction enough.

Maeve skipped training per Mal's instructions, despite her wounds being healed and her strength having returned. She helped unpacked Arianna's things, organizing them along her bookshelves.

Arianna slid a picture frame of their father between two sets of books. They stared at it in silence.

"What was it like," she asked softly, "when Arman killed Doggbind?"

Maeve looked over at her sister. She didn't meet her gaze.

"I can show you," said Maeve. "But you'll need to stay calm."

"You can always erase it if I don't want to remember it, right?" she asked.

Maeve shook her head. "I can block it, not erase it safely."

"She has flaws," said Arianna triumphantly.

Maeve rolled her eyes. "Do you want to see it?"

Arianna nodded. They took up in two armchairs facing one another. Maeve moved into her sister's mind with ease. She pulled forth the memory of Arman's betrayal of Doggbind, allowing it to meld into Arianna's own mind.

She gently slipped from her sister's memories. Arianna opened her eyes. She smiled wickedly.

They were not so different in some regards.

"What happened?" asked Maeve, crossing the threshold of The Tower of Fyren late in the night.

The windows along the west side of the foyer were shattered, all of the fires lights were burned out cold, and a Dark Magic lingered along the high ceilings.

She shivered in the freezing space and kept her gloves on.

"They don't know," said Belvadora. "Mr. Nommis says he was reading, Mrs. Nommis was upstairs asleep. Something came crashing through the windows."

"Where is he?" she asked.

"He's with Mal," she replied, pointing towards a slit of light shining down the hallway.

Maeve pressed down the hall, feeling hesitant to look up at the ceiling. She pushed open the door to the Nommis' study and stepped inside.

Mal's eyes met hers as Mr. Nommis continued speaking.

She clicked the door softly shut behind her.

Is he alright? she asked into his mind.

He's shaken up, replied Mal, *nothing more.*

Mr. Nommis turned and addressed Maeve. "I'm sorry for the disturbance Maeve," he said. "I hate to disturb you from sleep."

Maeve didn't tell him she rarely slept.

"What book were you reading?" she asked casually in an attempt to calm his nerves.

Mr. Nommis' brows pulled together. "Just something I found."

Maeve responded calmly. "You don't know what you were reading?"

Mr. Nommis shook his head, his expression almost ashamed.

"Fantasy? Fiction? Shakespeare? Cooking?" she asked.

"Vexkari," said Mr. Nommis.

Maeve's stomach plummeted. Her eyes shot to Mal.

"The only thing I know is. . .Vexkari."

Mal drew Mr. Nommis' attention back towards him. "How do you know that word?"

Mr. Nommis looked up at him and stammered. "I'm sorry, my Prince. I am not in my right mind."

Mr. Nommis' hand flew towards Maeve's throat. His fingers had barely bristled her skin when he collapsed to the floor in a loud thunk.

Maeve's hand instinctively crossed herself in protection. Her eyes shot to Mal.

"Astrea needs to assess him," said Mal. "He needs to be brought to Morana."

"He just moved to attack me, Mal," said Maeve, her voice slightly shaking. "I have known this man my entire life. He wouldn't hurt a bug in his tea."

Mal looked down at him.

He moved towards the door and entered the dark hallway. Maeve followed him, shutting the door and concealing Mr. Nommis in his unconscious state. The Bellator and Arman stood talking to Mrs. Nommis and examining the damage.

She moved towards the blown out windows.

Make them forget, Mal said into her mind.

Maeve's head whipped towards him.

"What?" she hissed.

Mal tugged her back into the darkness of the hallway.

Let me handle this how I need to, he said.

She looked up at him in the shadows. *You know exactly as I do this was not a coincidence, Mal. Something wanted him to find that book. And whatever was in it has been released. It's all over the room! I can't even bring myself to look at it.*

I know that, his voice said calmly, *but we cannot have them panicking over this. Make them forget before it gets out of control. And I will handle it all.*

Maeve ran her hands over her face and prepared to create multiple false memories and implant them one by one in the minds of everyone present.

It would be much simpler if you could alter them all at once, he said.

Maeve's throat tightened. She could. She'd done it before. She had used it shortly before Mal's coronation, to alter everyone's minds about her attacking Arianna with a deadly curse.

But Mal didn't know that. Only Reeve knew about her spell. Maeve hoped he'd forgotten the whole thing in the wake of her father's death and subsequent conflict.

Perhaps it was the feeling oozing from the Magic on the ceiling, the feeling she was being watched, that held her tongue. But in truth, Maeve had ample opportunity before then to tell Mal of her spell.

She just chose not to.

The Tower of Fyren was not the only strange occurrence in the coming weeks. Other restored Towers had similar unexplained damages and a lingering Dark Magic.

Maeve didn't argue when Mal instructed her to wipe the minds of the Sacred families living there. But the Sacred were not the only ones experiencing hostile Magic.

In The Beryl City there were reports of peculiar and unexplained disturbances as residents moved in and stores opened. Maeve erased those from memory, too. As the darkness of The Dread Lands seemed to fight him relentlessly, Mal remained confident in the path ahead of them.

Chapter 44

Maeve

Maeve.

Mal's voice rang out across her slumbering mind. Her eyes flew open as she sucked in a sharp breath. Maxius lay asleep beside her, undisturbed with even breaths. She cast a protective enchantment over him as Mal called her name once more.

Maeve pushed up out of bed and ran. She flew down the North Tower of Castle Morana, the grand spiraling staircase winding and winding down into the castle.

Mal stood in the Entrance Hall. His knees hit the stone tile and his head bowed. His Magic flickered and faded.

Maeve slid before him and grabbed his face at once, angling it up towards her. He was barely conscious.

"Mal," she said, panic flooding her voice.

He did not react. His skin, freezing against her palms, appeared drained. She rubbed her thumbs along his sharp cheekbones.

Mal, she said into his mind.

A heavy breath rose in his chest. With a gasp, his eyes opened to her.

"Hey," she said soothingly. "I'm here."

The whites of his eyes ran red. There was nothing in them but exhaustion. She had never felt his Magic so dull. She continued to stroke his face and pretend to be calm.

He needed her to be strong. And for him, she would be. But her insides were slipping further and further into fear.

"Have you called for Astrea?" she asked quickly.

He gave a small nod, and his eyes closed once more.

His body fell towards her, collapsing completely against her.

She supported him, cradling his head against her. Her heartbeat skyrocketed.

He was breathing.

He was alive.

But he was hurting. And she could feel it all. He was not slumbering. His body tensed and jerked in her arms. His face twisted in agony.

She slipped into his mind with ease.

Damnit, Mal, she whispered into his thoughts. *You cannot do this to yourself. Your shields are completely gone. Anyone can access your mind with such vulnerability.*

There came no reply. His mind lay blank.

She pressed further, searching for some indication of what caused him to be so paralyzed. There was nothing of his travels that night. No sign of anything past the gates of Castle Morana in the hours prior.

There was nothing but darkness, even then.

Maeve pulled from his mind. She held him tighter, placing her lips on his forehead.

"Please," she said softly. "I cannot lose you. Please let me help you fight this darkness. I never intended for you to carry this burden alone."

A dim flickering of light grew brighter from the West corridor. A moment later, Abraxas appeared. His silver-blond hair was perfect despite the late hour. His deep emerald robe shimmered against the candlelight in his outstretched arm as he crossed towards them.

"Is he alright, cousin?" he asked, kneeling beside her and examining Mal keenly.

Maeve nodded, her head still pressed against the top of his. "You have to talk sense into him, Brax."

Abraxas' face saddened.

"He won't listen to me," she continued.

"He wants to protect you, Maeve," said Abraxas gently.

"And who is protecting him?" she fired back. "How are we supposed to accept this new world if it tears him apart to get it?"

Abraxas placed his hand along her arm in sympathy. "I know, Maeve. I will do better as the Hand. I promise."

The Entrance Hall doors creaked open, sending pale green light across the dark hall. Astrea stepped inside without hesitation and briskly walked towards them, her robe trailing behind her.

Maeve pulled Mal tighter against her chest.

Astrea's eyes closed in frustration as a lengthy exhale blew from her lips. Mal lay on his chamber bed, still tormented by the Magic keeping him unconscious.

"If you can't do it just say so," said Maeve.

Astrea's hand tensed and her eyes opened, but she did not look at Maeve. She looked at Abraxas.

"Astrea," said Abraxas. "There is no shame in needing assistance. Call upon your mother."

Astrea didn't argue. She nodded at Abraxas and left the room without so much as a glance at Maeve.

Maeve's eyes never left Mal in the time it took Astrea to get to The Towers and wake her mother, Irma. She brushed her fingers along his cheek, softly petting his raven hair. Her chest caught each time his face contorted in pain.

Irma arrived, and Maeve watched her fail at waking their Dread Prince.

"This is dark," said Irma with a small shiver as she removed her healing hands from him. "Far darker than Magic I would care to know."

Alphard and Astrea's mother shook her fingers out and looked at Maeve.

"You should see for yourself," she said.

"I can feel it," said Maeve as she looked back over Mal.

Irma nodded. "Like calls to like."

Maeve took Mal's hand in her own. "Perhaps I can try."

"I'm not certain that's wise," said Abraxas tensely.

"On the contrary," began Irma, "I believe the Magic will respond well to Maeve's commands."

"Why?" questioned Abraxas.

Irma responded, "They are bonded."

"When I looked into his mind," began Maeve, "there was only darkness. Less than darkness. There was nothing but a feeling of. . .dread."

Irma nodded. "Call it to you. That thing which you feel that sits dark and deep in him, that which is keeping him closed from us, call it."

Maeve held Mal's hand tighter and shifted forward beside him. She took his Dread Locket in her other hand and closed her eyes.

His chambers vanished along with Abraxas' argumentative voice, and she was in his mind once more. The darkness held not even a glimmer of refraction.

She felt that darkness swell around her, feeling out her presence. She was not welcome there.

Mal, she called across his mind.

Something stirred for a brief moment, a glimpse of his Magic reached towards her.

Maeve, his voice distorted by another, called back.

She felt that sinister darkness slither around her.

Come to me, Mal, she called again, sending more of her Magic out.

He responded stronger, surging towards her. The darkness in his mind slashed out, severing the bond between her Magic and Mal's.

Maeve struck without thinking, allowing her anger and desire to protect Mal surge through her. Her Magic choked the darkness, which shattered instantly.

Light flooded the void around her. Images of Mal's past few hours flew through her mind, too fast to understand or comprehend. But she knew one thing: he was putting himself in too much danger.

And the darkness she severed was but a fraction of what he would need to take on to fully vanquish the blight in the land.

The floor beneath her grew soft, as Mal's strength surged to life. She pulled from his mind, spiraling back towards his chambers at Castle Morana.

He was awake, sitting upright, and breathing heavily with both his hands on her face. The whites of his eyes slowly returned, and his skin flushed with color.

Irma and Astrea stood on the other side of the bed. Abraxas kept his distance.

"You're alright," said Maeve, reassuringly.

His eyes scanned over her face, down her shaking body and back up at her eyes.

"Are you?" he asked with desperation.

She nodded in his grip. "I am now."

She pushed forward and wrapped her arms around his neck. His hands slid around her as she cried, "You cannot carry this burden alone."

He stroked the back of her head. "I cannot bear to see you take it."

Maeve held him tightly, her breaths stuck in her chest.

"Breathe," he said softly. "I am here."

They held one another silently. Irma spoke gently a moment later.

"I am sorry, my Prince. I could not wake you. It was I who encouraged her to try."

Mal didn't move. "It's alright, Irma," he said softly.

Maeve clung to him, relishing the steady breaths in his chest, intoxicated by his returned Magic. Mal did not move her.

"It's late," he said. "Thank you Irma. And you Astrea, for your devotion."

Abraxas repeated Mal's thanks as they left the room.

"My Prince," said Abraxas, with his fist over his heart. His footsteps receded as the door shut behind him.

"Maeve," said Mal smoothly.

She shook and lifted her head. "What is that thing?"

"What thing?"

"That thing in your mind. I've felt it before. I know it."

"Please, Maeve," he said weakly. "I don't want a lecture. Just let me hold you and-"

"No," she fired back. "No. I thought I was going to lose you."

"But you didn't."

"Not this time. But are you going to stop?"

Mal did not answer.

"You cannot bear for me to carry the burden, and I cannot bear to lose you for it."

"You are not going to lose me. There is Magic on our side. It is prophesied that I will restore these lands. It is written in Magic across us both that I will die before you. I swore it." He stroked her face. "I will not die in this battle. I can feel it."

Maeve ran her hands over his. "There are worse fates than death."

Mal didn't reply further. He pulled her close, and she accepted his affection without argument.

Chapter 45

Maeve

Arman danced Arianna slowly across the Ballroom floor. Her head rested against his chest with her eyes closed in peaceful bliss. The handsome Captain brought her hand to his lips, kissing them tenderly as they swayed.

"I still can't believe you thought you knew about them before me."

Abraxas appeared at her side. A cigar in one hand and a glass in the other.

Maeve smiled weakly. "At least you didn't have to walk in on them."

"How do you think I found out?" he muttered.

Maeve struggled to return his enjoyment.

"Cheer up, cousin," he said. "He's only been gone a few weeks. Look at Zimsy, having the time of her life dancing with that Bellator."

Maeve followed his gaze across the hall. Zimsy spun in a silver gown, smiling and laughing with a Supreme.

"She's so beautiful," said Maeve. "Sometimes I wonder how anyone could have ever desired to hurt her."

"Envy is an evil emotion," replied Abraxas.

Maeve often wondered how her beautiful friend came to be under an Enslavement Curse from a young age. There was no record of her being born on Earth, and she had served in many households in her earliest memories. There was nothing Maeve found in her mind that indicated a family that she was stolen from, or was sold from.

To which Zimsy took her hand and said, "You are my family."

Abraxas opened his mouth to speak, but Maeve stopped him.

"Just let me be frustrated, Brax." She looked over at him in appreciation. "Go enjoy yourself."

Abraxas flicked under her chin with a sympathetic smile, forcing her face up. He kissed her cheek swiftly. "Some good news, then, to brighten your night."

Maeve's brows raised.

"Lithandrian is coming here at last. She accepted Mal's invitation and will be here in a fortnight."

Maeve mustered the best smile she could for her cousin. "Can I leave soon?" she asked as he slipped away.

Abraxas turned back towards her. "Of course, cousin," he said with a fading smile. "You are not a prisoner here. If you wish to retire, I will not stop you."

"I'm just not certain how much longer I can pretend at these parties."

Abraxas stepped back towards her as cheers of excitement and welcome erupted through the hall. Their heads turned in unison as Reeve entered with a dazzling smile.

"He only comes here for the praise," muttered Maeve.

Abraxas smirked at her. "Weren't you going to bed?"

She narrowed her eyes at him and crossed the hall. Reeve's eyes slid to her as he crossed to the bar. Maeve stepped in his direction.

"Uh-uh," said Abraxas, stepping in front of her. "We have a plan, remember?"

"Ismail can still fawn over him once I've finished talking to him," she replied, stepping forward once more.

Abraxas countered. "Alright, fine," he said with a huff. "But don't get him all worked up. If you put him in a foul mood I worry he won't desire to. . .entertain Ismail."

"That's your plan?" asked Maeve dryly. "You think he'll fuck her?"

Abraxas opened his mouth but Maeve cut him off once more.

"Absolutely not," she said. "She didn't agree to that, she couldn't agree to that. She doesn't even have a choice in being here and we whore her out–"

"Seven Realms, shut up, cousin," snapped Abraxas. "How insulting. I merely meant she is going to speak to him and try to sense the Dread Stone. If something else happens or he fancies her, so be it.

But I did not command her to use her body for our gain, and to be quite honest, it's infuriating that you think I would ever do that to another. I'm uncertain if it's Mal's absence, Reeve's presence, or a combination of the two that makes you so irritable, but do not take it out on me."

Abraxas downed his drink and walked away, ignoring her call after him. Moments later, he was smiling and taking a round of shots with Alphard and Juliet. Victoria hung on Alphard's arm, already intoxicated and unable to drink more.

Maeve turned her attention back on Reeve, guilt swimming in her stomach. She'd use that guilt. It drove her every footstep towards Reeve where he leaned against the long bar.

She arrived at his side and Reeve looked her over.

"My, my, someone is in a mood," he said. "If you've come to spoil mine, I must ask that you withhold your endless questions."

"I only have one question where you are concerned that keeps me awake," she said hotly.

Reeve turned towards her. "Tell me more of how I occupy your mind on sleepless nights, kitten."

A breath of hatred rose through her. His satisfaction only grew.

"'Art thou afeard to be the same in thine own act and valor as thou art in desire?'" he asked. Reeve scanned her face. "Is she your favorite?"

Maeve raised her brows.

Reeve answered. "Lady Macbeth."

Maeve shook her head. "Always ready with a joke."

"She's rather fitting for you, don't you think?"

"You're the one who has resorted to using Shakespeare to distract me from my disdain for you."

"Is it me you disdain this week? Frankly, I can't keep up."

Maeve let loose a very shaky sigh as she scowled at him, at how easily he mocked her.

"Mm," he hummed. "Where is the Dread Prince this evening?"

"Don't pry, Reeve," said Maeve boredly. "It makes you look weak."

He laughed. "And you sniffing around me for months, desperate to find even a hint of who my Inheritor is, certainly makes you look strong."

Maeve spoke plainly, tired of the games. "Do you know who it is?"

Reeve watched her carefully for a moment. "No," he said finally.

A deception or truth she did not know. She no longer cared. The question was on the tip of her tongue. The one she so desperately wanted to ask him. The one Mal had forbidden her from asking.

Maeve looked back at the party. "I figured not."

Reeve took a swig of his drink. "I'm so curious, why do you think I don't know?"

"Because my father told me the Inheritor is a cruel Magic. One that delivers its presence in a crucial moment. I don't think you know who it is, because I don't think it's reached that moment. It's all barreling towards us still."

They held one another's gaze for a long moment.

"Where is Malachite, Maeve?" he asked.

"Someplace far from my protection," she replied. She swallowed and shook her head. "This is meaningless. It's all meaningless."

She left the Ballroom without apologizing for her abrupt departure.

Reeve followed her further into the castle. She felt each step of Magic towards her, hot on her heels.

"Goodnight, Reeve," she said dismissively, not bothering to look back at him.

"What is it that eats at you and yet will not slip from your tongue?"

Maeve shook her head, continuing towards the stairs.

"Maeve," he called after her with far too much concern in his voice.

"Did you know?" she asked, whipping towards him.

He stopped and took her in. His brows pulled together. "What?"

"Did you know that the goblet was poisoned?"

Reeve's chest fell. His face softened. "Maeve."

"Answer the fucking question," she hissed. "The question I have not been allowed to ask so Mal can assess if you are an enemy on his own terms. But I fear you already are *my* enemy."

Reeve's lip curled. "I had no way of knowing that goblet was still poisoned."

"So you admit you poisoned it to begin with?" she said, her blood turning hot.

"I poisoned the wine within the goblet," he relented, his voice growing frustrated. "How was I to know it would remain for hundreds of years?"

Maeve laughed in disbelief. It was hollow and empty. She scowled at him.

"Who could you have possibly been trying to kill with such lethal Magic?"

"Shadow!" Dark violet fire flared behind him in the shape of two wings. His hands wrapped in vines of pale flaming Magic.

Maeve stepped back from him.

He tilted his head back and rolled his neck. A lengthy few breaths later, and his eyes landed back on her. All flames gone.

His face moved like he was going to speak, but his lips curled in agony. With a soft growl, his breathing returned to normal.

"He was my friend. You think if I had known, I wouldn't have shattered that goblet with a blink?"

"And had it been in Mal's hands? What then?"

Reeve's face hardened. "It was not meant to kill the Dread."

"That's not an answer," she fired.

Reeve shook his head. "Your desire to paint me a villain is exhausting."

"Imagine how I feel. When the list keeps getting longer of those I cannot trust. Those who knowingly and unknowingly laid his death brick by brick."

Reeve scowled at her. "You blame me for the poison and not your Prince's inability to see how deadly it was in his hands? Has it even crossed your mind that he did, in fact,–"

"Enough!"

Electric Magic raced down her arm. Lightning swirled at her clenched fist. Reeve's eyes dropped to her hand as she shook.

"You think you know everything just because you're three

hundred years old."

"Three hundred twenty-six, thank you. And yes, one learns a thing or two over a couple centuries. Your mere existence is a blink to me."

"A blink?" She laughed. "You seem awfully obsessed with a blink."

"The blink is a pain in my ass. The blink has toppled governments I was allied with and killed many in her mere twenty and some years, so you can call it an obsession, but it is one that has been forced upon me."

"It was not my Magic that poisoned him. You forced your way into my world the moment you laced that goblet three hundred years ago."

His jaw loosened. His arrogant smile returned, and he returned to the party with a casual stride.

Chapter 46

Maeve

Maeve stepped into the Healing Chambers. Astrea stood over Mal, who lay collapsed in a chair and barely conscious. Astrea healed deep wounds that ran across his chest, self-inflicted marks of sacrifice that resonated with Dark Magic.

Maeve remained at a distance and watched as the blood vanished and the wounds slowly shrunk.

"Maeve," said Astrea, realizing she was there.

Other heads looked towards her. She didn't grant them the satisfaction of returning their speculative and curious gazes.

Mal was in worse condition than the last time. And the time before that. And by the look on Astrea's face, she knew it too.

Maeve strode towards him, her robes flowing behind her across the chamber. She met Astrea's face of concern before taking his face in her hands.

"What are you doing?" asked Mumford. He stepped forward, but Maeve ignored his guard dog mannerism.

Mal's conscience lurked just beneath the surface.

Her hands fell to her sides.

"Were you with him?" she asked Mumford.

He hesitated and then shook his head.

"I thought I told you to stay by him–" she started.

Mumford scowled. "He insisted on going alone. You seem to have forgotten his word supersedes your own."

Astrea dropped her hands. Mal's chest wounds were closed, and she had stopped the bleeding, but the skin remained marked.

She stood and stepped away, holding her arms tensely.

"I'm sorry, Maeve," she whispered. "They'll scar."

Maeve looked down at Mal's scarred torso, and her fingers lingered across his chest. "What is one more?" she muttered.

Maeve took in his mind and his latest excursion replayed in flashes. A shadowed cave. An ancient altar. A voice that whispered in a foreign tongue.

She pressed deeper into his mind as a doorway slipped open. A small movement brushed her leg. A misty hallway came into view. Old wooden floors and ample sunlight. A very young Maeve Sinclair walked by. She couldn't have been much older than ten. She pushed open a door as the scene changed.

A small room shifted into view. There was one tiny bed, and a desk covered with public library books, all Human stories of Magic and Mythology. Maeve's younger self hopped on the rickety bed and tucked her legs beneath her, facing a boy her same age.

Mal's handsome features were prominent even as a child. His eyes sparkled up at the young Maeve as they discussed the book before them in hushed voices.

You are not the only one who slips away to alternate realities in your mind, Mal's voice rang across the small space.

He allowed her to view the made up memory for a moment more, then darkness fell around her. Before her stomach could plummet from the sensation of Mal pushing her from his mind, she withdrew.

In a blink, she returned to the Healing Chambers. Mal's eyes were open, but completely glossed over in dark emerald swirls.

"Mal," said Maeve, calmly.

The whites of his eyes flooded with their proper color. Astrea stepped back from him. Maeve remained at his side, cupping his cheek.

With strained breath, he looked down at his chest.

"Your wounds are healed," said Astrea.

Mal nodded and thanked her with a small voice. She took her leave as Mumford stood and addressed him.

"You are alright, my Prince?" asked Mumford.

"Yes," replied Mal. He would not meet Maeve's eyes as she stared at him. "Leave us, Mumford."

Mumford didn't dare disobey a direct command.

As the door clicked shut behind him. Mal finally looked up at Maeve.

"What else did you see?"

"Nothing I understood."

His Magic pressed against her own mind. She allowed him to verify what she said to be true.

Mal leaned back in the chair with a weary sigh and ran his finger through his hair.

"Spit it out," he said.

"We have had this conversation many times."

"I said speak—"

"I do not think it is a good idea to continue down this road," said Maeve coolly.

"It is not for you to decide," sighed Mal.

His face and hands were as pale as Maeve had ever seen them. Soft green flecks of light remained in his dark eyes.

"You should rest," said Maeve.

"Not in an argumentative mood?"

Maeve didn't return his smirk. His face dropped.

"I don't need you to protect me," he said.

Maeve disagreed completely. "Get some rest," was all she said.

The tea Grandmother Agatha made was too hot to drink. Maeve stared at it as steam lifted from the dark brown liquid. Aunt Beatrice laid out the pastries and fruit Zimsy prepared. Arianna chattered endlessly about Arman. Abraxas teased her lightheartedly, but Maeve's sister was on too high of a cloud to even care about their cousin's crass jokes.

"Abraxas," said his mother, scolding him.

Abraxas shrugged with a smirk. "I am allowed a few, mother."

Anselm sat on his lap, while Aislin sat on Maeve's. They were growing quickly, and would forever be known as the first babies born in The Dread Lands in three hundred years.

Maxius played with Spinel around and under the table, knocking his head repeatedly. But he never seemed bothered.

Grandmother Agatha's chateau sat just outside The Beryl City, tucked on the edge of the Greywood. The house was Maeve's favorite of the old mansions. Pale pastels of spring decorated the rooms filled with plant life, creating a welcome juxtaposition to the darkening green twilight of the land.

"I suppose I do have some news, though," said Abraxas. He looked across the table at his mother and smiled, bouncing Anselm on his knee.

Beatrice sat her teacup down at once. "Don't toy with me, Abraxas Flint Rosethorn."

He smiled joyfully at his mother's rush of emotions.

"No toying, mother," he said softly. "Juliet is with child."

Beatrice squealed and made Agatha jump and spill some of her tea. The old Witch scowled at Beatrice. With a snap of her fingers the mess was gone. Beatrice rounded the table and threw her arms around Abraxas' neck, kissing the side of his face enthusiastically.

"That's wonderful, Brax," said Maeve as her cousin beamed and accepted his mother's affection.

"So these little ones will have a new friend soon enough," he said.

"Why isn't she here," asked Beatrice suddenly. "Is she alright?"

"Yes, mother," said Abraxas waving a hand at her, "she's fine. Spending the day with Astrea preparing their minds for motherhood and birth."

Maeve looked down at Spinel and Maxius on the rug. Maxius signing to the cat. Spinel observed him intently.

Mal worked with Maxius, when he was at Castle Morana, trying to draw some Magic from the boy. Maeve encouraged him as well, but not a single spark or flicker of power came from him.

Spinel's wide set eyes looked up at Maeve and Maxius' bright green ones landed on her as well.

Magic shot up her spine and down her arms.

The image came in a flash of white, but it was painfully there all the same.

Maxius was much smaller in the vision in her mind. His tiny hands reached towards her, gripping the fabric of her cloak as massive tears streamed his delicate face. The tall, hooded figure before her took him in their arms.

The image vanished, and Grandmother Agatha's tearoom returned to her vision. Maxius now stood beside her, with his head in her lap looking up at Aislin. She reached for his face and he smiled.

Arianna returned to talking about Arman, the corners of her mouth pulling up with every word. She played with her Sinclair family ring, the match to Maeve's, and spoke of another ring that was perhaps in her future.

Chapter 47

Maeve

The Elven Queen's presence in The Dread Lands was Abraxas' greatest achievement so far as Hand to the Prince. And she was not the only realm in attendance for a feast at Castle Morana. King Kier from Hiems brought his family and court, and Reeve never missed an opportunity to be the most powerful in the room.

Mal hooked a finger under Maeve's chin where they stood outside the door to Abraxas' study. "Best behavior. No outbursts. The three of them must kneel." He smiled softly. "And you make Lithandrian jumpy."

Maeve looked up at him. His eyes were completely natural save for a few small flecks of green that peeked through their deep hazel color.

Maeve relaxed into his hold. "Perhaps they should know when to jump."

Mal chuckled. "They do. But I need them enthralled for this to work. Not afraid. Magic is cunning, and I need them all to believe what I am selling them."

Maeve gestured towards the door. "After you, my Prince."

Mal's eyes slid to her bottom lip and he flicked his wrist in the air, opening the door to the study with ease.

Abraxas beamed at their entrance. "There they are."

Lithandrian, Kier, and Reeve sat with Abraxas at a small circular table. Mordred sat on his hind legs near Kier. Drystan was to Reeve's side, and an unfamiliar woman sat next to Lithandrian. Behind them, nearly filling Abraxas' study, were dozens of Elven soldiers.

Lithandrian stood gracefully with a smile. "Apologies, Dread Prince," she said. "They insisted on escorting their Queen."

Her gold and white hair spiraled down her shoulders in tight ringlets. A dainty silver tiara sat atop her head. Silken fabric draped from her sleeves and pooled at the floor.

"No need for apologies," said Mal with a humble smile.

"Yes," chimed Abraxas, "we are beyond ecstatic you are here."

Lithandrian laughed lightly as she took her seat. Her eyes landed on Maeve. "I trust you received my letters of regret for your father?"

Maeve's hand lingered on the back of the chair to Mal's right as she paused before taking her seat. "I did. Thank you."

"Oh," said Lithandrian. "I did not receive a reply."

"Mail travel between realms is quite tricky," said Abraxas. "If she didn't use my mother's jay, there's a chance the letters got lost."

Abraxas looked over at Maeve, a soft expectancy in his eyes. Her eyes lifted to Mal.

Best behavior, remember?

Maeve relaxed in her chair and bit her tongue. "I must not have. How foolish of me. Apologies."

Lithandrian seemed pleased, despite the obvious lie. She gestured to the woman beside her. Gold and silver jewels hung from her pointed ears, peeking out from behind straight dark hair.

"This is Evelina, Hand to the Queen."

"A pleasure," said Mal.

No one mentioned Xander, for that Maeve was grateful. Mal turned his attention to Reeve.

"Where is Eryx?" Mal asked Reeve casually.

"Downstairs, I'm sure," he said without concern. "Drinking. Eating. Dancing with Zimsy."

Maeve's eyes shot to him. He winked at her quickly. Maeve opened her mouth but Kier spoke first.

"An honor to be here, as always," he said, fawning at Mal between each word.

Mal smiled and turned to Abraxas.

"Shall we?" asked Mal.

Abraxas nodded.

Mal raised his hand, palm flat, and stretched it across the table. In one single motion, black mist slithered from the wooden tabletop beneath his hand. Sparkling like the night sky, the mist parted, and on the table sat three rings.

"Tokens of gratitude for your willingness to be here and work towards a better future," said Mal.

Each ring was uniquely different, one much more feminine than the others. All three screamed at Maeve. They were Mal's Magic. They were Vexkari.

"The Dread Prince has placed his own Magic in these rings," continued Abraxas, "and they are yours to use to advance your kingdoms and lives as you see fit."

Kier pushed to the edge of his seat with gleaming eyes. Lithandrian's dainty lips parted and her expression softened.

Reeve didn't look at the rings. He was relaxed in his chair, lazily looking at Mal.

Kier looked up at Mal. "You honor me once more."

Mal smiled. "You are worth honoring." He gestured towards the ring closest to Kier, one with an icy white band.

Kier grabbed the ring lustfully. He ran his fingers over the band. "Hiems hasn't seen new Magic in centuries."

Mal smiled. "Now you shall."

Kier slipped the ring on his hand, settling back into his chair with flushed cheeks.

Mal's attention turned to Lithandrian. "And how long has it been since the Elven Lands possessed such a power?"

Her glassy eyes looked up at Mal. She smiled and took a steadying breath. "Many moons."

Abraxas spoke. "There is more the Crown wishes to offer our friends from other kingdoms."

"I would hope so," said Lithandrian coyly. "I did not agree to come to gain Magic for myself alone."

Mal smiled diplomatically at her. "I know."

Lithandrian reached forward, her delicate fingers circled the thin band of Magic where it lay. A deep breath rose in her chest. "I want bloodlines."

"And bloodlines you shall have," replied Mal coolly.

Her gaze lifted to Mal, and then to Abraxas.

"My brother came to you desiring the same in my name."

Abraxas opened his mouth to speak but Mal held up his hand. They both looked at him.

"What your brother desired was never, and shall never, be on the table."

Lithandrian's hand rested delicately on the ring, though she did not pick it up. "I am aware he was too bold."

"That doesn't mean we don't have other options," said Abraxas. "There are many Magicals that are joyous at the prospect of a future in the Elven Lands and on Hiems."

Lithandrian's finger continued to circle the ring. "You want open borders?"

"Not necessarily," said Abraxas. "We want communication. We want regulated Portals between our realms. We want all four of us to flourish."

"With this Magic, Lithandrian," said Mal, "your people could even one day attend Vaukore. Magic blended seamlessly between realms that we all benefit from."

"What do you get out of it?" asked Evelina.

Mal looked at the Elven Queen's hand. "We too get bloodlines. Some of the strongest Senshi and Bellator are part Elven," he said, referring to Eryx and Larliesl. "We want to thrive here. Not merely survive."

Lithandrian lifted the ring off the table and admired it more. She smiled across the table at Mal. She dipped her head in admiration and held the ring in her lap, but she did not slip it on her finger.

"You are quiet, High Lord," said Mal at last. "Is my gift not enough for the one kissed by the Gods?"

Reeve smirked. With a slow inhale, he pressed forward and grabbed the ring meant for him. It was a dark band with pale markings. He passed it between each hand casually.

"Quite impressive Magic," said Reeve. "Even I do not understand the creation of Vexkari, and I am scarred with it."

Mal smirked in satisfaction. "You accept it so easily? When I know it is not a drop compared to your own Magic, nor that of your Senshi Warriors."

Reeve looked at Mal at last. Magic pulled tight and tense between them. "The gesture is a gracious one. I do not overlook it."

Maeve knew that ring would never sit on Reeve's finger. She had a suspicion that Mal knew as well. But they were all wrapped in a game of crowns and tricks, and everyone held their cards close.

Mal sat at the head of the long table made of deep emerald marble. Lithandrian and her husband sat to his one side, and Maeve on the other.

"I have never traveled to Hiems," said Lithandrian as Kier boasted his ideas for Hiems now that he had been offered even a slice of Mal's power.

"You'll need to wear more than that," laughed Kier, gesturing to the thin gown of fine fabric she wore. "Won't she, Maeve?"

Maeve looked over at Lithandrian and said dryly. "He's explaining to you that the ice planet is cold."

Lithandrian smiled at her, with what felt like a genuine understanding, for the first time.

"The last time Maeve visited us, she was freezing!" Kier continued, blissfully unaware of anything but his own joy. "She was shivering in that fitted bodice."

Mal's cool demeanor slipped for a moment as his eyes narrowed at Kier.

Best behavior, Maeve said into his mind.

His eyes snapped to hers as the corner of his mouth pulled up.

Next to her, Abraxas laughed and with a snap of his fingers, the empty bottles before them vanished and more liquor appeared on the table. Eryx poured two glasses. Maeve's chest rose as he extended one to the beauty across from him.

Zimsy.

She took it from him with her head cocked to the side playfully. Eryx pressed the rim of his glass against hers as they toasted one another.

Maeve leaned forward with her mouth agape and looked down, realizing Zimsy's little secret. Reeve's head moved forward, blocking her view.

He smiled at her in triumph. Maeve leaned over Abraxas, who sat between them, and hissed at Reeve. "Why is it you knew about my best friend's little flirtation and I didn't?"

Abraxas choked on his drink, nearly spitting on Maeve. Both Maeve and Reeve recoiled as he stared at Maeve, fully offended.

"I'm not your best friend?" asked Abraxas.

Maeve rolled her eyes and turned her attention back to Eryx and Zimsy a few seats down. Neither of them paid her any mind. Maeve smiled softly at the delight spread across Zimsy's face.

Abraxas huffed and poured himself another drink. Maeve looked back at Mal. Lithandrian's cheeks were flushed. Maeve's smile faded as Mal's Magic swirled around the Elven Queen.

Lithandrian's eyes glazed over as they locked on Mal, adoring his every small mannerism as he spoke to her softly.

She held forth her hand, pleased with his attention. His eyes never left hers as he slid the delicate silver ring onto her finger. Lithandrian's eyes fluttered to a close beneath the power of Mal's Magic flowing through her.

Maeve felt foolish as she watched his charming smile grow as his Magic settled around the Elven Queen. Mal's Pathokenesis abilities went unnoticed by all those around them as the light chatter and clinking of crystal echoed down the table.

Lithandrian's eyes opened and she looked down at the elegant band of Magic. She held her hand across her heart, with a small sigh of gratitude.

"An easy pledge to make," said Lithandrian. She raised her goblet gracefully. All followed suit without question or pause.

Mal's attention was on his newest ally, and so Maeve dared to glance down the table at Reeve. His eyes found hers briefly.

"To the Dread Prince," continued Lithandrian, "and to a new

world of Magic."

Reeve raised his goblet, his own gifted ring nowhere in sight.

Chapter 48

Maeve

"You promised not to use your Pathokenesis abilities on me, I will remind you," Maeve said as they walked the gardens at Castle Morana.

Mal eyed her. "I didn't merely promise it," he corrected her. "I swore it. In Magic."

A patter of footsteps drew their attention towards the castle.

Maxius bounded down the garden path, Zimsy close behind him.

"Lithandrian folded so easily beneath that Magic," said Mal quietly.

Maxius reached for Mal with eager arms long before he arrived between them. Mal kneeled and scooped him up. Maeve nodded at Zimsy, and she retreated into the castle. Spinel jumped high on a stone wall and surveyed them from above.

"Perhaps if I cannot convince you to stay, he can," said Maeve softly. "You are his favorite."

Mal looked from Maxius to her. He smiled. The small flecks of green in his eyes had vanished. "There is nothing that can stop me from perpetuating the future I see for us here."

Maeve opened her mouth as Mal's slender finger slipped over it.

He looked down at her. "I think I made up for my absence this morning, did I not? Or have you grown so insatiable—"

Maeve's eyes widened and she gripped his arm, hushing him.

Maxius was blissfully unaware of their conversation, reaching for a dying hydrangea in Mal's arm.

"That's what I thought," said Mal, his mouth hanging open.

Maeve playfully batted his hand away, but Mal swiftly took her chin in it once more. He pulled her to the tips of her toes and tipped her forward. His mouth consumed hers. Her stomach tightened at once, drawing up a deep inhale.

Maxius leaned further over Mal's shoulder towards the decaying blooms when Mal pulled his lips away and Maeve's eyes fluttered open. His grip on her chin remained.

"Maxius," said Mal.

The child slid back down into Mal's arm, his green eyes fixed on Mal.

"Are you going to practice your Magic while I am away?"

Maxius nodded.

Spinel jumped from the ledge and rubbed against Maeve's ankles, drawing Maxius' attention down. He pushed gently against Mal, a silent request to be set down. Mal placed him between them, and Maxius squatted down and reached for Spinel.

Together they looked at the mysterious child, and wondered if the Magic in him would ever manifest. Mal's Magic brushed under her chin, tugging her forward onto the balls of her feet.

His lips pressed into hers in an effortless kiss.

Mal,
I feel so far from you. I wish you would come home.

Her words remained on the enchanted piece of parchment they shared. They did not vanish. She marked the days he had been gone each night at midnight. Her marks piled up on the parchment before they disappeared and a single mark of his appeared.

Again and again her parchment filled up with marks, until she resorted to using both sides. Time at Castle Morana and beyond The Barrier grew farther and farther apart.

Maeve's nightmares and strange visions multiplied. She no longer slept in The Crown's Quarters. The gaunt, albino woman with long white hair found her nonetheless. She no longer relied on slumber and dreams to find Maeve.

She was often in the reflection of Maeve's breakfast tea. She was in the eyes of the Bellator she trained with. Maeve began a journal with her sightings. The ghostly figure never spoke. She watched her from the shadows with an ominous gaze.

And she never appeared around Maxius.

And, much to Maeve's dismay, she did not appear when Maeve took off the Dread Artifacts. It pained her to leave Mal's Dread Ring on her vanity, her Magic felt cold without it. But it was the only path to a peaceful sleep or afternoon Maeve could find.

At last, Mal's reply came, vanishing her one desperate plea for him to return to her.

How is Maxius?

Maeve stared at the words, fighting the selfish anger that rose through her.

Gone more often than not. For the sake of Magicals. Subjecting himself to horrors she knew not. While she spent most of her time lost in false memories of the world she longed to be in.

More words appeared in his elegant handwriting.

I imagine he is growing quickly at this age.

Everyday, she wrote back.

Her words vanished. A moment passed and Mal did not reply.

Are you alright? she wrote.

Yes.

Maeve swallowed hard as his single word faded.

Please Mal.

No reply came. The parchment lay blank. Maeve scribbled with a shaking hand.

Come home. Please.

The words did not vanish. He did not read them.

. . .

This place is foreign. It feels like a void. Come home and breathe life into it.

. . .

Maxius asks about you. At least, I think that's what he is signing. He is so fond of you. He still hasn't used Magic. I imagine if you worked with him, he could.

. . .

Darkness attacked The Beryl City. The shops are destroyed and the cafes lay in ruin. I wiped their minds. The Bellator are working to restore things.

. . .

I visited the unoccupied parts of the city today. Hundreds of shops and cafes. Their doors lay open. Window signs and paintings cracked and devoid of color. Their gilded and golden archways covered in decay. Viney thorns cover nearly every inch of stone, winding their way across bridges and sculptures. Some of the thresholds bear a lingering Magic, what I imagine was the last attempt of its inhabitants to fight off the blight.

The fountains are dry.

The flower beds, nothing but grey ash.

The sky remains dark.

I miss the bright blue sky on Earth. With giant white clouds gliding across it.

I miss the sound of the water crashing against the shoreline.

I miss the gardens. Your hydrangea are dead.

I miss the constellations and the moon.

I can't even see the moons here most days. There is only the same misty haze that has been lingering across these lands since the first time you brought me here.

In the city, there is what was once a tea shop. Inside there are two tall backed, oversized chairs by the remains of a black brick fire.

I wish it was restored to its former glory.

And I wish we were seated there. Perhaps reading, or recalling our day apart.

. . .

I'm running out of space. You made the parchment too small.

. . .

If you don't return soon, Mal, I am afraid I might break.

Chapter 40

Maeve

Maeve stared at the parchment crammed with her tiny words. It lay across a white marble table in Esmarelle's tea shop. Her words all vanished at once and a short reply scrolled across the pale paper.

Where are you?

She left Mal's ring and locket at Castle Morana when she Portaled to Earth.

His words disappeared as she read them. When she did not reply he wrote her once more.

Do not make me come find you.

Moments later, she stepped through her Portal and crossed the Entrance Hall of Castle Morana. Larliesl's and Arman's strength training had paid off. She barely felt a wobble as she closed it behind her.

She stepped into the Throne Room. Roswyn, Arman, and many of the Bellator gathered there.

Mal's eyes snapped to her. Roswyn stopped speaking at once.

Mal's voice was low. "Where have you been?"

"Earth," said Maeve happily, clapping her hands together.

A tight tension shifted through the hall. They all knew she had broken a rule. Mumford and Roswyn exchanged a glance.

"Leave us," Mal commanded.

All obeyed quickly. Mal stared at her in silence until the hall doors clicking closed echoed across the open archways. His eyes gleamed with faint spots of green.

She hated that green.

"I forbade you from going there, Maeve. I forbade all Earth travel. Do you not remember what happened last time you were on Earth?"

"I suppose it worked, though," she said.

Mal raised a brow.

"Here you are," she answered. "If I had known all it took was going to Earth I would have done it months ago."

The word "months" should have mattered to him. But he merely frowned.

"Here we are once more," she said. "My patience has all but diminished."

"What could you possibly desire there?"

"For fuck's sake Mal," she raised her voice. "The Cliffside in Scotland where I was raised!"

His eyes did not soften. He shook his head as though she was tricking him.

"Gardens, tea shops, parks of white stone statues surrounded by green life and color. Fucking color. Does the sun rise here? Ever? Or am I waiting on the impossible?"

"You have more power here than you ever did on Earth," he retorted.

"And I am lonely."

"You have your sister and Abraxas, teaching Maxius–"

"They are not you!"

Mal turned from her and rolled his neck.

"Things are different, you know they are," she pressed.

Mal didn't look at her. "I am The Dread Prince. You expect me to stay the same boy you met in school. But to be what I am, to give you all that I am, requires adaptation. The Dread Power was not meant for a mere Magical."

"Yes, but I didn't fall in love with a Prince. I fell in love with you."

Mal's eyes snapped to her, and she fell silent.

"You think it is not love that drives me to do this?"

Under the weight of his gaze, she couldn't find the courage to answer.

They stood silently until Mal finally spoke once more. "You have forgotten why we are here."

"We're here because this is our promised land–"

"We are here," Mal rounded on her, "for no other reason than that I am The Dread Descendant. I am the one who was prophesied to conquer the darkness in these lands. I am the one who will restore Magic here. Do you not see the sacrifices I am making? I must leave you and I expose myself to darkness and Magic that is volatile and unknown. And all you see is your own emotional state. When what we are doing is so much more than that, Maeve. This is greater than us—"

"You're damn right it is. And you are in jeopardy of failing at all of it. I see perfectly well what you are exposing yourself to. I see glimpses of that Magic which now occupies too much of your mind."

"That is my burden to bear."

"Then fuck it all! If it is going to consume you, then let's abandon this. We can go someplace else. Somewhere that doesn't require such a sacrifice from you, Mal."

"It is written in Magic. I cannot escape destiny."

"You once told me I shaped my own destiny. Why are you any different?"

He watched her carefully for a long and silent moment before uttering his truth.

"I want the glory."

Maeve nodded slowly, grateful for his honesty at last. "And all I want is you."

Mal stepped towards her, she countered away from him.

"You have spoken your mind, and now I must," she began. "I am afraid of the darkness that holds you. I am terrified of feeling it in my mind again."

"I won't allow that mistake a second time."

Maeve's chest tightened. "You shouldn't have allowed it in the first place."

Mal stepped towards her once more, and again she stepped back.

"You wanted me here so badly," he said, "and now you run."

Maeve looked up at him, fighting the shake building through her body.

"Do not move away from me again," he commanded. "That's an order."

He stepped towards her.

She obeyed, and remained in place.

Maeve looked up at him stubbornly.

A soft, pained, smile split across his face. "Please," he whispered as his hand moved to her face, "don't shut me out again."

His eyes were sincere. Maeve nodded.

Mal's hand cupped her cheek. "I can't feel your presence when you are out of the Dread Lands, not barely at all. It felt like your life force was dwindling out."

Maeve relaxed against his touch. "It was not my intention to scare you. I just. . ."

Mal's thumb bristled across her bottom lip. "Did you go home?"

She nodded and the tightness in her throat returned.

"There are hydrangea blooming around my father's gravesite now. Green hydrangea," she said, her voice constricting. "Vines of blooms in a quantity that take decades to blossom. Yet they are there within just a short time since I visited last."

He took her face fully in his hands. "They always will be."

Maeve pressed into him. "Please, Mal," she whispered, shakily.

"What, Little Viper?"

Maeve placed her hand over his and looked up at him.

"Please don't carry this alone. I am your Second. Your victor, your assassin, and your sword. I can't bear to watch you suffer alone. The darkness that dwells in Mount Morte cannot be yours to fight alone."

He tucked a finger under her chin. "How can I protect you if you are out there?"

"I am not the only one who needs protection."

Mal dropped his hands, and he stepped back from her. His Magic tensed around her. "How can I make you understand my word is final. You do not set foot near that mountain."

Maeve's temper swelled beneath her emotions. "Can you not see what this is doing to you?"

"I see it plainly, Maeve!" he fired back, his voice growing frustrated. "These lands speak to my very blood and tell me to turn back. I hear my ancestors each night I spend here, their ghosts of

Castle Morana warning me endlessly to run." He pointed towards the vaulted green glass windows, heated and angry now. "But that darkness out there says *your name.*"

Maeve's stomach twisted over. Mal continued.

"It taunts me with the knowledge that it will find you. On any planet. In any realm. And so, despite the warnings my Magic has offered me, despite every instinct to flee, I cannot, and will not. I will know I have kept you from the world of darkness that hunts you."

A long silence passed between them.

"My name?" she asked, her voice shaking.

Mal's shoulders dropped as he exhaled, regaining his normal cool and calm composure. He ran his fingers over his face and through his hair.

"Your name, Little Viper," he said with a sigh.

The Throne Room was suddenly too cold. And he was too far. She kicked her pride to the side and closed the space between them, throwing her arms around his neck. Mal's hands slid around her back, embracing her tightly.

One hand slid into his pocket and then ran along her arm. He pulled from her and took her left hand in his.

He slipped the Dread Ring back on her finger, its dark stone competing with her Sinclair family ring for attention as it glistened.

"You do not take this off again," he said, lacing his fingers through her own. "Not ever again."

Maeve prepared to argue and tell him of the ghostly gaunt woman in her mind who was only absent if she took off the ring, but her voice caught in her throat as Magic held her silent. Her brows relaxed as shock pooled down her body.

"You are going to swear to it," he said darkly. "In Magic."

Maeve shook her head and pulled on his hand. His grip tightened as green flooded his beautiful dark eyes.

"Yes," he said, not budging as she tried to fight against his Magic. "You are."

Chapter 50

Maeve

The floor was icy against Maeve's bare feet, growing colder with each step she took towards Mal's study. The Dread Ring on her finger weighed heavy on her Magic, her body, and her mind.

"You must wake him, Maeve," said Abraxas in a frazzled voice. "We are going to Hiems tonight and he must be in perfect form. The announcements are too important and too special to reschedule because he's unconscious."

"I know, Brax," she said weakly.

"It's just so important we solidify Kier's position on Hiems and the deals I've made–"

Maeve stopped and turned towards him. "I know."

Abraxas surveyed her for the first time since he'd pulled her from bed. Her Dread Mark burned with ice for long, ticking minutes, and she did not move to find Mal until Abraxas burst into her room.

"You're not sleeping, are you?" he asked quietly.

She didn't reply and continued towards Mal's study. She dreaded walking through those double doors and seeing what version of him was waiting on the other side.

He was no longer conscious. That much she could feel.

But when his eyes opened, would they be a calming shade of darkness, or filled with threatening flecks of green?

She was sure to hear from Roswyn that she was the last one to arrive at his side.

But there was no fear in her mind of him. Only fear for Mal.

She and Abraxas pushed open the doors, and Maeve sighed as Astrea poured a thick green substance down Mal's arms while he remained in a deep trance, not stirring or moving. Astrea struggled to heal him. The deep purple and red marks across his body were now more than just blood sacrifices or barters of Magic.

Maeve's heart sank.

They were Vexkari.

Maeve strolled over to him.

"Don't," snapped Astrea. "I can do this."

"I know," said Maeve coolly as she took Mal's chin. His head rolled limply in her hand. "But you are not accustomed to expelling such Dark Magic. This is different."

"Yes," muttered Astrea through a clenched jaw. "It is."

"Let me assist you where the darkness is concerned."

Astrea's hands halted. "How are you able to feel the darkness lingering that way?"

"Like calls to like," Maeve answered without looking at her. "Clear the room."

"He called us here. You don't dismiss us," said Roswyn.

"I won't be waking him until you're gone," said Maeve.

She couldn't let them see the state he could be in this time. Roswyn and his power hungry father were loyal to only one thing: strength.

And Mal was vulnerable.

Roswyn's jaw clenched when Maeve looked up at him.

"Come on," said Mumford without looking at her. Abraxas and Astrea were already gone.

When the door snapped behind them, Maeve reached out and touched Mal's face, entering his mind. Darkness enveloped her at once as her skin prickled with a chill.

The blurred and hazy image of an altar manifested once more. She'd seen it before in Mal's mind, but the image appeared sharper, more defined.

Blood dripped from the dark, glowing stones.

It is not enough.

Mal's pained voice slipped across her mind.

"What is not enough?" she asked him in reply.

A soft laugh of pity echoed across the space. Maeve's spine straightened. It was not Mal's.

Blood, it said.

Maeve stepped closer to the carnage of Mal's sacrifice. Her fingertips burned with desire for release. The Dread Ring on her finger hissed with warning against her skin.

"Who are you?" she asked.

No reply came.

It is not enough, Mal's voice returned.

Maeve pushed further into his mind, but the memory before her swiftly began collapsing as ivy needles pressed into her throat. With a gasp and a quickening pulse, she pulled herself from Mal's mind.

Her back pressed against the floor of his study. Mal hovered over her with a deadly grip on her throat and a wild expression. Fear poured from his Magic. His eyes swarmed with tiny flecks of green energy.

Wrong. They were so wrong. His eyes were a beautiful shade of chocolate in the dark. And a hazel dream in the light.

Maeve relaxed against him, taking in what breath she could.

"Mal," she said.

His grip tightened and more Magic slipped from all five fingers and his palm.

"Listen to my voice," she said as calmly as she could manage to fake. "It's me."

Mal's eyes scanned her face in rapid distress. He shook his head.

"Mal," she said smoothly with her last bit of air.

His eyes squeezed shut. His teeth slid together in agony.

Mal, my Prince. She pressed into his mind as her lips turned numb and her vision faded.

His eyes flew open. Their green color faded into darkness as his hands loosened and his face relaxed.

He lifted from her at once. She sucked in a sharp breath and pushed up on her elbows.

"It's alright," she said quietly.

His eyes darted around the room, as though he was unsure of where her voice was coming from

"Maeve?" he asked.

She nodded and moved to her knees, taking his face tenderly in her hands without fear or reservation. He flinched as her skin made contact with his. His eyes locked to hers like a magnet. Maeve tucked her legs beneath her. They kneeled before one another silently. She rubbed her fingers across his cheeks, through his raven hair and down his arms until his Magic relaxed, completely at rest, and his eyes closed.

"That's it," she encouraged.

"I'm so sorry," he said, the words pouring from him in a quiet embarrassment.

"It's not you," she said serenely.

Mal looked up at her with defeat in his eyes.

She shook her head. "The deeper you go, the harder it becomes for me to pull you out," said Maeve. "The deeper you go, Mal, the more of yourself you are losing."

Maeve's hair reached her lower back, despite Grandmother Agatha's desire for her to cut it. Her silver hairbrush snagged on a tangle as she distractedly combed through the long locks.

She stared at the gown Mal had sent to her chamber for the evening in the reflection of the vanity mirror as it hung across the room. It was stunning. Fit for a Queen.

But Maeve felt far from celebration. And far from comfortable wearing such a piece when its coloring looked so much like Mal's eyes as he lost control of himself.

It's not enough blood.

The voice from his mind whispered across her own.

The vanity mirror shifted. Black tendrils of Magic slithered along the edges and across her reflection. Her room darkened and Maeve felt the dark presence of *her* at once.

The albino gaunt woman was barely a shadow in the mirror, lingering behind her.

Maeve's legs turned heavy as she slipped onto the vanity stool, dropping the brush in her hand. It clattered silently into the vanishing floor.

It's not enough blood.

With shaking fingers, she reached towards the haunting reflection. Her fingers brushed the glass and it shattered into dozens of spiked, bloody, dripping shards.

Magic traced her darkened veins, sliding from her fingertips to her temple.

It's not enough blood.

Her eyes closed as the Magic overtook her mind in a haze.

It's not enough blood it's not enough blood it's not enough–

Pain ripped down her finger, slicing across the skin.

A delicate and distant muffled voice brought her eyes open with a pop. "Maeve!"

Maeve stared at Zimsy in the reflection of the unbroken vanity mirror.

Zimsy's eyes dropped to Maeve's bloodied finger.

The Dread Ring sat on the vanity.

Maeve held up her wounded ring finger. Multiple long cuts traveled down its length. Maeve looked back up at the mirror. No bloody cracks or slithering Magic. No apparition loomed over her.

"You swore not to take it off," Zimsy reminded her with a soft voice and her eyes on The Dread Ring.

"I can't stand the weight of it. I can't stand the things I see while wearing it. I can't stand that he's so easily in my head, despite being so far from me in every way imaginable."

Together they stared at the tiny bit of ancient Magic. Vexkari. Mal's and who knows who else's before him. The ring she'd once craved the feeling of, she now dreaded its cool band on her skin.

Blood dripped carelessly onto her lap, staining her clothes.

Her attention was on The Dread Ring where it sat, perfectly normal. No hidden barbs or spikes protruded from it. There was no damage to the elegant stone or smooth band.

Magic alone had ripped open the skin on her finger. Punishment for breaking her vow to never take it off.

She ran her free hand over the cuts, pushing healing Magic into them.

They didn't heal.

She inhaled slowly and released a shaking sigh.

The Dread Magic that wounded her ring finger would not heal with Magic. It would have to heal naturally.

Another scar for her collection.

She turned her hand over, palm up. Blood dripped down her finger and over the worn scar, sliced perfectly across her palm. Her blackened veins weaved seamlessly across the raised tissue.

Another mark of darkness forever on her skin.

"You need to get dressed for tonight," said Zimsy, her round eyes never leaving The Dread Ring where it lay untouched on Maeve's vanity. "And you'll have to put that back on."

Chapter 51

Maeve

"Maeve!" exclaimed Juliet as she stepped through the Portal to Hiems. "That color is stunning on you."

The Stalakta Fortress looked the same as her first visit. Ice encased every pillar and stone. She met eyes with the group of Bellator holding the Portal open for guests, feeling out of place in the elegant, long fabric when she'd grown so accustomed to her uniform as Dread Viper.

Maeve thanked Juliet but found it impossible to mean it. Her ring finger pulsed with pain.

"Evening, cousin," said Abraxas cheerfully as he kissed her cheek. "Haven't seen you in a gown in ages."

Mumford appeared at their side, with a girl Maeve didn't recognize.

Abraxas made a joke about Mumford's suit.

"It's what all the fashionable men in Aterna wear," said the girl on Mumford's arm defensively. She was American, like he was.

"Bet it is," sniggered Abraxas.

Maeve had never seen Reeve or any of his Senshi Warriors in such attire, but she'd never been to the cities in Aterna.

The girl turned to Maeve. She looked her over with an excited expression.

"Mm" said Abraxas, "apologies. Maeve this is Penelope Green. Penelope, Maeve Sinclair."

Penelope's head dipped.

Maeve was silent for a moment. "You need only bow to Mal."

Penelope smiled. "Mumford calls him that too," she said excitedly. "I am honored to meet you. At my school back home, or my old home I suppose, our dueling club was named after you."

Maeve smiled, and her brows pulled together. "What?"

Penelope nodded. "We just formed it last year. We call it Pure Sins. After you and The Dread Prince."

Maeve stared at her. "There is a Magical School in America? On Earth?"

Penelope nodded. "Founded three years ago by my parents."

Maeve looked to Abraxas. "Did you know about that?"

He nodded. "Mr. and Mrs. Green wrote me shortly after Mal's coronation. They are moving the school here to The Dread Lands."

Maeve looked back at Penelope. "I had no idea."

Penelope opened her mouth as the foyer of Stalakta darkened. She looked over her shoulder. The castle's icy entryway filled with a cosmic storm.

Mal stepped from the darkness, his eyes instantly on Maeve. Dressed in a stylish black set with The Dread Locket around his neck and The Dread Crown atop his raven hair, he didn't stop until he reached her side, ignoring all those who bowed as he crossed the Entrance Hall.

Penelope's head dropped lower than everyone else's at his arrival. Maeve didn't bow out of tradition or common occurrence. She never did.

He extended his arm to Maeve. She took it without looking at him.

He grabbed Maeve's hand and held it up, inspecting her sliced ring finger. She looked up at him, keeping her emotions in check as she took in the flecks of green swirling in his eyes.

"How'd that happen?" asked Mal with a smooth arrogance in his voice.

Maeve didn't respond.

He leaned in close to her ear and whispered, "The next time that ring slips off your finger, it will be more than blood I take from you."

Maeve's insides dulled to nothing. She did not feel the ice of Stalakta penetrate her exposed skin. She did not feel the throbbing in her wounded finger. She felt empty once more as Mal looked down at her.

"Smile," said Mal quietly as he kissed her cheek. "I didn't put you in emerald so you could frown all evening."

Mordred and his King's Guard trailed Mal from a distance all evening, more than they did Kier. They were the only Magical creatures in attendance. The rest of Kier's guests were Humans from Hiems with no Magic or connection to the rumored Magical creatures that occupied Hiems.

"You must understand," Kier had said, "most of them are wild beasts with no desire for such formal affairs. Not all have been touched by Fauna the way Mordred has."

Maeve lost count of the number of strangers who placed their hands together and dipped their heads respectfully at Mal, and then proceeded to tell her how honored they were to be in the Dread Viper's presence. Even a forced smile couldn't be found by the end of it. Mal didn't scold her. Perhaps the scowl across her face made his Second in command look fierce.

As one of Kier's councilmen introduced himself and his children, he said with a slight challenge in his voice, "Would be a honor to see all that Magic Kier claims you have."

Mal held his gaze with a blank stare for longer than was necessary and then said, "That can be arranged," as he let some of his lethal Dread Magic slip from him.

The councilman paled and dipped his head, attempting to scurry away.

"Now seems like a good time," said Mal. "What do you think?"

The councilman turned, his cheeks now red, and nodded anxiously. "Of course."

Mal extended his hand to Maeve. When she did not take it right away, his neck craned smoothly towards her.

"You want me to duel in a gown?" she asked quietly up at him.

He smiled. "It'll be like old times."

The councilman sighed with relief, as though he thought Mal was challenging him to duel despite having no Magical capabilities.

Maeve shook her head, sadness dripping from her voice. "We are far from old times, Mal," she muttered.

His smile faltered for a moment, but he recovered as she placed her hand in his and he led her to the center of the room.

Kier clapped his hands, and silence fell across the hall.

"Oh, wonderful!" he exclaimed. "Now you'll all get to see what I've witnessed within the Dread Prince."

Mal dropped her hand and continued across the hall. He turned back towards her and slid his fingers together, cracking each knuckle with his eyes locked on hers.

Maeve loosened her shoulders and planted her feet. A duel with Mal had once been a dance. A flirtation. Now, as too much of Mal slipped farther and farther from her, it was a burden to remember how effortless it had once been.

How he simply *was* and how she delighted in being near him. Simply near him.

Mal raised a single hand, and the room fell still. He gave Maeve a subtle nod.

She knew he wanted to show off and wipe that disbelieving grin off Kier's councilman's face. He wanted to show them all a taste of who he was.

And he did.

He blocked her advances before she fired. He countered her steps before she moved. He was ahead of her every step of the way, aweing the crowd like always. Her shields only withheld him because he allowed it. He did not fire on her fully, not once. But he made sure the crowd felt his power with each step cracking across the floor.

Before she could fire back against his fluid onslaught of spells, a hefty curse spiraled towards her chest. She slammed up a shield just as the spell reached her. It burst against her wall of Magic and sparkled across the room.

The party applauded excitedly as frustration swelled in Maeve. Mal did not smile at her or wait for her to fire again. Another hefty curse headed her way. She ducked to the floor and Obscured, rolling her knees against the ice floors of Hiems and appearing behind Mal.

Electric ice surged down her arm. He smiled as she pointed it towards him as the crowd screamed. With an explosion of cosmic mist he Obscured before her and grabbed her wrist. Mal held her lightning swarming hand high, drawing her to the tips of her toes.

He stared down at her with a wild expression, pressing sharp Magic through his fingers that dulled her electric Magic.

"What happens now that you can't use these two deadly little sinners to release all that fury?"

He pulled her higher, pressing his chest against hers. Maeve whined against him and placed her free hand on him, instinctively pushing him away. A bright green light burst from her as her palm pressed against him, knocking Mal backwards. Panic raced through her mind as Magic settled smoothly across the floor.

She looked down at her left hand in shock. The Dread Ring glistened atop her finger.

Whispers fluttered through the crowd at the equal look of surprise plastered across Mal's face. He shook it quickly and head cocked to the side. The room relaxed at his smile.

"Look at my Dread Viper, ladies and gentleman," he said, crossing towards Maeve. He applauded, giving them all approval to praise her triumph as well. "Learning new tricks, I see," he said quietly.

She opened her mouth to argue but his voice slid across her mind.

Smile.

Mal took her hand and turned to the crowd. Maeve forced a smile as he led her from the hall, thanking guests for their praise as they passed.

They rounded four corners before they were alone.

"I didn't do that," she hissed before he could stop her.

Mal pushed her back against the icy wall with one hand. She looked down at the firm contact between them. His sleeve pulled back slightly, exposing his wrist.

Maeve stopped resisting and relaxed into the wall. "When did you stop wearing the watch I gave you?" she asked quietly.

Mal's fingers slipped smoothly around her left hand. Cool steel slid down her finger. Her breath caught, anticipating the pain to come as he removed the Dread Ring. When his hand withdrew and he slid the ring on his own finger, she looked down, finding no fresh wounds. No new cuts of blood or scrapes of Magic. She looked up at him curiously.

"It's not a punishment if I do it," he said plainly.

She rested her head against the wall despite the fact that he'd dropped his hold on her. "I didn't do that, Mal."

He observed the ring for another moment and then his eyes met hers. She hated the bits of green floating through his eyes.

"I know," he said. "You'd never hurt your sworn Prince."

He left her in the icy glass corridor and returned to his party. She remained leaning against the wall and did not watch him go. At last, she pushed off the wall and ventured deeper into the ice castle.

She played with her empty ring finger, now feeling lonesome without it, as she absentmindedly explored down winding corridors until she came to a set of glass doors. They were a pale blue color, like ice. The frigid evening air struck her face as they clicked open.

Ice and snow covered everything as far as she could see, deep into the horizon.

"Maeve," said a voice.

She turned, and there stood Alphard Mavros. Wrapped in his arms, beneath most of his fur coat, was Victoria. Her bright red hair stood stark against the frozen land around the castle.

"Victoria," she said with a forced smile. "Alphard. It's been a while."

He nodded. "Funny how time moves differently between realms."

She laughed lightly. "I didn't mean to interrupt."

His eyes moved down to her left fingers, where fresh cuts were evident. She placed them behind her back smoothly.

Alphard's eyes met hers. His lips pulled tight. Maeve stepped towards them.

"How do you stand this cold, Victoria?" asked Maeve with an even more forced smile.

Victoria smiled brightly up at Alphard.

He looked down at her softly. "I keep her warm."

Maeve's stomach relaxed at her successful distraction. "I hope to see the pair of you in the Dread Lands soon."

"Very soon," said Alphard.

Maeve smiled. "I'm sure your parents have pulled out every bell and whistle imaginable for the wedding."

Victoria beamed and leaned closer to Alphard. "I am told the plans for the temple in The Dread Lands are nearly complete."

"Yes," said Maeve. "Mal has restored it fully. I'm certain the renovations will suit such an anticipated event."

"When is the announcement, Abraxas?" asked Juliet with a yawn as the night grew long. "I'm exhausted."

Abraxas' hand landed on her swollen belly.

"I know, love," he said. "Shouldn't be much longer. If you'd like to go now, I can escort you home myself."

"But you'll return here and I'll be all alone," she argued.

Abraxas smirked. "You're married to the Hand of the Prince."

She pressed towards him with a smile. "And being the Hand's wife, I happen to know a number of secrets about said Hand that might make him rethink sending me home alone."

Abraxas' smirk only widened. "Go on and tell them then. You were there. Then they'll all know the Hand's wife is just–"

Juliet's hand clamped over Abraxas' mouth as they laughed.

"Please," drawled Maeve, "be more sickening."

Mal's victorious moment arrived at last. Kier bent down on one knee, and swore his realm, his court, and his life to Mal.

Mal was a picture of grace as he took his first crown that did not belong to him.

Kier took Mal's hand in his own, Mal's snowy white band of Magic on his greedy fingers, and kissed the Dread Ring on Mal's hand.

Chapter 52

Maeve

The Dark Peaks grew blacker with each passing day. The green hazy twilight she had become accustomed to day in and day out in The Dread Lands slowly drifted into an endless night. Mount Morte loomed in the distance, calling her.

Like calls to like.

Her blood whispered thoughts of darkness as the peak of the mountain shifted back behind thick haze. The Dread Ring on her finger pulsed with warning in the all too quiet castle, drawing her from her balcony and down into the castle.

She stilled at the top of the stairs in the Entrance Hall.

Mal looked up at her with low shoulders as he staggered through the front doors. His eyes were a dark relief with no flecks of green visible. Maeve surged towards him, flying down the staircase. Mal only made it up a few steps before he fell, hardly catching himself. Maeve was at his side a moment later, pulling him up. His dark clothes were wet with blood.

"Why do you keep going out there?" she asked, running her hands along the bleeding mess of his chest.

He did not answer. She knew the answer. There was no changing his mind.

"I see the darkness growing in The Dark Peaks, Mal," she said. "I see what this is doing to you. One day you are mine and the next your mind and your Magic are foreign to me."

His eyes bore into hers, panic flooding them. "Am I losing my mind?"

Maeve's heart twisted. "No, My Prince," she said softly, brushing his hair from sweating forehead. "Allow me to help you."

Magic thrummed deep in her core, guiding her. She ran two

fingers across her palm, splitting the skin instantly. Cupping the back of his head with her clean hand, she placed her palm at his lips. His eyes widened as her blood hit his tongue.

One swallow and he collapsed in her arms.

Her bleeding hand fell as she held him close. Maeve gently wiped the blood that stained his lips and chin, ensuring his skin was perfectly clean.

When Astrea had arrived at her side, she did not know. She didn't hear the girl's muffled words as Alphard kneeled before them. Astrea took Maeve's bloodied hand smoothly and healed the wound with ease. A moment later, Mal was in Alphard's arms and he and Astrea were gone.

Roswyn kneeled before her. He mouthed something. And then again.

Maeve's eyes closed and when she opened them, Roswyn said her name a third time.

"Sinclair."

With a heavy breath, she looked up at him.

"What are you going to do?" he asked.

She didn't respond. She looked down where Mal had just been. Drops of her blood gleamed across the dark and shining stone stairs, mixed with his. Mal was suffering. And he may have been suffering for her, for all Magicals, but she wouldn't, no-she couldn't, go on watching him fade into darkness.

Roswyn stared at her. Maeve looked up at him once more, and then pushed off the stairs. She pulled her hair back, braiding the top section messily as she jogged down the stairs. Roswyn was on her heels. She stormed across the courtyards to the stables. Her father's horse, Spitfire greeted her silently, already saddled and ready for her.

"He specifically commanded you to remain here at Castle Morana,"said Roswyn as she swung her leg around her father's horse. The silver and grey speckled mare stood taller than the rest of the horses in the stables, save for Obsidian, Mal's black Clydesdale.

"Mal isn't in his right mind, Roswyn. You bloody well know it. I am sick of sitting in this castle pretending like we aren't about to lose him."

She yanked on Spitfire's reins as Roswyn snatched them up.

"You misunderstand. I'm coming with you," he said.

Maeve opened her mouth to snap at him and closed it quickly. Arman stepped hastily into the stables. With a sharp whistle, he stalked towards them. He grabbed a saddle as his horse trotted towards him. He looked at Roswyn.

"Hurry up, then," said Arman.

Roswyn straightened and obeyed at once.

As he pulled himself atop a horse, Arman looked over at Maeve, answering her unasked question.

"I saw Alphard carrying him to the Healing Chamber," he said.

Maeve looked away and straightened.

"Do you know what's out there? Beyond the Barrier?" he asked.

"No," said Maeve. "But we are about to find out. I am tired of hiding in these walls."

Roswyn moved to her other side.

Without another word, Maeve squeezed her legs together, and Spitfire charged forward. She barreled through the gardens of Castle Morana, which lay dead and devoid of life once more. The horses climbed the winding, narrow, paths of the Dark Peaks, leading to Mount Morte. They had not passed The Barrier when the sound of snapping twigs and branches cracked across the silent hills.

Maeve sat deeper in the saddle, slowing Spitfire. They waited a moment, all intently listening. She looked over her shoulder at Roswyn and Arman.

"I'll take the lead," said Roswyn as he pressed forward on his horse.

She'd never been so far into the mountains. Just as Roswyn had said, she'd been forbidden from the place. Dark Magic lingered in the air, delivering a clear message: they were not welcome.

The trail opened up into a small valley between peaks. With a sigh, Maeve brought them to a stop.

"There's nothing here," said Roswyn. "We should just go back."

Maeve navigated Spitfire around him, her eyes narrowed at the far wall of cliffs. "There's movement."

Arman pulled up next to her as the movement grew larger. Closer.

She could make out the faint shape of. . .three people.

"What are those things?" spat Roswyn.

The creatures crawled and limped closer, some of them missing entire limbs.

"Are those. . .people?" asked Arman quietly.

They drew closer, barreling towards them without pause.

"Look," said Roswyn, pointing past the trees, "there's others."

Four more of the strange creatures made their way towards them.

"Not people," said Maeve, as the Magic in her veins screamed danger.

The creatures had traits of a Human–of a Magical. Eyes, ears, fingers, and bodies just like theirs. But they were deformed, each in their own unique way. Skin hung from their bodies, some removed completely, exposing their bones.

A bright red shot of Magic whizzed between her and Arman. Their heads whipped to the side incredulously.

"Merlin and Primus," said Roswyn, "they have Magic."

Maeve gripped the reins on Spitfire as Arman threw up a shield. Another blast of Magic swirled towards them, shattering his shield at once.

"Seven fucking realms," said Roswyn, shocked that these gangly creatures broke through a Supreme like Arman's shield so easily.

Maeve hoisted her leg off Spitfire, and grabbed the horse's face. "Stay back."

Spitfire circled her once and trotted into the tree line. Arman and Roswyn followed her lead, dismounting their horses and preparing for the fight on foot.

Roswyn fired at once. His Magic ripped through one of the creatures, splitting its head from its body. It continued barreling towards them.

"What?" he barked, his eyes wide.

The groups of unusual creatures were nearly upon them. Maeve fired on them with three consecutive shots, each one having little effect on their pursuit.

Arman's brows pulled together. "Prepare for a physical battle."

Roswyn's fists clenched at his sides. "Each take one?" he asked, as the original three were yards away.

"Great," muttered Maeve.

They Obscured in sync, each landing face-to-face with the haggard creatures. Maeve's opponent lacked most of its left leg. Not that such a fact stopped its pursuit of her. With two fingers, she aimed at the creature's hip area, severing the limb entirely. It dropped to the rocky ground, the creature falling with it.

She stepped back in disgust as it continued to writhe towards her.

Arman and Roswyn dove for their creatures, pinning them to the ground. Their fists slammed into the creature's decaying faces, smashing its bones to nothing.

"Why. Won't. You. Die?" Roswyn seethed between Magical punches.

Arman placed his hands on the creature's chest, sending a blast of Magic potent enough to kill ten Magicals through it. Its bones exploded across the ground, but its flailing arms still gripped Arman, ripping his skin to shreds.

Arman's arms oozed blood. The Supreme seemed unaffected as he shoved off the twitching creature.

Maeve's spine prickled as swarms of the creatures crawled down the mountainside.

Roswyn Obscured further up the hill, taking on the set of four. Each blow of his Magic, knocked them back, sometimes even dislodging parts of their bodies, but they never lay dead.

Arman faced the horde of creatures crawling towards them boldly. "We cannot allow them to continue down the mountains towards Castle Morana."

Maeve nodded as he ran towards them, prepared to pummel them all, if that's what it took.

Lightning cracked at her fingers. She circled her arm in a whiplike motion, prepared to strike the line of creatures running at them. The band of lightning let loose–

Sharp needles wrapped her ankle. She hit the rocky terrain with force. Warmth trickled down the side of her head as it split open. Her lightning dissipated at once. The terrain spun as she twisted onto her back in agony. The creature holding her was half submerged in the earth as its bony and decayed hand gripped her leg, climbing higher from underground.

Sedating and nauseating Magic swirled up her leg. She fell against the earth with a groan. Her head rolled to the side and she saw the single creature she'd manage to hit with her lightning lay still. Its body dissolved to ash in a matter of seconds.

"It's fire," she said, realizing how to kill the creatures. "Arman," she called out as her vision blurred, "it's fi–"

More creatures broke free from underground. Breaking through dirt and roots and stone, they crawled towards her pinning her to the ground in a swarm. Hundreds of hands broke from the earth beneath her, all of them gripping her and dragging her across the unforgiving terrain further up the Dark Peaks. Each bony and chilled hand that seized her sent her further into darkness. She fought consciousness, shooting what Magic she could muster towards them.

It made no difference. She could barely open her eyes.

Her stomach flipped as warmth dripped across her face in little drops. The rugged ground was replaced with cold air. Some sensation returned to her as her eyes opened and she stumbled forwards. Arman's grip on her never faltered as he Obscured them only a few yards.

He fell to his knees, dropping Maeve with him. She lifted her head, enough to see the creatures barreling towards them from all sides.

"Arman we need to–" she began, as he slumped into her. More of her vision returned as they fell to the cold ground together, only then did she realize he was covered in blood. His blond hair was crimson across his forehead.

"Arman," she gasped, pulling herself towards him. Her legs were still completely useless. She hovered over him.

"Go," he said. "There is not time."

"What," she said groggily. "No–I can Obscure us–"

He smiled with blood stained teeth. "You can't."

Arman pushed himself up with a gut wrenching groan, ignoring Maeve's feeble attempt to keep him down. He faced the oncoming pack of creatures. There were hundreds.

"Don't you dare," said Maeve, fighting to speak coherently. "Obscure us again. Farther."

"I can't," he said, as his knees bent. He righted himself and held his chin up with a slow breath "It's alright," he said weakly. His trembling hand formed a fist and landed against his heart. "I am alright dying for the daughter of my Premier."

"No," she said fiercely.

"Yes," he replied. "Tell Arianna it has been her since- first m-moment I saw–"

Roswyn appeared at her side, grabbed her, and Obscured again. He teleported them down the hill. They tumbled across the rocky earth, slamming into thorny vines and jagged edges of stone.

Roswyn landed on all four and heaved. Maeve rolled further, barely able to push herself off the ground. Her body was numb.

"Don't you dare leave him," she seethed at Roswyn, her breathing low and sparse.

"I can only Obscure one of you," he said sharply, pulling his beaten body upright, "and maybe not even that with this Magic pressing down on us. In case you haven't noticed I also can barely feel my body. If I don't get you out of here, we'll both be dead."

"I can Obscure all three of us," she pushed her Magic out, sending a wave of spinning nausea through her.

"Not like this you can't," he snapped. "Now stop fucking fighting me."

His hands gripped her arms tightly as her stomach flipped and darkness encased them.

The courtyard at Castle Morana blurred into vision. Roswyn's grip loosened as she staggered sideways.

"Shit," said a familiar voice.

Strong arms slipped around her, supporting her.

"Where's Arman?" asked Alphard, holding Maeve close. "Shit, shit, shit."

She collapsed into him and pressed against his chest, trying to move back towards the gates.

"Take it easy," said Alphard as her legs wobbled beneath the numbing sensation still holding her captive.

Gravity shifted as he scooped the back of her knees up.

"Go back for him," she groaned in a mumble.

"Are you out of your mind?" Roswyn asked. "They were swarming us! Alphard and I cannot fight that off."

"Fuck you, Roswyn."

"Fuck me?!" The hot tempered blond screamed. "You are the one who failed."

"Shut the fuck up, both of you," said Alphard sharply.

Maeve pressed her fingertips to her chest. Alphard and Roswyn both sucked in sharply at the sensation.

She called to all the Bellator who now wore Mal's Dread Mark.

You are called to fight. Beyond the Barrier, Arman is wounded. Fight for your comrade.

She'd been so panicked she'd forgotten to tell him. . .

It's fire, she sent through her Dread Mark. Kill them with fire.

Alphard and Roswyn's bickering voices faded in and out as the dim firelights of Castle Morana blurred by.

"If she dies at either of our hands, Roswyn, we both die. You remember that, right?" snapped Alphard.

"You think I can't feel the reminder burning across my palm?" Roswyn fired back.

More firelights blurred by as she came in and out of consciousness.

Alphard set her on the soft bed in the Healing Chamber as a groan escaped her dry lips.

Abraxas rounded the corner with Astrea hot on his heels.

"Merlin, Gods, fuck," said Abraxas as his face paled at the blood coating her front.

He shoved Alphard aside and placed himself in front of her. Astrea rounded the raised bed and placed her hands on either side of Maeve's face.

Abraxas scanned over her quickly. "What happened, Roswyn?" He quickly scanned his body. "Do you need healing? What happened?"

"No. We got ambushed by a bunch of. . . I don't even know."

"Arman is out there still," said Alphard. "I'm going to join the rest of the Bellator."

"None of you are listening to me," said Roswyn hotly. "He's dead."

Abraxas' head whipped to Roswyn. "What?"

Alphard grabbed Roswyn by the front of his uniform and dragged him out of the hall.

Pressure built in Maeve's head, nearly unbearable.

Astrea's hands moved down to Maeve's throat, covered in developing bruises. Her legs and arms would be the same.

"These wounds are all different," said Astrea. "Multiple and of varying Magic. She was attacked by many. Dozens."

"Where's Mal," asked Abraxas.

"He's sedated," she answered. "For now."

The pressure in Maeve's head released as she breathed fully at last.

"Good," said Astrea encouragingly. "Another."

Maeve sucked in deeply.

Screams filled the castle. Maeve knew the cry well. The noise her sister made upon realizing their father was dead had been burned into the back of her mind. It played over and over on her sleepless nights while the gaunt apparition that haunted her evenings listened intently.

Maeve's clothes were sticky and stained with her own blood, as well as Roswyn's and Arman's. The crowd of Bellator parted as she passed. Some of them were kneeled, their heads hung in both silent and verbal prayers.

Arman's lifeless body lay rigid on the dark marble tile. Arianna lay next to him, her hands on his face.

Maeve stumbled towards them. Abraxas caught her.

Arianna's helpless sob filled the hall. Maeve reached for her, slipping on the blood that pooled beneath Arman. Fear plunged down her spine, and she reacted in the nick of time, throwing up a protective shield.

Lightning burst through the hall, but Maeve's hand was void of Magic.

Arianna glared up at her with enough hatred to bring Maeve to her knees. The impact of the floor went unfelt. Arman's blood was cold as it seeped through her pants.

Her own tears were just as cold as they slipped down her cheeks and pooled at her jaw.

Maeve ignored the electric Magic that cracked across Arianna's knuckles. She didn't care about an explanation of her sister's sudden burst of rare Magic. Magic only Maeve herself possessed.

Arianna sucked in multiple sharp sobs of uncontrolled breathing. She shook her head and squeezed her eyes shut.

One by one, the Bellator closed their fists over their hearts. With dirty and bloodied hands, Maeve took Arman's fingers and curled them under. She placed his fist on his chest in salute.

When her own fist sat over her heart, she said, "Milites."

"Mundi," rippled through the hall from hundreds of Magicals.

Chapter 53

Maeve

Maeve's eyes opened as Mal entered the candlelit bathroom. He leaned against the doorframe. She rolled her head along the edge of the bathtub. No crown sat atop his head.

"If you came to lecture me for going near Mount Morte," she began hoarsely, "can you postpone until the morning?"

He crossed towards her and pulled his long sleeve shirt over his head, followed by his pants. He draped his clothes across the tufted stool and bent over the edge of the tub. Maeve's head inclined to him.

His eyes were dark. No glowing flecks of green present. Her chest quaked with relief.

Her eyes traveled down his toned stomach, accented by the shadows in the darkened space. Scars ran down his arms and across his chest, little starbursts of scarred Magic. Dark Magic lingered across his pale skin.

"No lecture, Little Viper," he hummed. "Just let me hold you."

Maeve shifted in the warm water as he slid behind her. He wrapped his long arms around her front and pulled her against his chest.

Her throat constricted. Mal's lips pressed against her temple. "Let it out, Maeve," he hummed.

"I didn't want to run," she cried. "I wanted to fight."

"Knowing when to retreat is a valuable quality."

"I could have saved him," she argued, twisting towards him. "If Roswyn hadn't forced me to leave–"

"You could not have, Maeve. The blow he took for you was fatal."

Maeve pressed her face against his shoulder. "Is this what I am fated to endure? I cannot die, and yet those around me must suffer my failures." Mal's free hand moved up and down her back as she continued. "My power is greater than ever now, and yet I am no match for what lies out in that darkness. Arianna's hatred for me is solidified."

Mal took a glass bottle from the ledge of the tub and poured its contents into his hands. His slender fingers pressed against her scalp, lathering the floral scented shampoo into her hair. Maeve's eyes slid to a close as he worked his way through her hair, massaging gently.

"What were those things?" she asked quietly, turning once more and her back pressed against his front.

Mal's chest rose and fell. "They have been called many things across time. The Dreaded Dead. The Dead Walkers."

Maeve melted closer to him. "Des Inferius." she quoted. "From below."

His hands continued to move through her hair.

"That is why we could not kill them so easily," she said. "They are already dead."

Mal rinsed her hair silently. Maeve continued.

"But they attacked us—"

"They came for you," said Mal. "Roswyn made it clear. They did not try to take him or Arman. They wanted you."

She shifted and looked up at him, her brows pulled together as she faced him.

"You are being targeted," said Mal.

"Why?"

His hand moved to her face. His knuckles brushed along her jaw. "Because you are more mine than any facade of desire can conquer."

His eyes were sad. Conflicted.

"The darkness wants to hurt you?" she asked, her gaze darting between his eyes.

"It wants me to submit," he said. And then quietly, "It wants me alone."

Mal pulled her back down, her head resting on his chest as the water turned cold. Maeve slipped her arms snugly around him beneath the water.

"Children of Magic are never alone," she said softly.

Arman was buried with the highest honors in The Dread Lands. The first to die in their new world, Mal himself carved his tombstone with Magic. A new graveyard of Bellator began with him.

Arianna held Aislin and Anselm close, one in each arm. Their blonde hair stood stark against their black clothes of mourning.

Children so young shouldn't be mourning.

Grandmother Agatha sat in a new, elaborate chair with wheels. She placed one hand on Arianna's arm as Abraxas, and then Arman's father spoke. Arman's father shook Abraxas' hand as they exchanged places.

Maeve heard little of either speech. How could she when her mind only replayed his bleeding body and deadening eyes? She only heard Ariann's cry. The heartbroken sobs that ripped from her sister were, once again, her fault.

Maxius slipped from Zimsy's arms, pushing away from her with his eyes on Mal. Zimsy's eyes met Mal's silently. He gave her a soft nod, and she slid Maxius to the ground. He toddled towards them, reaching up for Mal with expectant arms and drooping eyes.

Mal's slender fingers brushed over the boy's hair. Maxius signed, '*up*'.

Mal bent forward and slipped an arm beneath his legs, hoisting him up against his chest. Maxius laid his head down, his eyes quickly closing.

Mal's cold and green-flecked eyes did not meet Maeve's gaze.

Arman's father's voice drifted into her thoughts, pulling her attention back to him where he stood looking down at his son's grave.

He was silent for a long moment, and then his light eyes met Maeve's, and he spoke words that made her sick.

"If my son had to die defending one of his own," he said, "I am glad it was Ambrose Sinclair's daughter."

Chapter 54

Maeve

Warmth flooded her finger, slipping into her hand. A clattering of metal filled her ears.

Maeve.

Her eyes opened into the dark corridor.

She didn't remember walking there.

Mal stood before her, the Dread Dagger in one hand and her bleeding finger in the other. But his green-flecked eyes were on the floor beneath them. He stepped to the side as Maeve realized what held his gaze.

Her blood dripped to the castle floor and then, against all bounds of physics, trailed along the corridor towards the black wall of stone before them. It ran along the flat floor, like a slithering snake and slipped into the cracks of the stones.

"What–" she began.

Mal concealed the dagger and placed her bleeding finger in his mouth. His eyes remained on her. Maeve looked up at him as her body began to shake, waiting for his explanation.

"It's not enough," he whispered, closing his eyes.

"What?"

His eyes opened. "It's not enough blood."

He dropped her hand and scanned up and down the blank wall. Maeve held her finger tenderly.

"Tell me what you saw to make you do that?"

Maeve stammered, her gaze pulled towards her blood that continued to crawl towards the door.

"I don't know," she admitted.

Mal remained silent for a moment, his eyes fixed on her blood.

"Why don't I remember how I got here?" She asked.

Mal didn't reply. He trailed his finger along his palm, thinly slicing it open and rotating his palm down. Slowly, small drops of his blood dripped to the floor.

The drops didn't move, or drift towards the stone wall.

He repeated the action with the Dread Dagger, and still his blood lay still.

Mal took her hand once more and flipped it palm up. He didn't ask as he ran his finger along her scarred palm, slicing it open just as he had his own. She winced as his grip grew tight against her pulsing hand. He turned it over as her blood fell to the floor on top of his.

It remained still.

Mal pulled the Dread Dagger back out. Maeve tensed against his grip, trying to pull her hand back.

"I don't think this is a good idea, Mal," she hissed.

He pressed the dagger against her twitching finger.

"Mal it's going to scar–"

He pressed the pointed tip into the tender skin at the tip of her finger and squeezed. A single drop of blood dropped to the floor.

And inched towards the wall.

"It's your blood," he said as the small drop slid across the floor. "Yours. Not mine."

Mal's grip on her tightened, pulling her towards the wall.

"Mal, no," she began, digging her feet into the floor. "We have no idea what's behind there."

Mal pulled her hand closer to the stone.

Electric Magic swelled at the fingers on her free hand, prepared to break his hold on her. The flecks of green in his eyes sparkled as he did not relinquish his grip. His Dread Magic pulsed through his skin into hers.

"We can do this one of two ways, Maeve," he said. "But you will reveal what Magic has concealed within this stone."

The sparks of Magic at her fingers remained. Mal dropped her hand.

"The hard way then," he said.

Maeve stepped away from him and the wall, clutching her bloodied hand.

"I have a bad feeling about this," she said. "I did not come here willingly. I did not slice my finger tip of my own volition—"

"That matters to you now?" he interrupted. "After all the minds you have violated? Now that it is you that is the victim, you are so against it?"

Maeve stepped away from him once more. "I will not open that door, Mal."

Mal crouched to the floor, his finger smearing the trail of her blood. "I wonder if Arianna's blood would work?"

Maeve's throat tightened. He continued.

"Arianna, who has already suffered so much."

Maeve darted towards him, no longer concerned with her bleeding hand. Mal stood tall and welcomed her challenge.

She pressed forward until they shared a breath. "Fine," she hissed. "You want my fucking blood?" She took his wrist, which still gripped the Dread Dagger, and held it to her stomach. "Why don't you just take it all?"

Mal's eyes rolled. "Always with the dramatics."

She pushed away from him, letting out a frustrated groan.

"Do not act as though I am being unreasonable," began Mal. "You swore an oath to me. I could demand it, and that Magic on your chest would punish you if you disobeyed. And yet, I desire you to do it willingly." He paused. "What if I could give you something in return? Something you've dreamed of since I met you?"

Maeve turned back towards him. "For my blood?"

Mal nodded. "You willingly give your blood for me."

Maeve's hands rested in defeat at her sides. The multiple stinging cuts throbbed through her.

Her eyes scanned the wall as she weighed her options.

Mal would get his way, in the end. Those green flecks in his eyes ensured he'd do so ruthlessly.

"You allow Zimsy and Arianna to take the children to the city, just until we know we aren't unleashing some hell upon the whole castle. And you swear not to use anyone else's blood for this. Not my sister. Not anyone."

Mal contemplated for a moment. Then he smiled at her. "Agreed." Magic snapped between them, binding her bargain just as much as his.

He breezed past her. "Go and wake them. Meet me back here."

"And what is it that you are so graciously giving me?" she called over her shoulder.

Mal didn't turn back towards her. "You will see. It'll be easiest once you're low on blood and vulnerable. I believe it'll be painful. Perhaps best if you're unconscious."

He disappeared into the dark castle corridor without another word.

Maeve stepped back towards the black stone as a faint whisper of Magic hissed from the wall.

More, it seemed to say.

"How much do you think it will take?" she asked as she stared at the blank, black wall deep in Castle Morana.

"I'm uncertain," Mal replied.

She looked up at him as he drew the Dread Dagger forth. His eyes still swam with green.

She never thought she'd come to hate the color.

"What if whatever is concealed here was not meant for us?" she asked quietly.

"You wound up standing in this spot with no memory of having gotten here."

"Doesn't that alarm you?"

"No more so than the other things I see and hear in this ancient place. Whether by the Magic in this door, or Castle Morana itself, you were meant to stand here."

He extended the Dread Dagger's hilt towards her. She didn't take it.

"Why not your blood?" she asked softly as her eyes traced the sharp blade. "You have royal Dread blood. And I am not even of Pureblood."

She looked up at him. Mal's vacant expression stung.

"Take the dagger, Maeve," was his only reply.

Maeve stared at him for a moment longer before she looked back down at the dagger.

"It's still given willingly," she began, "though I think I would prefer you to make the cut."

He flipped the dagger back into his own grip and placed his hand on her lower back, ushering her towards the blank wall.

She held her hand out, palm up, the skin already so marked and scared with Magic. What was another? Mal held her wrist and placed the cool edge of the blade against her scarred skin, forcing her fingers to wrap the sharpened steel.

His eyes met hers and with one smooth motion, he jerked the dagger through her skin. Needles of ice pierced her, weaving across her entire body. She squeezed the wound shut, spilling blood onto the floor.

It surged towards the wall at once. The blood slithered into the stone just as before, sliding into every crack and missing bit of stone. Maeve's vision shifted as she wobbled.

Mal took her palm and raised it high, forcing it flat against the wall. Magic thrummed from the stone, calling her Magic to provide more. She groaned against the unwanted feeling, nausea building at her core. Blood dripped from her wound, trailing down the wall in vine-like paths.

Maeve's head rolled forward. Mal caught her forehead before it slammed into the stone.

"You haven't lost that much yet, Maeve," he said.

She hated that the slight concern in his voice delighted her. She was starved for his protection.

"I know," she said with a tight breath. "But I feel so. . .empty."

The blood from the floor and the blood from her palm had not met yet. Mal's arm slid around her waist just as her legs wobbled. She groaned against him.

"You're burning up," he remarked.

"Please," she cried. "Please make it stop. I don't feel good."

"It's almost done, Little Viper," said Mal. "It is an honor to serve your Dread Prince in such a way," he hummed in her ear. "Is it not?"

It took all her strength to nod. This was not her Prince.

She shivered against him, despite his claim that her skin was hot.

At last, her blood met at the center of the wall. The dark red crimson began to glow, illuminating the dark corridor in a wash of red. Mal pulled her back and her arm fell slack.

A thunderous snap of Magic boomed from the wall as Magic released its seal. Warmth spread through her as Mal pulled her further back, completely supporting her. Her head rolled against his chest as the wall glowed red with every line and drop of her blood.

She understood then. It was Vexkari.

The markings dwelled only for a moment as they seeped into the wall, turning black and creating the archway of a large, rounded door. It clicked open in a dream-like swing.

Mal lowered her gently to the icy stone floor of the castle. He pressed his fingers to her temple.

"Sleep, Maeve," he said with a smile. "Your reward is forthcoming."

The final image of him stepping into a hazy green opening of light blurred into darkness.

Maeve opened her eyes in soft bedding. A light patter of Spinel's paws against the sheets brought her gaze to the foot of her bed, where Maxius and Spinel played with a large feather.

Spinel lunged for the feather, rolling over onto Maeve's legs.

Maeve pushed up, drawing both their attention towards her.

"Hi," she said with a small smile.

Maxius crawled towards her and kneeled beside her. Spinel

rubbed against his sides, purring loudly.

Maxius signed, *you've been asleep for a long time.*

"Days?" she asked.

He nodded and made a quick motion.

Maeve stretched then looked down at her cloth wrapped hand. It was still damp with whatever potion Astrea had surely soaked it in. The Dread Dagger's wound would have to heal naturally, but she was grateful for any relief from the pain she could get.

She turned her attention back to Maxius and pulled her arm around him, drawing him close. Spinel wiggled his way between them.

"I had to help Mal with something. Sometimes being his second means I make sacrifices."

Maxius' eyebrows pulled together as he looked up at her.

She questioned his understanding of the word. "Sacrifice?"

He shrugged.

"It means I am hurt so that you, and Zimsy, and everyone else here, is safe."

Maxius made the motion for *safe.*

"Exactly-"

You are not safe, he signed.

Maeve's stomach twisted. She tucked her head atop his.

Abraxas emerged from the open doors to her chamber. He beamed at her. "Marvelous, cousin. You are glowing."

Abraxas plopped himself on the side of the bed.

"Hello, Maxius," he said cheerfully.

Maxius buried his head further into Maeve's and pretended not to smile at Abraxas.

"You are awfully giddy," remarked Maeve.

Abraxas bit his lip. "Would you like for me to show you? Or tell you what you revealed in that empty wall?"

Maeve's heart kicked. "Everything's alright?" she asked hesitantly.

Abraxas laughed. "Oh my sweet cousin," he said with a laugh. "You found the Dread Spellbook."

Abraxas pulled her from the bed, and brought her to the hidden doorway her Magic revealed.

A library. Spotless, preserved with ancient Magic.

Books shot high into the ceiling, not a drop of dust or worn covers on them. Books bound with leather and silk. Books with stamped covers and handwritten titles, some large and some small.

Reading desks and oversized chairs lined the length of the library. Maeve smiled at the painted murals along the walls that depicted ancient stories and lore.

The ceiling portrayed a scene of creatures she'd never seen in any book, nor heard of in any story. They were large, dragon-like creatures, with shining slick, scale-less skin, long necks, and bat wings spread wide. They soared through pale green clouds of light, encircling a woman with white hair who wore the Dread Crown. She was glorious. Her eyes were bright green. They complimented her rosy cheeks and full pink lips. Her skin was as pale as her hair. She was depicted in the finest jewels and a black shimmering gown.

At the center of the room was an ornate pedestal. Magic still dripped from it.

"Mal has it?" she asked in regards to the spellbook.

"Yes," answered Abraxas.

"Where to even begin?" she muttered, taking in the room full of knowledge at her fingertips.

Abraxas looked over at her. "Thank you, Maeve," he said sincerely. He took her uninjured hand and squeezed once. "I'll leave you to it," he said with a smile.

How long she let herself be distracted by the endless amount of new knowledge and stories at her fingertips, she did not know. But the discovery of the library at Castle Morana was a win she was willing to take.

"And you were so adamant that you weren't going to reveal this place," came Mal's voice.

She looked up from her new book. He strode towards her with life in his step. Maeve set her apple and book aside.

"You look rested," she commented. "I'd like to talk to you about taking me to Mount Morte. There are texts here–"

"That mountain is still too dark and dangerous and is off limits to you," he said plainly.

Mal rounded the desk and took her face in his hands. His lips were on hers before she could blink. His touch was. . .genuine.

His Magic was calm and familiar, far from his state as of late.

Maeve rose out of her seat, desperate to be closer to him. She wound her fingers through his raven hair and he chuckled, pulling away from her.

She looked back and forth at his eyes. They were dark chocolate with swirling hazel. She doubted her own vision, as there was no trace of green in them at all.

"What?" she asked apprehensively as his expression shifted into shock.

His hands moved from her face and down to her waist. "You haven't kissed me like that in quite some time."

"I suppose I'm happy to see you looking like my Mal."

His finger tucked under her chin, craning her neck back. He clicked his tongue, a smile dancing at the corner of his lips. "I don't think your Dread Prince gave you permission to call him such a familiar name."

"Oh," she said softly, pushing herself closer to him. "And here I was hoping we'd become quite familiar in the next few minutes."

A dark smile pulled at his lips. He gripped her waist tightly. He lifted her and plopped her atop the desk, his lips finding hers once more.

Chapter 55

Maeve

Arianna and the twins were not present for their routine breakfast together.

Maeve didn't touch the breakfast spread before her. She barely sipped her tea. She was nose deep, scouring through the Dread Spellbook. The Magic described was not plain, nor simple. It wasn't spelled out in common words or instructions.

There was even a lengthy entry on Vexkari. She and Mal had been right about many things with Vexkari, but the Spellbook added even more insight to the dark transfer of Magic.

Mal understood parts of his Magic now more than ever. He pushed The Barrier farther and farther each day, reclaiming more of the Dread Lands than he had in months.

Maxius touched her hand gently, gathering her attention.

He signed *help* and pointed to the fruit too far for his reach.

Spinel paced up and down the table with his tail perked in a high curl.

"Try your Magic," said Zimsy encouragingly.

Maxius ignored her and patted Maeve's hand once more. Maeve slid the tray closer to him. He thanked her with a quick hand movement and carefully placed the bits he wanted on his plate.

Abraxas strolled into the room, brushing back his hair with one fluid movement.

"Good morning," he said in a clipped tone, not fully regarding Zimsy or Maxius. "Maeve."

She looked up at her cousin, who was so rarely frazzled. He bounced on the balls of his feet as his brows raised.

"Is it Mal?" she asked, closing the spellbook and already knowing the answer.

Abraxas nodded once. Maeve stood at once, clutching the book close to her. She followed Abraxas hastily into the corridor.

"Where is he?" she asked. "Why didn't I feel him call for me if he's hurt?"

"He's not hurt," her cousin replied.

"What then?"

Abraxas turned the corner and began their descent into the dungeons of Castle Morana.

"What is happening, Brax?" asked Maeve sharply.

They swiftly traveled deeper and deeper into darkness, the only source of light the dimmed firelights against the wall. Her Lux Charm illuminated at her wrist.

Distant wails filled the long hall before them. Maeve's pace quickened. The screams grew in their intensity. They followed the cries to a large cell, where the door stood wide open.

Mal stood over a hunched figure. The man fell to one knee, another shriek ripping from him.

Ismail stood nearby, looking horror-stuck. She looked frail in Roswyn's grip as he held her arms behind her back in one hand. Mordred's red eyes glimmered closely behind Mal.

"I'll ask once more," said Mal cooly. "Where is the Dread Stone?"

The man before Mal keeled over, exposing his face to Maeve.

Walter Brighton.

Her insides twisted with guilt. She'd ruined his life's work with one simple spell, effectively erasing his memory.

Mr. Brighton screamed, writhing on the floor beneath the torturous Magic resonating from Mal.

Maeve rushed towards them, placing herself between Mal and Mr. Brighton.

Mal's eyes were flecked with green.

"He doesn't remember anything, Mal!" Maeve begged, fighting for his attention. "I wiped it all, remember? I took it all."

"Why are you doing this?" cried Brighton behind her.

Maeve forced herself into Mal's line of vision.

Back down, Mal spoke into her mind.

No, was all she replied without hesitation.

"He knows nothing, Mal," she said gently.

"I am not asking him," was Mal's reply.

His eyes flicked up to Ismail, where she stood with splotchy skin and fear filled eyes.

Mal moved around her, still holding Mr. Brighton beneath his Magic.

"There are consequences for lying to me, Ismail."

"Please, Dread Prince," she said, her voice broken.

"Do you feel the Magic resonating from him?" Mal asked.

Ismail nodded stiffly.

"His life's work was dedicated to researching the Dread Artifacts," said Mal. "I know you can feel it."

Ismail's jaw tightened. "I cannot–" she began, her voice strained and breathless.

Another wave of pain crashed through Mr. Brighton. Ismail's eyes squeezed shut.

"I can enter her mind, Mal," said Maeve. "Determine if she is being truthful. Do you believe after all this, that if she knew, she wouldn't have relented by now? She is a ghost of herself, look at her!"

"Is that so, Ismail?" Mal asked.

The Witch nodded furiously, her cheeks flushing a deeper red with every strained breath she took.

Ismail's eyes opened. Her mouth twitched and her bottom lip trembled.

Mr. Brighton fell slack on the floor as Mal moved closer to Ismail. Maeve looked down at Brighton, his chest rose and fell slowly.

"You think she is being honest, Maeve?" He asked as he bent to Ismail's eyes level. "Let's find out."

With a giant gasp Ismail relaxed. Her eyes glassed over as she held Mal's gaze.

"Did you lie to me, Ismail?" Mal asked, his voice sultry and smooth.

A small smile of adoration blossomed at her lips. She nodded fervently.

Mal looked over his shoulder at Maeve. He merely raised his brows, and then turned his attention back to Ismail.

"You know where the Dread Stone is, don't you?" he asked.

Ismail's brows pulled together. She tried to smile, but the same agonizing twisting of her mouth returned. Her expression was a battle of devotion and discomfort.

Mal frowned.

"What Magic is this that fights me?" he asked.

Ismail twitched harder in Roswyn's grip, a low groan building in her throat.

Mal stood to his full height, casting a shadow over her. She continued to convulse, her eyes bulging and her mouth spilling out saliva. Mal did not relinquish his control over her as she struggled, fighting between Mal's Pathokenesis ability, and whatever Magic held her tongue.

Abraxas' hand slowly moved to cover his mouth. He swallowed and then ran his hand across his throat.

"Perhaps we should–" began Abraxas.

But as he spoke, Ismail's scream broke free from her, bouncing off the walls in the large cell.

Mal took her spasming face in his hands. "You are aware this means you are completely useless to me?" he said with a scowl.

Ismail smiled up at him through clattering teeth and twitching eyes.

"I advise you fight harder to release what desires to slip from your tongue, Ismail. Because either that Magic kills you, or I do."

Magic swarmed subtly at Maeve's finger tips, where she prepared to knock Ismail unconscious if that's what it took to release her from her misery.

Ismail's eyes jerked towards Maeve's fingers, the cry in her throat escalating higher and higher.

"Where is the Dread Stone?" Mal asked a final time.

Ismail's swollen eyes remained locked on Maeve's fingers swirling with Magic. She cried and screamed like a wounded animal twice her size. Her body thrashed and Mal dropped her face and stepped away from her.

His Pathokenesis abilities were not enough to bring forth the secret of the Dread Stone, but still he did not release her from his Magic.

"Maeve," called Mal, "come and search her mind for what she cannot speak."

Maeve stepped forward with relief.

But it was short lived.

In Ismail's next strained and convulsing breath, a shattering of Magic exploded across the cell. Roswyn recoiled, dropping his hold on her. She hit the floor face first, her skull slamming into the stone cell floor.

Maeve halted. Ismail did not breathe again.

Maeve stared down at her body, suddenly grateful she hadn't eaten any breakfast.

Mal looked back at Maeve.

"What the hell was that?" Roswyn asked.

"She knew where the stone was," said Mal, his eyes on Maeve. "Just as I said."

Maeve swallowed. "And now she's dead," she rasped.

Mal's attention had already moved back to Brighton.

"He's done nothing," said Maeve, stepping between Mal and where Brighton lay with labored breathing. "I already destroyed his life once, please don't make me complicit in such a finite way."

"And what will you give me in return?" countered Mal.

Maeve's mouth fell open. "Since when has everything become a bargain or a trade to you?"

"It must always be an even exchange," he reminded her.

"One death is enough. She is already dead. She tried to tell you from the start—"

"Stop it," snapped Abraxas from where he stood. His fingers pressed into his temples. "Both of you stop bickering."

Mal stared her down, the flecks of green in his eyes flickering with contempt.

At last he turned on his heel, without another glance at Brighton and made for the door of the cell. "It would be much easier if you'd all just cooperate," he said, Mordred and Roswyn trailing him silently.

Mal's steps drifted into silence.

Maeve looked up at her cousin. "We have entered dark days, Brax."

"The Dread Stone still remains out of reach, and we have no idea who Reeve's Inheritor is," began Abraxas at the long table in his study. "Given their desire for cooperation and a world utopia, what I have proposed is simple," began Abraxas. "In the hidden library I discovered an account from Dread Hands of the past. Before the blight, a touring tournament of duels and competitions took place on each realm, beginning in Aterna. Everything from fencing and archery to baking and craftmanship. Full cooperation and enjoyment for all," he said, sliding his journal closed. "Lithandrian wants an alliance with us, and has for some time now, but she is afraid of the will of the people who may not."

"And this is where we pretend everything is great?" asked Maeve dryly.

"The alternative is we invade Aterna," said Mal coolly. "And show them just how *great* we are."

"A beautiful utopia," she muttered.

Maeve did not look at him. She had not looked at him since Ismail's death.

"You think that's wise?" she asked Abraxas.

Her cousin swallowed. "I think the tournament is an easier way to win them over."

"We have been trying to win them over," muttered Maeve.

"Isn't there a faster way?" Roswyn asked.

"Like what?" asked Abraxas with a slight annoyance in his voice.

"Like Mal uses his Pathokenesis abilities on Reeve," he

suggested.

"The Aterna are immune to such Magic," said Mal.

Maeve looked over at him in a silent question.

"I've already tried," he confessed without remorse.

"But his people no longer possess Aterna Magic," argued Roswyn.

Mal looked over at him. "It's a thought."

"A bad one," said Maeve. "We don't even know if that's possible."

"Maeve then. She can alter his memory to think he serves you," offered Roswyn.

"It's not that simple," said Maeve. "I can't change his opinion. Even if I did alter his memory of past events, he would still, in his own heart, know what he desired. And those around him could also dispute his now false belief. There is nothing stopping him from realizing he doesn't serve Mal. I cannot alter hearts, only memories of what once was."

"So you'd have to alter them all one by one?" asked Abraxas.

"Yes," she lied, not divulging she'd altered groups of memories all together to one reality before. "But again-"

Abraxas tossed up his hand. "I heard you. Hearts and all." He sighed.

"Make no mistake," said Mal, "My ring sits on Lithandrian's finger. I can feel her desire to deny me dwindling each day. Kier's kingdom is already mine. It is only Aterna I am uncertain of."

Maeve shook her head. "And if this ruse of utopian cooperation fails, you will simply take Aterna?"

"Yes," he answered plainly.

"With what army do we attack theirs, Mal?" Maeve asked icily. "They have thousands upon thousands of Senshi Warriors."

"We have thousands of Bellator. The hundreds of wolves under Mordred's command. And soon, The Elven Army. The largest of them all."

"His citizens do not hold power. Their Magic is centuries gone, they are innocent in all of it."

"Innocence has yet to matter to our enemies, Maeve," replied Mal smoothly. "It should not impact your oath as my second."

Maeve looked away from him.

"Continue with your plan, Abraxas," said Mal.

Chapter 56

Maeve

All the realms graciously accepted Mal's proposal for a tournament. The Magical duels began in Aterna, with an exciting appearance from Lithandrian and the Elven court. Her gown was beaded, accenting her tall frame. Her white and gold hair hung long down her back with glistening jewels throughout. Her husband wore a matching set as they breezed along the crystal halls in Aterna, generously accepting the joyous praise of all Immortals.

All except one.

Reeve's eyes were on Maeve.

She stood alone, leaning against the pale crystal balcony as water from the Black Deep gently pushed against the steps around her in Reeve's palace. Her arms folded across her chest. She wore her attire as Mal's second, with the Dread Mark green cloak pinned at her shoulders.

The Dread Ring stood stark against her pale hands. Her Sinclair family ring glistened, matching the beauty of the crystal castle around her.

Reeve arrived at her side, and she did not look at him.

"If you've come to mock me," she said weakly. "I'd ask you to withhold your desire to toy with me."

Reeve did not reply to her statement. Instead, his eyes scanned over her and he said quietly, "Your eyes are red and swollen. Perhaps you need to retire."

Maeve was silent for a moment as she did not meet his gaze. She too ignored his words.

"Have you ever read 'Strange Case of Dr. Jekyll and Mr. Hyde?'" asked Maeve.

"Maeve," said Reeve with a low voice and far too much concern in it.

She looked up at him at last. His lips pulled together, and he fell silent for a long pause, before he said. "I've read it."

She looked back across the party where Mal stood, charming Immortals and the Elven people, with Lithandrian at his side. She ran her gloved hand up her throat, tracing the lines of Dark Magic in her veins.

"I am always steps behind, wondering what version of him I will come upon."

Reeve's voice was steady. "Do you think it's wise that you attend the opening ceremony? You appear under duress."

Maeve nodded as her mouth turned down. She looked up at him. "Is this the part where you sympathize and try to make me forget all the secrets you harbor? All the pain your careless choices caused me?" Maeve scoffed and laughed hollowly. "There's too much green in his eyes," she said. "If I leave, I'll regret it later."

"What?"

"If I leave–" she began.

"No," said Reeve. "What did you say before that?"

Maeve's brows pulled together.

"About his eyes?" pressed Reeve.

His face was calm, not an emotion out of place. But his questions gave him away, and Maeve realized the color of Mal's eyes suddenly mattered to Reeve.

More secrets he'd never tell her. More lies.

"I didn't say anything about his eyes," she said coolly.

Reeve held her gaze for a moment longer and then inhaled slowly before he spoke.

"Some advice, if you insist on staying: set right your face and do your job as his second. Because right now, you are only infuriating him more by not being at his side."

"And what of my fury?" she asked.

Reeve fought a smile. "A beautiful thing when used properly."

Maeve didn't have a chance to reply before he jerked his head towards Mal and the rest.

"Go," he said gently. "Try to enjoy your evening."

Reeve's welcome speech was grand. He toasted his Senshi Warriors and the Bellator about to compete in a series of duels. The winner was honored with more than glory. Reeve and Abraxas pulled together a large sum of gold for the top victors.

The open air coliseum was just as Maeve remembered it. Tall pillars of crystal carved out the stadium seating, where thousands of citizens from across Aterna, The Dread Lands, The Elven Lands and Hiems sat eager to see the duels.

Kier and Lithandrian were beside themselves, praising Abraxas for his brilliant and virtuous goal of inter-realm cooperation.

The realms and their courts were not seated with the citizens. They remained in the lavish hall of Crystalmore that overlooked the coliseum. Tables of food and wine were laid out on silk fabric, tufted leather seats lined the arena for a perfect view. A band of musicians played lightly.

Mordred and his wolves stole most of the attention from Reeve and Lithandrian's courts. They marveled at the oversized, Magical, talking beasts. Mordred kept his distance, observing from afar as he always did.

Thunderous cheers and applause erupted from the crowd as Reeve jogged up the smooth steps from the arena. Maeve's head rolled back against her seat as she watched him clap Abraxas on the back and congratulate him. Abraxas smirked and pulled two cigars from his pocket.

"We're going to need more than cigars," said Reeve, popping one in his mouth and motioning Alphard and Drystan over. "Where's the Aternian Absinthe?"

"Gods, no," said Abraxas with a sharp laugh. "Nope," he said, popping the P. "I can't allow you to do that to me this early."

Reeve grinned. "Who are you, and where's the real Abraxas

Rosethorn?"

"I am serious, Reeve," he said, lighting the tip of his cigar with the snap of his fingers. "These duels will last long into the night."

Reeve looked to Alphard, and they shared a grin. Reeve raised his brows.

"Just one," said Alphard.

Abraxas whined.

"Hush, Rosethorn," said Alphard.

Drystan poured three glasses.

"Will you all think so terribly of me–" began Abraxas, sick at the idea of being left out.

But Drystan was already pouring a fourth glass for him.

They clinked their glasses together all at once and tossed back the liquor.

Abraxas turned a slight shade lighter.

"And when will the Dread Viper be participating?" asked an airy voice.

Lithandrian stood beside her chair, her stare fixed on Maeve's attire.

"You certainly look ready to shatter minds," she finished.

Maeve didn't answer. She looked down at the ring on Lithandrian's finger. The elegant band and stone Mal gifted her radiated with his Dread Magic.

"Am I supposed to stand for you?" asked Maeve dryly.

"Of course not," Lithandrian replied, taking a seat opposite Maeve.

A loud clamor of Magic resonated from the arena, drawing their attention only for a moment.

Lithandrian turned her attention back to Maeve. "So?" she asked once more.

Mal's cool Magic brushed down her back, seeping through her clothes and chilling her skin. He appeared at her side a moment later.

"Maeve isn't dueling today," he said with a soft smile.

Lithandrian returned one. "I agree to come here after all this time, and you can't even let me see these fabled gifts she possesses."

Mal's eyes never left Lithandrian's as he said, "I promise you this, Lithandrian, you will see her power soon enough."

Lithandrian looked pleasantly unaware of the buried meaning within Mal's words. Maeve looked at the crown atop her head. A crown Mal craved.

A loud bang of Magic and a bright flash of light brought their attention back to the arena.

The Senshi Warriors duels were dissimilar in many ways from that of the Magicals. The people of Aterna held no Magic in their veins. Instead, the weapons they wielded were filled with Aterna's Magic from Reeve himself. Protective shields of Magic coated their plated armor, and once broken through, the duel ended.

They were elite, far superior than what Maeve had imagined.

"Drat," said Abraxas, looking down at his list of bets. "Already in the hole."

"Will you enter any horses into the games in my realm, Maeve? I hear your father's horse is quite fast. What's the beast's name?"

"Spitfire," she answered. "And yes, he's quite fast."

"Marvelous," the Elven Queen replied. "I simply can't wait. I've heard you are an excellent fencer, perhaps you'll give us a show?"

"Sure," said Maeve with great disinterest.

Mal's annoyance slipped towards her, intentional or not, she didn't know. His eyes scanned over her with a look of disdain.

"Perhaps you should return to Castle Morana and make yourself more presentable?"

Maeve did not look up at him. Her eyes remained on the two Senshi Warriors battling it out in the arena.

"Excuse me," said Maeve, pushing out of the chair.

She only made it a few steps before Mal snagged her arm. His Magic gripped her tight, sending burning ice into her skin.

"How disappointing it is to see the fire dull from your eyes," he whispered. "All that rebellion squashed with a single blow to your ego."

"Let go," she said weakly, turning away from him, desperate to be anywhere but at his torturous side.

He was like air too toxic to breathe.

Water that merely made her thirstier.

"Backing down so easily?" he asked. "It's a good thing Ambrose is dead and doesn't have to see how fucking weak you've become."

The tether that held her temper slipped free with ease in her next breath. She turned, furious, and drew two fingers at her side. Green lightning sparked across her knuckles, hot and prickling as it pulsed with rage.

The courts and guests around them fell silent with their eyes locked on the Magic radiating from her fingertips and her face of fury set on Mal. The band of musicians faded one by one.

Mal's chin lowered as tiny, dark swirls of green pierced from his narrowed eyes, daring her.

Don't.

The command rang clear across her mind, and Maeve froze.

For it wasn't Mal's voice that echoed past her impenetrable shields.

Mal had always been able to speak into her mind, but she allowed him entry. A fragment of his very soul ran through her veins. He was a part of her.

For another to speak into her mind without her permission. . .to break past the strongest mind wall of any Magical known.

She turned with horror. Her eyes lifted to the High Lord. Reeve stared casually at her across the hall.

Everyone between them and everything around them blurred. And there was only his presence. The world slammed to a halt.

And she forgot Mal. And his comment. She forgot that she lost her temper and nearly attacked her sworn Prince.

All that rang through her mind was the life altering and potentially catastrophic fact:

She was the High Lord of Aterna's fated mate.

Reeve's chin lowered slightly.

Don't, he said again.

Maeve's stomach dropped beneath her, nearly sending up her dinner.

Cold slender fingers wrapped around her arm, which was now collapsed limply at her side. Any and all trace of lightning were now gone. Maeve looked up at Reeve with wide eyes.

The hall snapped back into time, and tense murmurs whispered through the crowd.

Mal took her hand is his own and brought his lips to her ear.

"What are you going to do now?"

Maeve stammered, tearing her eyes away from Reeve. "I–"

Mal's grip tightened. *What are you going to do now that you've made a scene?*

Maeve couldn't form words.

Such a pity you can't alter their minds all at once, isn't it?

Fear prickled down her spine. Maeve steadied her breathing, desperate to control herself.

Mal laughed lightly, tossing his head back as he stood to his full height. He smiled down at her with easy charm. He released her from his tight hold and kissed her fingers.

"Fiercely loyal, this one," he announced to the room. "She thought I was in danger."

The mood shifted at once. Shoulders sighed in relief and the music resumed.

Mal kissed her fingers once more. As the attention on them faded, so did his smile. "You can thank me later. I have plenty of ideas."

He dropped her hand and turned on his heel. Maeve turned slowly, her body stiff and tight, to Reeve. But his attention was no longer on her. The High Lord swapped his drink for a new one, laughing with Eryx and some other warriors as though he hadn't just revealed yet another secret.

Damn him.

Her heart shook and air tightened across her chest.

He did not meet her gaze but his voice slid smoothly across her mind.

Stop staring at me and pull yourself together.

Maeve's lip curled upward. She turned and pushed through the crowd. They parted hastily around her. She did not announce her departure. She slipped through the Portal to the Dread Lands without a word of goodbye.

Reeve stood leaned against the bannister of her chamber balcony, his arms folded. Maeve scowled and crossed out into the cool night air.

"How are you in my head?" she demanded.

Reeve didn't look at her. "You know how."

"No," said Maeve. "That's ridiculous."

Reeve shot her a look. "Is it any more ridiculous than the charade happening all around us?"

Maeve tensed.

"How long have you known?" she asked.

"That doesn't really matter."

Maeve shook her head slightly and spoke sourly. "I must be a joke to you."

She leaned against the frame of the glass doors.

Reeve studied her, an arrogant look on his face. "Is that what you think?"

She didn't answer him. A cold breeze drifted between them. Maeve hugged herself tightly as clouds covered the moons, darkening the balcony.

"It doesn't mean anything," she said, her voice lacking its usual confidence.

"I know," he replied, his voice in perfect opposition to hers.

"I choose Mal," she added stubbornly. "I have faith he will pull through this."

"I know that too."

"You aren't owed me because of some ancient–"

"I never said I was," he interrupted quietly.

They stared at one another in a painful silence, longer than was comfortable. Finally, Maeve spoke.

"I can't tell him this."

Reeve made a face as though he agreed, though it annoyed him all the same. "I can promise I don't need your protection from–"

"Oh shut up," snapped Maeve. "This isn't just about you, or me."

A forced breath escaped her lips.

Another secret, one that would certainly plant more conflict between her and Mal, was the last thing she needed. Mal was so distant, so far from her.

Barely hanging by a thread.

If he knew that Reeve was standing before her in such a hidden and private way. . .

"Things are changing, Maeve," said Reeve, pulling her from her thoughts. "I know you can feel the darkness that is growing here."

Of course she did. But God's be damned if he didn't just be quiet.

Maeve tossed her head back and closed her eyes. "Shut. Up."

"I can feel it all the way across the Black Deep-"

"Did you not hear me say shut up?" asked Maeve.

"No, I did," snarled Reeve. "But say it again. I love hearing the hatred you harbor for me singing off your spoiled fucking tongue."

Maeve pushed off the doorframe and closed the gap between them, stopping short before they touched. Reeve's eyes swam with dark fire.

He bent until they shared one breath and whispered playfully. "You're too easy."

His body radiated warmth. She resisted the urge to step closer and allow herself to be shielded from the cold night air.

Maeve huffed and stepped back from him. "How did this even happen? I thought you already had a mate. I'm not even an Immortal."

"She was not my mate, despite the love we shared."

"But I thought," began Maeve. She sighed. "I asked you about her."

"You referred to her as my mate. I did not correct you."

Maeve stammered.

"I loved her, yes. Despite no Magical, fated bond, I loved her fully," he said. "Painfully and achingly so. The way you love your Dread Prince."

"You've known the whole time," said Maeve softly, reflecting on his first appearance at the Summer Solstice party the summer before her father died.

"I won't say anything." He leaned casually on the bannister.

"To anyone?"

Maeve's stomach twisted as Reeve answered. "It is not in my best interest to announce to the world that my mate is Malachite's Dread Viper."

Those words stung.

Maeve ran her fingers along the chilly stone bannister. "It is not, nor it cannot, come to good."

Reeve attempted a small smile, and failed. "You read Hamlet?"

Maeve nodded, avoiding his gaze. "You gave it such a glowing review."

"And?" he asked.

Maeve shrugged. "It was. . ."

Dark mist flared sharply around Reeve, reminiscent of his dragon form. Maeve gasped as soft prickles of ice crept from the nape of her neck and down her arms. Her eyes slipped closed as Mal's Magic crept in, taking over her senses.

Her eyes whipped open to Reeve, but he was gone, and in his wake was a swirling mass of black shadow and shining flecks of darkening starlight.

She walked briskly across the balcony. The glass doors clicked closed behind her with the slightest twist of two fingers at her side.

Mal appeared a moment later, sauntering across her bedroom chamber towards her.

"You're flustered."

"I'm fine," she lied.

He stopped short of her.

His eyes flicked up towards the balcony behind her, and then slowly moved back to hers.

Mal grabbed her face tightly between his fingers, Dark Magic pulsating into her skin. She closed her eyes and mustered her courage.

"Mal," she said calmly.

"I can't see into your mind," he said far too calmly.

"What would you like to see?" she asked, looking up at him.

"Don't," he said quietly, "toy with me."

He moved his hand away tensely and took her right hand in his own, holding up her two fingers as if they were on display.

The bits of green glowing in his eyes were smaller now, but still remained.

"You made to strike me."

"I was angry," said Maeve coolly.

Mal's head cocked slightly to the side. "And that gives you permission to strike your Prince?"

"No one even remembers. They'll think nothing of it."

Another lie. The lies between them were piling up.

"That is far from the point and you know it."

He discarded her hand and moved away from her, reclining in the loveseat.

"Sit," he commanded.

She obeyed, taking a seat opposite him.

"I'm done waiting. The time has come to solidify my supreme leadership."

"Kier is already under your control. Is that not enough?"

Mal did not answer. "You are so adamant that you will not fight Aterna."

"I did not say that," she argued carefully. "I said I didn't want to attack innocents."

"And you think Reeve is innocent? Despite his hand in your father's death."

"I believe the High Lord–"

"Don't call him that."

A sigh slipped from Maeve. "I believe Reeve is a smart ruler, who, unlike his father before him, isn't willing to sacrifice his people for his own power."

"Ambrose told you that?"

"Yes."

"Ambrose was a fool for putting so much faith in Reeve."

Acid boiled in Maeve's stomach.

Mal's eyes narrowed. "And you are as well."

Maeve leaned back in her seat, crossed her legs and whispered. "You are in a rare form tonight."

A small smile tugged at the corner of Mal's mouth, as though he delighted in throwing such an insult at her.

Crumbling. It was all crumbling.

Maeve saw it, she felt it all. And she knew. . . she was running out of time.

She abandoned all fear and pride. She stood and crossed the rug between them. Standing before the man she had sworn herself to in so many ways.

She dropped to her knees and placed her hands on his legs.

Mal's head inclined as he stared at her with green flecked eyes.

She was at risk of losing it all.

"I'm sorry for this evening," she whispered. "It may be a fool's errand to put Reeve's true colors to the test, but you must do so regardless. Even if you are certain he will not bow, that he will not give up that crown, I urge you to try. The adoration you will receive for it will abound."

"And what about the alternative?"

"The alternative is we take it all by force. And if that is what my Prince demands of me, it will be done. But as your second, I urge you to try for peace." Maeve sat up on her knees and moved between his legs. She placed her hands on his chest. "I want to be at your side and see you wear the only crown in all the realms. I want a future here where we have a life not plagued by constant battles. Try, for me, and for your loyal subjects here, try for peace. And if it does not work, I will burn every last monarchy and ruler down that opposes you until all that remains are the faithful."

Mal leaned over her, a prideful smirk playing on his lips. "Such a speech. You've been learning from Abraxas."

Her entire body relaxed. He took her chin in his hand. "I am not innocent tonight. I provoked you."

His lips moved closer to hers.

"You are quite good at it," she muttered.

"No one knows you like I do, Maeve." His hand drifted down her neck, tracing her black darkened veins. "And no one ever will."

Chapter 57

Malachite

As the Magical duels in Aterna came to a close, the victors of the duels collected their rewards and accolades with triumphant faces. First prize and third prize went to Senshi Warriors, with one of their Bellator stealing second place. Eryx and Drystan, Roswyn and Alphard all abstained from the tournament, giving others a chance to shine.

And shine they did.

The Senshi Warriors fought with a tenacity that gripped Mal's attention and consumed his mind. He thought of them endlessly. The power radiating from their swords and arrows. The agile and controlled strength they embodied.

He had to have it.

The Bellator were a wild mass of Magic, disciplined in an entirely different way of battle. Obscuring and tricks, bending nature and trapping the senses were their strengths. Their possibilities endless.

But the Senshi were designed for war. He could smell it.

They enjoyed their time with his Bellator. The Supremes in his ranks delighted in finding their power match in playful rivalry. They ate and danced together at Crystalmore, celebrating their triumphs and newfound comradery.

"We look forward to hosting you next," said Lithandrian, pulling Mal from his thoughts. "I have many contenders eager to match up against your Warrior's swordplay, High Lord."

"Their swords are only a part of their fight," said Reeve with a proud smile.

"Ah," replied Lithandrian, her eyes narrowing slightly, "but it is all of the Elven's strength. And in a battle of arms, I believe you'll see how greatly that matters."

Reeve toasted her. "It is not lost on me that Eryx has transformed their swordplay with the customs his father learned from your people."

Lithandrian seemed pleased with his remark. She excused herself as her husband inclined his head across the hall.

"I have an idea," said Mal.

Reeve cocked a brow, his effortless arrogance on full display.

"You and Maeve. A little display."

Reeve stalled.

"You want me to fight her?" asked Reeve, his smile fading.

"Why not?" Mal answered cooly. "A spectacle it will be, I'm sure."

Reeve nodded, licking across his front teeth.

"And here I was expecting you to place yourself," replied Reeve.

"Our day has not dawned," said Mal without missing a beat.

"Do you foresee it?" asked Reeve.

Mal smiled. "I am no seer."

"No," said Reeve. "You haven't got one of those I'm told."

Mal looked across the hall to Roswyn, where he and Alphard shared drinks with the Senshi. "Poor Emerie," was all he said.

"Yes," said Reeve dryly, following Mal's gaze. "Poor girl."

"Maeve has trained well," continued Mal. "You'd honor her to not hold back."

"A closing duel in the ancient times was a fight to the death."

Mal looked across the hall at her. Where she stood, leaned against the wall, watching guests with uneasy eyes. "You think she won't die for me?"

"No," said Reeve. "I'm certain she would. But you die before she does, correct?"

Mal's eyes snapped to Reeve, as though he had forgotten the High Lord was present for that Magical vow he made in the foyer at Sinclair Estates. He'd been emotional that day, terrified of losing her after Kietel took her.

And since that day, it was written in Magic: Mal would die before Maeve did.

Mal's cool demeanor returned as he looked away from Reeve.

"As I said," began Mal, "don't hold back."

He left Reeve without another word and crossed the hall towards Maeve. Her eyes flitted up to him and she pushed off the wall, meeting him halfway.

"The closing duel. You and Reeve."

Maeve's mouth fell open. Mal nearly chuckled.

"Don't worry, Little Viper. He won't kill you. But I expect to see you try to kill him."

"I'm not capable of killing him," she said softly.

"I said try. Bring that lightning out."

"I'm not angry enough for that."

Mal sighed and spoke with a sharp ease. "What do I need to do to provoke you?"

Maeve looked up into his dark eyes. There were barely any flecks of green in them.

"Is this punishment?" she asked.

Mal laughed softly. "What have you done deserving of punishment, Maeve? Move to attack me in front of all the other realms? Constantly question my place as your Prince?" He paused. "Look at me with such a soft disdain I hardly recognize you?"

Maeve's jaw loosened.

Mal's expression shifted as his eyes traced across her face. Sorrow swept across his green-flecked eyes, as they faded momentarily to their flawless natural color.

Maeve stepped towards him, hope swelling in her chest.

"Mal," she said softly.

His eyes lifted to hers, and with one breath, hope faded and the small flecks of green returned to his now hardened face.

"You best go prepare," he said.

Maeve

Mal's voice echoed across her mind as she stepped onto the pale ground of the arena, her eyes on Reeve where he waited for her at its center.

Do you so easily forget he placed that poison?

Maeve had not forgotten. She'd never forget.

If the Gods were cruel in nature, she must have been their favorite to mock.

Is it through negligence or naivety that you think he truly was unaware the goblet still held such a deadly curse?

A fated bond with the man ultimately responsible for the poison that killed her most beloved.

That perhaps, in your father's loyalty to me, Reeve felt threatened?

She wondered how long Reeve had known.

He'd kept their bond from her. He'd known and hadn't shared it with her. He could speak into her mind and had never been forthcoming with such important knowledge.

Reeve slid off his overcoat, revealing the black beaded tunic underneath. The finest clothes in Aterna. No shining armor in sight. His broad shoulders and fit frame looked deadly in all black. The jagged marks of Vexkari that ran along the side of his face and down his neck nearly glowed.

He contested my presence here, you said so yourself.

Reeve stepped across the arena, Magic pulsing from each step, until he stood in the middle of a large, black, seven-pointed star.

Its twin was a few steps away from Maeve.

It would be easy to find out.

I've never been in an Aterna's mind, Maeve replied to Mal.

It will bend to you, like they all do. See just how far you can go into his mind.

Mal slipped from her thoughts, and she closed the door that allowed him entry. She needed all her strength to last even a single spell in a duel with Reeve.

"You could surrender your win now," said Reeve with a practiced and perfected shining smile. "Save yourself the embarrassment."

"The only embarrassment I fear is that of cowardice." Maeve stepped into the black seven-pointed star in front of her and said cooly, "Do I look like a coward to you?"

"No," said Reeve with a small chuckle. "You look like your

father."

Maeve's insides twisted and plummeted, drawing rage from her core.

Rage that he wasn't present.

Rage that he lied to her.

Rage that she had no answers, nor an idea of who her mother was.

Rage that Mal was slipping into something twisted and she had no idea how to save him.

Lightning, electric and sharp, prickled at her fingertips.

They formally acknowledged one another with a small bow.

Reeve glanced down at her hand with an eager look in his eyes. "So be it," he said with a grin.

Lightning erupted from her fingers, refracting across the bright crystal walls encasing them. Cheers of excitement boomed around them.

Reeve was gone in a swirl of violet, fire-like mist before her Magic made contact. She whipped around; he stood at her backside.

With a single wave of his hand she stumbled sideways.

Maeve Obscured quickly before she hit the ground, righting herself a few feet away. She slammed up a shield as a small burst of Magic spiraled towards her. It slammed into her shield, sparkling to the ground.

Maeve's eyes narrowed at his purposefully weak attempt.

Reeve shrugged.

Maeve conjured Magic to her fingers, directly aiming for him as she simultaneously slammed into his mind.

Maeve recoiled against his mental shields. The Magic shooting from her hand vanished as she winced at the throbbing pain behind her eyes. His head cocked to the side playfully.

You want into my head? Reeve's voice echoed across her mind. *You have access. You need only use it.*

She'd never use that bond to connect with him. She hated that he was in her head at all. She pushed again, using every bit of strength to slice through his shields. This time, she fell to the pale crystal floor of the collegium with a smack.

Her palms cried at the impact of catching herself.

She withdrew her Magic pressing against his mental shields with a frustrated sigh and pushed up off the ground, glaring at him over her shoulder.

Too afraid to feel something other than hatred, Maeve? he taunted.

She stood tall and faced him.

Charged Magic spiked at her hand, bright blue and volatile, as she reared back.

He extended his hand, palm flat, as her lightning barreled towards him. He made no attempt to dodge her attack, in fact Reeve welcomed the deadly Magic into his palm with his eyes on her.

It did not dissipate, or slice through him. It snapped and jerked in his hand. He brought his hands together, a pained expression she'd never seen him wear rippling across his face as he held her lightning.

Maeve's mouth fell open and she froze.

The pale blue electric paths crackled around him as he took control of the energy, despite the agony it brought him. He held a tight breath as it moved through him, wrapping up his arms and illuminating more and more.

The crowd had grown completely quiet. The air buzzed with anticipation and shock. Pure awe and terror mixed across Maeve's expression. She didn't even attempt to hide her emotions as her arms fell slack at her sides.

Reeve's voice sounded across her mind. *You feel marvelous.*

She'd never win. He was always ahead of her in knowledge and in power.

Only he heard her as she fought the shake in her voice and whispered, "I do hate you."

Her lightning swarmed back to his hand.

"I know," he said with a quiet resolve.

Her vision shifted to the image of a dark night sky and the sound of a small cry.

Maxius' tiny hands reached towards her, gripping the fabric of her cloak as massive tears streamed his delicate face. The tall, hooded figure before her took him in their arms.

Maxius continued to reach for her in distress. Maeve's heart cracked open.

"This is not forever, Maeve," said the hooded figure.

His voice was familiar.

"Then why is my heart breaking?"

The hooded figure held Maxius tenderly.

"How am I supposed to walk away?" she asked, her voice breaking.

Warm wind swirled around them, settling Maxius against the hooded man's chest and calming him instantly. He breathed deeply as his eyes fluttered close beneath thick lashes.

The vision snapped back out of view, and Reeve stood before her in the coliseum once more.

Bright light blinded her.

Her body registered the shock in a delay as he flung her lightning back towards her. An invisible shield slammed up before her, not of her own Magic, dulling the blow. It was gone before she could understand whose Magic it was.

She cried out as her eyes squeezed shut against the burning hot Magic. The bit of lightning that clipped her shoulder throbbed as it courses through her body. Blood soaked through her clothes, damp and warm as it moved down her arm.

She peeked up at Reeve and realized she was on the ground, not having felt the fall. He stared down at her, his mask back in place and clicked his tongue.

"Your Viper is wounded, Dread Prince," announced Reeve loudly.

Maeve scowled up at him through the pain.

"You should stay down," said Reeve.

She pushed one foot into the ground, her other knee pulsing in pain. She pulled herself completely upright and staggered, gripping her stomach. The coliseum tilted and her view of Reeve blurred.

"You cannot win," he said. "It would be honorable for us both if you yield."

Maeve dug her heels in and did not reply.

Her father had taught her to never back down. Mal had trained her to never sacrifice her honor.

Please don't make me, he said into her mind. She didn't miss that his voice was wrought with pain. His face remained leisurely arrogant. *Yield.*

Maeve had never spoken to him through that ancient connection. And she didn't intend to start.

She pulled her spine tall, her chin proud, as what could only be described as heartbreak shattered across Reeve's face.

Her arms dropped to her side.

There came no apology as his divine Magic whipped across the arena. She had nothing left of a shield. She knew it would be an all but fatal blow.

But she would take it for her honor.

For her Dread Prince.

She'd do it to show Mal, as she always did, that her oath as his Second was never taken lightly. Even now, as her dreams of their future slipped away behind his dead eyes.

And to show Reeve that no matter what Magic lingered between them, she chose Mal.

What other choice was there? She would go down beside him, or not at all.

The side of her vision registered Maxius as he stepped towards her from a mass of dark swirling mist. In that same blink, a cracking sound rang through her ears, echoing off the now blurred walls of the arena as her jaw snapped, and darkness encased her.

Chapter 58

Reeve

Reeve yanked his Magic back, narrowly missing Maxius' small frame as the boy lunged forward. Magic ripped from his single pointed finger, shattering through the arena and throwing up a shield of dark energy around Maeve as her body hit the crystal floor, and didn't move again.

The coliseum froze.

Mal did not move to her side. The Dread Prince's eyes were set on Maxius, a look of shock plastered across his face.

The youngest Magical to point a single finger.

Even younger than Mal had been.

Tears streamed down the child's face as he turned silently towards Reeve.

"She is alive," said Reeve carefully, a tenderness in his voice. "I did not fatally wound her."

Maxius' look of fear and anger towards Reeve did not falter. Zimsy appeared at Maxius' side and took his hands in her own.

She drew the child's attention up at her, and he fell into her, bursting into tears. His dark shield of energy crumbled.

"Maxius." Mal's cool and calm tone rang across the arena.

The child looked up at him swiftly. He slipped from Zimsy's embrace and raced towards Mal, tears still streaming his round face.

Mal did not pick him up as he reached the floor of the arena, despite Maxius' raised arms. Mal took his head in his slender fingers.

"She is alright," said Mal. "Do you want to know how I know?"

Maxius sniffled and gripped the fabric of Mal's pants. Mal dropped his hand and scooped Maxius into his arms in a fluid motion.

Mal looked up at Reeve. "Because her blood flows for me."

Reeve's shoulders fell and his jaw relaxed. He looked back at Maeve. Tiny breaths rose and fell in her chest. Mal crossed towards her as Maxius buried his head against Mal's neck. Mal kneeled beside her and brushed his free hand down her cheek.

Maeve's first full breath sucked a year's worth of energy from Reeve as he finally felt her Magic swell back to life.

"Thank you for the hospitality, Reeve of Aterna," said Mal. "We will see you soon."

The three of them vanished in a dark cosmic haze.

Dread spiraled down Reeve's core. Mal moved off Crystalmore without a Portal, despite Reeve's own enchantments to prevent such Magic without his authorization. Reeve's eyes shot to Eryx. His second seemingly had the same realization: The Dread Prince found the Spellbook.

The colosseum released a collective breath as the mist cleared.

Abraxas joined Reeve at his side. "That seemed unnecessary," he said pointedly. "Was she alright?"

"I broke her jaw," said Reeve quietly, realizing how much power had slipped from him.

He had not intended to do such damage, and Maeve was sure to be sour for it.

Zimsy appeared at his other side, her steps even and slow. Her Elven beauty stood stark in the presence of so many Magicals and Immortals in attendance.

Abraxas ran his hand through his bright blond hair. "I suppose it needed to look convincing."

Reeve looked down at him, his head cocking to the side.

Abraxas didn't meet his gaze. His eyes remained on the guests whispering about Mal's sudden departure and such a deadly duel. "It's a curse really," he said quietly, "knowing everything."

Reeve steadied his breathing. She wouldn't have told her cousin. She was many things but reckless was not one of them.

Abraxas sighed, shaking his head. A soft, placating smile appeared on his lips. "I know you have good intentions here, High Lord. My uncle was your friend. I merely meant you likely didn't want to duel my cousin. But the Prince insisted."

Abraxas' voice was purely political. Reeve knew he wouldn't receive an honest and uncalculated response from The Dread Prince's hand, despite being Maeve's cousin, and so he chose to ignore the entire insinuation.

"She'll be fine," said Zimsy, watching Reeve. "Maeve has endured worse for less."

Chapter 59

Maeve

"To what do I owe the pleasure of such a rare visit?" asked Maeve as she pulled pins from her hair.

Mal stood in the doorway of her chamber. "Are you fully healed?"

She returned her gaze to the vanity mirror, still in her dueling attire.

"Yes," she answered.

"Astrea said a broken jaw is easily healed with a snap of her fingers. And that huge blast of lightning barely touched you."

Maeve did not reply, still sulking from her defeat.

"He was. . .merciful," said Mal.

"I suppose so," she replied shortly as the last of her braids fell.

She worked her fingers through them, untangling the woven hair.

"Now look who is punishing who," said Mal.

Maeve looked up at him.

"You knew I couldn't possibly win," she said bitterly.

Mal pushed off the door frame and crossed her chamber. "Perhaps I wanted to see it anyway."

He slid into an armchair and crossed one leg over the other casually. Maeve continued to brush through her hair and did not regard him.

"He certainly had your attention all evening prior to your duel."

Maeve scowled, cleverly quick with a reply. "I wasn't staring at him."

Mal's jaw tightened.

"I was staring at his date," she finished.

Mal's head tilted and his mouth opened ever so slightly, but Maeve didn't let him speak. She slipped off her jewelry. She spoke with calculated softness, continuing to pull Mal's mind away from

Reeve.

Away from the thoughts of him that ran across her mind.

"Do you know how infuriating it is to watch them waltz around with their everlasting beauty?" she asked. "When everyday my body is dying and changing with age."

Mal's eyes narrowed. "Hmm," he hummed. "That's interesting." He relaxed once more, his expression dripping back into his usual dark void of emotion.

Maeve reached for the back of her bodice, pulling on the laces as it fell loose around her shoulders. She caught the fabric swiftly, holding it at her chest, keeping herself covered, and looked up at Mal.

With one leg crossed over his knee, and an elbow on the arm of the chair, his long fingers propped up his chin as his attention lingered across her body. Slowly, his hungry eyes moved to hers. A silent command.

And her dueling uniform fell.

Maeve turned back towards the vanity, and slipped her legs free of the fitted clothing. Mal watched her silently in the mirror, with eyes that glowed green in small places.

She turned back towards him, and stepped across the fabric, now crumpled on the rug. When she was before him, her hands reached for the neckline of his top. She loosened the fabric slowly. With a soft snap of her fingers, each button on his shirt slipped open, exposing his lean and toned chest. She braced her arms on either side of the chair and bent towards his neck, planting her lips slowly and softly against his cold skin.

"Will you stay with me tonight," she whispered, kissing across his neck, moving towards his collarbone, "my Prince?"

Before Maeve could blink, darkness swirled around them, and her back touched down on velvet bedding. Mal kneeled between her legs and tossed his shirt aside.

"Say it again," he commanded.

Maeve obeyed. "Please, my Prince."

Mal pushed his hips into hers with a small groan. She felt his hardness through his pants at once.

"You'd think I wouldn't enjoy this, knowing you are merely manipulating me with this pretty body of yours," he said, taking her chin in between his fingers. "But, Primus and the Gods," he said darkly, grinding his hips against her once more, "it is so perfectly pretty."

His lips met hers as his fingers trailed across the Dread Mark on her chest.

The sensation shot to her toes and arched her body towards his.

"If you are so displeased with me," she said when their lips parted, "why is your body responding exactly how I want it to?"

Maeve pressed her Magic towards him, kissing him back with desperation. His mental shields were down, and she slipped through them with ease.

An idea struck her.

She pushed a memory gently towards him. It blossomed across his mind like a soft wind.

A floral sheet lay against soft grass, the edges lifting in the breeze. A small teapot and empty teacups sat near them. The summer sun beamed down upon them where they faced one another. Mal twirled a strand of her hair between his fingers while their lips danced on the edge of a kiss.

Maeve beamed as he whispered something.

She pulled out of Mal's mind, and she looked up at him where he hovered above her in the bed.

His eyes shifted to their natural color. Maeve inhaled deeply at the sight of his fully darkened eyes.

"Hi," she said softly, tears instantly threatening to fall down her cheeks.

Mal's expression faltered in confusion for a moment. He looked down at her body and his own arousal. His eyes dipped close, and he rested his forehead lightly on hers.

"Those feel like ancient versions of ourselves," he said.

Maeve nodded and brushed his hair back, running her fingers gently across the scar splitting his eye. "I want to go to Earth, Mal. I want to watch the sun rise through the glass in your old apartment… safe in your arms."

Mal hesitated to reply.

"Do you remember the sun, Mal?"

He nodded.

"Would you take me there?" she asked earnestly.

Mal pressed a kiss to her forehead and inhaled deeply. Darkness encased them as his arms moved around her body, one cradling the back of her head and the other around her waist.

They moved through time and space with ease. Mal's Magic was paramount, unlike anything he'd had when he became her tutor.

The darkness lifted, and the hazy blue moonlight of Earth filled the room. Soft sheets caressed her back in the bed at The Hapswitch House. Mal's old flat, formerly her Uncle's home, was rightfully his. Ambrose had ensured it.

Mal's eyes remained their true color as he held her close. She was certain it was a cruel dream. One that would be ripped from her at any moment. But they took their time worshipping one another and pretending, even if for a moment, that a nightmare didn't await them back in The Dread Lands.

Mal's shoulders rolled back and his eyes fluttered to a close. His skin gained a soft warmth and his heart beat steady against her chest. His Magic was calm.

Maeve traced her fingers tenderly along the starburst scars of Magic on his exposed chest. Sacrifices he'd made for her. For his destiny as their savior.

"I wanted to take you home," he said quietly. "I wanted to have you on every surface in that house. But I know you could not bear to be there, and nor can I."

"We should remain here," she said.

Mal brushed off the comment.

"I'm serious."

"I have a kingdom to rule, Maeve," said Mal, with a soft smile that did not meet his eyes.

Maeve propped herself up and took his face in her hands. "A Kingdom that is tearing you apart." His hands moved over hers. "It's tearing us apart, Mal."

"Nothing worth having comes to us with ease."

"No," she fired back. "I do not believe we should destroy it all for some possibilities on the other side."

"I am in control–"

Maeve yanked away from him and slid off the bed. She rubbed her eyes with her palms, turning towards the windows overlooking London. The morning sunlight was a soft, glowing yellow. The trees that lined the small street below bloomed with bright green leaves and soft brown bark. The cream-colored stones of the surrounding buildings looked like paintings.

The wooden floorboards creaked lightly beneath his steady steps. His arms circled around her, pulling her back into his chest. She rested her head against him.

"I can do this, Little Viper," he murmured into her temple after planting a small kiss.

"I don't want to go back there," she admitted, the words quiet and withdrawn.

Mal's lips pressed into the soft skin where her neck and shoulder joined. "The future is riding on our shoulders. We cannot abandon it now."

Chapter 60

Maeve

Maeve marked her enchanted parchment as days rolled by in Mal's absence when she unwillingly returned to Castle Morana after their visit to Earth. She scratched another mark as the delicate hands on her watch sat high at midnight.

The Dark Peaks were breathable. With all but the Dread Stone, Mal managed to drive the blight of the land back past Mount Morte, the tallest mountain in the realm.

She could no longer stay in the Crown's Quarters. Most nights she slept in the large bed in Zimsy's room with Maxius, who were both fast asleep on the upper floor of the castle as Maeve read in the library.

The firelights flickered as her eyelids grew heavy. She shook her head quickly and focused on the words before her.

The account was from a former servant of Orion the Dread, recalling the day a small and malnourished baby appeared at the gates of Castle Morana. She was swaddled in tattered fabric in the cold night air.

Shamefully, I hesitated to bring the babe inside. Orion was unlike a father in most manners, even his own children seldom saw his smile. Something drew me to the pale babe with white hair, and I did not care what Orion would say. We'd hide her in the kitchens if need be.

To my surprise, he favored her above all, even his heir and first born. She grew beautiful in her womanhood with charm that Orion lacked. Her Magic contradicted any tale or witness I bore of power. She ensnared his mind as a babe and never let go.

Father, she called him. Daughter, he called her.

His trueborn daughters mocked her pale skin and white hair with eyes to match. "Ghost," they called her in jealous whispers. As just a babe, I could not see it then, but as her hair grew and her skin never filled with warmth, I knew she was not malnourished when she wound up at the castle gates. She was an albino.

Maeve sat forward in her chair as warmth fled her own skin. She looked up at the mural ceiling. The woman depicted was surely too beautiful to be the gaunt woman who invaded her dreams.

Her eyes fell back to the text. She flipped the page to the next entry. Chunks of pages were ripped from the journal, leaving jagged edges of paper sitting up from the spine. The next entry was hardly even the same handwriting, much farther back in the book. It was messy and written with a shaking hand.

Today we laid to rest the last in the Dread Bloodline. They were burned, as is tradition. Their ashes were spread in the Greywood, as is tradition. Orion can barely stand. His eyes are so green now.

Ghost remains. She is always present. She is always watching my mind.

She tells him relentlessly she knows he bore another. One he kept secret.

She is always watching our minds.

Maeve flipped the page. There was nothing further. She closed the book with a discontent sigh. The possibilities of the missing, torn out pages ran through her mind.

Her gaze lifted back to the ceiling. It was unlikely there had been another like her- with such striking features-

In a blink, she was in Mal's study.

Standing in the center of the room.

No idea how she got there. No idea where she'd been before. Her eyes darted around the room. Mal stood shirtless over his desk, with disheveled hair as he clutched the Dread Goblet. He filled it with a dark, amber liquid.

Her body tensed. "What are you doing?" she asked quickly.

Mal ignored her. His skin gleamed with sweat as he gripped the goblet with trembling hands. Only then did Maeve see the brown liquid already dripping from the corner of his mouth.

"Stop it!" she screamed, Obscuring to him.

Mal downed the contents of the goblet at once, tossing back the dark liquid before she could knock it from his hands.

Maeve's stomach plummeted. Her hands tingled as fear overtook her. Mal gripped the Dread Goblet tightly and threw it across his study. It collided with the wall and hit the floor with one solid boom.

Maeve's eyes stung. Her pulse accelerated.

Mal looked up at her, his breathing heavy. No trace of green in his eyes. He stumbled backward, putting space between them. "Stay away."

Maeve disobeyed. She pressed him on shaking legs as he fell back against the wall. Tears slipped along his sunken cheek bones as he slid down to the floor.

Maeve fell to her knees before him.

"It won't kill me," he cried.

Maeve shook her head in a mixture of disbelief and comfort. "What?"

"The Dread Goblet cannot kill me."

Maeve looked across the study to where the gold goblet lay on the floor.

The Magic that had killed her father was completely dormant, not a trace of it lingering in Mal.

Ismail had said it. Even Reeve had. They just hadn't understood. "It was not meant to kill the Dread," she recited in a scattered whisper.

It was poisoned to kill someone…something else, Ismail had said.

Shadow, Reeve said. He intended to kill Shadow with such lethal Magic.

"How?" he stammered with dilated eyes. "How could it have so easily killed Ambrose when, no matter how many times I try to rid myself of this darkness, I cannot find release?"

"They never intended to kill House Dread," she said. "It was intended to save the Dread."

Mal beat his head against the wall behind him. Then again. Then again. Then again, until Maeve's hand swooped behind his damp hair, cradling his skull. Her knuckles took the brunt of the force as he slammed his head back once more. She didn't feel it.

"How many times have you tried to poison yourself?" she asked, her voice heartbreakingly soft.

Mal did not reply.

The whites of his eyes carried scattered red lines. Underneath them was dark purple, thin skin. Maeve touched his face with her free hand. His eyes snapped to her, but they remained their dark chocolate color.

"Come and rest, Mal," she said gently. "On Earth. With me."

His frightened eyes never left hers as he nodded.

A moment later, they arrived at Hapswitch House. Mal sunk into the sofa, his head rolling back into the dark leather.

"I want to try something," she said. "Something to make you relax."

He did not respond. Maeve pulled the Dread Dagger from its concealed spot on her thigh and sliced across her palm. His eyes snapped to the wound as the smell of blood singed their noses.

Maeve kneeled over him on the plush sofa as she brought her bleeding palm closer to his face.

He snagged her wrist weakly. "How do I know it's you?"

Her heart constricted. "Ask me something only I would know," she said with calm patience, hoping he couldn't see just how close to breaking she was.

His dark and lifeless eyes looked past her. After a moment he asked, "When did you know I loved you?"

She brought her woundless hand to his face. His eyes moved slowly back to hers. "When Vaukore fell, and you kissed me."

He did not smile. "And when did you fall in love with me?"

"The moment you said I was a Supreme," she said without hesitation. "As though you'd always known. As though you'd always seen me truly."

She brushed her fingers along his skin.

"One more," he said.

Maeve nodded.

"What was the song playing when I kissed you at the Summer Solstice party?" A small smile pulled at the corner of his lips.

Maeve smiled as blood pooled in her hand. "Symphony number nine."

"Yes," he said, recalling the memory.

His grip on her wrist released, and his arm fell limply to his side. Maeve cradled the back of his head and placed her bleeding palm at his mouth.

Mal slumbered deeply. His chest rose and fell in a heavy and full rhythm. She pressed her own fingers into the Dread Mark on Mal's chest. The Magic connecting all those with the mark flickered to attention at her command.

Intentional or not, Mal had created a bond between them all.

Maeve inhaled deeply and closed her eyes. She placed her other hand across her own mark, and spoke into all their minds.

Magic raced down thousands of Magical pathways.

The time has come to fight for your sworn Prince.

Maeve Portaled into the Entrance Hall at Castle Morana, leaving Mal on Earth. The castle was alive with haste. Bellator and healers rushed by Larliesl, who joined her at once. Abraxas and Astrea stood waiting for her with panicked expressions.

"The Beryl City is under attack," said Abraxas swiftly.

Maeve took a quick breath. "By who?"

Her cousin shook his head. "Not who. What."

Her lips pulled together. "The Dreaded Dead."

Abraxas nodded fearfully. "The Greywood is swarming with undead."

Maeve turned to Larliesl. "Gather all our forces at once," she commanded. "We move to attack."

He gave a short nod and waited for further instruction.

"Get as many as you can to the city at once. Healers too. And then we are going to Mount Morte, past the Barrier, to find whatever it is in those mountains that is trying to kill our Prince."

Larliesl took his leave at once.

"Remember, Professor," she called after him. "Flame, alone, can kill them."

Larliesl began shouting orders to varying officers.

Maeve turned to Abraxas and Astrea as Mumford and Roswyn appeared.

"Go to Earth and–"

"Earth travel is forbidden," began Mumford, but Maeve ignored him and continued addressing Abraxas and Astrea.

"–watch over him. I sedated him with my blood. I don't know how long he'll be out for."

Abraxas' eyes widened.

"How much blood did you give him?" Astrea asked.

"As much as possible before he fell unconscious." She turned towards Abraxas. "Take as many Bellator to ensure he's protected and stays there. He stays there, understood?"

Mumford spoke over her again. "You do not command and place his–"

Maeve whipped towards him at last, furious lightning crackling over her knuckles as the image of Mal, so destroyed and desperately drinking from the Dread Goblet, replayed in her mind. "I am second in command!" The room stilled as Mumford's jaw tightened. "I do not have time to waste on reminding you that you stand leagues beneath me in both rank and power. Fall the fuck in line."

She turned back towards Abraxas and Astrea. Neither of them held looks of shock or fear. "Go."

Abraxas vanished at once. Astrea spoke quietly.

"To give your blood to him. . .that is a different kind of Magic. We are truly desperate now, aren't we?"

Maeve reached forward, locking her hand around Astrea's forearm. "Fear is the absence of Magic."

Astrea gripped her arm tightly. "My boy," she began.

Maeve's stomach sank. Pyxis was his name. Emerie and

Roswyn's daughter. Arianna's twins: Anselm and Aislin. Maxius too.

"Belvadora!" called Maeve, as she spotted her pulling her long blonde hair back into a tight braid across the hall.

The newly Supreme soldier appeared at her side at once.

"Keep watch over the children. All of them. Your shields are the best of any Bellator."

The accounts of Orion's servant, the baby with unknown parents showing up at the Castle Gates, couldn't just be a coincidence. Maxius mattered in this mysterious land.

She just didn't know how.

Belvadora moved at once. Maeve grabbed her arm swiftly. "Find Zimsy. If Arianna gives you grief, remind her who you are, and who I am. Her pride and resentment will not stop me from protecting my family."

Belvadora placed her fist over her heart, over her Dread Mark, and nodded.

Bellator swarmed through the castle, some still pulling on their uniforms and talking frantically. Maeve welcomed the buzz of adrenaline that filled the air.

"We are heading to Mount Morte, correct?" asked Roswyn.

Maeve nodded. He wasn't dumb, despite his quick temper and brute nature.

"What?" exclaimed Mumford. "We were given specific commands to stay away from that very place."

Maeve looked over at him incredulously, but it was Roswyn who spoke. "It is stupidity or fear that you keep thinking we are playing by some rule book. This is real life Mumford."

Roswyn looked back at Maeve. "Alphard's in Aterna."

"Good," said Maeve. "Because I'm calling on Aterna to uphold their oath."

Roswyn shook his head slowly. "They never actually swore an oath to Mal."

That was true. They didn't have time. It had only been her father who vowed his Magical Militia to the Crown.

"They will come," she replied.

"We don't stand a chance out there without Mal–" began

Mumford. His lip curled as he tried to remain calm. "The last time you went out there, Arman, who is better than a hundred of us, died. This is a *suicide* mission!" He grit his teeth.

The word sent Magic spiraling down Maeve's arm. She pressed two fingers to his chest and stared fearlessly up at him. He stilled, his mouth falling slack.

"There is an enemy here," said Maeve. "You swore an oath to protect him." She pressed deeper into the mark on his chest, burning him. "Fucking uphold that vow."

She dropped her hand and looked at both of them. "Go suit up."

They obeyed with haste, Mumford muttering to Roswyn as they went.

"Are you certain this is wise," asked Abraxas, appearing at her side, with a large group of Bellator.

They began creating a Portal to Earth for Abraxas and Astrea.

"No," said Maeve. "I'm certain many are about to die. What choice do we have? What choice do I have?"

Abraxas grabbed the back of her head and pulled her in close. The cousins embraced, and when he pulled away, he looked at her with pride. "Usque ad Mortem, Sinclair."

Fire surged through Maeve's blood. Mal's Magic that ran through her darkened veins ignited with determination.

Chapter 61

Alphard

Alphard's chest tingled, icy and cold. Maeve's Magic pressed through the bond Mal had created with his Dread Mark between them all. There was no direct command. He didn't hear her voice, but he understood her command all the same.

He touched his chest. She felt like Antony now more than ever.

Alphard looked up at the High Lord of Aterna and Eryx.

Reeve's eyes were on his chest with a curious expression.

"The time has come, it seems," said Alphard. "You agreed to fight alongside us."

Reeve looked up at him.

"The Dread Viper calls you to aid her in battle," said Alphard.

Reeve downed the rest of his Elven Brandy and smiled. "I'm a bit rusty in battle."

Alphard laughed nervously. Reeve nodded down at Alphard's unfinished glass.

"That'll help," he said.

Alphard nodded and slammed back the drink. He hissed at the burn.

"Do you have a lady, Mavros?" Asked Reeve. "The redhead, yes?"

Alphard nodded.

"Go and kiss her. And tell the Dread Viper we will meet her at the Greywood."

Reeve

"Are you sure this is wise?" asked Eryx.

"Of course it's not wise," said Reeve, tightening the straps on his bracers.

"Then why are we going?"

Reeve stopped and looked over at his commander, his second.

Eryx's look of disappointment sliced through him. "Because it's her? Or because we are protecting ourselves?"

Reeve did not answer right away. Eryx continued.

"If it's a command, I will unsheathe my sword without question or pause. But as your friend, I urge you to consider the danger you are putting us in."

Reeve grabbed him by the shoulder in a brotherly gesture. Eryx mimicked the movement.

"The danger is on our doorstep if we stay or go," answered Reeve.

Eryx didn't press him further. He followed his command and left to gather a portion of the Senshi Army.

Drystan was already suited up, a slew of arrows at his back and a glossy bow in his hand.

"Is that new?" asked Reeve casually.

"Carved it in anticipation of this day," the small archer replied.

"It's not the same," said Reeve.

"No. This time is very different." Drystan crossed towards him and inspected his armor. "Eryx wasn't there. He doesn't know what that war was like. He doesn't know what any war is like. Don't be hard on yourself at the presence of his doubt and fear."

"And you?" asked Reeve. "Do you doubt my motives for running to their aid?"

Drystan grinned. "Brother, we've been alive for over three hundred years. You've proven you will fight and die and live for your people. But just this once, admit that you haven't closed us off completely from them and the darkness that lingers there because you can't let her go down with him." Drystan crossed the room and picked up Shadowslayer, turning and presenting it to Reeve. "She's going to go down with him, Reeve."

Reeve grabbed the Elven steel from Drystan's hands. "Not if I can help it," he snarled. "Was that admission enough?"

Drystan laughed. "Yes. Now, let's go slay some of those Dreaded Dead like old times."

The Beryl City was mayhem. Magicals fled from the city, desperate to escape the onslaught of Dreaded Dead swarming from the Greywood. They were just as Reeve remembered them. Gangly, bony creatures with tattered remains of clothing, some with more skin than others, all with one purpose: kill.

His Senshi Warriors tackled beheading them with fiery swords ablaze with his Aterna Magic. Magic that was rightfully theirs.

He longed to give it back to them. Selfishly, he longed to be unburdened of it.

Lightning cracked across the twilight sky, illuminating it with vibrant green scattered pops of color. Thunder rolled across the Greywood in great booms of Magic where Maeve and her Bellator were already fighting.

"Damn," said Drystan with a nod and an impressed expression. "Guess someone's rather angry."

The Dreaded Dead flooding the city lessened as Maeve and the Magicals succeeded in stopping their advance from the Greywood. Reeve and his Senshi moved through The Beryl City, ensuring every corner was rid of the undead. He applauded the Magicals who fought back, though futile it was if they didn't burn the corpses completely. Mordred and his wolves aided them, sniffing out the city for any stragglers.

Mere spells and hexes were nothing to the creatures reanimated with darkness.

While the entire metropolis had not been restored, the effort Mal and his Magicals had put into the revitalization of The Beryl City was worth commending. Even if Reeve felt a deadly set of eyes on him at all times.

Once they reached the Greywood, smoke and ash plumed high above the city and the trees from the burning bodies of the Dreaded Dead. The already barren land looked nothing short of apocalyptic.

Mordred and his wolves bolted ahead through the Greywood, prepared to rip and dismember the bodies of the undead. Magic was still required to end their cycle of reanimating permanently, but it slowed them down.

The Magicals were deep in battle in the forest when Reeve arrived. The undead were wild and untamed creatures of night, their sharp fingers dripping in deadly Magic as they attacked with relentless nature.

Lightning shot from Maeve's fingers, whipping through the swarms of Dreaded Dead coming up from the ground. They burst apart beneath her electric Magic and caught fire.

Alphard hollered a few yards away, commending her brutal attack as swirling orange flames shot from his fingers and wrapped the undead he faced.

"I must admit," said Eryx, stepping to Reeve's side, "she looks fearless."

Maeve's heart thumped out of beat. Erratic and filled with anger. Reeve felt it all. He didn't tear his eyes away from her as he said, "She's terrified."

With a single hand motion, the Senshi Warriors filed past Eryx.

Fire blazed around them, burning what remained of the dead trees. Maeve's eyes landed on Reeve as the creature before her turned to ash. Her shoulders dropped as her eyes scanned the line of Senshi Warriors joining their fight.

Maeve Obscured closer, setting fire to a crawling Dreaded Dead with a stomp on its back as she crossed toward them. Smoke blazed around them as the battle continued. If she noticed the dead Magicals littered across the floor of the forest, she did not look at them.

Reeve was certain she couldn't bring herself to.

Her eyes traced the Vexkari markings on the side of his face that traveled down his neck.

"Thank you," she said. "For coming."

"The city is secure," said Reeve.

Larliesl Obscured beside her. "There are hundreds more Maeve, coming from the waters on the south side of the Greywood."

"We can flank them from the north, circle back around," said Eryx. "If you can Obscure to the south and attack from there, we'll have a decent position."

Larliesl nodded. He and Eryx disappeared, shouting commands

and instructions.

"Do you know what prompted them to attack the city?" asked Reeve.

Maeve shook her head. "They've always remained behind Mal's barrier. Except once before…"

"And where is he?"

Maeve swallowed. "I left him on Earth."

He looked down at her tired eyes. She looked past him, beyond the Greywood and The Beryl City to where the Dark Peaks loomed ominously in the distance.

"I can no longer underestimate the cruelty of the world around me. I will not continue to stand by as my Prince alone faces the darkness that remains here." She tore her eyes away from the mountains and looked up at Reeve. "You've fought these creatures before, haven't you?"

Reeve nodded.

Black mist swirled in the middle of the fiery bloodshed. The Dread Prince appeared from the dark shadows, on his knees looking frail and drained.

Astrea Obscured at his side a moment later. He clutched his chest as she wrapped her arms around him, keeping him from collapsing.

"You are too weak, my Prince," she said, desperately. "You should not have done that."

Mal's eyes were hooded. His skin was pale and appeared thin.

Reeve knew at once. There was only one evil he'd ever seen claim such a powerful Magical that way. He felt her lingering and unmistakable presence in Mal's Magic.

Astrea frantically tried to heal him.

Mal pushed forward, falling back to the ground. Abraxas Obscured at his other side and supported his Prince as he faltered. With two pointed fingers, Abraxas fired on the enemy that crawled towards them. With little effort, the creature collapsed and turned to ash. He swirled his fingers high, creating a shield around them.

"Mal," said Abraxas sternly. "You cannot fight right now."

"Where is Maeve?" Mal asked, frantically.

Reeve turned to his side, where she had just been, with her eyes on The Dark Peaks. But she was gone. Horror that he'd not felt in years, decades, settled into his bones.

"She's going to open the tomb," said Mal weakly.

The hairs on the back of Reeve's neck shot to attention.

"She doesn't understand," continued Mal, his dark hazel eyes fighting for rest. "It needs her to do it. Mine is not enough blood. It's not enough blood, Brax, it's not enough it's not enough–"

Abraxas looked up at Reeve.

Mal fell into Abraxas fully, his arms limp at his sides.

"What does that mean?" Abraxas asked Reeve sharply.

Mal continued in a frantic and fading voice, "It's not enough–"

Astrea cursed loudly, overwhelmed by the chaos of battle around her. Chaos she was far from accustomed to.

"Take Mal and go back to Castle Morana," said Abraxas.

But Astrea had not heard him. She stepped past Abraxas' shield at the sight of her brother covered in blood, still fighting strongly despite his wounds.

Mal collapsed in Abraxas' arms, succumbing to his exhaustion.

But flames of violet fire had already consumed the High Lord of Aterna.

Abraxas let out a frustrated groan.

"Gods be with you, Maeve. Whatever you are doing," whispered Abraxas as Reeve vanished.

Chapter 62

Maeve

Mount Morte was quiet and still. Too much so.

Maeve looked back over her shoulder at the cavern's large opening, high on the mountain. The space was small and covered in a thick haze of green. She stepped deeper into the cavern and the hazy green mist cleared in the small space.

The altar she'd seen many times in Mal's mind moved into view. Ancient Magic oozed from it.

The Dread Viper arrives at last.

Maeve whipped around, turning in a quick circle. The cave remained empty and eerily still. The voice was not unfamiliar.

"I have heard your voice before," said Maeve. "I have felt you before."

Why have you come here?

"For Mal," she answered, still turning in a circle, looking for this unknown dark creature that spoke so easily into her thoughts.

You've come to save him. How valiant.

Maeve stepped towards the altar once more, feeling Magic tingle down her arms.

He's so very lost, isn't he?

She dared another step.

You alone can do it.

"Save him?" Maeve asked.

Save all of them.

"All?" she asked, her eyes still on the mesmerizing Magic radiating from the altar.

Maeve stepped again. The altar was a short reach away.

All. I know where your mother is.

Maeve's pulse shot to attention.

The room shifted before her. The altar vanished into mist,

forming a painfully beautiful scene. Snow fell outside the large windows at Sinclair Estates.

And there stood her mother.

Her birth mother.

Her father held her close by a fire.

Maeve crossed towards her parents.

A tiny version of herself played on the rug before them.

I can give you the life you deserve.

Antony rounded the corner with Arianna on his heels. They both concealed a large present behind their back.

Maeve looked back to her mother, her face still concealed as the child version of her siblings presented her with their gift.

Sinclair Estates twisted from view, and Hellming Hall at Vaukore shifted into focus. Antony and Arianna sat across the table from her. The three of them together at school.

Before Maeve could even take in the new scene it changed again.

There's so much you deserve to feel.

Her mother stood beside her, fixing her white lace veil.

Mal stood down the aisle waiting for her as Abraxas fixed his suit. Her father offered her his arm. Maeve's heart soared at the sight. They all vanished into grey smoke and darkness with her next breath.

"Wait," she said softly.

All of it is yours. I just need a little blood.

"My blood?" asked Maeve.

Your blood.

Maeve stood in the darkened space, yearning to see Mal's face as they vowed themselves to one another.

"But this is not reality," she said in a hushed voice. "It is but a dream."

Do the falsehoods you create within your mind feel like a dream?

Light infiltrated the darkness, creating a new scene around her.

She and Mal dined at Sinclair Estates. Mal reached over and touched her swollen belly.

They shared a smile.

Maeve's mouth fell open as her brows pulled together.

The vision shifted once more as the voice spoke.

Don't you want to remember carrying him?

Her mother and father sat out on the balcony at Sinclair Estates, taking turns holding a baby boy who she knew at once to be Maxius.

His first laugh? Holding him? Feeding him?

Icy tears slipped down Maeve's cheek and clung to her jaw.

"How could I have forgotten him?"

There is much you have forgotten. I can show it all to you.

Ambrose handed Maxius over to Mal. Her mother's back faced her, where she doted on Maxius. Her father cupped Maxius' cheek as Mal smiled up at her. Not a vision of her. Her.

Just a little blood.

"Maeve," said Mal in his perfectly velvety smooth voice. He was so beautiful. She'd forgotten just how full of life he once was. "Come," he called to her.

Just a little blood.

"Maeve, darling!" exclaimed her father upon noticing her.

More tears fell as her favorite voice in the world called her so affectionately.

Just a little blood. Just a little blood.

At last, her mother turned from Maxius, and Maeve saw her face fully.

She was glorious. A warm summer sunbathe and a cozy winter night. Her red lips smiled. It filled every crack inside Maeve's hollow soul.

Just a little blood, just a little blood, just a little–

Her mother's shoulders dropped with a content sigh. "My beautiful girl."

She extended her hand to Maeve.

"Come, my plus jeune serre-livre," said her father.

His littlest bookend.

Her mother nodded and reached further towards her. "Come, darling."

Just a little blood, just a little drop of blood, of blood, just a drop or all of it–

Maeve took her mother's hand.

Blinding, hot, fire surged through her stomach.

The balcony at Sinclair Estates dissolved into ash, taking Mal and Maxius, and the beloved image of her mother and father together at last, with it.

Maeve bent forward in a silent cry. Her knees collapsed into the floor of Mount Morte before the altar. Her hands shook as steel slipped from her grip and clattered to the ground. The Dread Dagger lay before her, soaked in bright crimson blood.

In her blood.

In the blood pouring from a full stab wound to her stomach.

Maeve sucked in a few strained breaths and felt the weight of her mistake brush past her before she fell unconscious on the ground of Mount Morte.

393

The explosion of Magic from Mount Morte was felt across all seven realms. Bright green light spiraled into the dark sky, creating a tower of cyclonic Magic above the mountain.

Reeve stood at the threshold of the path into the mountain, black wings of night slipped from his back. He was too late. His furious fist slammed against the invisible wall keeping him from Maeve. He poured all of Aterna's Magic into his sharpened claws that attempted to punch through the wall of Magic as he screamed her name.

The mountain did not move.

The ancient blight of Magic surged from Mount Morte and barreled across The Dread Lands at super speed, heading straight for Mal, where he lay unconscious in my arms. It sliced through the minds of dozens of Bellator in its path, shattering them in one pass. It penetrated my shield, knocking me backward, and swirled through Mal, wrapping his body in serpent-like bands of lethal Magic.

The Magic stilled. I shook and crawled away from the death lingering above Mal.

When the Dread Prince's eyes popped open with a sharp inhale, it was not fading and fleeting flecks of green that consumed them.

They were no longer a hazel dream.

They were a solid, piercing green nightmare.

-excerpt from recovered journal inside the Hand's chamber inside Castle Morana

PART THREE

Chapter 63

Reeve

Reeve's fist pounded relentlessly against the Magical barrier keeping him from Maeve. Her blood coated the ground around her in a halo pool.

"Hello, Reeve."

He turned. Mal stood behind him. His skin was no longer dull and lifeless. He was glowing with radiant Magic. And green eyes.

He'd seen those eyes before.

"No," breathed Reeve.

Mal smiled in a feline way. "Don't worry. I won't let her die."

He slipped past the barrier separating them and Maeve with ease, and turned back towards Reeve.

"Return to Aterna. I will call upon you when it's time to finally give me that crown you are so against wearing." He chuckled and turned back towards Maeve. He stepped through her blood without concern, and placed his hand on her chest. They Obscured out of Mount Morte, leaving nothing but a crimson stain of doom.

Crystalmore shook.

Eryx and Mely exchanged a look. She was nearly green in the face.

"If you're going to vomit again, please go in the other room," said Eryx.

"You reek of death," she muttered.

Eryx made an exasperated look. "You are the only one death affects."

The ground beneath them shook once more, rippling the liquid in their pale colored goblets.

"Go easy on her, Eryx," said Drystan. "It's not her fault she can sense such things."

Mely didn't smile at his mocking tone.

"What about those Dreaded Dead?" asked Drystan. "I killed at least fifty. Can you sense them too?"

"Yes," she said darkly.

Drystan's smile faded.

The palace shook again.

Eryx groaned, ignoring Mely and Drystan. "I wish he'd hurry up and get it out of his system," muttered Eryx.

Mely slammed her hands on the table. "Would you like to know who they were? Before Dark Magic fueled their never-ending nightmare?"

Eryx interjected. "I'd be more concerned with your High Lord, who likely wants to pitch you off the highest crystal tower right now."

Mely frowned and nearly gagged once more, but found it difficult to argue with him.

With one final quaking shake, Crystalmore stilled. A moment later, Reeve breezed through the open doors, ignoring their previous conversation.

Mely opened her mouth to speak, but as the High Lord's death toll slammed into her, she reeled and bent over the small trash can beside her chair.

Reeve slid into the chair and braced his arms on the table. Mely wiped her lips with a handkerchief and sat straight.

"You said you could sense her," said Reeve. "That means that she was dead when I put my sword through her three hundred years ago."

Mely looked down at the table between them. "I could feel her. . ."

Reeve's head lowered. "And now?"

Mely hesitated. "She is. . .changed."

"She's no longer dead?" asked Eryx.

Mely gave him a trepidatious glance.

"I don't think she ever was," said Reeve darkly.

"No," argued Mely. "I felt her. I know what I felt."

"No," said Reeve. "You don't. At her core, the core of Shadow Magic, is deception. I was a fool for believing any of it. What is three hundred more years for an ancient being of darkness? It was nothing for her to lie in wait for another to possess."

"Is the Sinclair girl dead?" asked Eryx.

"No," said Reeve.

"You said you watched Maeve bleed out?" Drystan questioned carefully.

Reeve nodded. "I did."

A moment passed between them.

"Why her blood?" asked Mely.

Reeve's mouth remained closed. Even if he wanted to divulge such a secret to them, the Magic binding his tongue made certain he couldn't.

Chapter 64

Maeve

It hadn't taken Maeve long for her weary eyes to focus on Mal, where he sat tall on his throne. The Dread Crown glistened on his head. His hair was perfectly fixed, and the dark circles beneath his eyes were gone. A rush of joy rose through her.

But then she saw his eyes.

Even from a distance, they glowed with wicked green intent.

Maxius sat on his lap, playing with the Dread Locket.

The visions she'd seen in Mount Morte slammed into her. She moved to stand, stalling as hot pain tensed in her stomach.

Mal's voice was smooth and calm. "It must heal naturally, remember?"

Maeve sucked in sharply. Shallow breaths were all the wound allowed her.

Maxius' eyes fell on her. The Dread Locket slipped from his tiny fingers. Mal caught it with ease, his eyes never leaving Maeve.

They alone occupied the Throne Room. Her least favorite part of the castle.

Maxius pushed off Mal's lap and gracefully slid to the floor. Mal placed the Dread Locket around his neck with care and looked up at her. Maxius moved down the marble steps.

Her son.

The desire to smile at him getting snuffed out by the fire in her stomach and the gleam in Mal's eyes was heartbreaking. In place of joy, she felt anguish. Where there should have been celebration, there was terror.

But his angelic face was so pure and perfect. A helpless feeling crashed down on her, bearing the weight of her mistake.

He reached the foot of the steps and broke into a small run towards her. Spinel slipped from behind the throne with his wide-set eyes on Maxius.

"Maxius," called Mal.

He stopped and turned back towards the throne. Mal made a quick motion with his hand. Maxius stilled and did not move towards her again.

"You look rather sentimental, Maeve," said Mal, standing from his throne and gracefully descending the dais steps. "Something you'd like to share?" Mal reached Maxius and halted.

Mal's green eyes remained on her. His brows raised.

"Perhaps that he is my son?"

Maeve shifted her legs beneath her, a pained whimper hissing between her teeth as the fire in her stomach built. She doubled over, afraid to grip the wound.

"Is that what refuses to slip from your tongue?" Mal looked at her boredly. "Were you hoping it was merely you that gained such knowledge?"

Mal flipped his hand over. Maxius placed his tiny hand in Mal's palm. They crossed the Throne Room together. Maxius' eyes scanned her as they moved closer.

He sucked in a small gasp and signed '*hurt*'.

Maeve pulled herself as tall as she could and braced her hands on the shining floor.

"I am alright," she said to him in a stuttering breath.

Maxius looked up at Mal, tugging his hand towards Maeve.

Help, he signed, pointing at Maeve.

Mal kneeled before Maeve. He dropped Maxius' hand and spoke plainly. "I cannot. She made quite the sacrifice. One that Magic cannot undo."

His green eyes met hers and Maeve lost all reserve. There was no trace of her Mal within his eyes. With a heaving cry, her eyes burned with tears. Mal's head cocked to the side as he watched her with dead eyes.

"It was just a little blood," he said coldly.

His hand cupped the back of Maxius' head gently. He continued addressing her. "You will attack Aterna without argument."

Hope crumbled, as Mal had found his leverage at last.

Chapter 65

Maeve

Guilt hovered over Maeve like a stalling storm cloud.

She was a selfish fool.

Mal concealed Maxius from her. He was hidden away to ensure her obedience. Even if she could get to him, she was at a loss. The newfound realization that he was her son settled into her slowly. Emotions rolled in like a shifting storm, uncertain and unpredictable.

Her self-inflicted stab wound from The Dread Dagger took its time healing, even with the stitches Astrea sewed her skin back together with.

"You could at least numb it," she had said through wincing breaths.

Astrea continued to pull the needle through Maeve's skin without stopping. "I was commanded not to," she had replied.

The attack plans for Aterna were laid out on a large table in Abraxas' study. Her cousin's eyes were bloodshot as he ran his fingers over the landscape of Crystalmore and Aterna.

Maeve didn't move. She didn't speak. Larliesl answered Abraxas' or Mal's questions about the Bellator. His voice was strained as he spoke of attacking citizens.

"Reeve will not take kindly to this," said Larliesl.

Mal spoke from the head of the table. "Reeve will see that either his people will die, or he will bend the knee. Do you think he will offer me his crown and power without some incentive?"

Larliesl shook his head. "No, my Prince."

"No," repeated Mal. "I am done waiting to discover the identity of his Inheritor. I will take the power of Aterna myself."

"And the Elven Lands?" asked Larliesl, looking back to Abraxas.

"One crown at a time," he replied darkly, not looking away from the map.

"Astrea," called Mal, causing the healer to startle. "How long until Maeve can break the shield in the Black Deep?"

"She's nearly back to her full strength," answered Astrea. "Give it two more days."

"Any arguments, Maeve?" he asked.

She shook her head in silent defeat.

"Marvelous."

She wondered how much of her Mal remained. How tight the grip this green-eyed darkness had on him was. Was her Mal buried just beneath the surface?

Play the game.

Her father's words. Abraxas' words.

Just play the game. She'd been prepared for the game her entire life. Born and bred for deception. Just as the darkness that now resided in Mal had deceived her.

She raised her hand, prepared to rap her knuckles against the door. It swung silently open. Maeve moved into the candlelit north tower.

Mal sat at his desk, a long owl feather quill scratching away at the parchment before him.

He offered her one glance before returning to his writing.

She closed the doors to his chamber with a gentle twist of her wrist.

"Why are you here?" he asked coolly.

"I figured you'd be asleep."

"That's not an answer."

Maeve crossed towards him. She slid between him and the desk, forcing him to pull away from his writing. He did not protest her presence as his green eyes scanned down her body. Maeve leaned against the desk.

"I'm lonely," she answered plainly.

Mal dropped the quill on the dark wood and leaned back in his chair. His legs brushed hers as he trapped her between them.

"Lonely?" he repeated, lust creeping into his tone.

"Mhmm," she replied.

"And your Prince cares about your loneliness, why?"

Maeve pulled on the soft satin bow that held her robe across her chest. "Because you look lonely, too."

Mal's eyes drifted down her front as she exposed her thin undergarments. His fingers crept down the back of her knee, gently teasing her skin.

"You are a wicked little thing, aren't you?" he asked, each word humming in the quiet space.

The robe fell from her shoulders and sprawled across the desk behind her.

"Do you aim to sway me from attacking Aterna," he said, "or to distract me from my anger at you?"

Maeve stilled, her performance nearly faltering. "You are angry with me?"

His eyes moved down to her legs, where his fingers slithered across her skin.

"You kept him from me."

Maeve resisted the urge to grab his beautifully haunting face. "I urge you to remember that someone hid him from me as well, Mal."

His name brought his eyes back to hers.

His fingers traveled slowly up her legs, his eyes dropping to her stomach.

"Marks on your body used to delight you," he said quietly, observing her most recent wound that would likely be her largest scar yet.

"How do you know this one doesn't?" she asked. His eyes snapped to hers through his thick lashes. "You think I went into that mountain with anything other than you in mind?"

A controlled breath rolled through him. He slid forward in the chair and placed a single hand on her chest and tilted her torso backwards, giving him a better view of the scar.

"I'll bleed out for you over and over," she said.

He bent over her stomach and brought his mouth to her skin, trailing down her sternum. Maeve's body tensed and ran wild with goosebumps. He licked over the scarred tissue of the Dread Dagger's wound. Ice pierced the tender skin beneath his tongue, drawing a hiss from her lips.

He snagged her wrist at once before she could push his head away.

His eyes lifted to hers. His tongue flicked over the raised skin once more, bringing her teeth together, never releasing her wrist.

"I want to show you something I remembered," she whispered.

Mal's cold eyes scanned her face.

"Please?" she asked with a soft smile.

Mal did not return it.

"You want me to be tender and good, Little Viper? You want me to stroke your face and tell you everything will be fine?" His head cocked to the side. "You think you can manipulate me, of all people, with your pretend innocence?"

Maeve sucked in a tight breath and relented. She snatched her hand from his and pushed off the desk with a glare. Mal's hand moved to her throat at once, pressing their bodies together and holding her hostage.

"You've never fucked with hatred, Maeve? Oh, that's right. No one has fucked you but me. Do you know why that is?"

"Because I'm yours?" she asked with a scowl.

With a devilish smile and a shake of his head, his teeth sunk into her skin, clamping down on the tender area between her shoulder and her neck. Maeve rose to the tips of her toes, desperate to alleviate the sting.

His mouth withdrew and two fingers shoved inside her mouth. "It's because there is no match for you besides me. There is not a soul alive who could handle such a rebellious, arrogant ego. No one else has fucked you, Maeve, because you know they'd never be crawling through your skin like I am. They'll never force you the way I'm willing to force you. Because what you want most, is to not be in control. Day in and day out you stand above the rest in control. You fight the battle of control in your own mind of doubt. I take your control away. And you worship me for it."

White light erupted across her eyes.

"This is not forever, Maeve," said the hooded figure, as Maxius reached towards her with frantic tears.

His voice was still familiar, and impossible to place.

"Then why is my heart breaking?"

The hooded figure held Maxius tenderly.

"How am I supposed to walk away?" she asked, her voice breaking.

Warm wind swirled around them, settling Maxius against the hooded man's chest and calming him instantly. Maxius breathed deeply as his eyes fluttered close beneath thick lashes.

The figure's hood began to slip back–

Maeve groaned as her mind slammed back into Mal's chamber. She fell backward into his desk.

Mal staggered and gripped the sides of his head. He turned his back on her.

"It was you," he said quietly. "You tried to take him from me."

Maeve shook her head, unable to argue, unable to understand. "Mal," she said, her voice quivering.

"That night he appeared," he continued, "I knew then it was somehow you. With the blood coating your upper lip, just as it had been with Kietel, I knew you were the coordinate. Emerie's prophecy . . ."

Maeve stilled. "What?"

He stumbled across the room and caught himself on the bedpost. His breathing was sharp and uneven.

"What prophecy?" she asked, not moving towards him as she pushed up from his desk.

Mal did not answer her. Maeve gripped the desk beneath her with white knuckles.

"She had another prophecy, didn't she?" asked Maeve quietly, her Magic at the ready. "One about Maxius."

Mal gripped the sides of his head and groaned as his green eyes flickered with darkness.

"Mal," she snapped, stepping towards him.

He whipped towards her, scowling.

"What. Prophecy."

Mal was on her in a flash. She threw up a shield just in time to separate their Magic, propelling them each backwards, her heels sliding across the floor and flipping over his desk. Papers and books slid to the floor with her.

The room fell silent.

He had moved to attack her.

The blood in her veins stilled. The electric Magic pleading to fight at her fingertips dissipated in one breath. Ink spilled across the dark floor beside her.

When she looked up at him, his eyes were dark, not a trace of green in them.

"What. . ." Mal's voice was barely above a whisper.

The freezing air assaulted her overly exposed skin. She coiled her trembling fingers in.

"Hey," she said softly, trying not to sound too eager. "I'm fine."

Mal shook his head.

"It's okay," she said gently. "I want to help you, Mal. But we need to get to Earth okay?"

His head tilted back at the ceiling. "You can't, Maeve. I keep trying to tell you."

She moved to stand and his eyes snapped to her. She stood on shaking legs and extended her hand towards him.

"Earth," she said. "We can talk about it there."

Mal's eyes narrowed. Green flecks of light surged through them.

"Take us to Earth," said Maeve frantically. "Now!"

"It's too late," he said. "If I go to Earth, I bring her with me. You should run."

Her chest tightened, pressure shooting up her jaw. Every bit of her trembled as she choked out, "No."

"You are not listening to me. . ."

"You're goddamn right," she said, sniffling and suppressing the tears ready for release. "If you won't take us, I will."

She prepared her Magic to create a Portal as black night swirled around her, knocking her to the floor. Mal pinned her body down, holding her right hand hostage, dulling the Magic ready to manifest their way out of Castle Morana.

Maeve looked up at his solid green eyes as sharp, slicing Magic cut into her wrist. An agonizing and devastating scream raked across her throat until her insides were so raw, no scream came.

He was gone once more. Maeve squeezed her eyes shut and shook her head. Warm, wet tears streaked her cheeks.

"I want to go home, Mal," she cried in a broken voice. "I want to go home."

She looked up at his vacant expression.

"You have lost," said Mal, his voice not his own. "You will never go home. You are alone."

The sides of her face and hair were wet with tears as she said, "Children of Magic are never alone."

Mal's eyes slammed shut. His brows pulled together and his lip curled. He pushed off her and ran his long fingers over his face, pressing into his eyes.

Maeve slipped from beneath him, scooted back against the wall and pulled her legs in tight.

"Don't do this to me," she whimpered as Mal's eyes opened and were void of any green color.

He fell back on his knees, his chest heaving.

"You're hurt," he said, his eyes on the blood coming from her wrist.

Maeve shook her head. "Stop it," she said weakly.

Mal looked up at her, confusion plastered across his wild expression.

"Maeve?" he asked.

"Stop it," she repeated, angry tears streaking her face. "Whatever, whoever, you are–stop."

Mal raised his hand and ran his thumb across his fingers. His eyes saddened, still on the blood coming from her wrist. "I did that."

It wasn't a question. It was a fearful and gut wrenching

realization.

He didn't look away from the wound.

His eyes flickered like an igniting green fire, the color deepening rapidly. His head rolled back, and Maeve prepared herself for another switch.

She pointed two fingers at him and fired. His shield slammed up as she dove into his mind, successfully distracting him for just a fleeting moment.

Darkness consumed her, dripping in bloody black nothingness all around her.

"You will not take him from me," she said boldly.

I already have, replied the voice from Mount Morte.

Deadly Magic swirled around her. The doorway slipped open like it always did. Maeve took a steadying breath. . .and jumped.

A grey room with wet dripping stones misted before her.

"Judyth," a wretched voice snapped.

A child with skin paler than snow, and hair whiter than ice, looked up. Her pale eyes were covered in thick, transparent lashes.

The young beauty did not respond.

Smack.

She barely recoiled as the back of the wretched woman's hand collided with her face. The hit knocked her sideways, the chains and cuffs binding her wrists and ankles clattered as she fell.

Metal on metal reverberated in Maeve's ears, changing the scene completely.

Smoke plumed into the sky from piles of ash. Bodies lay scattered, fresh with still bleeding wounds.

Metal scraped against metal with a slithering sound.

The child was older, a woman now. The albino woman that haunted her dreams and was painted in the library mural stood in beautiful white clothes. The Dread Crown sat between woven braids of curled pale hair, cascading down to her radiant skin.

She pointed a sword at Reeve. Not just any sword.

His sword. The one the Bellator fawned over and always hung at his side.

She smiled. It was entrancing.

"Hello, Reeve of Aterna."

Reeve's head lowered with vengeful eyes. Blood and dirt coated his face as he sucked in shallow breaths. "Shadow."

Maeve's heart slammed to a stop.

Shadow laughed. "A generous term of affection. I must say what an even more generous sight," remarked Shadow. "The heir on his knees. Too weak to even stand."

Reeve's chest compressed. Blood splattered from his mouth in a suppressed cough.

She vanished and reappeared behind him, placing the large blade at his throat.

The Magic that pulsed from Shadow set Maeve's skin crawling with terror. Her blood screamed and begged for her to escape.

She pulled herself from Mal's mind with a heavy blink, her stomach flipping at the sudden release of such potent Magic.

Mal shifted uneasily on his feet and covered his mouth.

"My potions," muttered Mal as he yanked open draws, flinging their contents behind him.

"Mal," said Maeve.

He slammed open the door of the armoire and ripped his suits and cloaks from their hangers, frantically rummaging through the pockets.

"I have to have them-I-I-" he stammered.

Maeve crossed towards him and attempted to take his hands.

He whipped away from her and moved towards the bed. He swung his arm across the bedside table, sending numerous empty potions bottles shattering to the floor.

"Mal, please," she started, her voice cracking.

He growled in frustration and whipped around towards her. His breathing was heavy and his stare intense.

Maeve kept her arms calm at her side. "Please, Mal," she said as her throat tightened. "Tell me what to do. Tell me how to free you from this wicked curse."

His eyes narrowed. His chest rose and fell with haste and a scowl moved across lips. "I cannot be saved, Maeve. You should run. You should take Maxius—"

Her insides twisted. She stepped towards him as a hiss of warning escaped his mouth. Maeve halted at once.

"No," she said, with a slow shake of her head. "I can save you."

Mal laughed, kicking his head back madly. "Save me? This is your doing!"

The door slammed open, ripping from its place in the wall. It clattered to the floor with a bang. Astrea stood barely ten steps away on the other side of the threshold. The potion in her hand flew across the room and into Mal's outstretched fingers. The glass stopper disappeared, and he downed the swirling contents at once. His eyelids drooped and his jaw relaxed. He stumbled and braced himself on the post of his bed frame.

He looked up at Maeve one more time before falling sideways onto the plush bed.

Astrea stepped calmly into the room.

Magic swelled up through Maeve, all the way from her toes to her chest. The tightness in her throat exploded with a furious cry. Warmth filled her cheeks and her eyes squeezed close.

She ran her hands over her face. Her warm tears streaked the backs of her fingers. When she looked up, Astrea slid Mal's dangling legs onto the bed. She propped his head on the feathered pillows and pulled the duvet around him.

"That potion should kill him," Astrea said under her breath. "But it doesn't. And he keeps telling me to make them stronger and stronger. I fear I will run out of ways to sedate him."

Astrea looked down at her sworn Prince with a tight expression.

Maeve steadied her breathing and moved towards what remained of the door, her discarded robe flying to her outstretched hand. "Come. We need to talk."

Chapter 66

Maeve

"Did you know?" asked Maeve.

Abraxas' brows raised.

"Emerie made a prophecy about my son?"

Her cousin's eyes widened, and he looked at Emerie.

She ran her hands through her long blonde hair with shaking fingers. She looked down at the table. "He commanded me to be silent."

Abraxas exhaled tensely. "What was the prophecy?"

"I'll only ask once more Brax: you didn't know?" asked Maeve.

Abraxas looked back at her and took her hand in his own and spoke sincerely. "I swear it, cousin. I knew nothing of a prophecy that was made about you." He rubbed his fingers across her cold knuckles and looked back at Emerie. "Recite it," he instructed.

Emerie looked at Astrea from the corner of her eye and shook her head. "You are not the only ones with children to consider," she snapped. "Astrea and I have babies, their lives depend on ours. I am not so foolish as to disobey the crowned Prince at a time when–"

Maeve didn't hesitate. The Dread Magic, and Mal's own Magic inside the Dread Ring she wore, swelled under her command. She moved into Emerie's mind with ease, cracking her Pureblood defenses at once.

She called forth the memory in question and watched as a terrified and soaked in sweat Emerie recited her first prophecy with a thousand voices not her own:

"The blood of the Crowned Prince that was prophesied will join the blood of another and, in their bond, create Magic that is unstoppable. He will be the catalyst that plunges the Magicals deeper into darkness, but he will break the curse of this land and unite all the realms. There is no victory before his manifestation. There is no

triumph until his Dread Magic is one with the crowned Prince's."

Maeve yanked herself out of Emerie's mind. Her body felt feverish as her arms tingled. She gripped Abraxas' hand tightly.

"How dare you," began Emerie.

"Fuck you," spat Maeve.

They stared at once another in contempt. Maeve's stomach turned over and over as anxiety and fear made their way into her mind.

Emerie looked away in shame.

Abraxas placed his elbow on the table and covered his mouth. "Fuck," he muttered. "Maxius is your son? Yours and Mals?"

Maeve nodded, barely hearing him as he asked another question.

Maeve recited Emerie's hidden prophecy from start to finish in her mind. Twice. She played it over and over again in her head.

"This doesn't make any sense," said Astrea. "Though. . . I can feel the truth in such Magic. You did not birth him, but I know he is yours made flesh. I didn't understand what I was feeling in him until now. He is Mal made over a hundred times stronger. And he is you in every essence possible. But you did not birth him. You did not carry him."

Abraxas looked over at Maeve and blurted out, "How long have you been able to alter everyone's memory to your desired outcome?"

Maeve's eyes slid to his. Her cousin's face was soft, void of all anger or judgment.

"Since before my father died," she answered honestly.

Emerie and Astrea's mouths fell open at the implication.

"I've only used it once," continued Maeve. "At a ball, it wasn't even significant."

Abraxas shook his head. "How do you know you've only used it once? If you altered your mind to forget, just like everyone else's, how would you know?"

"Gods," muttered Astrea, her hand clamped over her mouth.

"The possibilities are endless," said Abraxas, straightening in his chair, "and there is no use trying to figure out exactly how many times you've done this. How many things have you altered trying to stop something from happening? All that matters is that you tried to hide him for some reason. And I am willing to bet that reason is directly related to this prophecy."

Something deep in Maeve's stomach twisted and turned without reprieve.

Emerie spoke. "There is no victory before his manifestation. There is no triumph until his Dread Magic is one with the crowned Prince's."

No one spoke the understood implications of Emerie's prophetic words. Maeve knew, deep in her core, she was no longer trying to save Mal just for his sake. For their sake.

It would be to save Maxius' life, too.

Whatever resided in Mal, whatever or whoever she had so foolishly released in Mount Morte, wouldn't stop with Mal. If Maxius was the key to their salvation. . .

Maeve turned her attention towards Astrea.

"Can you heal him? Can you, and your mother if need be, expel the darkness that has taken up residency in his mind?"

Astrea bit her thumbnail and stared down at the table. "Potions and healing spells aren't what he needs. This is Magic I am not equipped to handle. Nor is my mother." Her fingers gravitated towards her chest, where her own Dread Mark lay beneath her clothes. "Even with the powers of Dread Mal has allowed me, I cannot do this." Her eyes grew large. "What about the Dread Spellbook?"

"I have already searched every page," said Maeve. "There is nothing it has to offer us where reversing Magic is concerned. What if I could get someone here who could help?"

"Who?" asked Abraxas quickly.

"Reeve mentioned it to me once. He said, in Aterna, that they have Healers. Power ordained from the Gods, I think he said." Her hands crept up her neck, over her blackened veins. "When I was sick, when that Dark Magic had hold of me, he said the Healers there could help me."

"Yes," said Astrea quickly. "Do it. Every moment that I battle this darkness in him it is damaging my very soul." Her fingers twitched nervously. "I haven't seen my boys in weeks. I am too afraid of transferring this darkness to them."

"I'll write to him at once," said Abraxas.

"No," said Maeve solemnly. "There isn't time."

Maeve pushed out of her chair and hastily made her way across Castle Morana with a single thought echoing across her mind: How long have we really been here? How much time has truly passed?

Chapter 67

Maeve

She paced across her chamber, shifting through the Magic that coursed through her. Reeve had done it before-spoken into her mind. She wasn't sure how, as she had sworn to never call upon him that way.

But Mal needed her.

Maxius needed her.

She swore under her breath. With a wave of her hand the curtains along the wall of her chambers pulled tightly closed, blocking all moonlight. She snapped her fingers and all the candles sparked into little glowing flames.

She sank to the floor, crossing her legs under herself. She brushed her hair behind her shoulders and looked down at her palm.

She closed her eyes and controlled her breathing. In and out, in and out, until her heartbeat was steady.

"Worth a try," she muttered, opening her eyes.

With two pointed fingers she sliced across her palm in a willing sacrifice.

Show me how to call to him. Mind to mind.

Dark Magic moved through her. It was cold and relentless as it ripped through the wound, taking her offering in exchange for knowledge. Her teeth cracked together as the Dark Magic took more payment than ever before.

She felt it then. A soft glow of warm Magic. It was brittle, barely held together. It smelled like Reeve. It breathed like Reeve.

She called his name across that Magic.

Reeve?

The air around her shifted. Warmth flitted into the room, steady, like a heartbeat.

Are you alright?

His voice moved through her mind in an echo. His tone was casual, but she sensed his concern shift through her.

Yes, she replied into the void. *Is there someplace I can meet you?*

Now? he replied.

Yes.

Silence fell. She wondered if she had lost him.

"Sanctum."

"What?"

The void shifted, her head spun slightly.

I'm already there now. Just come to me.

I don't know how.

Yes, you do.

She pulled his warmth towards her, tendrils of it circled up her arm. Magic swirled around her, Obscuring her out of her chamber.

Three trees twisted together before her as her feet landed on smooth white stone. Their limbs wrapped one another in supple wood. She'd been there before. The memory was ash in her mouth. Behind the trees stood Reeve. She ascended white stone steps towards him. Clear water slipped around the winding roots and ran beneath the floor.

"Have you been here before?" asked Reeve, his eyes on the trees.

Maeve nodded, unwilling to elaborate. "Though I do not know what it is, or why it is."

Reeve looked up at the altar. "Highest point on the planet," he said softly.

"So it's a temple?"

Reeve nodded. "You could say that."

"Are we in The Dread Lands or Aterna?"

"Neither," he answered. "We are standing on neutral ground."

"I need a Healer," she blurted.

"What?" asked Reeve, snapping to attention. "You look fine."

"It's not for me."

"Then who?"

Maeve looked up at him. "For Mal."

Reeve's face hardened, and he paused a moment. "Alright."

"You'll allow it?" she asked.

Reeve scoffed. "Am I truly the villain in your mind? You think I would deny him a Healer?"

Maeve didn't answer right away. "When can the Healer come to Castle Morana?"

"They won't travel to the Dread Lands now. He will have to come to the House of Healing in Aterna."

"He'll never agree to that," she argued. "They'll have to come to us. And possibly. . .in secret."

Reeve's face hardened once more. "They won't, Maeve. They aren't going to come there. Some of them were there the last time the throne was occupied and they haven't forgotten it."

She stepped towards him. "Then make them come."

"That is not the ruler I am."

"Then you sentence him," she seethed, "and if he falls, I will hold you personally responsible."

"So be it," said Reeve with a calm reserve. "It's pointless anyway. I will not sacrifice my people for him. Nor for you. Not a single one. This is not the curse of some mere Magical or a flesh wound. The healing he needs cannot be done by even the greatest Healers in Aterna."

"What was in that mountain?" she asked quietly. "What is it that occupies his mind? That poisons him against me? That speaks to me in shadows of whispers? I know that you know."

He spoke in a hushed tone. "The darkness I drove into those lands was that of nightmares."

"It's her isn't it?" she asked, her voice nearly breaking. "That Shadow you spoke of."

Reeve paused. "I believe it is her, yes."

"You didn't kill her."

"I may have thought I did. But I was never prophesied to destroy her. That is not my destiny."

"What if it's not real?" asked Maeve. "What if these prophecies are just that? And I am a fool for hoping he can still conquer this evil?"

"You already know what you did, Maeve. You already know who you released on Mount Morte. Why do you doubt it?"

"Because you once told me Shadow Magic was deception and lies. I can no longer believe my own reality. Maxius. . ."

Reeve's face saddened, but he smiled softly at her.

Maeve eyed him. "Do you know?"

"That he is your son?" He nodded. "Strange though, I am only just remembering. Like shards of Magic slowly chip away around his existence."

Her breathing hitched. "I cannot protect him. I have never felt so completely incapable."

Reeve looked over at the three intertwined trees.

"Do you know why The Dark Planet sits empty, void, and eradicated of Shadow Magic?"

Maeve shook her head.

"They once occupied this realm with Dread and Aterna, when Magicals outgrew Vaukore's realm. All was neutral ground. All three branches of Magic lived amongst one another. Shadow Magic rose above the rest. There have been many wars across Magic. Shadow Magic died because there were those who sought to eradicate it. It didn't happen by chance or circumstance."

"They were killed," she stated plainly, understanding his words as she looked down at the three stars branded in Magical dark ink on her wrist.

Shadow Magic. Aterna Magic. Dread Magic.

"They were enslaved. Destroyed and broken. To be of Shadow Magic was a curse."

"Who waged war on them?"

Reeve hesitated. "The Dread and Aterna at first. They lost their place in this realm and were forced to The Dark Planet. But their misery did not end there. The Dragons of The Dark Planet did not take kindly to them either. They wanted to put an end to the lies of Shadow Magic and all its deception."

"The same dragons my family hunted and slaughtered to their own extinction?"

"The very ones," said Reeve.

"Is the cycle of death and destruction ever going to end?"

Reeve smiled softly, in pity. "Maybe one day. But that is not a future history predicts if we are to believe in its repetition."

Maeve grew quiet. "I think I've seen her. She is what haunts my dreams and–"

Reeve's eyes widened. He looked like he may take a step back.

Maeve looked up at him. "Show her to me."

"No," said Reeve quickly. "You have already seen her. You know it's her."

"Why won't you let me see?"

Reeve shook his head. "I cannot let you inside my head."

Maeve scoffed. "Now who paints the villain?"

"We were painted long ago," said Reeve with a grin, "and keep smudging the paint, never allowing it to dry."

Maeve sighed.

Reeve continued. "She poisoned the last Dread Descendant, just as I imagine she has poisoned Mal. Sooner or later, she will have hold over it all once more."

"Ghost, his children called her," she said quietly. "I think she destroyed them, too."

The Library at Castle Morana held nothing about Shadow except the servant's account from Orion the Dread.

"But then how does Mal exist?" she muttered.

"Because Orion hid them. While Shadow was trying to take my head, his ancestors were fleeing to Earth. Willingly abandoning all Dread Magic in their veins in hopes that she wouldn't want to consume their Magic if they had none."

Maeve's nostrils flared. "And you knew all of this," she said. Her hands lifted in defeat and then fell to her sides. "So easily held your tongue all this time."

Reeve did not glare at her like she anticipated. He inhaled and smiled. "Spells are breaking left and right."

Silence fell between them. Maeve relinquished her pride and accepted that the circumstances were irrelevant to what she must achieve.

"I want to save him, Reeve. I believe I can save him."

He looked away from her and spoke with genuine sadness. "I know you do."

Warmth flitted towards her. She could so easily step into it, into him, and have a moment of respite from the perpetual chill she'd grown accustomed to.

Reeve's eyes moved back to hers. The Vexkari running down the side of his face and across his neck made her lonely and despairing thoughts drift further than she could allow.

The most powerful being alive. Not anymore. Not now that Shadow returned. He may not have been her enemy, but her father had taught her that it would rarely be so black and white.

Trusting Reeve seemed impossible.

"Maybe there's something in your Library that could help Astrea heal him."

His head fell backwards in defeat.

Maeve shook her head with a slow sigh. "I see," she said quietly.

Reeve trusting her seemed equally impossible.

"If one good deed in all my life I did, I do repent it from my soul," he recited the Shakespeare without looking at her.

"Titus Andronicus," she said. "My mother didn't care for that one."

"I imagine not," he replied stiffly.

Maeve rubbed her eyes in exhaustion. "Is there anything I can do?"

Reeve looked down at her. "You can run."

Maeve looked away from him. "That's what Mal said," she whispered.

"Then you might heed his words. Despite all else, I do not dispute that he cares deeply for you. Buried though it may be."

Maeve shook her head and touched her chest, where, under her clothes, lay her own Dread Mark. The first he'd ever given. "I swore an oath. It is not in my blood to run. Usque ad Mortem, Sinclair," said Maeve.

A smile spread across Reeve's lips. "Yes. I know you not to be of cowardice."

"Could I take her?"

Reeve's eyes widened. "Have you gone mad?"

"I'm genuinely asking–"

"No, Maeve," he said hastily. "I'm sorry, but you are not strong enough. If Malachite succumbed to her, then you are no match for her. I was barely a match for her. I got lucky. Very lucky."

"I don't care," she said at once.

Reeve shook his head. "Well, I do. You will die at the hand of that darkness."

"Then help me!"

"I have tried," he fired back. "You do not like my solutions."

Maeve turned her back on him and marched down the white steps past the trees.

"Maeve!" he called after her.

She didn't turn back towards him.

"Are you able to see what I saw in this temple? Does it show you the curses it once showed me?"

Maeve didn't answer.

She buried the images of Dark Magic deep in her mind and refused to acknowledge their presence. There was too much darkness already. She could not harbor more.

She Obscured, and stepped into the Healing Hall, her eyes scanning the room for Astrea. Alphard stood at her side. Abraxas sat kicked back in an armchair, smoking a cigar with tired eyes.

Astrea's eyes widened upon seeing her. "Well?"

"There's nothing he can do," said Maeve plainly.

Astrea's gaze fell to the floor.

"What's your plan?" she asked Astrea. She looked at Abraxas. "Does anyone have a plan?"

Abraxas set his cigar aside. "We move forward until a way to help Mal has been found."

"We attack Aterna you mean?" snapped Maeve.

"Yes," he snapped back. "Do you have another way to keep us all alive? You are likely the only one able to Portal off realm at this point. Mal has blocked the Magic altogether. And even if you did manage to create a Portal for the thousands upon thousands of citizens here, Mal would know in a heartbeat. And even if, and it's a rather large if, cousin, you managed to get all the Magicals in the Dread Lands to Earth, then what? We bring a planet conquering blight to the innocent Humans?"

"Alright," said Maeve, her temper desperate to slip out.

Abraxas' mouth pulled into a thin line as he looked away from her.

"Come with me, Astrea," said Maeve.

"No," she said at once. "Not if you are taking me to him."

Maeve shook her head. "You are his healer, Astrea. It's sworn and burned across your chest, just as it is mine. Just as it is Abraxas' and Alphard's."

"I studied Practical Magic with an emphasis on healing at Vaukore, Maeve. I learned to heal from my mother and Healer Kimmerance. There was no class on expelling an ancient and wicked phantom of Magic!"

"Fine," she said. "I'll go to your mother."

"No!" shrieked Astrea. "You can't. She has Pyxis. He has to stay far away from all this."

Maeve's eyes narrowed in disbelief. "You think this isn't going to affect them because they're in some fancy tower? You think The Beryl City isn't about to be a ruin of civilization once more?"

Astrea stood and boldly crossed towards her. Maeve's brows raised at the look of fury on Astrea's face. Magic swirled at Astrea's hand.

Maeve's eyes dipped to Astrea's fist.

"Watch yourself, Astrea," said Maeve coldly. "Your rage does not stand alone."

Astrea's chest rose and fell in broken breaths. "Tell me you won't seek my mother for this."

"I can't promise you that," said Maeve. "I am trying to save our Prince and my son."

Astrea's mouth turned down. "What of my son?"

"Then do better!" hissed Maeve. "Figure out a way to heal him."

Astrea fired on her, Magic exploding from her hand.

Maeve didn't block it, but shot a single spell straight at Astrea, which shattered her Magic. Alphard and Abraxas moved between them at once, Alphard taking the hit from Maeve's curse.

He winced and grabbed his sister, forcing her ready-to-re-fire hands down at her sides.

"Astrea, no," grunted Alphard. "You idiot, she'll destroy you."

Abraxas stepped into her line of vision. Both his hands gripped her wrists and spread them wide.

His face was pained. "Stop," he whispered. "Before you take it too far."

Maeve pushed against him. She'd forgotten how strong Abraxas' Magic was. He rarely used it for more than lighting the tip of a cigar. But it was there, steadily flickering against her own.

Maeve relaxed, but Abraxas remained restraining her.

"I'm stronger than you, you know?" Maeve pushed against him.

"That's a bloody understatement," he replied.

Maeve inhaled slowly and closed her eyes. Abraxas' hold on her wrists disappeared.

Abraxas took her hand in his own. "Let's take a walk."

Chapter 68

Maeve

The water was like an ice bath. Her legs shook as she found her footing on the rocks beneath the dark water of the Black Deep. The wall of Magic isolating the Dread Lands from Aterna wafted in an ethereal glow across the black water.

It reflected back at them, the illusion that there was nothing beyond it. She could not see Aterna's lands.

It was no regular shield. It would take nearly all of her Magic. Mal wore the crown, the locket and the ring, so she'd have no Dread Magic to help her. Though, her mind was quiet without the Dread Ring, and so she welcomed the absence of dark energy.

If his own strength was not enough, what if together they still were not enough?

The water's temperature traveled up her body, chilling even the parts of her not submerged. She shook in the freezing lake.

Mal's instructions were clear. She was to break the shield, and retreat to Castle Morana. The rest of their Bellator, the Supremes now formally named The Dread Knights, would advance to one of the smaller cities of Aterna.

She was commanded not to go.

Command or not, she was certain she'd be unconscious soon enough.

She stood beside Mal. Mordred stood at his other side. His wolves were eager. Too eager. She held her arm out at her side, two fingers at the ready. Mal mirrored her.

Mal didn't look at her. "On my count, Sinclair," he said calmly. "Not a moment sooner."

The use of her last name burned in her throat.

"You do not falter until it is collapsed or you are."

She steadied herself and prepared her mind to be drained of every ounce of Magic she had. Mal moved behind her. His fingers slid down her arm until his palm rested atop her hand. He extended their arms towards the wall of Magic, arranging his single finger with her two.

Her eyes lingered on The Dread Ring gleaming on his slender finger above her own. Power undulated from the jewel, thrumming at her core.

It'll be back on your finger soon enough, he said into her mind. *I put more Magic in it. I know you feel it begging to be one with yours.*

The pulse of Magic from the Dread Ring fell into sync with her own. Or perhaps her heart slowed to match its rhythm.

Maeve looked up at the wall of Magic that had stood for three centuries. Reeve's Magic radiated from the floating, glowing Magic. It resembled Crystalmore, with its pillars of pale stones that gleamed like a moon.

"Three," he said, pulling her from thoughts of Reeve.

She closed her eyes, letting electric ice travel down her arm and swirl at her fingertips.

Reeve would never forgive her for what she was about to do.

"Two."

She'd never forgive herself.

A bit of Dread Magic slipped into her own, popping her eyes open at the unexpected sensation.

"One."

Their combined blast was catastrophic. It surged from them, parting the water and crackling the wall of Magic. She let all the walls of her own Magic down, and flowed every bit of herself into the volatile and destructive Magic pouring from her fingers.

The wall of Aterna Magic ripped open with a deafening and shrill break of Magic.

Maeve's legs turned to nothing. The skin on her fingers burned and melted away. The bright lightning fizzled out as she stumbled.

Mal withdrew his Magic.

Water crashed back and surged around them, knocking her footing loose and sending her sideways. The onyx colored water encased her only for a moment as slender arms wrapped around her, pulling her from the waves. Bitter water prickled down her skin. The water grew colder and colder until she was certain she no longer had legs. Mal pulled her close. Her head rolled limply against his chest, her destroyed fingers pulsing with each slow heartbeat.

Castle Morana was quiet when her eyes opened again. The Crown's Quarters felt like a tomb. She'd been laid on the bed, her fingers healed, and left in the castle alone.

Mal was advancing on Aterna in the south. The attack would be quick, it was meant as a warning, not carnage.

If I destroy it all, who will bow? he had said.

She sat up. Beside the bed were three empty potions, all of them to ensure she healed quickly. The Dread Ring sat back on her finger.

There was a chance she could get to Reeve, and return to the castle before anyone knew.

It was worth a try.

If he cared about the future of Aterna, and she knew he did, perhaps there was a chance he'd listen to her. Perhaps she was selfish, and wanted to persuade his forgiveness from him before it could fester into hatred.

She pushed up from the bed. She'd been there before. Obscuring onto the precipice of Crystalmore was easy with a breach in their shields. The swarm of Senshi Warriors that surrounded her moments after her feet touched down were not as easily handled.

Eryx pushed his way between them. He stood tall in his full armor. His long Elven hair was slicked back in tight braids and numerous earrings connected to the silver necklaces he wore.

"I knew you'd come here," he spat.

"I just want to talk to Reeve," she replied.

Eryx's scowl never faltered as he raised a single hand. The surrounding Senshi drew their swords in one fluid and synchronized movement.

Maeve sighed and cocked her head to the side. "I'm not very good at the whole 'injure don't kill' thing," she said. "And I do not want to hurt your warriors. So perhaps you should stand down?"

"Dozens of Senshi Warriors against one Magical. I'll take my odds."

"Tell them to stand down," she repeated. "Do not sign their death warrant."

They pressed towards her.

Maeve flew into the closest Warrior's mind, holding him on the edge.

"Please," she said. "I don't want to hurt them."

Eryx's eyes were on the captive Senshi. The Warriors continued to advance towards her. They moved as one, in a calculated dance.

"I don't have much time, please," she said, her teeth grinding together.

Eryx's expression did not change.

Only a few more seconds and she would have to act.

A shot of air fizzed past her, so close a loose strand of her hair whipped across her face. Her eyes widened at the archer atop the steps. He opened both his eyes and lowered his bow.

"Enough, Eryx," said Drystan.

The most skilled archer in the realms missed her by a hair. From a short distance.

Maeve dropped her hold on the Senshi Warrior's mind as the small framed archer made his way towards them with an arrogant smile.

He missed on purpose.

She hadn't felt his oncoming attack at all. No threatening Magic made itself known. No surge of energy came with that arrow.

It was. . .just an arrow.

A lengthy breath escaped Maeve's lips. So lengthy she wondered how long she'd been holding it.

Eryx drew both his swords and positioned himself defensively, ready to protect Drystan.

"We can't beat her today," said Drystan, who appeared at his side, and made no attempt to reach for another arrow.

Maeve's eyes traced along the tattoo-like scars that ran through his under-shave. She'd seen such marks many times now since she first made his acquaintance. She herself wore traces of Dark Magic.

Of Vexkari.

"Today?" asked Maeve, peeling her eyes away from the markings she was so curious about.

Drystan nodded. "I have faith your demise will come at your own hand. Though I am uncertain if it will be for your pride, or because of your stubbornness."

"Enough cryptic bullshit," snarled Eryx, his Elven eyes set with daggers. "Since when do you miss shots?"

"That's Elven steel," she remarked at Eryx. "Fine jewels for an army captain."

"Smart words from a Second draped with Dread Artifacts she is unworthy to wear."

"What do you want?" asked Drystan.

Maeve looked out across the waters, to Dark Peaks. Dawn was on the verge of breaking.

"To talk," she said. "To Reeve."

"You aren't getting anywhere near him," said Eryx. "Not today, not ever again."

Maeve squinted at the horizon. A faint yellow line traced the peaks of the mountains. Like. . .sunlight breaking the day.

A warm heartbeat pulsed in her chest.

"He's already here," she muttered.

A burst of wind slammed around them. Reeve appeared before her in a swirl of violet fire. His dragon form towered over her as snarling flames erupted from his snout. His neck was long, like that of an eel, and covered in the same pointed spikes and barbs his long back and tail were. Thousands of glittering amethyst scales bore the same markings that traced along his Human skin.

His own Vexkari.

He was divinely horrible.

Black steel claws scraped across the pale crystal stone. His demonic eyes were locked on her.

But her gaze was fixed on the mountains behind him.

"The sun," she muttered in disbelief.

Violet fire exploded around her. She threw up her arms across her face, but her shield was too slow.

Reeve's flames burned around her, burning her in a perfect swirling pattern up her arm. She snapped her eyes shut and pushed against his Magic. She didn't move to strike back at him.

How dare you, he snarled into her mind.

Maeve steadied her breathing and gripped her burned arm closely. She looked up as his Human form emerged from the tall flames.

"Leave," he commanded Drystan and Eryx without a glance their way.

Eryx turned and sulked away, taking the Senshi Warriors with them. Drystan lingered only for a moment, and then obeyed Reeve.

Maeve looked back at the Dark Peaks, which were drenched in morning light. Soft grays and blues shadowed the mighty rocks, as vibrant orange beams pressed over the peaks.

"The sun shines here," she said.

Reeve's Magic cracked impatiently towards her, ringing through her ears. She turned towards him.

His claws were balled into fists at his side. Maeve met his furious eyes.

"Come to Castle Morana in three night's time. And if you bend the knee, there will be no more attacks, no bloodshed, no war."

Reeve scoffed. "Now you no longer desire an alliance? Merely dominance? When not one moon cycle ago you were begging for my help? Now you want my throne?"

Maeve didn't answer. She looked back at the sunrise. Reeve laid into her further.

"I know it is not of your own accord that you are here attacking my lands, my Warriors. I know that your mind is lost where reason and logic are concerned."

Her eyes darted to him defensively. "It is not my mind that is lost," she whispered. "I warned you. I did indeed beg for your help —"

Reeve heaved a sigh. "Get out."

"Will you come?" she asked.

Reeve didn't answer. She turned towards him fully.

"For me?" she continued softly.

Reeve's jaw loosened.

"For me, will you come? I fear the horizon before us if you will not bend."

"Before us?" he seethed into the word. "There is no longer an us. There is only you. Alone."

Maeve stepped towards him. He didn't counter. He allowed her to be an arm's length away from him.

"Please," she said quietly. "You must come and you must bend the knee."

Reeve bent forward until their noses were an inch from touching. "Your wide eyes and soft voice do not work on me, Witch. I know what it is you are."

Maeve's face remained poised. "Then it will be war."

The light in Reeve's eyes dimmed. "It already was destined from the moment he was born. Fulfilled in the moment he claimed you."

"Is that what this is? Your elitist pride in that you cannot have what that beastly instinct of yours desires to claim?"

"It is far from my nature to want you, the arrogant Dread Viper, as a mate."

"Arrogant? It is you whose pride will be our destruction." Her throat tightened. "The utopia I dreamed of slips away from me with each passing hour. The night grows darker and the hour grows late."

"It is you who has darkened it! It is you who has re-created this never-ending cycle of destruction. I warned you what those lands would do to Malachite–"

"Stop it!" She cried.

Her arms pulsed with fiery needles. Her body was hot. Too hot.

She looked back towards the Dark Peaks. The endless twilight across their side of the realm nearly erased the memory of sunlight from her mind. The color was calming, like the hydrangea that grew year round at Sinclair Estates.

Reeve's harsh voice snapped her out of her trance.

"This is my invitation to submit? His war Viper on my balcony, more preoccupied with the sunrise than the one who she asks the unthinkable."

"I haven't seen a sunrise in. . .truthfully I have no idea."

She gripped her arm and stepped towards the edge of the balcony. Reeve continued to lay into her.

"That city you just attacked is full of citizens of Aterna who hold no ill will towards you. Most of them talk about you as if you are a work of fiction, praise ringing through their voices. How incredible The Dread Prince's Viper is. How she is a marvel of Magic, and how she can traverse minds with ease. And now that image of you will be forever replaced with one of fear."

"I should be feared," she fired back.

"There is only one man who should fear you, and he is a blind fool who does not."

"You are not afraid of me?" she asked.

"I cannot allow myself to fear. Fear is the absence of Magic."

She looked back at him. "Fear is the absence of Magic," she repeated, softly. Her arm burned all the way to her stomach. "Hmm."

"Look at me," his low voice commanded.

Maeve turned and faced him without argument. The fire burning deep in her core brought the corners of her vision dark.

"This is the end, Maeve," he said. "This is the only time I will offer what I am about to. Return to Earth with your son and leave this war behind you. I will not pursue you. Do what you must to run far from the darkness that now resides in your Prince. Or you will fall, and I will not catch you."

"I swore an oath," she said. "It is scarred across my body."

"Greater Magic has been broken."

She shook her head. "When the raven from Abraxas arrives shortly, respond with acceptance. Come, and hear Mal's terms."

"Raven?"

Maeve nodded.

Reeve heaved a sigh. "You are not meant to be here."

She didn't reply. Reeve continued with the shake of his head. "You came without his permission."

"Come," she repeated one last time, preparing her palm flat behind her to Portal back to Castle Morana, fearful if she Obscured she'd vomit and pass out. "Please."

Reeve watched her with sad eyes. Maeve's footing faltered slightly.

"Your fire burns deep," she said with a small laugh of exhaustion.

"Tell the Mavros girl you need a panacea potion to heal it. I am sorry. I was not aiming to burn you. Rage is. . .a deceitful being."

Maeve stepped into the Portal. "So it seems."

Chapter 69

Maeve

The Portal outside the gates of Castle Morana swirled out of existence behind her. She pushed herself forward, despite the sweat building on the back of her neck and across her palms.

The winding path past the gates had never felt longer. She fell into the massive doors, knocking them open and falling to her hands and knees.

Maeve looked up. Mal stood at the center of the hall with his hands tucked casually behind his back. Abraxas whispered hurriedly in his ear. A hushed chaos ensued around them. Astrea stood over a Bellator, chanting healing spells in a vibrating tone.

Not even Mal's cold stare, and the temperature of Morana to match, lessened the burning in her core. Her skin was aflame with Reeve's fire.

"Astrea," said Mal coolly, his eyes never leaving Maeve as he interrupted Abraxas.

Astrea withdrew from the Bellator at once, following his gaze to Maeve.

"Maeve is hurt," said Mal.

He stared at the burns on her arm with an unreadable expression.

Abraxas met her tired eyes for a moment, shock rolling over his face as he realized the only way she could have received such a wound.

Maeve swallowed hard, averting her eyes back to the floor.

Astrea stood before her. "Let me see your arm," she said briskly.

"Don't you dare touch me," panted Maeve.

Mal spoke with royal control. "Maeve. Astrea will heal your arms." He turned on his heel and didn't look back as he said. "That's an order. Ensure they don't scar, Astrea. Come, Abraxas."

Abraxas didn't hesitate to fall in step with Mal. Their footsteps faded down the corridor.

"An order," said Astrea. "You aren't used to getting those. What did you do out there to deserve the cold shoulder?"

A sigh slipped from Astrea. Maeve looked up at her. They remained locked in a glare until Alphard appeared. He stepped behind Maeve and slid his arms under hers, pulling her off the floor.

"No—" she began with a groan, the heat of Reeve's Magic shifting through her quickly. Alphard swirled her around towards him and gripped her shoulders tightly.

"What were you thinking going to Reeve like that?" he hissed down at her, disdain running through his eyes.

Maeve took him in through blurred vision. One side of his chest was coated in dried blood around a tear in the fabric of his uniform.

"Are you alright?" she asked without hesitation.

Alphard merely nodded. His grip loosened, but he did not let her go. His gaze traveled to her ripped sleeves and the scorched skin along her arm.

"You aren't," he said.

"I'm not like you," said Maeve. Her head bobbed over her shoulder at Astrea. "I don't need her. I can do it myself. Like most things, it seems."

Astrea's nostrils flared.

"Astrea," said Alphard, "go heal the rest."

"Her arms, Al," his sister started. "I was given a direct order—"

"I don't give a fuck if her arm rots and falls off. We will all die in the explosion if you touch her."

Astrea didn't argue further with her brother. She stormed in the other direction without a word.

"Why are you so stubborn?" noted Mal boredly as she slumped into a chair in his study. Abraxas sat at his desk, hunched over and scribbling quickly, with a cigar in his mouth.

Maeve didn't answer. She laid her burned arm on the armrest and began healing herself in silence. Mal nearly rolled his eyes as he batted her hand away, ripped away what remained of her sleeve and wrapped his fingers around her forearm.

Prickles of ice weaved their way into her skin, sewing up the wound, stopping the blood flow and numbing the pulsating pain. Maeve's eyes slid to a close, and she melted back into the chair, letting the cool leather stick to her clammy skin.

Mal's fingers slid lower, pulling a soft moan from her throat.

She rolled her head to the side and opened her eyes up at him. Despite their solid green color that brought her an uneasiness, he looked down at her softly. His free hand moved to her face, and she welcomed his gentle, fleeting touch.

His Magic brushed across her skin, negating the flush of her cheeks. His eyes traced down to her healed arm. He withdrew his hands and turned from her, leaving her empty once more.

"What do you make of the Senshi Army?" Maeve asked Abraxas as he poured wax onto the envelope and pressed Mal's seal into the spreading green liquid.

He pulled his cigar from his lips and didn't smile. "Obviously worth their salt." He took another pull. "Or you wouldn't have gotten wounded."

He looked up at her and smirked playfully.

"Do you enjoy seeing my Dread Viper bleeding, Abraxas?" asked Mal dryly.

"Not at all," said Abraxas. "But naturally I enjoy her lack of usual perfection."

"Any Second that isn't quick enough to react from a physical assault is far from perfect."

Maeve looked up at him. There was no denying they were burn marks, and there was only one other being powerful enough to wound her in such a way.

Mal took a seat and placed his hands in his lap. "So what did Reeve of Aterna say to you?"

Abraxas stopped smoking, frowned, and looked over at Maeve. "You saw him?"

"She went to see him," Mal corrected.

"Don't talk about me like I'm not here," she said coolly. "And yes. I did."

Abraxas shook his head back and forth quickly. He sat up with a straight back and put out his cigar. "What for? That wasn't part of the plan."

"It makes no difference if it was I or a raven."

"You are incredibly wrong about that," said Mal icily.

Maeve looked over at him. "I hoped if I asked him personally to submit that, it could sway him."

Mal's head shifted to one side. "And why would you think your word would impact him so?"

Maeve rested her head against the chair-back. "I assisted in breaking his shields," said Maeve. "You told me not to advance on the southland. You never said I couldn't deliver the message personally."

Mal nearly smiled, and looked away unable to argue. It was Abraxas who was in a tizzy.

"What did he say?" pressed Abraxas.

"He didn't exactly," she replied.

Abraxas groaned. "Maeve."

"Brax, ambushed by our request to bend the knee or not, it will make no difference."

"That is not your decision to make," said Abraxas. "There are so many things in motion. You cannot just take it upon yourself to change the course of things I have laid out."

"How could you possibly know the course of things?" she questioned. "You don't know if he will bend or not."

"That's not the point," he said, whipping out another scroll of parchment. "It wasn't your place."

Chapter 70

Maeve

"Where is Maxius?" she asked, hoping her voice sounded casual as she prepared to enter the great hall of Castle Morana.

Mal looked over at her. "Is he the only thing keeping you obedient?"

Maeve attempted to smile. "I have always struggled with obedience."

Mal did not look amused. Her fake smile faded.

"Best behavior," he said.

Maeve nodded and moved to go around him. Mal snagged her chin between his fingers. She looked up at him in defeat as his green eyes slid back and forth between hers.

"Maxius is with Zimsy," he said at last.

Relief washed over her.

"And where are they?" she asked softly, pushing the bit of him that chose to reprieve some of her worries.

His eyes darkened in their green color, and his grip tightened. Maeve tensed beneath him.

"Nevermind," she breathed. "Thank you."

His fingers loosened and became tender. "If he does not bend the knee," began Mal, "will you take his crown in my name?"

The Dread Mark on her chest prickled, a reminder of the oath she swore. A reminder that there was only one acceptable reply.

She nodded, and the set of double doors opened with a lazy wave of his hand.

Reeve came to Castle Morana alone.

No Eryx or Drystan.

No Senshi Warriors.

Just himself and Shadowslayer hanging on his hip. He sat, with crossed arms, and watched the councilmen of Hiems bicker amongst themselves as Mal sauntered across the hall.

Mordred lurked close on Maeve's heels, he and his wolves escorted a hobbling Kier to his seat.

Kier's hair had grown stringy and grey. His once brown beard was a coarse mess of untamed and unshaven bush. His lids hung heavy, nearly concealing his glazed over eyes. Mal's ring on his finger radiated Dread Magic as Kier held a vacant and distant expression. His nails had grown long and dirty.

"I'm sorry, Reeve," said Mal. "You were meant to have my undivided attention this morning." His eyes slid to the stern faces of Kier's council. "But it seems there are urgent matters at hand."

Reeve's expression of boredom and disgust didn't so much as twitch.

Mordred withdrew from Kier and joined his guard of wolves that paced along the hall. Their silent footsteps and glowing eyes remained in constant rotation.

Kier's council exchanged slick glances with one another at Kier's appearance.

"Fauna's fire," muttered one councilman with a shake of his head.

"Please," said Mal, raising his brows and offering a smile, "sit."

Kier's council took their seats in the large wooden chairs, their eyes nervously shifting between Mal and Reeve.

"Apologies, High Lord of Aterna," said the same councilman. "I did not realize we were overstepping your presence at court today."

Reeve's eyes slid to him. "And you are?"

"Coryenn," he replied. "King Kier's royal counselor."

Reeve merely looked back to Mal, refusing to meet Maeve's eyes.

Mal looked up at her from where he sat. He smirked and loosed a laugh. "Sit, Maeve."

She obeyed in silence, slipping into the chair at his side.

"We haven't even begun and she's on edge," said Mal smoothly. He looked her over with a wickedly soft grin and then averted his attention to Coryenn. "My Hand tells me you have grievances."

Coryenn looked at him fearlessly. His second mistake. His first was coming to Castle Morana to begin with.

"I can't imagine what those are," hummed Mal.

"We are here to discuss the future of Hiems," Coryenn blurted out, as though it should have been obvious. He turned his attention to Kier. "You have been away for quite a time. Might you return to Hiems soon?"

Kier did not respond, nor did he even acknowledge his counsel. His distant gaze was fixed on the floor.

"Darkness is brewing on Hiems, my King," Coryenn continued.

Mal smiled playfully, as playful as something laced with venom could be, and cocked his head to the side. "Your what?"

The councilman's face hardened farther. He swallowed. "My King," he repeated.

"Oh," said Mal with a quiet, unsettling laugh. "I thought for certain I misheard you."

Coryenn's eyes snapped back to Kier. "There are those of us on Hiems who have reservations about. . ."

Mal's hands remained casually placed in his lap, but that didn't stop Kier's council from eyeing his deadly weapons with apprehension.

"All sorts of creatures are changing," he continued. "There are reports of cruel acts and dark sacrifices. Even the trees grow volatile. We are concerned for your health, my King-"

"Mordred," called Mal, smoothly interrupting him.

The white wolf slunk from behind Mal's chair.

"Does Kier look incapacitated to you?" Mal asked Mordred, his gaze fixed on Coryenn.

Mordred did not even observe Kier. His glowing, dark red eyes were latched on Kier's royal counselor. "He's never looked better, my Prince," rasped the wolf.

"I couldn't agree more," said Mal cooly.

Mordred sat back on his hind legs with watchful eyes.

The rest of his wolves slowly closed in on the circle of councilmen. Their glowing eyes popping out from the shadows. Many of the Hiemsmen tensed, swallowing hard and twisting their hands together.

Coryenn shook his head, red flooding his skin. "We cannot sit by as Hiems becomes a wasteland of bloodthirsty creatures of darkness!" He pleaded desperately at Kier. "You are not yourself, my King," He stood hastily and stepped towards Kier. "If you will not remove that ring from your finger, I will."

Mordred stepped forward between Mal and Kier, snapping once at the councilman and snarling with rows of deadly, barred teeth.

Coryenn halted, fear quaking through his body. Another councilman spoke.

"You were meant to protect our King, Mordred. What evil has brought you to break such honorable oaths?"

Mal sighed. "Mordred, the next time one of our guests refers to Kier as a king, claw out their throat."

Mordred's teeth remained bared as he watched Coryenn, daring him to step forward.

"And you," said another councilman shakily, turning his attention to Reeve, "you are part of this deception?"

"You would be wise to accept your *king's* decision to abdicate to Malachite," was all Reeve said.

Mal's eyes narrowed at Reeve.

Coryenn paled, whispers exchanging amongst his constituents. "You are going to hand over Aterna to this darkness?" he asked, terror ringing through his tone.

Reeve looked up at Maeve at last, and did not reply to Kier's advisor.

"It seems Reeve has not yet made up his mind," said Mal. "Perhaps we should persuade him, shouldn't we, Mordred?"

Red painted the floor before Maeve could even look away from Reeve. Neither of them watched as Mordred and his wolves ripped apart every last member of Kier's council. Maeve didn't hear their snapping bones or flaying flesh. She didn't hear the way the wolves teeth cracked together between snarls.

Silence encased her mind, shielding her from the sound of carnage, as Reeve's voice delicately said, *What keeps you sitting there and not running to me now?*

Maxius, she replied without a hesitation.

A pause. And then, *You don't know where he is.*

Please, she said, *Bend. The. Knee.*

Reeve's eyes darted to Mal.

"How long will this go on?" asked Reeve with a shrug.

Mordred snarled, jerking his head to the side in one sharp motion. Coryenn's neck snapped, and he did not move again.

"Wonderful," said Reeve. "Now that the show is out of the way, let's discuss your plans to continue to attack my cities. When can I expect an apology and an agreement you will never attack the innocents of my home again? How long does that game last?"

"Until you break," said Mal frankly. "Until you yield."

Reeve's chest rose and fell. The metallic taste of blood sat in the air.

Mal's playful demeanor vanished and he stood. "Until you kneel."

Mal's voice rang across her mind. *Show him that new dose of Dread Magic at your fingertips, Dread Viper.*

Dread Magic that last time it had been fused with her fingers caused them to disintegrate completely.

Maeve Obscured with a swish of Magic and appeared across the hall before Reeve. He looked her over as she appeared before him, and for a moment she thought something like relief swept over his handsome face.

"Et tu, Brute?" asked Reeve, clinging to his mask of carefree arrogance.

Maeve did not smile. "Then fall, Caesar."

Shadow swirled around her once more and she was at Reeve's side, two deadly fingers placed on his throat.

The High Lord's skin turned cold beneath her touch. His face drained of its color.

He looked up at her in horror.

"My, my," said Reeve, his voice slightly shaking. "What a surprise."

With Mal's Dread Ring on her finger, and the locket around her neck, there was perhaps a chance of her wounding Reeve.

Mal dismissed Mordred. He and his wolves escorted Kier from

the hall.

Mal looked at Reeve calmly. "I would say I hate to do it this way, but I do not."

Reeve's eyes never left Mal. "Remove your fingers, Maeve."

Maeve stared at Mal, waiting for his call.

Reeve sighed. "Come now, Malachite, call off your dog."

Mal's face twisted into a scowl, but Maeve laughed. Mal gave her a small nod.

She dropped her fingers.

Maeve walked around the chair and faced Reeve. His eyes traveled quickly up and down her body, his mouth slightly agape. A look of bewilderment danced across his eyes. Something he knew, but she didn't.

Maeve's face scrunched. "What–" she began softly.

His intense stare dropped. He spoke over her as she opened her mouth to question him.

"So," said Reeve, quickly discarding his look of shock. "Some meeting."

"I tried to tell you," said Maeve coolly.

"Don't condescend to me, kitten," he replied with the wave of his hand as he crossed an ankle over a knee. "Now. What's all the show for, Mal? Your new wolves couldn't have killed them another time?"

Mal's charming, although slightly unhinged, demeanor returned, and he tucked his hands behind his back. "I've come to enjoy the show."

"Shocking," said Reeve. He looked around the hall. "This place just oozes death, doesn't she?" He looked back at Mal and scowled. "You just had to have the glory, didn't you? You just had to fulfill some foolish prophecy. And now it will cost you everything."

"I have lost nothing," said Mal.

Reeve's eyes moved to Maeve. "Not yet."

"Lithandrian sends her regards," said Mal, "and regrets she could not be here for such a historic moment today."

"Does she?" asked Reeve. "That pretty ring you forced on her finger tell you that?"

"Among other things."

Reeve held his glare. "Bet you were sour when you couldn't affect me with those powers of persuasion." Reeve smiled. "I tossed that ring in the Black Deep."

"Enough," drawled Mal. "Will you bend the knee?"

Reeve chuckled lightly, and a small rumble of Magic rippled through the room. "An Immortal bends to no one."

"Haven't you heard?" asked Mal with a grin. "I have all but one Dread Artifact. The Magic these lands have gifted me will last forever. I practically am immortal now."

Maeve's head whipped towards him with wide eyes. Mal and Reeve ignored her.

"History is littered with crowns that believed they were eternal," said Reeve. "Immortal you may claim to be, but you do not have the birthright of Immortality. I don't know what it is you are anymore."

Mal's charming smile didn't falter as he spoke with an icy quality. "You will find out."

Maeve watched each of them carefully, most of her attention on Reeve, ready to strike at a moment's notice.

Reeve's eyes traveled to her again. "What will you do? Wipe my memory, force me to comply? I know those sweet fingers harbor more power than merely killing." His voice darkened, his eyes gleamed over with bubbling anger. "And I know that you are hesitant to shatter and control minds because it takes such a toll on you. Isn't that right? You nearly killed yourself in that self-righteous display of Magic, bringing the Orator here and then shattering the minds of all those disloyal to you. Even the St. Beveraux girl wounded you for days. Such a shame," he taunted. "All that power and you can't use it or it'll rip you apart. So, I ask again, what will you do?"

But it was Mal who answered. "It's up to you how this plays out."

Reeve pushed off the chair and stepped casually over the bodies that lay before him.

"Give me something in return," said Reeve. "You have given the others gifts for their allegiance, I am sure."

"I gave you a ring of Dread power just as I gave Kier and Lithandrian," said Mal with a scowl. "It sits at the bottom of the

Black Deep, apparently."

"You bewitched Lithandrian with your silver tongue. I desire more than a ring of Magic."

Mal gestured his arms out, enjoying their banter. "What would you ask?"

Reeve spoke without missing a beat He pointed at Maeve. "Her."

Maeve's face turned cold, icy chills shot down her body as she inhaled sharply.

I do not need your saving, she spoke into his mind.

Oh, I beg to differ, he replied.

It was Mal who laughed this time, not Maeve. She stared at Reeve with trepidation.

"Something reasonable," said Mal with another small laugh.

"Is that not reasonable?" replied Reeve.

He looked over at her, the playful and flirtatious way he normally corresponded with her long gone. His tone was that of a wartime ruler negotiating. "My armies for a bride?"

Maeve neared the end of her patience. Mal's Magic hissed at her warningly.

"Apologies," said Reeve nastily as he took in the angry power pushing to burst inside her. "Is there a bad taste in your mouth about being given to a man in exchange for breeding?"

Maeve's two fingers cracked together as electricity shot through her body, gathering at her fingertips in bright green light.

"Maeve," growled Mal.

But her eyes didn't leave Reeve.

"Listen to your master," mocked Reeve, taunting her.

This is your last chance, Maeve, he spoke to her silently. *Or I promise you, I will not save you.*

Enough," snapped Mal.

"Is that still a no?" Reeve asked with his eyes on Maeve.

"That's a never," said Mal darkly. "She is not yours."

Maeve did not answer him. He spoke into her mind one last time.

So be it.

Reeve looked back at Mal. "She is mine, though, isn't she?"

Mal's brows flicked up.

"She never did tell you?"

"Reeve," said Maeve shakily. Green lightning swarmed her fingertips.

"I said no, Maeve," hissed Mal, his eyes never leaving Reeve.

Without missing a beat, Reeve spat the words that made Maeve's stomach plummet through the floor. "She's my mate."

"He's lying," snapped Maeve.

Mal snapped back. "He's not lying and you know it."

Maeve's eyes whipped to Mal. His were already on her.

"You think I can't feel the pull? You think that the greatest Supreme Magical who ever lived cannot see your Magic calling out to him?"

Maeve swallowed in shock. "You knew?"

"And you both lied," said Mal. "At any rate, I don't see the relevance of your bond. She denies the Magic between you, so what importance is it to me?"

"What if I don't intend to deny it?" answered Reeve as he looked between them.

"Then you'll die on a fool's errand," answered Mal. "She belongs to me."

His words didn't bring a smile to her face. They didn't send fluttering Magic through her core.

"I do not intend to bend to you," said Reeve.

"Then you sentence your kingdom to ash."

White light slammed into Maeve's mind.

Maxius reached for her in distress as a hooded figure held him.

"This is not forever, Maeve," said the hooded figure.

"Then why is my heart breaking?"

The hooded figure held Maxius tenderly.

"How am I supposed to walk away?" she asked, her voice quivering.

Warm wind swirled around them, settling Maxius against the hooded man's chest and calming him instantly. He breathed deeply as his eyes fluttered close beneath thick lashes.

The figure's hood slipped back.

"Because you are protecting your child," said Reeve, his hand

sliding to the back of Maxius' head.

Maeve looked up at him from Maxius' slumbering face.

"On your life," she reminded him.

"In Magic," he finished for her.

Blinding white light returned, shooting her back into Reeve and Mal's negotiations.

"Did you think I had forgotten it?" snarled Reeve. "Your spell?"

Maeve's hands shot to her head as she wobbled slightly. It was Reeve. She'd taken Maxius to Reeve for protection.

"What?" she asked, barely hearing his words.

"The spell your father told me of," repeated Reeve.

Maeve's heart sank and her eyes snapped up at him. The spell she had likely used for Mal to forget Maxius. The spell she kept secret from Mal.

No, no, no, no, she begged into Reeve's mind.

But the High Lord was good on his word. If he heard her, he did not reply.

A mighty roar filled the hall as black and amethyst swirling fire encapsulated Reeve. A dragon size shadow cast over them. With a fearsome screech and an explosion of Magic, he vanished and the smoke dissipated.

The High Lord of Aterna was gone.

Maeve's blood rushed through her, sending her skin aflame. He had not forgotten the spell as she hoped. He had not bent the knee as she had hoped.

Mal's face full of fury did not falter as she walked towards him, prepared to beg his forgiveness and plead to see her son.

"What spell?" Mal asked slowly.

Maeve stopped before him. "Please, listen to me. I didn't—"

His eyes narrowed and his voice filled with bitter betrayal. "What. Spell."

"My Father told him, I did not—"

"I will only ask you once more."

Maeve swallowed. "A memory spell I created." She continued her confession before her courage failed. "To alter multiple minds at once. To create a false reality collectively within those minds—"

"And it works?"

She nodded.

The temper that rarely slipped from his deadly calm demeanor flared to the surface. "Reeve knows how to alter the entire world's memory at once and you didn't think it was important I knew that? That I had that capability as well?"

"The entire world?" she questioned.

"Did you think he was not capable of such a thing? That you are not?"

"I had hoped–" said Maeve as her voice shook.

"You hoped?" he hissed, closing the gap between them. "You hoped I wouldn't be absolutely furious that you've kept this from me for-for how long now? You hoped that Reeve–"

Gold, spiraling orbs screamed into the hall. Maeve's stomach plummeted. She gripped Mal's arms. "No, no, no."

There were endless possibilities for Reeve's spell. She prayed that perhaps he found it in his heart to mend Mal's mind.

But even a lie so strong as one created by Reeve wouldn't stand a chance against the darkness in her Dread Prince's head.

Mal threw up his strongest shield around them, but there was no shielding this spell. The golden beams of light sliced through his black wall of Magic with ease.

Mal looked down at Maeve. "What have you done?"

Mal threw up another shield. It swirled around them in cosmic majesty. It was futile, for in their next drawn breath, Maeve Sinclair, and the rest of all living things, would cease to remember Aterna, the Immortal People, and their Immortal High Lord, The Senshi Warrior, Dragon of the Aterna, Reeve.

Chapter 71

Malachite

If you won't save her, please take her from me. Drive her far from this evil that haunts me. I cannot live knowing she will come to hate me. I cannot die, for this plague is eternal, everlasting in its insatiable need for my blood. Golden blood she has not, and the shadow wants her, despite my pleadings for her life to be spared.

I have given it all. My mind. My body. My very soul.

And now the boy.

My boy.

I am going mad with the knowledge the prophecy is not fulfilled until our Magic is one. The shadow of my mind craves him more than she ever craved me. He is far from Castle Morana and I pray he never returns.

I will deny Maeve her motherhood if he is kept secret from this darkness. My own heart aches at the lack of his smile.

There is Magic in the Greywood that I cannot grasp. The Dark Peaks now wrap The Dread Lands, when I swear there was once something beyond. Magic is so very deceitful in the Greywood. I think I have found it, mastered this unknown call of Magic, but I never do.

Something tells me there is more to these lands. More beyond the endless Greywood I wander through.

Someone who could protect my Little Viper and my even smaller viper too.

The shadow does not want my Little Viper to be mine. She thirsts for a crown of her own. A queen, she says she will be.

I never wanted a crown.

If one thing in my life I did desire, it was only her. To breathe her air was satisfactory.

I must make her run. I must make her dare to disobey the call of Magic between us. Her fear and hatred will be a welcome alternative for death.

Even now I feel the shadow's breath upon my neck, and I will be punished for my unfaithful writing.

Deliver Maeve from this hell. I beg, I beg, I beg.

The Dream is not dead. . .it has been buried alive.

Please, I beg...

I beg...

Chapter 72

Maeve

Snow started falling in The Dread Lands and it did not stop. The Greywood's spindly branches looked more dead than ever against the icy backdrop. Castle Morana was colder than Stalakta on Hiems, even with the layered clothes and coats they now wore and the pale green fires that blazed through the halls.

Mordred and his wolves lurked at every corner, ready to report to Mal any talk against his plans to invade The Elven Lands or any questioning his sanity.

Earth, in the time it had been abandoned, entered a time where the power-hungry Magicals who remained there created gangs of forceful law. There were still Magical Militia on Earth, still thousands of citizens who chose to remain there, trapped in a lawless realm.

Mal showed little care for them. He said it was their punishment for not coming to The Dread Lands when it was offered.

Many of the Sacred and Magicals stood behind him earnestly. Mal was on the cusp of full domination. With Kier already having denounced his titles and given Mal the entire realm of Hiems, and his complete control of Vaukore Academy and its realm, it was only natural that the Elven Lands were next.

"I will not go," said Maeve.

Mal did not verbally acknowledge her from his throne, but his Magic tapped on her mental shields. She debated for a moment, and then resigned, allowing him entry.

You will mind your tongue in my court, and remember your son.

Maeve's eyes narrowed across the long table in the Throne Room, rage barreling through her as he continued discussing his plan for invading The Elven Lands.

Rage he unleashed in her. Rage he tamed.

Maeve placed her elbows on the table and leaned forward, facing him fully. "I. Am. Not. Going," she seethed, her teeth scraping together.

No one in attendance looked at either one of them. No one dared speak.

Mal's neck craned towards her. Green, glimmering eyes dared her a step further as she spoke into his mind.

I know the prophecy. It is not finished.

Yet, he finalized with a scowl.

Maeve leaned back in her seat, satisfied to have won such a small battle.

A battle was all that remained between them.

Mal, her Mal, came in glimpses and glances. The war inside his mind was futile. The darkness of Shadow that possessed him was as strong as his eyes were green.

"You do not deserve that mark on your chest," he said, addressing her for the first time in the tense meeting.

"Then take it," she fired back, gesturing her arms wide. "Oh, but then how will you track my every move and emotion? How will you remain one step ahead of me?"

Mal's eyes traveled down to her neck, to her inky black veins. "There are other ways in which you belong to me. I am in your veins, in your skin, wedged between your bones."

"If only I could bleed you out," she said.

"Enough," he drawled.

"You are talking about waging war on innocents," said Maeve, ignoring his command to be silent.

"Then so be it," he replied. "There will only be one crown in the six realms. And it will be mine."

"You have the power to take it all yourself, why force me?"

"Because oaths will not so easily be forgotten in my kingdom."

"And what of the oaths you swore me?" she asked. "What of your promises?"

"Perhaps we should reconvene another time," said Abraxas quietly, his eyes on the scrolls of parchment across the table.

"My promises?" Mal repeated darkly, ignoring his Hand entirely. "You forget endlessly what I have accomplished."

"If only forgetting were that easy," said Maeve.

The rocky beaches of The Black Deep turned into a thin layer of ice, choppy and jagged, as the water pushed and pulled beneath it. The black water spread as far as the eye could see, becoming one with the dark horizon.

Snow flurries touched down on the stone railing of her balcony, adding to the layer of ice forming along the railing.

Maeve.

Mal's voice called, searching for her.

She released her Magic, drawing him to her.

A black swirl of cosmic night flitted across the balcony. It swirled high, evaporating and revealing Mal. His unkempt hair and his unbuttoned shirt, exposing his scarred chest, proved his weakened state. His green eyes pleaded with a lost desperation.

He crossed towards her, unaffected by the flying drops of ice hitting his bare skin. Mal's hand landed on her hips, sliding down her thighs as he kneeled before her.

"Just a little," he said.

She touched his face tenderly, sending his eyes closed as she ran her fingers over the scar splitting his eye. The scar she'd given him. "Why can't you always be like this?"

Snow piled in tiny white drops in his dark hair and on his shoulders.

"Where's Maxius?" she asked.

His hands tensed on her thighs. "Don't talk about him. It's not safe."

"Then no blood for you," she replied.

Mal's head fell back as he looked up at her, his brows pulled together as his lips parted. He fisted the fabric at her legs and yanked her to her knees before him. Ice crunched beneath her.

"Do you enjoy that I have to beg you?" he asked, his hands moving to her face.

"No," she replied solemnly. "I enjoy nothing of watching your possession."

"Then help me sleep," he said, "help me rid her–"

His eyes squeezed shut and his hands fell to his lap as he hung his head with a slow breath.

Maeve tucked her fingers beneath his chin, forcing his gaze back up at her. His face twitched in agony beneath Shadow's spell, punishment for daring to speak against her.

"It's not your fault," she said with heavy eyes, as she looked across the Black Deep. A warm trickle of wind caressed her skin, gone so quickly she questioned its existence at all. "It's my fault."

Bright white light erupted in her vision, pulling her deep into Mal's mind. Darkness swam around her in misty trails of Magic. Toxic and deadly.

A flash of a moment scattered in broken pieces across the darkness. She felt the vision more than she saw it. She knew the face, though it was brief and distant and changed. Older now was the boy before her. His name was Jude, the child from Mal's orphanage on Earth.

Maeve's eyes widened and a rush of joy flooded her skin as she realized where Mal hid Maxius away. She now knew where her son was.

Satisfied?

Maeve's fleeting joy vanished at the voice.

Darkness consumed her once more, swirling up around her, feeling for her Magic. Shadow's voice echoed across the void of Mal's mind. It lingered, repeating into silence with an unsettling vibration.

Shadow knew where Maxius was.

"You've known all along," said Maeve, her voice flat in the darkened space.

Her teeth snapped together as she shook her head. Shadow had tricked her once before. She would not fail again.

"You may think this a game, but you will not play it better than me," said Maeve.

A game? A game of crowns? A game of broken hearts? A game of death? I win them all.

"I don't believe you. I don't believe you know where he is."

The cunning Magic circling her smiled. Her eyes squeezed shut at the uncomfortable and invasive sensation.

Consider it a parting gift. You are in the way of my crown.

Maeve pressed her Magic out, slowly and carefully. Shadow's mind was everywhere at once, with no place to latch onto.

Laughter filled the space. Maeve flinched, withdrawing at once.

You think you can shatter my mind without shattering his? We are one now. What you inflict on my mind, you inflict on his.

A glow of pale light illuminated behind her, as ice prickled down her spine. Maeve turned over her shoulder.

Do you know my name?

Many names popped into Maeve's head, but the image of her as a child, with chained legs and ankles stood stark in her mind.

"Judyth," said Maeve softly to the pale and striking woman.

She looked nothing like her portrait on the library ceiling and everything like the ghost of Maeve's nightmares. Her long white hair and fingers dipped into sticky, swirling shadow.

Her icy brows tugged together. Her pale lips did not move as her voice resounded towards Maeve. *I haven't been called that name for many centuries.*

"It really is you," said Maeve in a soft breath. "Shadow."

Her expression shifted. Her eyes narrowed as she said, *I have been called that name before, but not by you. Strange Magic, Shadow Magic. They were wise to fear it. We've met before, remember? You so graciously offered me your blood on Mount Morte.*

"I'll never forget such a costly mistake."

Shadow smiled, the beauty that was buried beneath her gaunt appearance shining through.

"If you truly know where Maxius is, why wouldn't you move to bring him back here."

I do not want him here. Just as I do not want you here, Dread Viper.

Maeve didn't dare look away from the deceptive creature.

You have no future here. You can either let the Prince go, or I will take him from you.

"Haven't you already?"

A hiss bounced across the void. *I have not even hardly begun.*

Maeve's chest tightened. She wasn't even certain she'd said the traitorous words until Shadow responded.

"If I let Mal go. . .you will let me go?"

Admiration swelled around her in Magic. *At last, you chose yourself. I was disappointed with how selfless you've been up to now.*

"You haven't hurt Maxius because you don't want to risk his Magic joining Mal's and fulfilling Emerie's prophecy."

The admiration vanished, replaced by fury. Shadow's face darkened. Maeve continued.

"Isn't that what you want? Mal for yourself, and Maxius gone?"

Shadow's eyes traced over Maeve.

"I will make you a deal."

Laughter scattered around her. *She bargains with me?*

"Or not."

The laughter subsided. Maeve continued.

"I will remove myself from your way. And you will let me and my son go."

Silence fell. Maeve waited for her reply with bated breath and worsening resentment.

You stay away from the Dread Prince, and I will stay away from your son.

"Swear it," said Maeve quickly, desperate to solidify her bargain before her heart broke and prevented her from the necessary choices.

I want your eyes.

"What?" snapped Maeve.

The color. I want the color of your eyes.

Maeve stammered a reply, and then closed her mouth.

She had her father's eyes.

"And what color will mine be?" she asked at last.

The darkness smiled. *We will trade.*

Vacant pale eyes of ice stared back at her. Beautiful though Shadow had been, and still was in her own haunting way, Maeve was not certain Shadow's pale white eyes would suit her.

For all your scars you remain vain.

Maeve took a long breath.

"Fine," she relented, holding up her palm to strike across the scarred skin. "But not until we are safe from here. Agreed?"

Certainly. You will need those pretty blue eyes one more time.

"And you will not kill Mal," she commanded, adding to their deal.

The arrogance around her faded. Tears threatened to slip from the corners of her eyes at the weight of her weakness.

"If you want a crown, it will be at his side. Not at his demise."

Contemplation shifted across the void, turning to anger.

You do not command me.

"Today I do," said Maeve. "Or I will withdraw from his mind, and if it is done with my last breath, I will ensure his Magic becomes one with Maxius', fulfilling the prophecy you so desperately fear."

Shadow's frustrated Magic swirled around her, closing some of the gap between them as the pale woman was suddenly closer.

"You will not hurt him, or there is no bargain," said Maeve, a shake in her voice. "Is that understood?"

Magic sliced across her outstretched hand, sealing their deal.

Ice burned into her throat, her chest, her face, flooded her lungs.

Go and shatter his heart of ice, Little Viper, Shadow mocked.

The void of her mind shifted and frigid stone pressed into her back. Mal hovered above her on the snowy balcony of Castle Morana.

"You cannot," he cried through a clamped jaw, constricting her throat. "You cannot leave me."

"All that I do is done for you!" she rasped, hot tears soaking her cheeks.

His hands joined as one, squeezing and blocking all air flow. His face relaxed in terrifying control. His breaths became slow as she pushed her Magic against him.

"You swore to fight for me," he said coolly, the whites of his eyes scattered with red.

Maeve's eyes squeezed shut against the pressure. He overpowered her in every way.

Jealousy spiraled around them in the form of a great shadow.

"You swore," he said again, his voice growing colder and more distant.

He pulled her from the floor, never releasing her throat until they kneeled before one another. Maeve's arms hung limply at her sides. Resistance was pointless. She looked up at him, sucking in what tiny gasps she could.

"I have done it all for you," he said smoothly, his nostrils flaring. "And I am not enough."

The jealous cloud of Magic circling them grew darker. Maeve's brows pulled together. The Magic laced through it was not Mal's.

"How can I love you if you will not let me?" he asked as the circling shadow cast over them.

His grip loosened and slacked. His eyelids drooped.

Maeve moved her hands to her face. "Remember my words, Mal," she whispered. "In the darkness, remember my vow." Their eyes met as she swore to him, unbreakable Magic snapping between them. "Pour toujours."

Maeve pressed her lips to his as they faded into darkness, the feeling of his lips slipping from her. Black night fell upon them as Shadow claimed him. The darkness lifted, and she was alone with wet, stinging cheeks.

À tout jamais, Mal's voice echoed across her mind.

Chapter 73

Maeve

She would play the game to achieve her goal. To ensure the deal she'd made with Shadow succeeded.

"You've lost your mind," hissed Abraxas as she confessed her plan to him.

"Ironic words," muttered Maeve as she slid into the seat of her vanity, inspecting the already forming bruises and pops of burst blood vessels across her neck and chest.

Her breastbone pulsed with each sharp breath she took.

"I'll go get Astrea," said Abraxas

"I'm going to leave it," said Maeve, looking at her reflection with red and puffy eyes. "I need it for what I'm about to do."

Maeve looked closely at the small, dark red and purple dots that scattered across her cheekbones and around her eyes. They nearly blended into her subtle freckles.

The skin around her neck, swollen and marred from Mal's hands, would form bruises. Maeve followed them down to the faint black lines that shot up her throat, markings she had worn proudly, just as her father encouraged her to.

Mal's devastated face burned into her mind. She prayed he'd hold onto her final words, despite the Magic she was preparing to unleash.

Abraxas paced behind her.

"How are you going to Portal off realm without him realizing it?" he asked in a hushed tone. "The moment he cannot feel your Magic here, he will come for you. You cannot move in secret. I cannot even make a Portal to the next room without him knowing."

"I can with your help," said Maeve.

"How?" he asked in exasperation as a hand slipped through his bright hair and he stopped pacing

"Mal is not the only one with the knowledge of Vexkari," she answered plainly.

Abraxas' eyes met hers in the mirror. She slipped her Sinclair family ring off her finger and placed it on the vanity.

"You actually are mad," he said quietly.

"No," said Maeve. "I am determined I can pull this off."

"And how will any of this heal Mal's mind? How will any of this expel the darkness inside of him?"

Maeve traced her fingers over the ring's band and the sapphire stone. "This is the only way I see."

"We are moments away from waging war on The Elven world," he said desperately. "How can you run like this? I need you here."

Maeve turned on the stool and faced her cousin. "I will still be here," she said softly. "Just. . .not the same. If I abandon Mal, she will abandon her desire for Maxius."

Abraxas swallowed.

"I believe Mal can be saved," said Maeve. "This is the only way I know how."

She turned back towards the ring. "Now," she began, "Do you still have your mother's jaybird that can make her own Portals?"

The Tower Alphard picked for himself was, as expected, one of the largest of those restored under Mal's reign. Second only to Abraxas' own small castle he rarely occupied.

Of course, none of them compared to Castle Morana.

She crossed the threshold of Magic protecting Alphard's home and the gates slipped open for her. Dark vines covered the pathway, like most of what remained of the lost civilization of Magic. An unsettling feeling crept from those vines and their lack of color. Not a bloom in sight, and yet they were alive. Covered in thorns and ready to draw blood.

She stopped and stood in front of the large black door, slowly wrapping her fingers around the silver serpent knocker, and knocked three times.

The sound echoed across the open lawn. She withdrew her shaking hands and pulled the hood of her cloak in tightly, shadowing most of her face.

Alphard Mavros swung open the door calmly, his hair disheveled and wild. He squinted and then frowned upon recognizing her features beneath her hood.

"Great," said Alphard dryly. "What do you want? More orders for me to assassinate those disloyal to the Prince?"

"I just want to talk," said Maeve.

Alphard studied her for a moment and shook his head. He turned and rolled his eyes briefly, leaving the door open. Maeve didn't need to be told that was the closest thing to an invitation she would get. She stepped inside as he rounded the corner through an archway.

His house was ornately decorated, but Maeve recognized the taste to be his mother Irma's. With maybe a touch of Abraxas' control over the restoration of the beautiful houses.

She turned the corner into the sitting room.

"Care for a drink?" asked Alphard, making his way over to the small bar in the corner.

"No," said Maeve, lowering her hood.

"I'm sure you're here to congratulate me," said Alphard, without looking at her. "It being the eve of my wedding, and all."

Alphard poured himself a glass of Dragon Whiskey and turned back towards her.

His eyes widened.

"Fuck," said Alphard, freezing upon seeing the damage to her neck and face and letting the glass slip through his hands and shatter across the marble floor.

Maeve looked back at him, not even attempting to hide her fear any longer. Her whole body began to shake.

His mouth hung open slightly, unable to find the words to say to her.

"I need to know something," said Maeve.

"What happened?" asked Alphard.

"It doesn't matter I need to–"

"The bloody fucking hell it doesn't," he said sharply.

"Would you still marry me?" Maeve blurted out, her voice breaking.

Alphard stood silently for a moment. "What?"

"Would you still marry me?" she repeated.

"Maeve. . ." Alphard shook his head in disbelief and looked down. He ran his fingers through his hair. "I don't understand."

"It's not a trap," she said. "I want to know if you would have it be so? Of your own will? If that's what I needed."

Alphard breathed loud and heavy. "I am hours away from finally marrying her."

His words cracked something in her chest. Perhaps it was the fact that she didn't care that it would break his heart, what she was asking. Perhaps it was her own jealousy at the love Alphard and Victoria truly shared. Or that she was prepared to deny him of it.

Maeve doubled over with her face in her hands. Real tears streaked her cheeks.

Alphard shot to her and pulled her to the sofa, setting her down gently. He kneeled in front of her, taking her face in his hands.

"Tell me what's happened," said Alphard, pushing her hair out of her face and looking into her blue eyes.

"I can't," cried Maeve. "I just need to know–"

"Of course I would," he said softly, interrupting her. "I made a promise to protect you, many years ago." His hand withdrew and showed her a very faint jagged scar along his palm. "I made it in blood. I always intended to keep that promise until it was clear you didn't need my hand."

"With who? My father?"

Alphard shook his head. "Antony."

Maeve swallowed and let out a tense breath. "What if I needed it now?"

Alphard brushed her fallen hair behind her ear once more and examined her bruisings. "Mal did this."

"There is a darkness that has taken him, Alphard," she cried. "I cannot extinguish it. I am lost. He is lost. I cannot stay here. Maxius cannot be subjected to this evil."

"There is no realm you can travel to that he won't find you." His hand moved from her face and he placed one pointed finger at her chest where her Dread Mark lay. His own in the same spot on his body. "That ensures it."

Her breaths caught in her chest as she tried to keep her tears at bay.

"What if I had a way?" she asked in a whisper.

Alphard's eyes closed. He pulled from her and stood. "You're serious."

Maeve wiped her face, sniffling.

"Why me?"

Maeve didn't answer. "That's not relevant."

He turned on her, his temper slipped out. "You are asking me to give up everything. It's not irrelevant."

"It is," she argued. "You admitted it. It's written in Magic and in blood: you will not ignore the call no matter how you may desire to."

"Perhaps a foolish bond I made when I thought you were my duty, mine to claim. The world has changed, you ensured it. You wrote the new rules you now wish to run from."

"It is for Maxius that I run–" she began fiercely.

"Then admit it!" he yelled. "For once admit that you are being selfish. I will take your hand, I will protect your son but I just want you to say–"

"Fine," she cried. "I picked you because the alternatives are grim. There is no one else that would do this willingly. No one that cares for me for as long as you have. No one else understands the position I am in, that would make such a sacrifice–"

Alphard held his hand up. He turned away from her. "You're going to alter my memories," he said, and then shook his head. "No, not just mine. You're going to alter everything."

Maeve's tears dried.

A soft breath escaped his lips. "I knew you had some secret up your sleeve."

Maeve looked down at the floor. "Mal doesn't know."

They remained silent for a long moment until Alphard finally spoke.

"Give me tonight with Victoria. And tomorrow, I am yours."

Alphard didn't look back at her as he left her. She heard the front door open and close.

She didn't dare move to touch the Dread Mark beneath her clothes.

Greater Magic has been broken, echoed across her mind in a familiar voice she couldn't place.

Chapter 74

Maeve

Maeve's body felt light, with weightless bones and a dizzy head. She played with her ring finger, unaccustomed to the way her finger felt without the gold band and sapphire stone.

The act of Vexkari had been every bit as nauseating and excruciating as Mal made it seem. But in a place as potent and swarming with Magic as Castle Morana, Magic was easily commanded. As every ounce of her Magic sat in her ring back at Castle Morana, the only way for her to move off realm in secret, she walked down a foggy alleyway in London as the sun set behind the city.

She couldn't let herself dwell on the emptiness she felt without her Magic or the unbridled terror not having it.

Fear is the absence of Magic, she repeated to herself as she crossed a darkened alley in London.

But there was more than just her own Magic in her veins. The feeling of Mal's Magic alone coursing through her was euphoric. It tingled like their first kiss. The weight of it was like his protectiveness when Vaukore fell. Those versions of herself and Mal were scarred with war and death and darkness.

They were but a memory.

A beautiful memory that propelled her across a stone paved street. Spring was in full bloom on Earth. Jude stood tall on the other side of the gates at Finchley Orphanage.

"Hello, Jude," said Maeve.

He squinted at her. "Hello," he replied skeptically.

"You don't recognize me," she said as she took in his expression.

Jude shook his head.

"Do you know Maxius?"

Jude's eyes widened, and he swallowed. "No."

Maeve smiled. "Please don't lie to me," she said softly. "I know he is here."

Jude straightened. "You can't come in."

"That's alright," she said. "Can you bring him here?"

"No," said Jude. "I promised to help watch over him."

Maeve watched him for a moment. "You promised Mal you'd watch over him?"

Jude frowned at her and tried to look brave. "Yes."

Maeve smiled in appreciation. "That was very kind of you to do."

Jude shook his head. "You can't come in. You can't cross the gates. No one can except him. He said he sealed it with Magic. His Magic. He said he's the most powerful Wizard ever. And it's real! I saw it. He told me himself that no Magic but his can cross."

"Hmm," said Maeve, inhaling deeply. "I think you might be correct. But Magic is. . ." She lifted two fingers as the metal bars of the gates clinked apart. "Clever," she finished, as they swung wide.

Jude's cheeks turned red as he stepped backward. "What are you doing?"

Maeve closed her eyes and called upon every bit of Mal that ran free in her blood. Her darkened veins turned black as night as Mal's Magic seeped from her. She stepped between the tall iron gates and crossed the shield of Magic surrounding the orphanage.

Jude scurried backward along the path. Maeve pressed forward, closing the gates behind her with a soft push of her palm.

Past the front door of the orphanage, Zimsy stood immediately. Her face was both fearful and thrilled as she took Maeve in.

She looked her over once before dropping the book in her hands and jetting around the table towards her. Maeve slammed into her as Zimsy flung her arms around her neck.

Maeve held her tightly. "Maxius is here, yes?"

Zimsy nodded and pulled away. Her large eyes lingered on the bruises across Maeve's throat. She opened her mouth to speak, but Maeve cut her off.

"We don't have much time," she said.

Zimsy nodded and took her hand. "I must tell you first," she said. Her lips and brows pulled together as she squeezed her hand. "Just as before, when we were on Earth and Mal was in The Dread

Lands. . .time moves differently."

Maeve's shoulders dropped. "Alright," she said bravely. "I don't want to know how long, Zimsy. I can't know. I have to keep moving forward."

Zimsy pulled her into a hallway as a stomping thud landed at the foot of the stairs.

Maeve's throat tightened as joy exploded through her.

Maxius' smile faded and his mouth fell open.

He was older, but Maeve's heart swelled. He was still a small child.

"Do you remember me?" she asked hesitantly.

Her stomach turned to acid at the reality of her words.

He was at least four now. She'd missed so much of his life. Again.

Maeve kneeled down as Spinel trotted down the stairs and wrapped himself between Maxius' legs.

Maeve's suppressed cry spiraled into a relieved laugh. "I should have known."

She looked back at Maxius.

We go home? he signed.

Maeve's breathing hitched as she saw a gold band on his wrist—a watch with an emerald inlay and two serpent hands. She opened her arms to him. "Come here."

Maxius fell into her as she wrapped her arms around his small frame, tucking her head atop his. She couldn't lose him again. She couldn't erase it all and not know where he was, who he was.

Not with Shadow at her back.

She closed her eyes and allowed herself just a moment of pretend peace. Soon she'd have the time with him they both deserved. To make memories of their own.

More lies it would all be, but she'd settle for them in such dark times.

"We should stay here," said Zimsy. "On Earth."

"No," said Maeve, not opening her eyes. "This orphanage is only safe because Mal made it so. Shadow and I have a deal, though I'm not stupid enough to believe she'll uphold it."

Zimsy's eyes grew large. "You made a deal with that darkness? Oh, Maeve."

Maeve held Maxius tight.

There was no place safer than at her side. Mal may have placed the strongest protections around the orphanage, but Shadow would find a way, just as Maeve had, deal or no deal.

There was only one way to beat the dark reality upon them. Even if it only bought them time.

Her Lux Charm illuminated in the darkness.

Sinclair Estates was quiet. Like a shadowed memory of something that once was. Despite the elegant beauty the home was, stepping across its foyer was far from the warm welcome home she'd received without fail in the past. Each echoing step across the white marble was a reminder that she was completely alone.

The furniture and paintings were covered in thick tarps of fabric. The ornate fireplaces only held ash.

She twisted her fingers and ignored the cry of Magic in her darkened veins. It begged her to remain loyal. It pleaded with her to keep trying to save him, as she had sworn to do. The Dread Mark on her chest thrummed with a sinister threat, as though it could feel she was about to break her vows.

Reversing Vexkari wasn't in the Dread Spellbook. There were no counter-curses in the ancient text. The Dread Magic it boasted was final and irreversible.

But Vexkari was more than just Dread Magic. It was greater and older than all three types of Magic. And Maeve was certain that if it were possible to alter the brand of Magic on her chest, and reverse such deep vows, the Library at Sinclair Estates would have the knowledge to do so.

What little light the sliver of the moon provided slipped in through the skylights of the vaulted room. The sky was clear, allowing for a picturesque view of the stars.

She stalled, allowing herself a moment to admire the moonlit collection of wisdom before her. Her Lux Charm gently hummed with pale white light.

Time wasn't limitless, and she counted on Abraxas to ensure, if Mal returned to Castle Morana, that he did not note her absence. With a long and hopeful breath, she stepped down the aisle.

A soft crackling sound flittered by her ear. Her Lux Charm dissipated, dissolving into nothing as a warm blue glow encompassed the air around her. The firelight at the first row of books illuminated with a soft flame. Small, bright blue, crackling fire mounted the golden sconce.

She stepped deeper into the Library.

Another hiss as the end cap on the second row of books glowed just like the first.

Maeve's heart stilled. And she smiled.

Row after row went by, flames bursting to life, as she ventured deeper into the Library at a quickened pace. Her eyes stung with tears and her chest tightened beneath the safe and familiar Magic blossoming around her.

She'd never understood before, just as she hadn't understood Vaukore's Magic.

Sinclair Estates was its own Vexkari.

It was alive with the Magic of her ancestors. Her father and his brothers. Her grandmother and her sisters. She opened herself to feel it all.

The house's Magic infiltrated her with warmth. It was births and celebrations of life. It was card games in the sunroom and children's first steps in the gallery. It was stolen glances of courting and tea served just right. It was the telling of the same family stories again and again, ones that always ensured smiles.

It was a memory of time so beautiful it ought to have shattered her.

But there was no sorrow in her now. There was only gratitude to be part of something so holy and raw.

She held onto that Magic until at last, she stepped past a row of books and no firelight burst into existence. She stopped and turned. The rows of books behind her remained illuminated. She looked down the darkened row and understood at once.

She stepped down the aisle, smiling as more firelights guided her way with each step.

She held tightly to the Magic of her blood, the Magic of her ancestors, and knew they would protect her from what was next.

A single book slipped from the shelf and slammed into the floor with a reverberating thud. Its pages whipped violently open, flipping to a single page.

The Library illuminated with the glow of a hundred lights all around her.

Maeve fell to her knees before the book.

There would be no sacrifice of blood or exchange needed for this spell. It was her ancestors who already paid the price for her. Magic swirled around her, swallowing all sound.

A small portal swirled into existence in the air. From it, swooped a jaybird with her Sinclair family ring in its beak. The dainty blue and white bird flapped its wings before her. Tied to its leg was a small roll of parchment, which slid to the floor and opened elegantly.

See you on the other side.

Your favorite,

Brax

Maeve took her ring from the feathered creature's beak and slipped it on her finger.

Vexkari consumed her, drenching her in Magic. *Her* Magic.

With a fearless voice, and without hesitation, she placed two fingers on her chest where the Dread Mark lay and recited the spell stamped across the tattered page.

The fabric of her blouse shredded open above the mark.

The smell of cinnamon cigars flitted up around her and numbed the pain of the expulsionary Magic required to remove the oath she took.

Chapter 75

Malachite

Mal clutched his chest, the pain having brought him to his knees in Mount Morte. His teeth slid together with a snap.

The albino serpent slithered around him, her translucent, smooth body coiled up his arm as she hissed at him. Her words were distant and muddled.

He exhaled sharply, his fingers finding his temple where a dull pounding resonated through his body.

"She destroyed her mark," he gasped, panting.

Traitor, the serpent hissed in his mind.

Mal relaxed back on his knees, still clutching his chest.

He hadn't noticed her slip to Earth. How had she moved between realms so easily without his knowledge? To remove her mark…

Gold orbs of light screamed into the cave, spiraling towards him, ready to erase reality.

He knew at once what she had done.

He understood that in a moment's time, he'd forget he'd tasted her sweet lips and called her his.

She never deserved you, hissed the serpent.

If Maeve was destined to push him away, he was destined to make her come crawling back. She was his. And his alone.

Dark Magic sliced across his mind in warning. *I will be your queen,* it said.

Mal laughed darkly, despite his shadow's possession. "You can run from me, Little Viper. But you cannot hide from me."

473

end of book two

THE
DREAD SERIES

continue reading with

THE DREAD KING

THE DREAD PRINCE

Excerpt from book three in The Dread Series
The Dread King

I am not yours, and you are not mine.

The voice forced its way into the cracks of her mind with desperation.

The feeling of smooth, cool skin brushed against her cheek in the darkness. His voice continued, low and filled with something between a promise and a threat.

And yet, I want you all the same.

She inhaled sharply as Magic slipped down her spine. That same desperate, seeking feeling trying to take root.

Another voice, entirely different, one she could name, entered her mind.

"Maeve."

Alphard Mavros' voice cut through her mind, yanking her eyes open, leaving the prickling skin on her cheek feeling bare. Her eyes settled on the teacup before her, steam swirling above the amber liquid.

"Maeve," Alphard said again, his voice unbothered and absent.

She looked up at last, the entire breakfast room coming into focus. Maxius sat next to her, eating his food with careful precision. Alphard looked through their mail, setting aside the newspaper.

"Have you taken your potion today?" he asked, flipping through the various envelopes.

Maeve didn't answer. Her hand moved to her cheek, where the Magic she'd felt slowly faded at her touch. At last, Alphard's eyes landed on her.

He slid a vial of pale liquid across the breakfast table. "Drink."

Maeve took it without argument, realizing she couldn't remember how long she'd been taking them. A side effect of the "episodes," Astrea would remind her.

Rebelliously, Maeve left some at the bottom of the bottle, bitter she needed Astrea to make her potions at all. Her fingers slipped into her pocket, brushing against a small strip of blank parchment. Something that unexplainably grounded her on days when her mind felt far from her own.

Her mind settled, and the voice she'd heard felt like a fast-fading dream she could hardly even recall.

"A royal invitation," said Alphard, tossing a glowing square of parchment on the table.

"A royal invitation, where?" asked Maeve with a groan, already knowing the answer.

"Castle Morana," answered Alphard.

Maeve frowned. "I hate going there," she muttered.

"I know," said Alphard.

"You can just go without me," she replied.

"Doubtful," said Alphard as he looked up at her and slid the parchment across the breakfast table towards her.

Beneath the swirling and performative invitation to a ball at Castle Morana was Abraxas' elegant stamped seal. Beneath that was a brief note.

Non-negotiable, cousin.
Brax

"He really does know everything," said Alphard as he stood.

Alphard's fingers twisted gently through Maxius' hair in the seat next to him. Maxius barely noticed; he was fixated on Spinel pawing relentlessly at the window. Ice edged on the large panes as endless snow fell in the bitter cold. It had been winter for as long as Maeve could remember. Never-ending ice and snow covered everything from the Greywood to the Dark Peaks.

"How are things?" asked Maeve, before Alphard could leave.

Alphard's brows raised.

"Abraxas says you are likely to return to the front lines of The Elven Lands soon if their capital doesn't fall."

Alphard frowned. Maeve hadn't forgotten how he'd come back the first time he'd been sent off to fight. How distant. How on edge he was.

"You neglected to tell me that," said Maeve pointedly.

Alphard sighed. "I don't want to talk about this in front of Maxius."

"Your son deserves to know if you are heading into war," she replied. "Even if you don't think I do."

Maxius peeled his eyes away from the window and looked up at Alphard at last.

"He's six." Alphard's eyes narrowed slightly at Maeve as he dropped his affectionate hold on Maxius. "The Dread Prince has been away for some time. Until he returns, I have no idea where I'll be."

With that, he left them in silence.

After a moment, Maxius' attention returned to the window where Spinel begged for entry.

Maxius signed, *Open*, with his small hands.

Maeve raised her brows at Maxius. "Go on," she said, nodding her head towards the window. Maxius' lips pulled together. He blinked once, but the window remained closed, despite Spinel's frantic pawing.

At his initial failure, Maxius looked up at her with frustrated eyes. She felt no Magic radiating from him. Maeve smiled softly. Maxius returned his attention to the window and tried once more.

Nothing.

Maeve's eyes drifted to the locket that hung around his neck. Thoughts threatened to slip into her mind, thoughts that bordered on reality, but she knew to be false.

Maxius stood in frustration and slammed his fist on the table. The glass shattered with a sharp ring.

Maxius startled and then quickly smiled up at Maeve in triumph. Spinel jumped onto the floor and fussed at them before slinking away to find warmth with Maxius hot on his heels.

Maeve shook her head and muttered, "That's one way to do it," as she relented and downed the rest of her daily potion.

Zimsy rounded the corner of the breakfast room, narrowly dodging Spinel and Maxius. She immediately pulled her robe tightly around her with a quick shiver. "It's freezing in here."

Maeve breathed a laugh and repaired the broken window with a quick twist of her wrist. "Yes, but at least he's performing Magic."

"Oh, good!" she chimed, taking a seat at the table. "What's this?" she asked, snagging the invitation between two of her delicate fingers.

"A royal invitation," answered Maeve grimly.

Zimsy read over the elegant square of parchment. "It's a month away. Gives you plenty of time to fake an illness."

Maeve laughed. "Brax is too sharp for that."

"Looks like it's a rather important event," said Zimsy, placing the invitation down and pouring herself some tea. "Any idea what they could be announcing?"

"No," said Maeve. "Maybe they expect the war will be over then."

"Maybe the Elven Army finally surrendered."

Maeve knew Zimsy didn't approve of the war in the Elven Lands. Maeve didn't concern herself with politics and war, but since Zimsy was passionate about it, she had already decided to agree with her friend.

"How long has it been now?" asked Zimsy.

Maeve's brows raised.

"Since the Elven Queen was overthrown by her own people," elaborated Zimsy.

"Over a year," said Maeve.

Over a year since Lithandrian's people staged a mutiny and established militant control. How the Elven Army managed to obtain Magic no one knew.

Their sudden ability to fight with Magic was a mystery to all citizens of the Dread Lands. Not even Abraxas himself understood. Not that it mattered to Maeve.

She never thought of her crowned Prince beyond the occasional reminder of his existence. They hadn't been close at Vaukore, and in the years she and Alphard had lived in the Dread Lands, she'd never even laid eyes on Malachite Peur. In fact, rumor had it the Crowned Prince had been away for some time, searching for an explanation and counter to the Elven people's newfound Magic.

ABOUT THE AUTHOR

Hi! I'm Lauren Cate (yes I have a double first name, but the good news is if that blows your mind you can call me LC. All the cool kids do.)

I write fiction about the messed up and toxic love you should stay away from in real life (but he's fictional. . . so enjoy) and baddie women. Even if they are the villain. Still baddie.

I've been a performing artist my whole life until publishing. I have two cats and I am obsessed with cats.

You can follow my socials and my website for more information about me and my other works!

Thank you so much for reading! It means the world to me to have gotten Maeve's story into your hands.

XOXO
LC

TikTok @authorlaurencateleake
Instagram @laurencateleake
Facebook: Author Lauren Cate Leake

ALSO BY LAUREN CATE LEAKE

THE DREAD DESCENDANT SERIES
THE DREAD DESCENDANT
THE DREAD PRINCE
THE DREAD KING
DREADFULLY YOURS

MURDEROUS LOVE: AN ANTHOLOGY
FEATURING MARRY, KISS, KILL